Collector's Library

Collector's Library

THE MAN WHO WOULD BE KING

and other stories

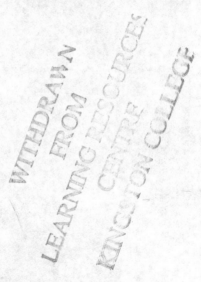

THE MAN WHO WOULD BE KING

and other stories

Rudyard Kipling

with an Afterword by

JOHN GRANT

Collector's Library

The stories selected for this volume were
first published between 1885 and 1909
This edition published in 2005 by
Collector's Library
an imprint of CRW Publishing Limited
69 Gloucester Crescent, London NW1 7EG

ISBN 1 904919 55 3

2 4 6 8 10 9 7 5 3 1

Typeset in Great Britain by Antony Gray
Printed and bound in China by Imago

Contents

The Phantom 'Rickshaw

May no ill dreams disturb my rest,
Nor Powers of Darkness me molest.

Evening Hymn

One of the few advantages that India has over England is a great knowability. After five years' service a man is directly or indirectly acquainted with the two or three hundred civilians in his province, all the messes of ten or twelve regiments and batteries, and some fifteen hundred other people of the non-official caste. In ten years his knowledge should be doubled, and at the end of twenty he knows, or knows something about, every Englishman in the Empire, and may travel anywhere and everywhere without paying hotel-bills.

Globetrotters who expect entertainment as a right, have, even within my memory, blunted this open-heartedness, but none the less today, if you belong to the inner circle and are neither a bear nor a black sheep, all houses are open to you, and our small world is very, very kind and helpful.

Rickett of Kamartha stayed with Polder of Kumaon some fifteen years ago. He meant to stay two nights, but was knocked down by rheumatic fever, and for six weeks disorganised Polder's establishment, stopped Polder's work, and nearly died in Polder's bedroom. Polder behaves as though he had been placed under eternal obligation by Rickett, and yearly sends the little Ricketts a box of presents and toys. It is the same everywhere. The men who do not take the trouble to conceal from you their opinion that you are an incompetent ass, and the women who blacken your character and misunderstand your wife's amusements, will work themselves to the bone in your behalf if you fall sick or into serious trouble.

Heatherlegh, the doctor, kept, in addition to his regular practice, a hospital on his private account – an arrangement of loose-boxes for incurables, his friends called it – but it was really a sort of fitting-up shed for craft that had been damaged by stress of weather. The weather in India is often sultry, and since the tale of bricks is always a fixed quantity, and the only liberty allowed is permission to work overtime and get no thanks, men occasionally break down and become as mixed as the metaphors in this sentence.

Heatherlegh is the dearest doctor that ever was, and his invariable prescription to all his patients is, 'Lie low, go slow, and keep cool.' He says that more men are killed by overwork than the importance of this world justifies. He maintains that overwork slew Pansay, who died under his hands about three years ago. He has, of course, the right to speak authoritatively, and he laughs at my theory that there was a crack in Pansay's head and a little bit of the Dark World came through and pressed him to death. 'Pansay went off the handle,' says Heatherlegh, 'after the stimulus of long leave at home. He may or he may not have behaved like a blackguard to Mrs Keith-Wessington. My notion is that the work of the Katabundi Settlement ran him off his legs, and that he took to brooding and making much of an ordinary P&O flirtation. He certainly was engaged to Miss Mannering, and she certainly broke off the engagement. Then he took a feverish chill and all that nonsense about ghosts developed. Overwork started his illness, kept it alight, and killed him, poor devil. Write him off to the system that uses one man to do the work of two and a half men.'

I do not believe this. I used to sit up with Pansay sometimes when Heatherlegh was called out to patients and I happened to be within claim. The man would make me most unhappy by describing, in a low, even voice, the procession that was always passing at the bottom of his bed. He had a sick man's command of language. When he recovered I suggested that he should write out the whole affair from beginning to end, knowing that ink might assist him to ease his mind.

He was in a high fever while he was writing, and the blood-and-thunder magazine diction he adopted did not calm him. Two months afterwards he was reported fit for duty, but, in spite of the fact that he was urgently needed to help an undermanned commission stagger through a deficit, he preferred to die; vowing at the last that he was hag-ridden. I got his manuscript before he died, and this is his version of the affair, dated 1885, exactly as he wrote it.

My doctor tells me that I need rest and change of air. It is not improbable that I shall get both ere long – rest that neither the red-coated messenger nor the midday gun can break, and change of air far beyond that which any homeward-bound steamer can give me. In the meantime I am resolved to stay where I am; and, in flat defiance of my doctor's orders, to take all the world into my confidence. You shall learn for yourselves the precise nature of my malady, and shall, too, judge for yourselves whether any man born of woman on this weary earth was ever so tormented as I.

Speaking now as a condemned criminal might speak ere the drop-bolts are drawn, my story, wild and hideously improbable as it may appear, demands at least attention. That it will ever receive credence I utterly disbelieve. Two months ago I should have scouted as mad or drunk the man who had dared tell me the like. Two months ago I was the happiest man in India. Today, from Peshawar to the sea, there is no one more wretched. My doctor and I are the only two who know this. His explanation is that my brain, digestion, and eyesight are all slightly affected; giving rise to my frequent and persistent 'delusions'. Delusions, indeed! I call him a fool; but he attends me still with the same unwearied smile, the same bland professional manner, the same neatly-trimmed red whiskers, till I begin to suspect that I am an ungrateful, evil-tempered invalid. But you shall judge for yourselves.

Three years ago it was my fortune – my great misfortune – to sail from Gravesend to Bombay, on return from long leave, with one Agnes Keith-Wessington, wife of an officer on the Bombay side. It does not in the least concern you to know what manner of woman she was. Be content with the knowledge that, ere the voyage had ended, both she and I were desperately and unreasonably in love with one another. Heaven knows that I can make the admission now without one particle of vanity! In matters of this sort there is always one who gives and another who accepts. From the first day of our ill-omened attachment, I was conscious that Agnes's passion was a stronger, a more dominant, and – if I may use the expression – a purer sentiment than mine. Whether she recognised the fact then, I do not know. Afterwards it was bitterly plain to both of us.

Arrived at Bombay in the spring of the year, we went our respective ways, to meet no more for the next three or four months, when my leave and her love took us both to Simla. There we spent the season together; and there my fire of straw burnt itself out to a pitiful end with the closing year. I attempt no excuse. I make no apology. Mrs Wessington had given up much for my sake, and was prepared to give up all. From my own lips, in August 1882, she learnt that I was sick of her presence, tired of her company, and weary of the sound of her voice. Ninety-nine women out of a hundred would have wearied of me as I wearied of them; seventy-five of that number would have promptly avenged themselves by active and obtrusive flirtation with other men. Mrs Wessington was the hundredth. On her neither my openly-expressed aversion nor the cutting brutalities with which I garnished our interviews had the least effect.

'Jack, darling!' was her one eternal cuckoo cry: 'I'm sure it's all a mistake – a hideous mistake; and we'll be good friends again someday. *Please* forgive me, Jack, dear.'

I was the offender, and I knew it. That knowledge transformed my pity into passive endurance and, eventually, into blind hate – the same instinct, I suppose, which prompts a man to savagely stamp on the spider he has but half killed. And with this hate in my bosom the season of 1882 came to an end.

Next year we met again at Simla – she with her monotonous face and timid attempts at reconciliation, and I with loathing of her in every fibre of my frame. Several times I could not avoid meeting her alone; and on each occasion her words were identically the same. Still the unreasoning wail that it was all a 'mistake';

and still the hope of eventually 'making friends'. I might have seen, had I cared to look, that that hope only was keeping her alive. She grew more wan and thin month by month. You will agree with me, at least, that such conduct would have driven anyone to despair. It was uncalled for; childish; unwomanly. I maintain that she was much to blame. And again, sometimes, in the black, fever-stricken night-watches, I have begun to think that I might have been a little kinder to her. But that really *is* a 'delusion'. I could not have continued pretending to love her when I didn't; could I? It would have been unfair to us both.

Last year we met again – on the same terms as before. The same weary appeals, and the same curt answers from my lips. At least I would make her see how wholly wrong and hopeless were her attempts at resuming the old relationship. As the season wore on, we fell apart – that is to say, she found it difficult to meet me, for I had other and more absorbing interests to attend to. When I think it over quietly in my sickroom, the season of 1884 seems a confused nightmare wherein light and shade were fantastically intermingled: my courtship of little Kitty Mannering; my hopes, doubts, and fears; our long rides together; my trembling avowal of attachment; her reply; and now and again a vision of a white face flitting by in the 'rickshaw with the black-and-white liveries I once watched for so earnestly; the wave of Mrs Wessington's gloved hand; and, when she met me alone, which was but seldom, the irksome monotony of her appeal. I loved Kitty Mannering; honestly, heartily loved her, and with my love for her grew my hatred for Agnes. In August Kitty and I were engaged. The next day I met those accursed 'magpie' *jhampanis* at the back of

Jakko, and, moved by some passing sentiment of pity, stopped to tell Mrs Wessington everything. She knew it already.

'So I hear you're engaged, Jack, dear.' Then, without a moment's pause: 'I'm sure it's all a mistake – a hideous mistake. We shall be as good friends someday, Jack, as we ever were.'

My answer might have made even a man wince. It cut the dying woman before me like the blow of a whip. 'Please forgive me, Jack. I didn't mean to make you angry; but it's true, it's true!'

And Mrs Wessington broke down completely. I turned away and left her to finish her journey in peace, feeling, but only for a moment or two, that I had been an unutterably mean hound. I looked back, and saw that she had turned her 'rickshaw with the idea, I suppose, of overtaking me.

The scene and its surroundings were photographed on my memory. The rain-swept sky (we were at the end of the wet weather), the sodden, dingy pines, the muddy road, and the black powder-riven cliffs formed a gloomy background against which the black-and-white liveries of the *jhampanis*, the yellow-panelled 'rickshaw, and Mrs Wessington's down-bowed golden head stood out clearly. She was holding her handkerchief in her left hand and was leaning back exhausted against the 'rickshaw cushions. I turned my horse up a bypath near the Sanjowlie Reservoir and literally ran away. Once I fancied I heard a faint call of 'Jack!' This may have been imagination. I never stopped to verify it. Ten minutes later I came across Kitty on horseback; and, in the delight of a long ride with her, forgot all about the interview.

A week later Mrs Wessington died, and the inexpressible burden of her existence was removed from my life. I went plainsward perfectly happy. Before three months were over I had forgotten all about her, except that at times the discovery of some of her old letters reminded me unpleasantly of our bygone relationship. By January I had disinterred what was left of our correspondence from among my scattered belongings and had burnt it. At the beginning of April of this year, 1885, I was at Simla – semi-deserted Simla – once more, and was deep in lovers' talks and walks with Kitty. It was decided that we should be married at the end of June. You will understand, therefore, that, loving Kitty as I did, I am not saying too much when I pronounce myself to have been, at that time, the happiest man in India.

Fourteen delightful days passed almost before I noticed their flight. Then, aroused to the sense of what was proper among mortals circumstanced as we were, I pointed out to Kitty that an engagement ring was the outward and visible sign of her dignity as an engaged girl; and that she must forthwith come to Hamilton's to be measured for one. Up to that moment, I give you my word, we had completely forgotten so trivial a matter. To Hamilton's we accordingly went on the 15th of April 1885. Remember that – whatever my doctor may say to the contrary – I was then in perfect health, enjoying a well-balanced mind and an *absolutely* tranquil spirit. Kitty and I entered Hamilton's shop together, and there, regardless of the order of affairs, I measured Kitty for the ring in the presence of the amused assistant. The ring was a sapphire with two diamonds. We then rode out down the slope that leads to the Combermere Bridge and Peliti's shop.

While my Waler was cautiously feeling his way over the loose shale, and Kitty was laughing and chattering at my side, – while all Simla, that is to say as much of it as had then come from the plains, was grouped round the reading-room and Peliti's verandah, – I was aware that someone, apparently at a vast distance, was calling me by my Christian name. It struck me that I had heard the voice before, but when and where I could not at once determine. In the short space it took to cover the road between the path from Hamilton's shop and the first plank of the Combermere Bridge I had thought over half a dozen people who might have committed such a solecism, and had eventually decided that it must have been some singing in my ears. Immediately opposite Peliti's shop my eye was arrested by the sight of four *jhampanis* in 'magpie' livery, pulling a yellow-panelled, cheap, bazar 'rickshaw. In a moment my mind flew back to the previous season and Mrs Wessington with a sense of irritation and disgust. Was it not enough that the woman was dead and done with, without her black-and-white servitors reappearing to spoil the day's happiness? Whoever employed them now I thought I would call upon, and ask as a personal favour to change her *jhampanis'* livery. I would hire the men myself, and, if necessary, buy their coats from off their backs. It is impossible to say here what a flood of undesirable memories their presence evoked.

'Kitty,' I cried, 'there are poor Mrs Wessington's *jhampanis* turned up again! I wonder who has them now?'

Kitty had known Mrs Wessington slightly last season, and had always been interested in the sickly woman.

'What? Where?' she asked. 'I can't see them anywhere.'

Even as she spoke, her horse, swerving from a laden mule, threw himself directly in front of the advancing 'rickshaw. I had scarcely time to utter a word of warning when, to my unutterable horror, horse and rider passed *through* men and carriage as if they had been thin air!

'What's the matter?' cried Kitty; 'what made you call out so foolishly, Jack? If I *am* engaged I don't want all creation to know about it. There was lots of space between the mule and the verandah; and, if you think I can't ride – There!'

Whereupon wilful Kitty set off, her dainty little head in the air, at a hand-gallop in the direction of the bandstand; fully expecting, as she herself afterwards told me, that I should follow her. What was the matter? Nothing indeed. Either that I was mad or drunk, or that Simla was haunted with devils. I reined in my impatient cob, and turned round. The 'rickshaw had turned too, and now stood immediately facing me, near the left railing of the Combermere Bridge.

'Jack! Jack, darling!' (There was no mistake about the words this time: they rang through my brain as if they had been shouted in my ear.) 'It's some hideous mistake, I'm sure. *Please* forgive me, Jack, and let's be friends again.'

The 'rickshaw-hood had fallen back, and inside, as I hope and pray daily for the death I dread by night, sat Mrs Keith-Wessington, handkerchief in hand, and golden head bowed on her breast.

How long I stared motionless I do not know. Finally, I was aroused by my syce taking the Waler's bridle a nd asking whether I was ill. From the horrible to the commonplace is but a step. I tumbled off my horse and dashed, half fainting, into Peliti's for a glass of cherry-brandy. There two or three couples were gathered round the coffee-tables discussing the gossip of the day. Their trivialities were more comforting to me just then than the consolations of religion could have been. I plunged into the midst of the conversation at once; chatted, laughed, and jested with a face (when I caught a glimpse of it in a mirror) as white and drawn as that of a corpse. Three or four men noticed my condition; and, evidently setting it down to the results of overmany pegs, charitably endeavoured to draw me apart from the rest of the loungers. But I refused to be led away. I wanted the company of my kind – as a child rushes into the midst of the dinner-party after a fright in the dark. I must have talked for about ten minutes or so, though it seemed an eternity to me, when I heard Kitty's clear voice outside enquiring for me. In another minute she had entered the shop, prepared to upbraid me for failing so signally in my duties. Something in my face stopped her.

'Why, Jack,' she cried, 'what *have* you been doing? What *has* happened? Are you ill?' Thus driven into a direct lie, I said that the sun had been a little too much for me. It was close upon five o'clock of a cloudy April afternoon, and the sun had been hidden all day. I saw my mistake as soon as the words were out of my mouth; attempted to recover it; blundered hopelessly, and followed Kitty in a regal rage out of doors, amid the smiles of my acquaintances. I made some excuse (I have forgotten what) on the score of my feeling faint; and cantered away to my hotel, leaving Kitty to finish the ride by herself.

In my room I sat down and tried calmly to reason out the matter. Here was I, Theobald Jack Pansay, a well-educated Bengal civilian in the year of grace 1885, presumably sane, certainly healthy, driven in terror from my sweetheart's side by the apparition of a woman who had been dead and buried eight months ago. These were facts that I could not blink. Nothing was farther from my thought than any memory of Mrs Wessington when Kitty and I left Hamilton's shop. Nothing was more utterly commonplace than the stretch of wall opposite Peliti's. It was broad daylight. The road was full of people; and yet here, look you, in defiance of every law of probability, in direct outrage of Nature's ordinance, there had appeared to me a face from the grave.

Kitty's Arab had gone *through* the 'rickshaw: so that my first hope that some woman marvellously like Mrs Wessington had hired the carriage and the coolies with their old livery was lost. Again and again I went round this treadmill of thought; and again and again gave up baffled and in despair. The voice was as inexplicable as the apparition. I had originally some wild notion of confiding it all to Kitty; of begging her to marry me at once, and in her arms defying the ghostly occupant of the 'rickshaw. 'After all,' I argued, 'the presence of the 'rickshaw is in itself enough to prove the existence of a spectral illusion. One may see ghosts of men and women, but surely never coolies and carriages. The whole thing is absurd. Fancy the ghost of a hillman!'

Next morning I sent a penitent note to Kitty, imploring her to overlook my strange conduct of the previous afternoon. My divinity was still very wroth, and a personal apology was necessary. I explained, with a fluency born of nightlong pondering over a falsehood, that I had been attacked with a sudden palpitation of the heart – the result of indigestion. This eminently practical solution had its effect; and Kitty and I rode out that afternoon with the shadow of my first lie dividing us.

Nothing would please her save a canter round Jakko. With my nerves still unstrung from the previous night I feebly protested against the notion, suggesting Observatory Hill, Jutogh, the Boileaugunge road – anything rather than the Jakko round. Kitty was angry and a little hurt; so I yielded from fear of provoking further misunderstanding, and we set out together towards Chota Simla. We walked a greater part of the way, and, according to our custom, cantered from a mile or so below the convent to the stretch of level road by the Sanjowlie reservoir. The wretched horses appeared to fly, and my heart beat quicker and quicker as we neared the crest of the ascent. My mind had been full of Mrs Wessington all the afternoon; and every inch of the Jakko road bore witness to our old-time walks and talks. The boulders were full of it; the pines sang it aloud overhead; the rain-fed torrents giggled and chuckled unseen over the shameful story; and the wind in my ears chanted the iniquity aloud.

As a fitting climax, in the middle of the level men call the Ladies' Mile the Horror was awaiting me. No other 'rickshaw was in sight – only the four black-and-white *jhampanis*, the yellow-panelled carriage, and the golden head of the woman within – all apparently just as I had left them eight months and one fortnight ago! For an instant I fancied that Kitty *must* see what I saw – we were so marvellously sympathetic in all things. Her next words undeceived me – 'Not a soul in sight! Come along, Jack, and I'll race you to the reservoir buildings!' Her wiry little Arab was off like a bird, my Waler following close behind, and in this order we dashed under the cliffs. Half a minute brought us within fifty yards of the 'rickshaw. I pulled my Waler and fell back a little. The 'rickshaw was directly in the middle of the road; and once more the Arab passed through it, my horse following. 'Jack! Jack dear! *Please* forgive me,' rang with a wail in my ears, and, after an interval: 'It's all a mistake, a hideous mistake!'

I spurred my horse like a man possessed. When I turned my head at the reservoir works the black-and-white liveries were still waiting – patiently waiting – under the grey hillside, and the wind brought me a mocking echo of the words I had just heard. Kitty bantered me a good deal on my silence throughout the remainder of the ride. I had been talking up till then wildly and at random. To save my life I could not speak afterwards naturally, and from Sanjowlie to the church wisely held my tongue.

I was to dine with the Mannerings that night, and had barely time to canter home to dress. On the road to Elysium Hill I overheard two men talking together in the dusk. – 'It's a curious thing,' said one, 'how completely all trace of it disappeared. You know my wife was insanely fond of the woman (never could see anything in her myself), and wanted me to pick up her old 'rickshaw and coolies if they were to be got for love or money. Morbid sort of fancy I call it; but I've got to do what the Memsahib tells me. Would you believe that the man she hired it from tells me that all four of the men – they were brothers – died of cholera on the way to Hardwar, poor devils; and the 'rickshaw has been broken up by the man himself! Told me he never used a dead Memsahib's 'rickshaw. Spoilt his luck. Queer notion, wasn't it? Fancy poor little Mrs Wessington spoiling anyone's luck except her own!' I laughed aloud at this point; and my laugh jarred on me as I uttered it. So there *were* ghosts of 'rickshaws after all, and ghostly employments in the other world! How much did Mrs Wessington give her men? What were their hours? Where did they go?

And for visible answer to my last question I saw the infernal Thing blocking my path in the twilight. The dead travel fast, and by short cuts unknown to ordinary coolies. I laughed aloud a second time and checked my laughter suddenly, for I was afraid I was going mad. Mad to a certain extent I must have been, for I recollect that I reined in my horse at the head of the 'rickshaw, and politely wished Mrs Wessington 'Good-evening.' Her answer was one I knew only too well. I listened to the end; and replied that I had heard it all before, but should be delighted if she had anything further to say. Some malignant devil stronger than I must have entered into me that evening, for I have a dim recollection of talking the commonplaces of the day for five minutes to the Thing in front of me.

'Mad as a hatter, poor devil – or drunk. Max, try and get him to come home.'

Surely *that* was not Mrs Wessington's voice! The two men had overheard me speaking to the empty air, and had returned to look after me. They were very kind and considerate, and from their words evidently gathered that I was extremely drunk. I thanked them confusedly and cantered away to my hotel, there changed, and arrived at the Mannerings' ten minutes late. I pleaded the darkness of the night as an excuse; was rebuked by Kitty for my unlover-like tardiness; and sat down.

The conversation had already become general and, under cover of it, I was addressing some tender small talk to my sweetheart when I was aware that at the farther end of the table a short, red-whiskered man was describing, with much broidery, his encounter with a mad unknown that evening

A few sentences convinced me that he was repeating the incident of half an hour ago. In the middle of the story he looked round for applause, as professional storytellers do, caught my eye, and straightway collapsed. There was a moment's awkward silence, and the red-whiskered man muttered something to the effect that he had 'forgotten the rest', thereby sacrificing a reputation as a good storyteller which he had built up for six seasons past. I blessed him from the bottom of my heart, and – went on with my fish.

In the fullness of time that dinner came to an end; and with genuine regret I tore myself away from Kitty – as certain as I was of my own existence that It would be waiting for me outside the door. The red-whiskered man, who had been introduced to me as Dr Heatherlegh of Simla, volunteered to bear me company as far as our roads lay together. I accepted his offer with gratitude.

My instinct had not deceived me. It lay in readiness in the Mall, and, in what seemed devilish mockery of our ways, with a lighted headlamp. The red-whiskered man went to the point at once, in a manner that showed he had been thinking over it all dinner-time.

'I say, Pansay, what the deuce was the matter with you this evening on the Elysium Road?' The suddenness of the question wrenched an answer from me before I was aware.

'That!' said I, pointing to It.

'*That* may be either DT or eyes for aught I know. Now you don't liquor. I saw as much at dinner, so it can't be DT. There's nothing whatever where you're pointing, though you’re sweating and trembling with fright like a scared pony. Therefore, I conclude that it’s eyes. And I ought to understand all about them. Come along home with me. I’m on the Blessington lower road.’

To my intense delight the ’rickshaw, instead of waiting for us, kept about twenty yards ahead – and this, too, whether we walked, trotted, or cantered. In the course of that long night ride I had told my companion almost as much as I have told you here.

‘Well, you’ve spoilt one of the best tales I’ve ever laid tongue to,’ said he, ‘but I’ll forgive you for the sake of what you’ve gone through. Now come home and do what I tell you; and when I’ve cured you, young man, let this be a lesson to you to steer clear of women and indigestible food till the day of your death.’

The ’rickshaw kept steadily in front; and my red-whiskered friend seemed to derive great pleasure from my account of its exact whereabouts. ‘Eyes, Pansay – all eyes, brain, and stomach. And the greatest of these three is stomach. You’ve too much conceited brain, too little stomach, and thoroughly unhealthy eyes. Get your stomach straight and the rest follows. And all that’s French for a liver pill. I’ll take sole medical charge of you from this hour, for you’re too interesting a phenomenon to be passed over.’

By this time we were deep in the shadow of the Blessington lower road, and the ’rickshaw came to a dead stop under a pine-clad, overhanging shale cliff. Instinctively I halted too, giving my reason. Heatherlegh rapped out an oath.

‘Now, if you think I’m going to spend a cold night on the hillside for the sake of a stomach-*cum*-brain-*cum*-eye illusion – Lord, ha’ mercy! What’s that?’

There was a muffled report, a blinding smother of dust just in front of us, a crack, the noise of rent boughs, and about ten yards of the cliff-side – pines, undergrowth, and all – slid down into the road below, completely blocking it up. The uprooted trees swayed and tottered for a moment like drunken giants in the gloom, and then fell prone among their fellows with a thunderous crash. Our two horses stood motionless and sweating with fear. As soon as the rattle of falling earth and stone had subsided, my companion muttered: 'Man, if we'd gone forward we should have been ten feet deep in our graves by now. "There are more things in heaven and earth" . . . Come home, Pansay, and thank God. I want a peg badly.'

We retraced our way over the Church Ridge, and I arrived at Dr Heatherlegh's house shortly after midnight.

His attempts towards my cure commenced almost immediately, and for a week I never left his sight. Many a time in the course of that week did I bless the good fortune which had thrown me in contact with Simla's best and kindest doctor. Day by day my spirits grew lighter and more equable. Day by day, too, I became more and more inclined to fall in with Heatherlegh's 'spectral illusion' theory, implicating eyes, brain, and stomach. I wrote to Kitty, telling her that a slight sprain caused by a fall from my horse kept me indoors for a few days; and that I should be recovered before she had time to regret my absence.

Heatherlegh's treatment was simple to a degree. It consisted of liver pills, cold-water baths, and strong exercise, taken in the dusk or at early dawn – for, as he sagely observed: 'A man with a sprained ankle doesn't walk a dozen miles a day, and your young woman might be wondering if she saw you.'

At the end of the week, after much examination of pupil and pulse, and strict injunctions as to diet and pedestrianism, Heatherlegh dismissed me as brusquely as he had taken charge of me. Here is his parting benediction: 'Man, I certify to your mental cure, and that's as much as to say I've cured most of your bodily ailments. Now, get your traps out of this as soon as you can; and be off to make love to Miss Kitty.'

I was endeavouring to express my thanks for his kindness. He cut me short.

'Don't think I did this because I like you. I gather that you've behaved like a blackguard all through. But, all the same, you're a phenomenon, and as queer a phenomenon as you are a blackguard. No!' – checking me a second time – 'not a rupee, please. Go out and see if you can find the eyes-brain-and-stomach business again. I'll give you a lakh for each time you see it.'

Half an hour later I was in the Mannerings' drawing-room with Kitty – drunk with the intoxication of present happiness and the foreknowledge that I should never more be troubled with Its hideous presence. Strong in the sense of my new-found security, I proposed a ride at once; and, by preference, a canter round Jakko.

Never had I felt so well, so overladen with vitality and mere animal spirits, as I did on the afternoon of the 30th of April. Kitty was delighted at the change in my appearance, and complimented me on it in her delightfully frank and outspoken manner. We left the Mannerings' house together, laughing and talking, and cantered along the Chota Simla road as of old.

I was in haste to reach the Sanjowlie reservoir and

there make my assurance doubly sure. The horses did their best, but seemed all too slow to my impatient mind. Kitty was astonished at my boisterousness. 'Why, Jack!' she cried at last, 'you are behaving like a child. What are you doing?'

We were just below the convent, and from sheer wantonness I was making my Waler plunge and curvet across the road as I tickled it with the loop of my riding-whip.

'Doing?' I answered; 'nothing, dear. That's just it. If you'd been doing nothing for a week except lie up, you'd be as riotous as I.

'Singing and murmuring in your feastful mirth,
    Joying to feel yourself alive;
Lord over Nature, Lord of the visible Earth,
    Lord of the senses five.'

My quotation was hardly out of my lips before we had rounded the corner above the convent, and a few yards farther on could see across to Sanjowlie. In the centre of the level road stood the black-and-white liveries, the yellow-panelled 'rickshaw, and Mrs Keith-Wessington. I pulled up, looked, rubbed my eyes, and, I believe, must have said something. The next thing I knew was that I was lying face downward on the road, with Kitty kneeling above me in tears.

'Has it gone, child?' I gasped. Kitty only wept more bitterly.

'Has *what* gone, Jack dear? What does it all mean? There must be a mistake somewhere, Jack. A hideous mistake.' Her last words brought me to my feet – mad – raving for the time being.

'Yes, there *is* a mistake somewhere,' I repeated, 'a hideous mistake. Come and look at It.'

I have an indistinct idea that I dragged Kitty by the wrist along the road up to where It stood, and implored her for pity's sake to speak to It; to tell It that we were betrothed; that neither Death nor Hell could break the tie between us: and Kitty only knows how much more to the same effect. Now and again I appealed passionately to the Terror in the 'rickshaw to bear witness to all I had said, and to release me from a torture that was killing me. As I talked I suppose I must have told Kitty of my old relations with Mrs Wessington, for I saw her listen intently with white face and blazing eyes.

'Thank you, Mr Pansay,' she said, 'that's *quite* enough. *Syce ghora láo*.'

The syces, impassive as Orientals always are, had come up with the recaptured horses; and as Kitty sprang into her saddle I caught hold of her bridle, entreating her to hear me out and forgive. My answer was the cut of her riding-whip across my face from mouth to eye, and a word or two of farewell that even now I cannot write down. So I judged, and judged rightly, that Kitty knew all; and I staggered back to the side of the 'rickshaw. My face was cut and bleeding, and the blow of the riding-whip had raised a livid blue weal on it. I had no self-respect. Just then, Heatherlegh, who must have been following Kitty and me at a distance, cantered up.

'Doctor,' I said, pointing to my face, 'here's Miss Mannering's signature to my order of dismissal and – I'll thank you for that lakh as soon as convenient.'

Heatherlegh's face, even in my abject misery, moved me to laughter.

'I'll stake my professional reputation – ' he began.

'Don't be a fool,' I whispered. 'I've lost my

life's happiness and you'd better take me home.'

As I spoke the 'rickshaw was gone. Then I lost all knowledge of what was passing. The crest of Jakko seemed to heave and roll like the crest of a cloud and fall in upon me.

Seven days later (on the 7th of May, that is to say) I was aware that I was lying in Heatherlegh's room as weak as a little child. Heatherlegh was watching me intently from behind the papers on his writing-table. His first words were not encouraging; but I was too far spent to be much moved by them.

'Here's Miss Kitty has sent back your letters. You corresponded a good deal, you young people. Here's a packet that looks like a ring, and a cheerful sort of a note from Mannering Papa, which I've taken the liberty of reading and burning. The old gentleman's not pleased with you.'

'And Kitty?' I asked dully.

'Rather more drawn than her father from what she says. By the same token you must have been letting out any number of queer reminiscences just before I met you. Says that a man who would have behaved to a woman as you did to Mrs Wessington ought to kill himself out of sheer pity for his kind. She's a hot-headed little virago, your mash. Will have it too that you were suffering from DT when that row on the Jakko road turned up. Says she'll die before she ever speaks to you again.'

I groaned and turned over on the other side.

'Now you've got your choice, my friend. This engagement has to be broken off; and the Mannerings don't want to be too hard on you. Was it broken through DT or epileptic fits? Sorry I can't offer you a better exchange unless you'd prefer hereditary insanity. Say the word and I'll tell 'em it's fits. All Simla knows about that scene on the Ladies' Mile. Come! I'll give you five minutes to think over it.'

During those five minutes I believe that I explored thoroughly the lowest circles of the Inferno which it is permitted man to tread on earth. And at the same time I myself was watching myself faltering through the dark labyrinths of doubt, misery, and utter despair. I wondered, as Heatherlegh in his chair might have wondered, which dreadful alternative I should adopt. Presently I heard myself answering in a voice that I hardly recognised –

'They're confoundedly particular about morality in these parts. Give 'em fits, Heatherlegh, and my love. Now let me sleep a bit longer.'

Then my two selves joined, and it was only I (half-crazed, devil-driven I) that tossed in my bed tracing step by step the history of the past month.

'But I am in Simla,' I kept repeating to myself. 'I, Jack Pansay, am in Simla, and there are no ghosts here. It's unreasonable of that woman to pretend there are. Why couldn't Agnes have left me alone? I never did her any harm. It might just as well have been me as Agnes. Only I'd never have come back on purpose to kill *her*. Why can't I be left alone – left alone and happy?'

It was high noon when I first awoke; and the sun was low in the sky before I slept – slept as the tortured criminal sleeps on his rack, too worn to feel further pain.

Next day I could not leave my bed. Heatherlegh told me in the morning that he had received an answer from Mr Mannering, and that, thanks to his (Heatherlegh's) friendly offices, the story of my affliction had travelled through the length and breadth of Simla, where I was on all sides much pitied.

'And that's rather more than you deserve,' he concluded pleasantly, 'though the Lord knows you've been going through a pretty severe mill. Never mind; we'll cure you yet, you perverse phenomenon.'

I declined firmly to be cured. 'You've been much too good to me already, old man,' said I; 'but I don't think I need trouble you further.'

In my heart I knew that nothing Heatherlegh could do would lighten the burden that had been laid upon me.

With that knowledge came also a sense of hopeless, impotent rebellion against the unreasonableness of it all. There were scores of men no better than I whose punishments had at least been reserved for another world; and I felt that it was bitterly, cruelly unfair that I alone should have been singled out for so hideous a fate. This mood would in time give place to another where it seemed that the 'rickshaw and I were the only realities in a world of shadows; that Kitty was a ghost; that Mannering, Heatherlegh, and all the other men and women I knew were all ghosts; and the great grey hills themselves but vain shadows devised to torture me. From mood to mood I tossed backwards and forwards for seven weary days; my body growing daily stronger and stronger, until the bedroom looking-glass told me that I had returned to everyday life, and was as other men once more. Curiously enough my face showed no signs of the struggle I had gone through. It was pale indeed, but as expressionless and commonplace as ever. I had expected some permanent alteration – visible evidence of the disease that was eating me away. I found nothing.

On the 15th of May I left Heatherlegh's house at eleven o'clock in the morning; and the instinct of the bachelor drove me to the club. There I found that every man knew my story as told by Heatherlegh, and was, in clumsy fashion, abnormally kind and attentive. Nevertheless I recognised that for the rest of my natural life I should be among but not of my fellows; and I envied very bitterly indeed the laughing coolies on the Mall below. I lunched at the club, and at four o'clock wandered aimlessly down the Mall in the vague hope of meeting Kitty. Close to the bandstand the black-and-white liveries joined me; and I heard Mrs Wessington's old appeal at my side. I had been expecting this ever since I came out, and was only surprised at her delay. The phantom 'rickshaw and I went side by side along the Chota Simla road in silence. Close to the bazar, Kitty and a man on horseback overtook and passed us. For any sign she gave I might have been a dog in the road. She did not even pay me the compliment of quickening her pace, though the rainy afternoon might have served for an excuse.

So Kitty and her companion, and I and my ghostly Light-o'-Love, crept round Jakko in couples. The road was streaming with water; the pines dripped like roof-pipes on the rocks below, and the air was full of fine driving rain. Two or three times I found myself saying to myself almost aloud: 'I'm Jack Pansay on leave at Simla – at *Simla*! Everyday, ordinary Simla. I mustn't forget that – I mustn't forget that.' Then I would try to recollect some of the gossip I had heard at the club: the prices of So-and-So's horses – anything, in fact, that related to the workaday Anglo-Indian world I knew so well. I even repeated the multiplication-table rapidly to myself, to make quite sure that I was not taking leave of my senses. It gave me much comfort, and must have prevented my hearing Mrs Wessington for a time.

Once more I wearily climbed the convent slope and entered the level road. Here Kitty and the man started off at a canter, and I was left alone with Mrs Wessington. 'Agnes,' said I, 'will you put back your hood and tell me what it all means?' The hood dropped noiselessly, and I was face to face with my dead and buried mistress. She was wearing the dress in which I had last seen her alive; carried the same tiny handkerchief in her right hand, and the same card-case in her left. (A woman eight months dead with a card-case!) I had to pin myself down to the multiplication-table, and to set both hands on the stone parapet of the road, to assure myself that that at least was real.

'Agnes,' I repeated, 'for pity's sake tell me what it all means.' Mrs Wessington leaned forward, with that odd, quick turn of the head I used to know so well, and spoke.

If my story had not already so madly overleaped the bounds of all human belief I should apologise to you now. As I know that no one – no, not even Kitty, for whom it is written as some sort of justification of my conduct – will believe me, I will go on. Mrs Wessington spoke, and I walked with her from the Sanjowlie road to the turning below the Commander-in-Chief's house as I might walk by the side of any living woman's 'rickshaw, deep in conversation. The second and most tormenting of my moods of sickness had suddenly laid hold upon me, and, like the Prince in Tennyson's poem, 'I seemed to move amid a world of ghosts'. There had been a garden-party at the Commander-in-Chief's, and we two joined the crowd of homeward-bound folk.

As I saw them it seemed that *they* were the shadows – impalpable fantastic shadows – that divided for Mrs Wessington's 'rickshaw to pass through. What we said during the course of that weird interview I cannot – indeed, I dare not – tell. Heatherlegh's comment would have been a short laugh and a remark that I had been 'mashing a brain-eye-and-stomach chimera'. It was a ghastly and yet in some indefinable way a marvellously dear experience. Could it be possible, I wondered, that I was in this life to woo a second time the woman I had killed by my own neglect and cruelty?

I met Kitty on the homeward road – a shadow among shadows.

If I were to describe all the incidents of the next fortnight in their order, my story would never come to an end, and your patience would be exhausted. Morning after morning and evening after evening the ghostly 'rickshaw and I used to wander through Simla together. Wherever I went there the four black-and-white liveries followed me and bore me company to and from my hotel. At the theatre I found them amid the crowd of yelling *jhampanis*; outside the club verandah, after a long evening of whist; at the Birthday Ball, waiting patiently for my reappearance; and in broad daylight when I went calling. Save that it cast no shadow, the 'rickshaw was in every respect as real to look upon as one of wood and iron. More than once, indeed, I have had to check myself from warning some hard-riding friend against cantering over it. More than once I have walked down the Mall deep in conversation with Mrs Wessington, to the unspeakable amazement of the passers-by.

Before I had been out and about a week I learned

that the 'fit' theory had been discarded in favour of insanity. However, I made no change in my mode of life. I called, rode, and dined out as freely as ever. I had a passion for the society of my kind which I had never felt before; I hungered to be among the realities of life; and at the same time I felt vaguely unhappy when I had been separated too long from my ghostly companion. It would be almost impossible to describe my varying moods from the 15th of May up to today.

The presence of the 'rickshaw filled me by turns with horror, blind fear, a dim sort of pleasure, and utter despair. I dared not leave Simla; and I knew that my stay there was killing me. I knew, moreover, that it was my destiny to die slowly and a little every day. My only anxiety was to get the penance over as quietly as might be. Alternately I hungered for a sight of Kitty, and watched her outrageous flirtations with my successor – to speak more accurately, my successors – with amused interest. She was as much out of my life as I was out of hers. By day I wandered with Mrs Wessington almost content. By night I implored Heaven to let me return to the world as I used to know it. Above all these varying moods lay the sensation of dull, numbing wonder that the seen and the unseen should mingle so strangely on this earth to hound one poor soul to its grave.

August 27. – Heatherlegh has been indefatigable in his attendance on me; and only yesterday told me that I ought to send in an application for sick leave. An application to escape the company of a phantom! A request that the Government would graciously permit me to get rid of five ghosts and an airy 'rickshaw by going to England! Heatherlegh's proposition moved me to almost hysterical laughter. I told him that I should await the end quietly at Simla; and I am sure that the end is not far off. Believe me that I dread its advent more than any word can say; and I torture myself nightly with a thousand speculations as to the manner of my death.

Shall I die in my bed decently and as an English gentleman should die; or, in one last walk on the Mall, will my soul be wrenched from me to take its place for ever and ever by the side of that ghastly phantasm? Shall I return to my old lost allegiance in the next world, or shall I meet Agnes loathing her and bound to her side through all eternity? Shall we two hover over the scene of our lives till the end of Time? As the day of my death draws nearer, the intense horror that all living flesh feels toward escaped spirits from beyond the grave grows more and more powerful. It is an awful thing to go down quick among the dead with scarcely one half of your life completed. It is a thousand times more awful to wait as I do in your midst, for I know not what unimaginable terror. Pity me, at least on the score of my 'delusion', for I know you will never believe what I have written here. Yet as surely as ever a man was done to death by the Powers of Darkness, I am that man.

In justice, too, pity her. For as surely as ever woman was killed by man, I killed Mrs Wessington. And the last portion of my punishment is even now upon me.

'The Finest Story in the World'

Or ever the knightly years were gone
With the old world to the grave,
I was a king in Babylon
And you were a Christian slave.

W. E. Henley

His name was Charlie Mears; he was the only son of his mother who was a widow, and he lived in the north of London, coming into the City every day to work in a bank. He was twenty years old and was full of aspirations. I met him in a public billiard-saloon where the marker called him by his first name, and he called the marker 'Bullseye'. Charlie explained, a little nervously, that he had only come to the place to look on, and since looking on at games of skill is not a cheap amusement for the young, I suggested that Charlie should go back to his mother.

That was our first step towards better acquaintance. He would call on me sometimes in the evenings instead of running about London with his fellow-clerks; and before long, speaking of himself as a young man must, he told me of his aspirations, which were all literary. He desired to make himself an undying name chiefly through verse, though he was not above sending stories of love and death to the penny-in-the-slot journals. It was my fate to sit still while Charlie read me poems of many hundred lines, and bulky fragments of plays that would surely shake the world.

My reward was his unreserved confidence, and the self-revelations and troubles of a young man are almost as holy as those of a maiden. Charlie had never fallen in love, but was anxious to do so on the first opportunity; he believed in all things good and all things honourable, but at the same time, was curiously careful to let me see that he knew his way about the world as befitted a bank-clerk on twenty-five shillings a week. He rhymed 'dove' with 'love' and 'moon' with 'June', and devoutly believed that they had never so been rhymed before. The long lame gaps in his plays he filled up with hasty words of apology and description, and swept on, seeing all that he intended to do so clearly that he esteemed it already done, and turned to me for applause.

I fancy that his mother did not encourage his aspirations; and I know that his writing-table at home was the edge of his washstand. This he told me almost at the outset of our acquaintance – when he was ravaging my bookshelves, and a little before I was implored to speak the truth as to his chances of 'writing something really great, you know'. Maybe I encouraged him too much for, one night, he called on me, his eyes flaming with excitement, and said breathlessly: 'Do you mind – can you let me stay here and write all this evening? I won't interrupt you, I won't really. There's no place for me to write in at my mother's.'

'What's the trouble?' I said, knowing well what that trouble was.

'I've a notion in my head that would make the most splendid story that was ever written. Do let me write it out here. It's *such* a notion!'

There was no resisting the appeal. I set him a table;

he hardly thanked me, but plunged into his work at once. For half an hour the pen scratched without stopping. Then Charlie sighed and tugged his hair. The scratching grew slower, there were more erasures, and at last ceased. The finest story in the world would not come forth.

'It looks such awful rot now,' he said mournfully. 'And yet it seemed so good when I was thinking about it. What's wrong?'

I could not dishearten him by saying the truth. So I answered: 'Perhaps you don't feel in the mood for writing.'

'Yes I do – except when I look at this stuff. Ugh!'

'Read me what you've done,' I said.

He read, and it was wondrous bad, and he paused at all the specially turgid sentences, expecting a little approval; for he was proud of those sentences, as I knew he would be.

'It needs compression,' I suggested cautiously.

'I hate cutting my things down. I don't think you could alter a word here without spoiling the sense. It reads better aloud than when I was writing it.'

'Charlie, you're suffering from an alarming disease afflicting a numerous class. Put the thing by, and tackle it again in a week.'

'I want to do it at once. What do you think of it?'

'How can I judge from a half-written tale? Tell me the story as it lies in your head.'

Charlie told, and in the telling there was everything that his ignorance had so carefully prevented from escaping into the written word. I looked at him, wondering whether it were possible that he did not know the originality, the power of the notion that had come in his way? It was distinctly a Notion among notions. Men had been puffed up with pride by ideas not a tithe as excellent and practicable. But Charlie babbled on serenely, interrupting the current of pure fancy with samples of horrible sentences that he purposed to use. I heard him out to the end. It would be folly to allow his thought to remain in his own inept hands, when I could do so much with it. Not all that could be done indeed; but, oh so much!

'What do you think?' he said at last. 'I fancy I shall call it "The Story of a Ship".'

'I think the idea's pretty good; but you won't be able to handle it for ever so long. Now I – '

'Would it be of any use to you? Would you care to take it? I should be proud,' said Charlie promptly.

There are few things sweeter in this world than the guileless, hot-headed, intemperate, open admiration of a junior. Even a woman in her blindest devotion does not fall into the gait of the man she adores, tilt her bonnet to the angle at which he wears his hat, or interlard her speech with his pet oaths. And Charlie did all these things. Still it was necessary to salve my conscience before I possessed myself of Charlie's thoughts.

'Let's make a bargain. I'll give you a fiver for the notion,' I said.

Charlie became a bank-clerk at once.

'Oh, that's impossible. Between two pals, you know, if I may call you so, and speaking as a man of the world, I couldn't. Take the notion if it's any use to you. I've heaps more.'

He had – none knew this better than I – but they were the notions of other men.

'Look at it as a matter of business – between men of the world,' I returned. 'Five pounds will buy you any number of poetry books. Business is business, and you may be sure I shouldn't give that price unless – '

'Oh, if you put it *that* way,' said Charlie, visibly moved by the thought of the books. The bargain was clinched with an agreement that he should at unstated intervals come to me with all the notions that he possessed, should have a table of his own to write at, and unquestioned right to inflict upon me all his poems and fragments of poems. Then I said, 'Now tell me how you came by this idea.'

'It came by itself.' Charlie's eyes opened a little.

'Yes, but you told me a great deal about the hero that you must have read before somewhere.'

'I haven't any time for reading, except when you let me sit here, and on Sundays I'm on my bicycle or down the river all day. There's nothing wrong about the hero, is there?'

'Tell me again and I shall understand clearly. You say that your hero went pirating. How did he live?'

'He was on the lower deck of this ship-thing that I was telling you about.'

'What sort of ship?'

'It was the kind rowed with oars, and the sea spurts through the oar-holes, and the men row sitting up to their knees in water. Then there's a bench running down between the two lines of oars, and an overseer with a whip walks up and down the bench to make the men work.'

'How do you know that?'

'It's in the tale. There's a rope running overhead, looped to the upper deck, for the overseer to catch hold of when the ship rolls. When the overseer misses the rope once and falls among the rowers, remember the hero laughs at him and gets licked for it. He's chained to his oar of course – the hero.'

'How is he chained?'

'With an iron band round his waist fixed to the bench he sits on, and a sort of handcuff on his left wrist chaining him to the oar. He's on the lower deck where the worst men are sent, and the only light comes from the hatchways and through the oar-holes. Can't you imagine the sunlight just squeezing through between the handle and the hole and wobbling about as the ship moves?'

'I can, but I can't imagine your imagining it.'

'How could it be any other way? Now you listen to me. The long oars on the upper deck are managed by four men to each bench, the lower ones by three, and the lowest of all by two. Remember it's quite dark on the lowest deck and all the men there go mad. When a man dies at his oar on that deck he isn't thrown overboard, but cut up in his chains and stuffed through the oar-hole in little pieces.'

'Why?' I demanded amazed, not so much at the information as the tone of command in which it was flung out.

'To save trouble and to frighten the others. It needs two overseers to drag a man's body up to the top deck; and if the men at the lower deck oars were left alone, of course they'd stop rowing and try to pull up the benches by all standing up together in their chains.'

'You've a most provident imagination. Where have you been reading about galleys and galley-slaves?'

'Nowhere that I remember. I row a little when I get the chance. But, perhaps, if you say so, I may have read something.'

He went away shortly afterwards to deal with booksellers, and I wondered how a bank-clerk aged twenty could put into my hands with a profligate abundance of detail, all given with absolute assurance, the story of extravagant and bloodthirsty adventure, riot, piracy, and death in unnamed seas. He had led his hero a desperate dance through revolt against the overseers, to command of a ship of his own, and at last to the establishment of a kingdom on an island 'somewhere in the sea, you know'; and, delighted with my paltry five pounds, had gone out to buy the notions of other men, that these might teach him how to write. I had the consolation of knowing that this notion was mine by right of purchase, and I thought that I could make something of it.

When next he came to me he was drunk – royally drunk on many poets for the first time revealed to him. His pupils were dilated, his words tumbled over each other, and he wrapped himself in quotations – as a beggar would enfold himself in the purple of emperors. Most of all was he drunk with Longfellow.

'Isn't it splendid? Isn't it superb?' he cried, after hasty greetings. 'Listen to this:

> "Wouldst thou" – so the helmsman answered,
> "Know the secret of the sea?
> Only those who brave its dangers
> Comprehend its mystery."

By gum!

> "Only those who brave its dangers
> Comprehend its mystery," '

he repeated twenty times, walking up and down the room and forgetting me. 'But *I* can understand it too,' he said to himself. 'I don't know how to thank you for that fiver. And this; listen:

I remember the black wharves and the slips
And the sea-tides tossing free;
And the Spanish sailors with bearded lips,
And the beauty and mystery of the ships,
And the magic of the sea.

I haven't braved any dangers, but I feel as if I knew all about it.'

'You certainly seem to have a grip of the sea. Have you ever seen it?'

'When I was a little chap I went to Brighton once; we used to live in Coventry, though, before we came to London. I never saw it,

When descends on the Atlantic
The gigantic
Storm-wind of the Equinox.'

He shook me by the shoulder to make me understand the passion that was shaking himself.

'When that storm comes,' he continued, 'I think that all the oars in the ship that I was talking about get broken, and the rowers have their chests smashed in by the oar-heads bucking. By the way, have you done anything with that notion of mine yet?'

'No. I was waiting to hear more of it from you. Tell me how in the world you're so certain about the fittings of the ship. You know nothing of ships.'

'I don't know. It's as real as anything to me until I try to write it down. I was thinking about it only last night in bed, after you had lent me *Treasure Island*; and I made up a whole lot of new things to go into the story.'

'What sort of things?'

'About the food the men ate; rotten figs and black

beans and wine in a skin bag, passed from bench to bench.'

'Was the ship built so long ago as *that*?'

'As what? I don't know whether it was long ago or not. It's only a notion, but sometimes it seems just as real as if it was true. Do I bother you with talking about it?'

'Not in the least. Did you make up anything else?'

'Yes, but it's nonsense.' Charlie flushed a little.

'Never mind; let's hear about it.'

'Well, I was thinking over the story, and after a while I got out of bed and wrote down on a piece of paper the sort of stuff the men might be supposed to scratch on their oars with the edges of their handcuffs. It seemed to make the thing more lifelike. It *is* so real to me, y'know.'

'Have you the paper on you?'

'Ye–es, but what's the use of showing it? It's only a lot of scratches. All the same, we might have 'em reproduced in the book on the front page.'

'I'll attend to those details. Show me what your men wrote.'

He pulled out of his pocket a sheet of notepaper, with a single line of scratches upon it, and I put this carefully away.

'What is it supposed to mean in English?' I said.

'Oh, I don't know. I mean it to mean, "I'm beastly tired." It's great nonsense,' he repeated, 'but all those men in the ship seem as real as real people to me. Do do something to the notion soon; I should like to see it written and printed.'

'But all you've told me would make a long book.'

'Make it then. You've only to sit down and write it out.'

'Give me a little time. Have you any more notions?'

'Not just now. I'm reading all the books I've bought. They're splendid.'

When he had left I looked at the sheet of notepaper with the inscription upon it. Then I took my head tenderly between both hands, to make certain that it was not coming off or turning round. Then . . . but there seemed to be no interval between quitting my rooms and finding myself arguing with a policeman outside a door marked *Private* in a corridor of the British Museum. All I demanded, as politely as possible, was 'the Greek antiquity man'. The policeman knew nothing except the rules of the Museum, and it became necessary to forage through all the houses and offices inside the gates. An elderly gentleman called away from his lunch put an end to my search by holding the notepaper between finger and thumb and sniffing at it scornfully.

'What does this mean? H'm,' said he. 'So far as I can ascertain it is an attempt to write extremely corrupt Greek on the part' – here he glared at me with intention – 'of an extremely illiterate – ah – person.' He read slowly from the paper, '*Pollock*, *Erckmann*, *Tauchnitz*, *Henniker*' – four names familiar to me.

'Can you tell me what the corruption is supposed to mean – the gist of the thing?' I asked.

'I have been – many times – overcome with weariness in this particular employment. That is the meaning.' He returned me the paper, and I fled without a word of thanks, explanation, or apology.

I might have been excused for forgetting much. To me of all men had been given the chance to write the most marvellous tale in the world, nothing less than the story of a Greek galley-slave, as told by himself.

Small wonder that his dreaming had seemed real to Charlie. The Fates that are so careful to shut the doors of each successive life behind us had, in this case, been neglectful, and Charlie was looking, though that he did not know, where never man had been permitted to look with full knowledge since Time began. Above all, he was absolutely ignorant of the knowledge sold to me for five pounds; and he would retain that ignorance, for bank-clerks do not understand metempsychosis, and a sound commercial education does not include Greek. He would supply me – here I capered among the dumb gods of Egypt and laughed in their battered faces – with material to make my tale sure – so sure that the world would hail it as an impudent and vamped fiction. And I – I alone would know that it was absolutely and literally true. I – I alone held this jewel to my hand for the cutting and polishing! Therefore I danced again among the gods of the Egyptian court till a policeman saw me and took steps in my direction.

It remained now only to encourage Charlie to talk, and here there was no difficulty. But I had forgotten those accursed books of poetry. He came to me time after time, as useless as a surcharged phonograph – drunk on Byron, Shelley, or Keats. Knowing now what the boy had been in his past lives, and desperately anxious not to lose one word of his babble, I could not hide from him my respect and interest. He misconstrued both into respect for the present soul of Charlie Mears, to whom life was as new as it was to Adam, and interest in his readings; and stretched my patience to breaking point by reciting poetry – not his own now, but that of others. I wished every English poet blotted out of the memory of mankind. I blasphemed the mightiest names of song because they had drawn

Charlie from the path of direct narrative, and would, later, spur him to imitate them; but I choked down my impatience until the first flood of enthusiasm should have spent itself and the boy returned to his dreams.

'What's the use of my telling you what *I* think, when these chaps wrote things for the angels to read?' he growled, one evening. 'Why don't you write something like theirs?'

'I don't think you're treating me quite fairly,' I said, speaking under strong restraint.

'I've given you the story,' he said shortly, re-plunging into 'Lara'.

'But I want the details.'

'The things I make up about that damned ship that you call a galley? They're quite easy. You can just make 'em up for yourself. Turn up the gas a little, I want to go on reading.'

I could have broken the gas globe over his head for his amazing stupidity. I could indeed make up things for myself did I only know what Charlie did not know that he knew. But since the doors were shut behind me I could only wait his youthful pleasure and strive to keep him in good temper. One minute's want of guard might spoil a priceless revelation: now and again he would toss his books aside – he kept them in my rooms, for his mother would have been shocked at the waste of good money had she seen them – and launched into his sea-dreams. Again I cursed all the poets of England. The plastic mind of the bank-clerk had been overlaid, coloured, and distorted by that which he had read, and the result as delivered was a confused tangle of other voices most like the mutter and hum through a City telephone in the busiest part of the day.

He talked of the galley – his own galley had he but known it – with illustrations borrowed from the 'Bride of Abydos'. He pointed the experiences of his hero with quotations from 'The Corsair', and threw in deep and desperate moral reflections from 'Cain' and 'Manfred', expecting me to use them all. Only when the talk turned on Longfellow were the jarring cross-currents dumb, and I knew that Charlie was speaking the truth as he remembered it.

'What do you think of this?' I said one evening, as soon as I understood the medium in which his memory worked best, and, before he could expostulate, read him nearly the whole of 'The Saga of King Olaf'.

He listened open-mouthed, flushed, his hands drumming on the back of the sofa where he lay, till I came to the Song of Einar Tamberskelver and the verse:

> 'Einar then, the arrow taking
> From the loosened string,
> Answered, "That was Norway breaking
> 'Neath thy hand, O King." '

He gasped with pure delight of sound.

'That's better than Byron, a little?' I ventured.

'Better! Why it's *true*! How could he have known?'

I went back and repeated:

> ' "What was that?" said Olaf, standing
> On the quarterdeck,
> "Something heard I like the stranding
> Of a shattered wreck." '

'How could he have known how the ships crash and the oars rip out and go *z-zzp* all along the line? Why only the other night . . . But go back, please, and read "The Skerry of Shrieks" again.'

'No, I'm tired. Let's talk. What happened the other night?'

'I had an awful dream about that galley of ours. I dreamed I was drowned in a fight. You see we ran alongside another ship in harbour. The water was dead still except where our oars whipped it up. You know where I always sit in the galley?' He spoke haltingly at first, under a fine English fear of being laughed at.

'No. That's news to me,' I answered meekly, my heart beginning to beat.

'On the fourth oar from the bow on the right side on the upper deck. There were four of us at that oar, all chained. I remember watching the water and trying to get my handcuffs off before the row began. Then we closed up on the other ship, and all their fighting men jumped over our bulwarks, and my bench broke and I was pinned down with the three other fellows on top of me, and the big oar jammed across our backs.'

'Well?'

Charlie's eyes were alive and alight. He was looking at the wall behind my chair. 'I don't know how we fought. The men were trampling all over my back, and I lay low. Then our rowers on the left side – tied to their oars, you know – began to yell and back water. I could hear the water sizzle, and we spun round like a cockchafer, and I knew, lying where I was, that there was a galley coming up bow-on to ram us on the left side. I could just lift up my head and see her sail over the bulwarks. We wanted to meet her bow to bow, but it was too late. We could only turn a little bit because the galley on our right had hooked herself on to us and stopped our moving. Then, by gum! there was a crash! Our left oars began to break as the other galley, the moving one y'know, stuck her nose into them. Then the lower-deck oars shot up through the deck planking, butt first, and one of them jumped clear up into the air and came down again close at my head.'

'How was that managed?'

'The moving galley's bow was plunking them back through their own oar-holes, and I could hear no end of a shindy in the decks below. Then her nose caught us nearly in the middle, and we tilted sideways, and the fellows in the right-hand galley unhitched their hooks and ropes, and threw things on to our upper deck – arrows, and hot pitch or something that stung – and we went up and up and up on the left side, and the right side dipped, and I twisted my head round and saw the water stand still as it topped the right bulwarks, and then it curled over and crashed down on the whole lot of us on the right side, and I felt it hit my back, and I woke.'

'One minute, Charlie. When the sea topped the bulwarks, what did it look like?' I had my reasons for asking. A man of my acquaintance had once gone down with a leaking ship in a still sea, and had seen the water-level pause for an instant ere it fell on the deck.

'It looked just like a banjo-string drawn tight, and it seemed to stay there for years,' said Charlie.

Exactly! The other man had said: 'It looked like a silver wire laid down along the bulwarks, and I thought it was never going to break.' He had paid everything except the bare life for this little valueless piece of knowledge, and I had travelled ten thousand weary miles to meet him and take his knowledge at second hand. But Charlie, the bank-clerk on twenty-five shillings a week, who had never been out of sight of a made road, knew it all. It was no consolation to me that once in his lives he had been forced to die for his gains. I also must have died scores of times, but behind me, because I could have used my knowledge, the doors were shut.

‘And then?’ I said, trying to put away the devil of envy.

‘The funny thing was, though, in all the row I didn’t feel a bit astonished or frightened. It seemed as if I’d been in a good many fights, because I told my next man so when the row began. But that cad of an overseer on my deck wouldn’t unloose our chains and give us a chance. He always said that we’d all be set free after a battle, but we never were; we never were.’ Charlie shook his head mournfully.

‘What a scoundrel!’

‘I should say he was. He never gave us enough to eat, and sometimes we were so thirsty that we used to drink salt water. I can taste that salt water still.’

‘Now tell me something about the harbour where the fight was fought.’

‘I didn’t dream about that. I know it was a harbour, though, because we were tied up to a ring on a white wall and all the face of the stone under water was covered with wood to prevent our ram getting chipped when the tide made us rock.’

‘That’s curious. Our hero commanded the galley, didn’t he?’

‘Didn’t he just! He stood by the bows and shouted like a good ’un. He was the man who killed the overseer.’

‘But you were all drowned together, Charlie, weren’t you?’

'I can't make that fit quite,' he said, with a puzzled look. 'The galley must have gone down with all hands, and yet I fancy that the hero went on living afterwards. Perhaps he climbed into the attacking ship. I wouldn't see that, of course. I was dead, you know.'

He shivered slightly and protested that he could remember no more.

I did not press him further, but to satisfy myself that he lay in ignorance of the workings of his own mind, deliberately introduced him to Mortimer Collins's *Transmigration*, and gave him a sketch of the plot before he opened the pages.

'What rot it all is!' he said frankly, at the end of an hour. 'I don't understand his nonsense about the Red Planet Mars and the King, and the rest of it. Chuck me the Longfellow again.'

I handed him the book and wrote out as much as I could remember of his description of the sea-fight, appealing to him from time to time for confirmation of fact or detail. He would answer without raising his eyes from the book, as assuredly as though all his knowledge lay before him on the printed page. I spoke under the normal key of my voice that the current might not be broken, and I knew that he was not aware of what he was saying, for his thoughts were out on the sea with Longfellow.

'Charlie,' I asked, 'when the rowers on the galleys mutinied how did they kill their overseers?'

'Tore up the benches and brained 'em. That happened when a heavy sea was running. An overseer on the lower deck slipped from the centre plank and fell among the rowers. They choked him to death against the side of the ship with their chained hands quite quietly, and it was too dark for the other overseer to see what had happened. When he asked, he was pulled down too and choked, and the lower deck fought their way up deck by deck, with the pieces of the broken benches banging behind 'em. How they howled!'

'And what happened after that?'

'I don't know. The hero went away – red hair and red beard and all. That was after he had captured our galley, I think.'

The sound of my voice irritated him, and he motioned slightly with his left hand as a man does when interruption jars.

'You never told me he was red-headed before, or that he captured your galley,' I said, after a discreet interval.

Charlie did not raise his eyes.

'He was as red as a red bear,' said he abstractedly. 'He came from the north; they said so in the galley when he looked for rowers – not slaves, but free men. Afterwards – years and years afterwards – news came from another ship, or else he came back – '

His lips moved in silence. He was rapturously retasting some poem before him.

'Where had he been, then?' I was almost whispering that the sentence might come gently to whichever section of Charlie's brain was working on my behalf.

'To the Beaches – the Long and Wonderful Beaches!' was the reply after a minute of silence.

'To Furdurstrandi?' I asked, tingling from head to foot.

'Yes, to Furdurstrandi,' he pronounced the word in a new fashion. 'And I too saw – ' The voice failed.

'Do you know what you have said?' I shouted incautiously.

He lifted his eyes, fully roused now. 'No!' he snapped. 'I wish you'd let a chap go on reading. Hark to this:

> But Othere, the old sea captain,
> He neither paused nor stirred
> Till the king listened, and then
> Once more took up his pen
> And wrote down every word.
>
> And to the King of the Saxons
> In witness of the truth
> Raising his noble head,
> He stretched his brown hand and said,
> "Behold this walrus tooth."

By Jove, what chaps those must have been, to go sailing all over the shop never knowing where they'd fetch the land! Hah!'

'Charlie,' I pleaded, 'if you'll only be sensible for a minute or two I'll make our hero in our tale every inch as good as Othere.'

'Umph! Longfellow wrote that poem. I don't care about writing things any more. I want to read.' He was thoroughly out of tune now, and raging over my own ill-luck, I left him.

Conceive yourself at the door of the world's treasure-house guarded by a child – an idle, irresponsible child playing knucklebones – on whose favour depends the gift of the key, and you will imagine one half my torment. Till that evening Charlie had spoken nothing that might not lie within the experiences of a Greek galley-slave. But now, or there was no virtue in books, he had talked of some desperate adventure of the Vikings, of Thorfin Karlsefne's sailing to Wineland, which is America, in the ninth or tenth century. The battle in the harbour he had seen; and his own death he had described. But this was a much more startling plunge into the past. Was it possible that he had skipped half a dozen lives, and was then dimly remembering some episode of a thousand years later? It was a maddening jumble, and the worst of it was that Charlie Mears in his normal condition was the last person in the world to clear it up. I could only wait and watch, but I went to bed that night full of the wildest imaginings. There was nothing that was not possible if Charlie's detestable memory only held good.

I might rewrite the Saga of Thorfin Karlsefne as it had never been written before, might tell the story of the first discovery of America, myself the discoverer. But I was entirely at Charlie's mercy, and so long as there was a three-and-sixpenny Bohn volume within his reach Charlie would not tell. I dared not curse him openly; I hardly dared jog his memory, for I was dealing with the experiences of a thousand years ago, told through the mouth of a boy of today; and a boy of today is affected by every change of tone and gust of opinion, so that he must lie even when he most desires to speak the truth.

I saw no more of Charlie for nearly a week. When next I met him it was in Gracechurch Street with a bill-book chained to his waist. Business took him over London Bridge, and I accompanied him. He was very full of the importance of that book and magnified it. As we passed over the Thames we paused to look at a steamer unloading great slabs of white and brown marble. A barge drifted under the steamer's stern and a lonely ship's cow in that barge bellowed. Charlie's face changed from the face of the bank-clerk to that of an unknown and – though he would not have believed this – a much shrewder man. He flung out his arm across the parapet of the bridge and laughing very loudly, said: 'When they heard *our* bulls bellow the Skroelings ran away!'

I waited only for an instant, but the barge and the cow had disappeared under the bows of the steamer before I answered.

'Charlie, what do you suppose are Skroelings?'

'Never heard of 'em before. They sound like a new kind of seagull. What a chap you are for asking questions!' he replied. 'I have to go to the cashier of the Omnibus Company yonder. Will you wait for me and we can lunch somewhere together? I've a notion for a poem.'

'No, thanks. I'm off. You're sure you know nothing about Skroelings?'

'Not unless he's been entered for the Liverpool Handicap.' He nodded and disappeared in the crowd.

Now it is written in the Saga of Eric the Red or that of Thorfin Karlsefne, that nine hundred years ago when Karlsefne's galleys came to Leif's booths, which Leif had erected in the unknown land called Markland, which may or may not have been Rhode Island, the Skroelings – and the Lord He knows who these may or may not have been – came to trade with the Vikings, and ran away because they were frightened at the bellowing of the cattle which Thorfin had brought with him in the ships. But what in the world could a Greek slave know of that affair? I wandered up and down among the streets trying to unravel the mystery and the more I considered it the more baffling it grew. One thing only seemed certain, and that certainty took away my breath for the moment. If I came to full knowledge of anything at all, it would not be one life of the soul in Charlie Mears's body, but half a dozen – half a dozen several and separate existences spent on blue water in the morning of the world!

Then I reviewed the situation.

Obviously if I used my knowledge I should stand alone and unapproachable until all men were as wise as myself. That would be something, but, manlike, I was ungrateful. It seemed bitterly unfair that Charlie's memory should fail me when I needed it most. Great Powers Above – I looked up at them through the fog-smoke – did the Lords of Life and Death know what this meant to me? Nothing less than eternal fame of the best kind, that comes from One, and is shared by one alone. I would be content – remembering Clive, I stood astounded at my own moderation – with the mere right to tell one story, to work out one little contribution to the light literature of the day. If Charlie were permitted full recollection for one hour – for sixty short minutes – of existences that had extended over a thousand years, I would forgo all profit and honour from all that I should make of his speech. I would take no share in the commotion that would follow throughout the particular corner of the earth that calls itself 'the world'. The thing should be put forth anonymously. Nay, I would make other men believe that they had written it. They would hire bull-hided self-advertising Englishmen to bellow it abroad. Preachers would found a fresh conduct of life upon it, swearing that it was new and that they had lifted the fear of death from all mankind. Every Orientalist in Europe would patronise it discursively with Sanskrit and Pali texts. Terrible women would invent unclean variants of the men's belief for the elevation of their sisters. Churches and religions would war over it. Between the hailing and restarting of an omnibus I foresaw the scuffles that would arise among half a dozen denominations all professing 'the doctrine of the True Metempsychosis as applied to the world and the New Era'; and saw, too, the respectable English newspapers shying, like frightened kine, over the beautiful simplicity of the tale. The mind leaped forward a hundred – two hundred – a thousand years. I saw with sorrow that men would mutilate and garble the story; that rival creeds would turn it upside down till, at last, the western world which clings to the dread of death more closely than the hope of life, would set it aside as an interesting superstition and stampede after some faith so long forgotten that it seemed altogether new. Upon this I changed the terms of the bargain that I would make with the Lords of Life and Death. Only let me know, let me write, the story with sure knowledge that I wrote the truth, and I would burn the manuscript as a solemn sacrifice. Five minutes after the last line was written I would destroy it all. But I must be allowed to write it with absolute certainty.

There was no answer. The flaming colours of an Aquarium poster caught my eye, and I wondered whether it would be wise or prudent to lure Charlie into the hands of the professional mesmerist then, and whether, if he were under his power, he would speak of his past lives. If he did, and if people believed him . . . but Charlie would be frightened and flustered, or made conceited by the interviews. In either case he would begin to lie through fear or vanity. He was safest in my own hands.

'They are very funny fools, your English,' said a

voice at my elbow, and turning round I recognised a casual acquaintance, a young Bengali law student, called Grish Chunder, whose father had sent him to England to become civilised. The old man was a retired native official, and on an income of five pounds a month contrived to allow his son two hundred pounds a year, and the run of his teeth in a city where he could pretend to be the cadet of a royal house, and tell stories of the brutal Indian bureaucrats who ground the faces of the poor.

Grish Chunder was a young, fat, full-bodied Bengali, dressed with scrupulous care in frock coat, tall hat, light trousers, and tan gloves. But I had known him in the days when the brutal Indian Government paid for his university education, and he contributed cheap sedition to the *Sachi Durpan*, and intrigued with the wives of his fourteen-year-old schoolmates.

'That is very funny and very foolish,' he said, nodding at the poster. 'I am going down to the Northbrook Club. Will you come too?'

I walked with him for some time. 'You are not well,' he said. 'What is there on your mind? You do not talk.'

'Grish Chunder, you've been too well educated to believe in a God, haven't you?'

'Oah, yes, *here*! But when I go home I must conciliate popular superstition, and make ceremonies of purification, and my women will anoint idols.'

'And hang up *tulsi* and feast the *purohit*, and take you back into caste again, and make a good *khuttri* of you again, you advanced Freethinker. And you'll eat *desi* food, and like it all, from the smell in the courtyard to the mustard oil over you.'

'I shall very much like it,' said Grish Chunder unguardedly. 'Once a Hindu – always a Hindu. But I like to know what the English think they know.'

'I'll tell you something that one Englishman knows. It's an old tale to you.'

I began to tell the story of Charlie in English but Grish Chunder put a question in the vernacular, and the history went forward naturally in the tongue best suited for its telling. After all, it could never have been told in English. Grish Chunder heard me, nodding from time to time, and then came up to my rooms, where I finished the tale.

'*Beshak*,' he said philosophically. '*Lekin darwaza band hai.* [Without doubt; but the door is shut.] I have heard of this remembering of previous existences among my people. It is of course an old tale with us, but, to happen to an Englishman – a cow-fed *Mlechh* – an outcast. By Jove, that is *most* peculiar!'

'Outcast yourself, Grish Chunder! You eat cow-beef every day. Let's think the thing over. The boy remembers his incarnations.'

'Does he know that?' said Grish Chunder quietly, swinging his legs as he sat on my table. He was speaking in his English now.

'He does not know anything. Would I speak to you if he did? Go on!'

'There is no going on at all. If you tell that to your friends they will say you are mad and put it in the papers. Suppose, now, you prosecute for libel.'

'Let's leave that out of the question entirely. Is there any chance of his being made to speak?'

'There is a chance. Oah, yes–s! But *if* he spoke it would mean that all this world would end now – *instanto* – fall down on your head. These things are not allowed, you know. As I said, the door is shut.'

'Not a ghost of a chance?'

'How can there be? You are a Christi-án, and it is forbidden to eat, in your books, of the Tree of Life, or else you would never die. How shall you all fear death if you all know what your friend does not know that he knows? I am afraid to be kicked, but I am not afraid to die, because I know what I know. You are not afraid to be kicked, but you are afraid to die. If you were not, by God! you English would be all over the shop in an hour, upsetting the balances of power, and making commotions. It would not be good. But no fear. He will remember a little and a little less, and he will call it dreams. Then he will forget altogether. When I passed my First Arts Examination in Calcutta that was all in the cram-book on Wordsworth. "Trailing clouds of glory", you know.'

'This seems to be an exception to the rule.'

'There are no exceptions to rules. Some are not so hard-looking as others, but they are all the same when you touch. If this friend of yours said so-and-so and so-and-so, indicating that he remembered all his lost lives, or one piece of a lost life, he would not be in the bank another hour. He would be what you call sacked because he was mad, and they would send him to an asylum for lunatics. You can see that, my friend.'

'Of course I can, but I wasn't thinking of him. His name need never appear in the story.'

'Ah! I see. That story will never be written. You can try.'

'I am going to.'

'For your own credit and for the sake of money, *of* course?'

'No. For the sake of writing the story. On my honour that will be all.'

'Even then there is no chance. You cannot play with

the gods. It is a very pretty story now. As they say, let it go on that – I mean at that. Be quick; he will not last long.'

'How do you mean?'

'What I say. He has never, so far, thought about a woman.'

'Hasn't he, though!' I remembered some of Charlie's confidences.

'I mean no woman has thought about him. When that comes; *bus – hogya* – all up! I know. There are millions of women here. Housemaids, for instance. They kiss you behind doors.'

I winced at the thought of my story being ruined by a housemaid. And yet nothing was more probable.

Grish Chunder grinned.

'Yes – also pretty girls – cousins of his house, and perhaps *not* of his house. One kiss that he gives back again and remembers will cure all this nonsense, or else – '

'Or else what? Remember he does not know that he knows.'

'I know that. Or else, if nothing happens he will become immersed in the trade and the financial speculation like the rest. It must be so. You can see that it must be so. But the woman will come first, *I* think.'

There was a rap at the door, and Charlie charged in impetuously. He had been released from office, and by the look in his eyes I could see that he had come over for a long talk; most probably with poems in his pockets. Charlie's poems were very wearying, but sometimes they led him to speak about the galley.

Grish Chunder looked at him keenly for a minute.

'I beg your pardon,' Charlie said uneasily; 'I didn't know you had anyone with you.'

'I am going,' said Grish Chunder.

He drew me into the lobby as he departed.

'That is your man,' he said quickly. 'I tell you he will never speak all you wish. That is rot – bosh. But he would be most good to make to see things. Suppose now we pretend that it was only play' – I had never seen Grish Chunder so excited – 'and pour the ink-pool into his hand. Eh, what do you think? I tell you that he could see *anything* that a man could see. Let me get the ink and the camphor. He is a seer and he will tell us very many things.'

'He may be all you say, but I'm not going to trust him to your gods and devils.'

'It will not hurt him. He will only feel a little stupid and dull when he wakes up. You have seen boys look into the ink-pool before.'

'That is the reason why I am not going to see it any more. You'd better go, Grish Chunder.'

He went, insisting far down the staircase that it was throwing away my only chance of looking into the future.

This left me unmoved, for I was concerned for the past, and no peering of hypnotised boys into mirrors and ink-pools would help me to that. But I recognised Grish Chunder's point of view and sympathised with it.

'What a big black brute that was!' said Charlie, when I returned to him. 'Well, look here, I've just done a poem; did it instead of playing dominoes after lunch. May I read it?'

'Let me read it to myself.'

'Then you miss the proper expression. Besides, you always make my things sound as if the rhymes were all wrong.'

'Read it aloud, then. You're like the rest of 'em.'

Charlie mouthed me his poem, and it was not much worse than the average of his verses. He had been reading his books faithfully, but he was not pleased when I told him that I preferred my Longfellow undiluted with Charlie.

Then we began to go through the manuscript line by line, Charlie parrying every objection and correction with: 'Yes, that may be better, but you don't catch what I'm driving at.'

Charlie was, in one way at least, very like one kind of poet.

There was a pencil scrawl at the back of the paper, and 'What's that?' I said.

'Oh, that's not poetry at all. It's some rot I wrote last night before I went to bed, and it was too much bother to hunt for rhymes; so I made it a sort of blank verse instead.'

Here is Charlie's 'blank verse':

We pulled for you when the wind was against us
 and the sails were low.
 Will you never let us go?
We ate bread and onions when you took towns, or
 ran aboard quickly when you were beaten back
 by the foe.
The captains walked up and down the deck in fair
 weather singing songs, but we were below.
We fainted with our chins on the oars and you did
 not see that we were idle for we still swung to
 and fro.
 Will you never let us go?
The salt made the oar-handles like shark-skin; our
 knees were cut to the bone with salt cracks; our
 hair was stuck to our foreheads; and our lips

were cut to our gums, and you whipped us
because we could not row.
Will you never let us go?
But in a little time we shall run out of the port-
holes as the water runs along the oar-blade, and
though you tell the others to row after us you
will never catch us till you catch the oar-thresh
and tie up the winds in the belly of the sail. Aho!
Will you never let us go?

'H'm. What's oar-thresh, Charlie?'

'The water washed up by the oars. That's the sort of song they might sing in the galley y' know. Aren't you ever going to finish that story and give me some of the profits?'

'It depends on yourself. If you had only told me more about your hero in the first instance it might have been finished by now. You're so hazy in your notions.'

'I only want to give you the general notion of it – the knocking about from place to place and the fighting and all that. Can't you fill in the rest yourself? Make the hero save a girl on a pirate-galley and marry her or do something.'

'You're a really helpful collaborator. I suppose the hero went through some few adventures before he married.'

'Well then, make him a very artful card – a low sort of man – a sort of political man who went about making treaties and breaking them – a black-haired chap who hid behind the mast when the fighting began.'

'But you said the other day that he was red-haired.'

'I couldn't have. Make him black-haired of course. You've no imagination.'

Seeing that I had just discovered the entire principles upon which the half-memory falsely called imagination is based, I felt entitled to laugh, but forbore for the sake of the tale.

'You're right. *You're* the man with imagination. A black-haired chap in a decked ship,' I said.

'No, an open ship – like a big boat.'

This was maddening.

'Your ship has been built and designed, closed and decked in; you said so yourself,' I protested.

'No, no, not that ship. That was open or half-decked because – By Jove, you're right. You made me think of the hero as a red-haired chap. Of course if he were red, the ship would be an open one with painted sails.'

Surely, I thought, he would remember now that he had served in two galleys at least – in a three-decked Greek one under the black-haired 'political man', and again in a Viking's open sea-serpent under the man 'red as a red bear' who went to Markland. The devil prompted me to speak.

'Why "of course", Charlie?' said I.

'I don't know. Are you making fun of me?'

The current was broken for the time being. I took up a notebook and pretended to make many entries in it.

'It's a pleasure to work with an imaginative chap like yourself,' I said, after a pause. 'The way that you've brought out the character of the hero is simply wonderful.'

'Do you think so?' he answered, with a pleased flush. 'I often tell myself that there's more in me than my mo – than people think.'

'There's an enormous amount in you.'

'Then, won't you let me send an essay on "The Ways of Bank-Clerks" to *Tit-Bits*, and get the guinea prize?'

'That wasn't exactly what I meant, old fellow: perhaps it would be better to wait a little and go ahead with the galley story.'

'Ah, but I shan't get the credit of that. *Tit-Bits* would publish my name and address if I win. What are you grinning at? They *would*.'

'I know it. Suppose you go for a walk. I want to look through my notes about our story.'

Now this reprehensible youth who left me, a little hurt and put back, might for aught he or I knew have been one of the crew of the *Argo* – had been certainly slave or comrade to Thorfin Karlsefne. Therefore he was deeply interested in guinea competitions. Remembering what Grish Chunder had said I laughed aloud. The Lords of Life and Death would never allow Charlie Mears to speak with full knowledge of his pasts, and I must even piece out what he had told me with my own poor inventions while Charlie wrote of the ways of bank-clerks.

I got together and placed on one file all my notes; and the net result was not cheering. I read them a second time. There was nothing that might not have been compiled at second-hand from other people's books – except, perhaps, the story of the fight in the harbour. The adventures of a Viking had been written many times before; the history of a Greek galley-slave was no new thing, and though I wrote both, who could challenge or confirm the accuracy of my details? I might as well tell a tale of two thousand years hence. The Lords of Life and Death were as cunning as Grish Chunder had hinted. They would allow nothing to escape that might trouble or make easy the minds of men. Though I was convinced of this, yet I could not leave the tale alone. Exaltation followed reaction, not once, but twenty times in the next few weeks. My moods varied with the March sunlight and flying clouds. By night or in the beauty of a spring morning I perceived that I could write that tale and shift continents thereby. In the wet windy afternoons, I saw that the tale might indeed be written, but would be nothing more than a faked, false-varnished, sham-rusted piece of Wardour Street work in the end. Then I blessed Charlie in many ways – though it was no fault of his. He seemed to be busy with prize competitions, and I saw less and less of him as the weeks went by and the earth cracked and grew ripe to spring, and the buds swelled in their sheaths. He did not care to read or talk of what he had read, and there was a new ring of self-assertion in his voice. I hardly cared to remind him of the galley when we met; but Charlie alluded to it on every occasion, always as a story from which money was to be made.

'I think I deserve twenty-five per cent, don't I, at least?' he said, with beautiful frankness. 'I supplied all the ideas, didn't I?'

This greediness for silver was a new side to his nature. I assumed that it had been developed in the City, where Charlie was picking up the curious nasal drawl of the underbred City man.

'When the thing's done we'll talk about it. I can't make anything of it at present. Red-haired or black-haired heroes are equally difficult.'

He was sitting by the fire staring at the red coals. '*I* can't understand what you find so difficult. It's all as clear as mud to me,' he replied. A jet of gas puffed out between the bars, took light, and whistled softly. 'Suppose we take the red-haired hero's adventures first, from the time that he came south to my galley and captured it and sailed to the Beaches.'

I knew better now than to interrupt Charlie. I was out of reach of pen and paper, and dared not move to get them lest I should break the current. The gas-jet puffed and whinnied, Charlie's voice dropped almost to a whisper, and he told a tale of the sailing of an open galley to Furdurstrandi, of sunsets on the open sea, seen under the curve of the one sail evening after evening when the galley's beak was notched into the centre of the sinking disc, and 'we sailed by that for we had no other guide', quoth Charlie. He spoke of a landing on an island and explorations in its woods, where the crew killed three men whom they found asleep under the pines. Their ghosts, Charlie said, followed the galley, swimming and choking in the water, and the crew cast lots and threw one of their number overboard as a sacrifice to the strange gods whom they had offended. Then they ate seaweed when their provisions failed, and their legs swelled, and their leader, the red-haired man, killed two rowers who mutinied, and after a year spent among the woods they set sail for their own country, and a wind that never failed carried them back so safely that they all slept at night. This, and much more, Charlie told. Sometimes the voice fell so low that I could not catch the words, though every nerve was on the strain. He spoke of their leader, the red-haired man, as a pagan speaks of his God; for it was he who cheered them and slew them impartially as he thought best for their needs; and it was he who steered them for three days among floating ice, each floe crowded with strange beasts that 'tried to sail with us', said Charlie, 'and we beat them back with the handles of the oars'.

The gas-jet went out, a burnt coal gave way, and the fire settled with a tiny crash to the bottom of the grate. Charlie ceased speaking, and I said no word.

'By Jove!' he said at last, shaking his head. 'I've been staring at the fire till I'm dizzy. What was I going to say?'

'Something about the galley book.'

'I remember now. It's twenty-five per cent of the profits, isn't it?'

'It's anything you like when I've done the tale.'

'I wanted to be sure of that. I must go now. I've – I've an appointment.' And he left me.

Had not my eyes been held I might have known that that broken muttering over the fire was the swan-song of Charlie Mears. But I thought it the prelude to fuller revelation. At last and at last I should cheat the Lords of Life and Death!

When next Charlie came to me I received him with rapture. He was nervous and embarrassed, but his eyes were very full of light, and his lips a little parted.

'I've done a poem,' he said; and then, quickly: 'It's the best I've ever done. Read it.' He thrust it into my hand and retreated to the window.

I groaned inwardly. It would be the work of half an hour to criticise – that is to say, praise – the poem sufficiently to please Charlie. Then I had good reason to groan, for Charlie, discarding his favourite centi-pede metres, had launched into shorter and choppier verse, and verse with a motive at the back of it. This is what I read:

The day is most fair, the cheery wind
  Halloos behind the hill,
Where he bends the wood as seemeth good,
  And the sapling to his will!
Riot, O wind; there is that in my blood
  That would not have thee still!

She gave me herself, O Earth, O Sky;
  Grey sea, she is mine alone!
Let the sullen boulders hear my cry,
  And rejoice tho' they be but stone!

Mine! I have won her, O good brown earth,
  Make merry! 'Tis hard on Spring;
Make merry; my love is doubly worth
  All worship your fields can bring!
Let the hind that tills you feel my mirth
  At the early harrowing!

'Yes, it's the early harrowing, past a doubt,' I said, with a dread at my heart. Charlie smiled, but did not answer.

Red cloud of the sunset, tell it abroad;
  I am victor. Greet me, O Sun,
Dominant master and absolute lord
  Over the soul of one!

'Well?' said Charlie, looking over my shoulder.

I thought it far from well, and very evil indeed, when he silently laid a photograph on the paper – the photograph of a girl with a curly head and a foolish slack mouth.

'Isn't it – isn't it wonderful?' he whispered, pink to the tips of his ears, wrapped in the rosy mystery of first love. 'I didn't know; I didn't think – it came like a thunderclap.'

'Yes. It comes like a thunderclap. Are you very happy, Charlie?'

'My God – she – she loves me!' He sat down repeating the last words to himself. I looked at the hairless face, the narrow shoulders already bowed by desk-work, and wondered when, where, and how he had loved in his past lives.

'What will your mother say?' I asked cheerfully.

'I don't care a damn what she says!'

At twenty the things for which one does not care a damn should, properly, be many, but one must not include mothers in the list. I told him this gently; and he described Her, even as Adam must have described to the newly-named beasts the glory and tenderness and beauty of Eve. Incidentally I learned that She was a tobacconist's assistant with a weakness for pretty dress, and had told him four or five times already that She had never been kissed by a man before.

Charlie spoke on and on, and on; while I, separated from him by thousands of years, was considering the beginnings of things. Now I understood why the Lords of Life and Death shut the doors so carefully behind us. It is that we may not remember our first and most beautiful wooings. Were this not so, our world would be without inhabitants in a hundred years.

'Now, about that galley story,' I said still more cheerfully, in a pause in the rush of the speech.

Charlie looked up as though he had been hit. 'The galley – what galley? Good heavens, don't joke, man! This is serious! You don't know how serious it is!'

Grish Chunder was right. Charlie had tasted the love of woman that kills remembrance, and the finest story in the world would never be written.

With the Night Mail

A story of 2000 AD *together with extracts from the magazine in which it appeared*

At nine o'clock of a gusty winter night I stood on the lower stages of one of the GPO outward mail towers. My purpose was a run to Quebec in 'Postal Packet 162 or such other as may be appointed'; and the Postmaster-General himself countersigned the order. This talisman opened all doors, even those in the despatching-caisson at the foot of the tower, where they were delivering the sorted Continental mail. The bags lay packed close as herrings in the long grey underbodies which our GPO still calls 'coaches'. Five such coaches were filled as I watched, and were shot up the guides to be locked on to their waiting packets three hundred feet nearer the stars.

From the despatching-caisson I was conducted by a courteous and wonderfully learned official – Mr L. L. Geary, Second Despatcher of the Western Route – to the Captains' Room (this wakes an echo of old romance), where the mail captains come on for their turn of duty. He introduces me to the captain of '162' – Captain Purnall, and his relief, Captain Hodgson. The one is small and dark; the other large and red; but each has the brooding sheathed glance characteristic of eagles and aeronauts. You can see it in the pictures of our racing professionals, from L. V. Rautsch to little Ada Warrleigh – that fathomless abstraction of eyes habitually turned through naked space.

On the notice-board in the Captains' Room, the pulsing arrows of some twenty indicators register, degree by geographical degree, the progress of as many homeward-bound packets. The word 'Cape' rises across the face of a dial; a gong strikes: the South African mid-weekly mail is in at the Highgate Receiving Towers. That is all. It reminds one comically of the traitorous little bell which in pigeon-fanciers' lofts notifies the return of a homer.

'Time for us to be on the move,' says Captain Purnall, and we are shot up by the passenger-lift to the top of the despatch-towers. 'Our coach will lock on when it is filled and the clerks are aboard.'

'No. 162' waits for us in Slip E of the topmost stage. The great curve of her back shines frostily under the lights, and some minute alteration of trim makes her rock a little in her holding-down slips.

Captain Purnall frowns and dives inside. Hissing softly, '162' comes to rest as level as a rule. From her North Atlantic Winter nose-cap (worn bright as diamond with boring through uncounted leagues of hail, snow, and ice) to the inset of her three built-out propeller-shafts is some two hundred and forty feet. Her extreme diameter, carried well forward, is thirty-seven. Contrast this with the nine hundred by ninety-five of any crack liner, and you will realise the power that must drive a hull through all weathers at more than the emergency speed of the *Cyclonic*!

The eye detects no joint in her skin plating save the sweeping hair-crack of the bow-rudder – Magniac's rudder that assured us the dominion of the unstable air and left its inventor penniless and half-blind. It is calculated to Castelli's 'gullwing' curve. Raise a few feet of that all but invisible plate three-eighths of an inch and she will yaw five miles to port or starboard ere she is under control again. Give her full helm and she returns on her track like a whiplash. Cant the whole forward – a touch on the wheel will suffice – and she sweeps at your good direction up or down. Open the complete circle and she presents to the air a mushroom-head that will bring her up all standing within a half mile.

'Yes,' says Captain Hodgson, answering my thought, 'Castelli thought he'd discovered the secret of controlling aeroplanes when he'd only found out how to steer dirigible balloons. Magniac invented his rudder to help war-boats ram each other; and war went out of fashion and Magniac he went out of his mind because he said he couldn't serve his country any more. I wonder if any of us ever know what we're really doing.'

'If you want to see the coach locked you'd better go aboard. It's due now,' says Mr Geary. I enter through the door amidships. There is nothing here for display. The inner skin of the gas-tanks comes down to within a foot or two of my head and turns over just short of the turn of the bilges. Liners and yachts disguise their tanks with decoration, but the GPO serves them raw under a lick of grey official paint. The inner skin shuts off fifty feet of the bow and as much of the stern, but the bow-bulkhead is recessed for the lift-shunting apparatus as the stern is pierced for the shaft-tunnels. The engine-room lies almost amidships. Forward of it, extending to the turn of the bow tanks, is an aperture – a bottomless hatch at present – into which our coach will be locked. One looks down over the coamings three hundred feet to the despatching-caisson whence voices boom upward. The light below is obscured to a sound of thunder, as our coach rises on its guides. It enlarges rapidly from a postage-stamp to a playing-card; to a punt and last a pontoon. The two clerks, its crew, do not even look up as it comes into place. The Quebec letters fly under their fingers and leap into the docketed racks, while both captains and Mr Geary satisfy themselves that the coach is locked home. A clerk passes the waybill over the hatch coaming. Captain Purnall thumb-marks and passes it to Mr Geary. Receipt has been given and taken. 'Pleasant run,' says Mr Geary, and disappears through the door which a foot-high pneumatic compressor locks after him.

'A-ah!' sighs the compressor released. Our holding-down clips part with a tang. We are clear.

Captain Hodgson opens the great colloid underbody porthole through which I watch over-lighted London slide eastward as the gale gets hold of us. The first of the low winter clouds cuts off the well-known view and darkens Middlesex. On the south edge of it I can see a postal packet's light ploughing through the white fleece. For an instant she gleams like a star ere she drops toward the Highgate Receiving Towers. 'The Bombay Mail,' says Captain Hodgson, and looks at his watch. 'She's forty minutes late.'

'What's our level?' I ask.

'Four thousand. Aren't you coming up on the bridge?'

The bridge (let us ever praise the GPO as a repository of ancientest tradition!) is represented by a view of Captain Hodgson's legs where he stands on the Control Platform that runs thwartships overhead. The bow colloid is unshuttered and Captain Purnall, one hand on the wheel, is feeling for a fair slant. The dial shows 4300 feet. 'It's steep tonight,' he mutters, as tier on tier of cloud drops under. 'We generally pick up an easterly draught below three thousand at this time o' the year. I hate slathering through fluff.'

'So does Van Cutsem. Look at him huntin' for a slant!' says Captain Hodgson. A fog-light breaks cloud a hundred fathoms below. The Antwerp Night Mail makes her signal and rises between two racing clouds far to port, her flanks blood-red in the glare of Sheerness Double Light. The gale will have us over the North Sea in half an hour, but Captain Purnall lets her go composedly – nosing to every point of the compass as she rises.

'Five thousand – six, six thousand eight hundred' – the dip-dial reads ere we find the easterly drift, heralded by a flurry of snow at the thousand fathom level. Captain Purnall rings up the engines and keys down the governor on the switch before him. There is no sense in urging machinery when Aeolus himself gives you good knots for nothing. We are away in earnest now – our nose notched home on our chosen star. At this level the lower clouds are laid out, all neatly combed by the dry fingers of the East. Below that again is the strong westerly blow through which we rose. Overhead, a film of southerly drifting mist draws a theatrical gauze across the firmament. The moonlight turns the lower strata to silver without a stain except where our shadow underruns us. Bristol and Cardiff Double Lights (those statelily inclined beams over Severnmouth) are dead ahead of us; for we keep the Southern Winter Route. Coventry Central, the pivot of the English system, stabs upward once in ten seconds its spear of diamond light to the north; and a point or two off our starboard bow The Leek, the great cloud-breaker of St David's Head, swings its unmistakable green beam twenty-five degrees each way. There must be half a mile of fluff over it in this weather, but it does not affect The Leek.

'Our planet's over-lighted if anything,' says Captain Purnall at the wheel, as Cardiff–Bristol slides under. 'I remember the old days of common white verticals that 'ud show two or three hundred feet up in a mist, if you knew where to look for 'em. In really fluffy weather they might as well have been under your hat. One could get lost coming home then, an' have some fun. Now, it's like driving down Piccadilly.'

He points to the pillars of light where the cloud-breakers bore through the cloud-floor. We see nothing of England's outlines: only a white pavement pierced in all directions by these manholes of variously coloured fire – Holy Island's white and red – St Bees' interrupted white, and so on as far as the eye can reach. Blessed be Sargent, Ahrens, and the Dubois brothers, who invented the cloud-breakers of the world whereby we travel in security!

'Are you going to lift for the Shamrock?' asks Captain Hodgson. Cork Light (green, fixed) enlarges as we rush to it. Captain Purnall nods. There is heavy traffic hereabouts – the cloud-bank beneath us is streaked with running fissures of flame where the Atlantic boats are hurrying Londonward just clear of the fluff. Mail-packets are supposed, under the Conference rules, to have the five-thousand-foot lanes to themselves, but the foreigner in a hurry is apt to take liberties with English air. 'No. 162' lifts to a long-drawn wail of the breeze in the fore-flange of the rudder and we make Valencia (white, green, white) at a safe 7000 feet, dipping our beam to an incoming Washington packet.

There is no cloud on the Atlantic, and faint streaks of cream round Dingle Bay show where the driven seas hammer the coast. A big SATA liner (*Société Anonyme des Transports Aériens*) is diving and lifting half a mile below us in search of some break in the solid west wind. Lower still lies a disabled Dane: she is telling the liner all about it in International. Our General Communication dial has caught her talk and begins to eavesdrop. Captain Hodgson makes a motion to shut it off but checks himself. 'Perhaps you'd like to listen,' he says.

'*Argol* of St Thomas,' the Dane whimpers. 'Report owners three starboard shaft collar-bearings fused. Can make Flores as we are, but impossible further. Shall we buy spares at Fayal?'

The liner acknowledges and recommends inverting the bearings. The *Argol* answers that she has already done so without effect, and begins to relieve her mind about cheap German enamels for collar-bearings. The Frenchman assents cordially, cries '*Courage, mon ami*,' and switches off.

Their lights sink under the curve of the ocean.

'That's one of Lundt & Bleamers's boats,' says Captain Hodgson. 'Serves 'em right for putting German compos in their thrust-blocks. *She* won't be in Fayal tonight! By the way, wouldn't you like to look round the engine-room?'

I have been waiting eagerly for this invitation and I follow Captain Hodgson from the control-platform, stooping low to avoid the bulge of the tanks. We know that Fleury's gas can lift anything, as the world-famous trials of '89 showed, but its almost indefinite powers of expansion necessitate vast tank room. Even in this thin air the lift-shunts are busy taking out one-third of its normal lift, and still '162' must be checked by an occasional down-draw of the rudder or our flight would become a climb to the stars. Captain Purnall prefers an overlifted to an underlifted ship; but no two captains trim ship alike. 'When *I* take the bridge,' says Captain Hodgson, 'you'll see me shunt forty per cent of the lift out of the gas and run her on the upper rudder. With a swoop upwards instead of a swoop downwards, *as* you say. Either way will do. It's only habit. Watch our dip-dial! Tim fetches her down once every thirty knots as regularly as breathing.'

So is it shown on the dip-dial. For five or six minutes the arrow creeps from 6700 to 7300. There is the faint 'szgee' of the rudder, and back slides the arrow to 6000 on a falling slant of ten or fifteen knots.

'In heavy weather you jockey her with the screws as well,' says Captain Hodgson, and, unclipping the jointed bar which divides the engine-room from the bare deck, he leads me on to the floor.

Here we find Fleury's Paradox of the Bulk-headed Vacuum – which we accept now without thought – literally in full blast. The three engines are HT&T assisted-vacuo Fleury turbines running from 3000 to the Limit – that is to say, up to the point when the blades make the air 'bell' – cut out a vacuum for themselves precisely as over-driven marine propellers used to do. '162's' limit is low on account of the small size of her nine screws, which, though handier than the old colloid Thelussons, 'bell' sooner. The midships engine, generally used as a reinforce, is not running; so the port and starboard turbine vacuum-chambers draw direct into the return-mains.

The turbines whistle reflectively. From the low-arched expansion-tanks on either side the valves descend pillarwise to the turbine-chests, and thence the obedient gas whirls through the spirals of blades with a force that would whip the teeth out of a power saw. Behind, is its own pressure held in leash or spurred on by the lift-shunts; before it, the vacuum where Fleury's Ray dances in violet-green bands and whirled tourbillions of flame. The jointed U-tubes of the vacuum-chamber are pressure-tempered colloid (no glass would endure the strain for an instant) and a junior engineer with tinted spectacles watches the Ray intently. It is the very heart of the machine – a mystery to this day. Even Fleury who begat it and, unlike Magniac, died a multimillionaire, could not explain how the restless little imp shuddering in the U-tube can, in the fractional fraction of a second, strike the furious blast of gas into a chill greyish-green liquid that drains (you can hear it trickle) from the far end of the vacuum through the eduction-pipes and the mains back to the bilges. Here it returns to its gaseous, one had almost written sagacious, state and climbs to work afresh. Bilge-tank, upper tank, dorsal-tank, expansion-chamber, vacuum, main-return (as a liquid), and bilge-tank once more is the ordained cycle. Fleury's Ray sees to that; and the engineer with the tinted spectacles sees to Fleury's Ray. If a speck of oil, if even the natural grease of the human finger touch the hooded terminals, Fleury's Ray will wink and disappear and must be laboriously built up again. This means half a day's work for all hands and an expense of one hundred and seventy-odd pounds to the GPO for radium-salts and such trifles.

'Now look at our thrust-collars. You won't find much German compo there. Full-jewelled, you see,' says Captain Hodgson as the engineer shunts open the top of a cap. Our shaft-bearings are CMC

(Commercial Minerals Company) stones, ground with as much care as the lens of a telescope. They cost £37 apiece. So far we have not arrived at their term of life. These bearings came from 'No. 97', which took them over from the old *Dominion of Light* which had them out of the wreck of the *Perseus* aeroplane in the years when men still flew tin kites over oil engines!

They are a shining reproof to all low-grade German 'ruby' enamels, so-called 'boort' facings, and the dangerous and unsatisfactory alumina compounds which please dividend-hunting owners and drive skippers crazy.

The rudder-gear and the gas lift-shunt, seated side by side under the engine-room dials, are the only machines in visible motion. The former sighs from time to time as the oil plunger rises and falls half an inch. The latter, cased and guarded like the U-tube aft, exhibits another Fleury Ray, but inverted and more green than violet. Its function is to shunt the lift out of the gas, and this it will do without watching. That is all! A tiny pump-rod wheezing and whining to itself beside a sputtering green lamp. A hundred and fifty feet aft down the flat-topped tunnel of the tanks a violet light, restless and irresolute. Between the two, three white-painted turbine-trunks, like eel-baskets laid on their side, accentuate the empty perspectives. You can hear the trickle of the liquefied gas flowing from the vacuum into the bilge-tanks and the soft gluck-glock of gas-locks closing as Captain Purnall brings '162' down by the head. The hum of the turbines and the boom of the air on our skin is no more than a cotton-wool wrapping to the universal stillness. And we are running an eighteen-second mile.

I peer from the fore end of the engine-room over the

hatch-coamings into the coach. The mail-clerks are sorting the Winnipeg, Calgary, and Medicine Hat bags; but there is a pack of cards ready on the table.

Suddenly a bell thrills; the engineers run to the turbine-valves and stand by; but the spectacled slave of the Ray in the U-tube never lifts his head. He must watch where he is. We are hard-braked and going astern; there is language from the Control Platform.

'Tim's sparking badly about something,' says the unruffled Captain Hodgson. 'Let's look.'

Captain Purnall is not the suave man we left half an hour since, but the embodied authority of the GPO. Ahead of us floats an ancient, aluminium-patched, twin-screw tramp of the dingiest, with no more right to the 5000-foot lane than has a horse-cart to a modern road. She carries an obsolete 'barbette' conning tower – a six-foot affair with railed platform forward – and our warning beam plays on the top of it as a policeman's lantern flashes on the area sneak. Like a sneak-thief, too, emerges a shock-headed navigator in his shirtsleeves. Captain Purnall wrenches open the colloid to talk with him man to man. There are times when Science does not satisfy.

'What under the stars are you doing here, you sky-scraping chimney-sweep?' he shouts as we two drift side by side. 'Do you know this is a Mail-lane? You call yourself a sailor, sir? You ain't fit to peddle toy balloons to an Eskimo. Your name and number! Report and get down, and be – !'

'I've been blown up once,' the shock-headed man cries, hoarsely as a dog barking. 'I don't care two flips of a contact for anything *you* can do, Postey.'

'Don't you, sir? But I'll make you care. I'll have you towed stern first to Disko and broke up. You can't recover insurance if you're broke for obstruction. Do you understand *that*?'

Then the stranger bellows: 'Look at my propellers! There's been a wulli-wa down below that has knocked us into umbrella-frames! We've been blown up about forty thousand feet! We're all one conjuror's watch inside! My mate's arm's broke; my engineer's head's cut open; my Ray went out when the engines smashed; and . . . and . . . for pity's sake give me my height, Captain! We doubt we're dropping.'

'Six thousand eight hundred. Can you hold it?' Captain Purnall overlooks all insults, and leans half out of the colloid, staring and snuffing. The stranger leaks pungently.

'We ought to blow into St John's with luck. We're trying to plug the fore-tank now, but she's simply whistling it away,' her captain wails.

'She's sinking like a log,' says Captain Purnall in an undertone. 'Call up the Banks Mark Boat, George.' Our dip-dial shows that we, keeping abreast the tramp, have dropped five hundred feet the last few minutes.

Captain Purnall presses a switch and our signal beam begins to swing through the night, twizzling spokes of light across infinity.

'That'll fetch something,' he says, while Captain Hodgson watches the General Communicator. He has called up the North Banks Mark Boat, a few hundred miles west, and is reporting the case.

'I'll stand by you,' Captain Purnall roars to the lone figure on the conning-tower.

'Is it as bad as that?' comes the answer. 'She isn't insured. She's mine.'

'Might have guessed as much,' mutters Hodgson. 'Owner's risk is the worst risk of all!'

'Can't I fetch St John's – not even with this breeze?' the voice quavers.

'Stand by to abandon ship. Haven't you any lift in you, fore or aft?'

'Nothing but the midship tanks, and they're none too tight. You see, my Ray gave out and –' he coughs in the reek of the escaping gas.

'You poor devil!' This does not reach our friend. 'What does the Mark Boat say, George?'

'Wants to know if there's any danger to traffic. Says she's in a bit of weather herself, and can't quit station. I've turned in a General Call, so even if they don't see our beam someone's bound to help – or else *we* must. Shall I clear our slings? Hold on! Here we are! A Planet liner, too! She'll be up in a tick!'

'Tell her to have her slings ready,' cries his brother captain. 'There won't be much time to spare . . . . Tie up your mate,' he roars to the tramp.

'My mate's all right. It's my engineer. He's gone crazy.'

'Shunt the lift out of him with a spanner. Hurry!'

'But I can make St John's if you'll stand by.'

'You'll make the deep, wet Atlantic in twenty minutes. You're less than fifty-eight hundred now. Get your papers.'

A Planet liner, east bound, heaves up in a superb spiral and takes the air of us humming. Her underbody colloid is open and her transporter-slings hang down like tentacles. We shut off our beam as she adjusts herself – steering to a hair – over the tramp's conning-tower. The mate comes up, his arm strapped to his side, and stumbles into the cradle. A man with a ghastly scarlet head follows, shouting that he must go back and build up his Ray. The mate assures him that he will find a nice new Ray all ready in the liner's engine-room. The bandaged head goes up wagging excitedly. A youth and a woman follow. The liner cheers hollowly above us, and we see the passengers' faces at the saloon colloid.

'That's a pretty girl. What's the fool waiting for now?' says Captain Purnall.

The skipper comes up, still appealing to us to stand by and see him fetch St John's. He dives below and returns – at which we little human beings in the void cheer louder than ever – with the ship's kitten. Up fly the liner's hissing slings; her underbody crashes home and she hurtles away again. The dial shows less than 3000 feet.

The Mark Boat signals we must attend to the derelict, now whistling her death-song, as she falls beneath us in long sick zigzags.

'Keep our beam on her and send out a General Warning,' says Captain Purnall, following her down.

There is no need. Not a liner in air but knows the meaning of that vertical beam and gives us and our quarry a wide berth.

'But she'll drown in the water, won't she?' I ask.

'Not always,' is his answer. 'I've known a derelict up-end and sift her engines out of herself and flicker round the Lower Lanes for three weeks on her forward tanks only. We'll run no risks. Pith her, George, and look sharp. There's weather ahead.'

Captain Hodgson opens the underbody colloid, swings the heavy pithing-iron out of its rack, which in liners is generally cased as a smoking-room settee, and at two hundred feet releases the catch. We hear the whir of the crescent-shaped arms opening as they descend. The derelict's forehead is punched in, starred across, and rent diagonally. She falls stern first, our beam upon her; slides like a lost soul down that pitiless ladder of light, and the Atlantic takes her.

'A filthy business,' says Hodgson. 'I wonder what it must have been like in the old days?'

The thought had crossed my mind, too. What if that wavering carcass had been filled with the men of the old days, each one of them taught (*that* is the horror of it!) that after death he would very possibly go for ever to unspeakable torment?

And scarcely a generation ago, we (one knows now that we are only our fathers re-enlarged upon the earth), *we*, I say, ripped and rammed and pithed to admiration.

Here Tim, from the control platform, shouts that we are to get into our inflators and to bring him his at once.

We hurry into the heavy rubber suits – the engineers are already dressed – and inflate at the air-pump taps. GPO inflators are thrice as thick as a racing man's 'flickers', and chafe abominably under the armpits. George takes the wheel until Tim has blown himself up to the extreme of rotundity. If you kicked him off the control platform to the deck he would bounce back. But it is '162' that will do the kicking.

'The Mark Boat's mad – stark ravin' crazy,' he snorts, returning to command. 'She says there's a bad blow-out ahead and wants me to pull over to Greenland. I'll see her pithed first! We wasted half an hour fussing over that dead duck down under, and now I'm expected to go rubbin' my back all round the Pole. What does she think a postal packet's made of? Gummed silk? Tell her we're coming on straight, George.'

George buckles him into the Frame and switches on

the Direct Control. Now under Tim's left toe lies the port-engine Accelerator; under his left heel the Reverse, and so with the other foot. The lift-shunt stops stand out on the rim of the steering-wheel where the fingers of his left hand can play on them. At his right hand is the midships engine lever ready to be thrown into gear at a moment's notice. He leans forward in his belt, eyes glued to the colloid, and one ear cocked toward the General Communicator. Henceforth he is the strength and direction of '162', through whatever may befall.

The Banks Mark Boat is reeling out pages of ABC Directions to the traffic at large. We are to secure all 'loose objects'; hood up our Fleury Rays; and 'on no account to attempt to clear snow from our conning-towers till the weather abates'. Underpowered craft, we are told, can ascend to the limit of their lift, mail-packets to look out for them accordingly; the lower lanes westward are pitting very badly, 'with frequent blowouts, vortices, laterals, etc.'.

Still the clear dark holds up unblemished. The only warning is the electric skin-tension (I feel as though I were a lace-maker's pillow) and an irritability which the gibbering of the General Communicator increases almost to hysteria.

We have made eight thousand feet since we pithed the tramp and our turbines are giving us an honest two hundred and ten knots.

Very far to the west an elongated blur of red, low down, shows us the North Banks Mark Boat. There are specks of fire round her rising and falling – bewildered planets about an unstable sun – helpless shipping hanging on to her light for company's sake. No wonder she could not quit station.

She warns us to look out for the backwash of the bad vortex in which (her beam shows it) she is even now reeling.

The pits of gloom about us begin to fill with very faintly luminous films – wreathing and uneasy shapes. One forms itself into a globe of pale flame that waits shivering with eagerness till we sweep by. It leaps monstrously across the blackness, alights on the precise tip of our nose, pirouettes there an instant, and swings off. Our roaring bow sinks as though that light were lead – sinks and recovers to lurch and stumble again beneath the next blowout. Tim's fingers on the lift-shunt strike chords of numbers – 1:4:7: – 2:4:6: – 7:5:3, and so on; for he is running by his tanks only, lifting or lowering her against the uneasy air. All three engines are at work, for the sooner we have skated over this thin ice the better. Higher we dare not go. The whole upper vault is charged with pale krypton vapours, which our skin-friction may excite to unholy manifestations. Between the upper and lower levels – 5000 and 7000, hints the Mark Boat – we may perhaps bolt through if . . . Our bow clothes itself in blue flame and falls like a sword. No human skill can keep pace with the changing tensions. A vortex has us by the beak and we dive down a two-thousand-foot slant at an angle (the dip-dial and my bouncing body record it) of thirty-five. Our turbines scream shrilly; the propellers cannot bite on the vexed air; Tim shunts the lift out of five tanks at once and by sheer weight drives her bulletwise through the maelstrom till she cushions with jar on an up-gust, three thousand feet below.

'*Now* we've done it,' says George in my ear: 'Our skin-friction, that last slide, has played Old Harry with the tensions! Look out for laterals, Tim; she'll want some holding.'

'I've got her,' is the answer. 'Come *up*, old woman.'

She comes up nobly, but the laterals buffet her left and right like the pinions of angry angels. She is jolted off her course four ways at once, and cuffed into place again, only to be swung aside and dropped into a new chaos. We are never without a corposant grinning on our bows or rolling head over heels from nose to midships, and to the crackle of electricity around and within us is added once or twice the rattle of hail – hail that will never fall on any sea. Slow we must, or we may break our back, pitch-poling.

'Air's a perfectly elastic fluid,' roars George above the tumult. 'About as elastic as a head sea off the Fastnet, ain't it?'

He is less than just to the good element. If one intrudes on the Heavens when they are balancing their volt-accounts; if one disturbs the High Gods' market-rates by hurling steel hulls at ninety knots across tremblingly adjusted electric tensions, one must not complain of any rudeness in the reception. Tim met it with an unmoved countenance, one corner of his underlip caught up on a tooth, his eyes fleeting into the blackness twenty miles ahead, and the fierce sparks flying from his knuckles at every turn of the hand. Now and again he shook his head to clear the sweat trickling from his eyebrows, and it was then that George, watching his chance, would slide down the life-rail and swab his face quickly with a big red handkerchief. I never imagined that a human being could so continuously labour and so collectedly think as did Tim through that Hell's half-hour when the flurry was at its worst. We were dragged hither and yon by warm or frozen suctions, belched up on the tops of wulli-was, spun down by vortices and clubbed aside by laterals under a dizzying rush of stars in the company of a drunken moon. I heard the rushing click of the midships engine-lever sliding in and out, the low growl of the lift-shunts, and, louder than the yelling winds without, the scream of the bow-rudder gouging into any lull that promised hold for an instant. At last we began to claw up on a cant, bow-rudder and port-propeller together; only the nicest balancing of tanks saved us from spinning like the rifle-bullet of the old days.

'We've got to hitch to windward of that Mark Boat somehow,' George cried.

'There's no windward,' I protested feebly, where I swung shackled to a stanchion. 'How can there be?'

He laughed – as we pitched into a thousand-foot blowout – that red man laughed beneath his inflated hood!

'Look!' he said. 'We must clear those refugees with a high lift.'

The Mark Boat was below and a little to the sou'west of us, fluctuating in the centre of her distraught galaxy. The air was thick with moving lights at every level. I take it most of them were trying to lie head to wind, but, not being hydras, they failed. An under-tanked Moghrabi boat had risen to the limit of her lift, and, finding no improvement, had dropped a couple of thousand. There she met a superb wulli-wa, and was blown up spinning like a dead leaf. Instead of shutting off she went astern and, naturally, rebounded as from a wall almost into the Mark Boat, whose language (our G.C. took it in) was humanly simple.

'If they'd only ride it out quietly it 'ud be better,' said

George in a calm, while we climbed like a bat above them all. 'But some skippers *will* navigate without enough lift. What does that Tad-boat think she is doing, Tim?'

'Playin' kiss in the ring,' was Tim's unmoved reply. A Trans-Asiatic Direct liner had found a smooth and butted into it full power. But there was a vortex at the tail of that smooth, so the TAD was flipped out like a pea from off a fingernail, braking madly as she fled down and all but over-ending.

'Now I hope she's satisfied,' said Tim. 'I'm glad I'm not a Mark Boat . . . Do I want help?' The General Communicator dial had caught his ear. 'George, you may tell that gentleman with my love – love, remember, George – that I do not want help. Who *is* the officious sardine-tin?'

'A Rimouski drogher on the lookout for a tow.'

'Very kind of the Rimouski drogher. This postal packet isn't being towed at present.'

'Those droghers will go anywhere on a chance of salvage,' George explained. 'We call 'em kittiwakes.'

A long-beaked, bright steel ninety-footer floated at ease for one instant within hail of us, her slings coiled ready for rescues, and a single hand in her open tower. He was smoking. Surrendered to the insurrection of the airs through which we tore our way, he lay in absolute peace. I saw the smoke of his pipe ascend untroubled ere his boat dropped, it seemed, like a stone in a well.

We had just cleared the Mark Boat and her disorderly neighbours when the storm ended as suddenly as it had begun. A shooting-star to northward filled the sky with the green blink of a meteorite dissipating itself in our atmosphere.

Said George: 'That may iron out all the tensions.' Even as he spoke, the conflicting winds came to rest; the levels filled; the laterals died out in long, easy swells; the airways were smoothed before us. In less than three minutes the covey round the Mark Boat had shipped their power-lights and whirred away upon their businesses.

'What's happened?' I gasped. The nerve-storm within and the volt-tingle without had passed: my inflators weighed like lead.

'God, He knows!' said Captain George soberly. 'That old shooting-star's skin-friction has discharged the different levels. I've seen it happen before. Phew: What a relief!'

We dropped from ten to six thousand and got rid of our clammy suits. Tim shut off and stepped out of the Frame. The Mark Boat was coming up behind us. He opened the colloid in that heavenly stillness and mopped his face.

'Hello, Williams!' he cried. 'A degree or two out o' station, ain't you?'

'Maybe,' was the answer from the Mark Boat. 'I've had some company this evening.'

'So I noticed. Wasn't that quite a little draught?'

'I warned you. Why didn't you pull out north? The east-bound packets have.'

'Me? Not till I'm running a Polar consumptives' sanatorium boat. I was squinting through a colloid before you were out of your cradle, my son.'

'I'd be the last man to deny it,' the captain of the Mark Boat replies softly. 'The way you handled her just now – I'm a pretty fair judge of traffic in a volt-flurry – it was a thousand revolutions beyond anything even *I*'ve ever seen.'

Tim's back supples visibly to this oiling. Captain George on the control platform winks and points to the portrait of a singularly attractive maiden pinned up on Tim's telescope bracket above the steering-wheel.

I see. Wholly and entirely do I see!

There is some talk overhead of 'coming round to tea on Friday', a brief report of the derelict's fate, and Tim volunteers as he descends: 'For an ABC man young Williams is less of a high-tension fool than some . . . Were you thinking of taking her on, George? Then I'll just have a look round that port-thrust – seems to me it's a trifle warm – and we'll jog along.'

The Mark Boat hums off joyously and hangs herself up in her appointed eyrie. Here she will stay, a shutterless observatory; a lifeboat station; a salvage tug; a court of ultimate appeal-cum-meteorological bureau for three hundred miles in all directions, till Wednesday next when her relief slides across the stars to take her buffeted place. Her black hull, double conning-tower, and ever-ready slings represent all that remains to the planet of that odd old word authority. She is responsible only to the Aerial Board of Control – the ABC of which Tim speaks so flippantly. But that semi-elected, semi-nominated body of a few score of persons of both sexes controls this planet. 'Transportation is Civilisation,' our motto runs. Theoretically, we do what we please so long as we do not interfere with the traffic *and all it implies*. Practically, the ABC confirms or annuls all international arrangements and, to judge from its last report, finds our tolerant, humorous, lazy little planet only too ready to shift the whole burden of public administration on to its shoulders.

I discuss this with Tim, sipping maté on the control

platform while George fans her along over the white blur of the Banks in beautiful upward curves of fifty miles each. The dip-dial translates them on the tape in flowing freehand.

Tim gathers up a skein of it and surveys the last few feet, which record '162's' path through the volt-flurry.

'I haven't had a fever-chart like this to show up in five years,' he says ruefully.

A postal packet's dip-dial records every yard of every run. The tapes then go to the ABC, which collates and makes composite photographs of them for the instruction of captains. Tim studies his irrevocable past, shaking his head.

'Hello! Here's a fifteen-hundred-foot drop at fifty-five degrees! We must have been standing on our heads then, George.'

'You don't say so,' George answers. 'I fancied I noticed it at the time.'

George may not have Captain Purnall's catlike swiftness, but he is all an artist to the tips of the broad fingers that play on the shunt-stops. The delicious flight-curves come away on the tape with never a waver. The Mark Boat's vertical spindle of light lies down to eastward, setting in the face of the following stars. Westward, where no planet should rise, the triple verticals of Trinity Bay (we keep still to the Southern route) make a low-lifting haze. We seem the only thing at rest under all the heavens; floating at ease till the earth's revolution shall turn up our landing-towers.

And minute by minute our silent clock gives us a sixteen-second mile.

'Some fine night,' says Tim, 'we'll be even with that clock's Master.'

'He's coming now,' says George, over his shoulder. 'I'm chasing the night west.'

The stars ahead dim no more than if a film of mist had been drawn under unobserved, but the deep air-boom on our skin changes to a joyful shout.

'The dawn-gust,' says Tim. 'It'll go on to meet the Sun. Look! Look! There's the dark being crammed back over our bows! Come to the after-colloid. I'll show you something.'

The engine-room is hot and stuffy; the clerks in the coach are asleep, and the Slave of the Ray is ready to follow them. Tim slides open the aft colloid and reveals the curve of the world – the ocean's deepest purple – edged with fuming and intolerable gold. Then the Sun rises and through the colloid strikes out our lamps. Tim scowls in his face.

'Squirrels in a cage,' he mutters. 'That's all we are. Squirrels in a cage! He's going twice as fast as us. Just you wait a few years, my shining friend, and we'll take steps that will amaze you. *We*'ll Joshua you!'

Yes, that is our dream: to turn all earth into the Vale of Ajalon at our pleasure. So far, we can drag out the dawn to twice its normal length in these latitudes. But some day – even on the Equator – we shall hold the Sun level in his full stride.

Now we look down on a sea thronged with heavy traffic. A big submersible breaks water suddenly. Another and another follows with a swash and a suck and a savage bubbling of relieved pressures. The deep-sea freighters are rising to lung up after the long night, and the leisurely ocean is all patterned with peacock's eyes of foam.

'We'll lung up, too,' says Tim, and when we return to the control platform George shuts off, the colloids are opened, and the fresh air sweeps her out. There is no hurry. The old contracts (they will be revised at the end of the year) allow twelve hours for a run which any packet can put behind her in ten. So we breakfast in the arms of an easterly slant which pushes us along at a languid twenty.

To enjoy life, and tobacco, begin both on a sunny morning half a mile or so above the dappled Atlantic cloud-belts and after a volt-flurry which has cleared and tempered your nerves. While we discussed the thickening traffic with the superiority that comes of having a high level reserved to ourselves, we heard (and I for the first time) the morning hymn on a Hospital boat.

She was cloaked by a skein of ravelled fluff beneath us and we caught the chant before she rose into the sunlight. 'Oh, ye Winds of God,' sang the unseen voices: 'bless ye the Lord! Praise Him and magnify Him for ever!'

We slid off our caps and joined in. When our shadow fell across her great open platforms they looked up and stretched out their hands neighbourly while they sang. We could see the doctors and the nurses and the white-button-like faces of the cot-patients. She passed slowly beneath us, heading northward, her hull, wet with the dews of the night, all ablaze in the sunshine. So took she the shadow of a cloud and vanished, her song continuing. 'Oh, ye holy and humble men of heart, bless ye the Lord! Praise Him and magnify Him for ever.'

'She's a public lunger or she wouldn't have been singing the *Benedicite*; and she's a Greenlander or she wouldn't have snow-blinds over her colloids,' said George at last. 'She'll be bound for Frederikshavn or one of the Glacier sanatoriums for a month. If she was an accident ward she'd be hung up at the eight-thousand-foot level. Yes – consumptives.'

'Funny how the new things are the old thing I've read in books,' Tim answered, 'that savages used to haul their sick and wounded up to the tops of hills because microbes were fewer there. We hoist 'em into sterilised air for a while. Same idea. How much do the doctors say we've added to the average life of a man?'

'Thirty years,' says George, with a twinkle in his eye. 'Are we going to spend 'em all up here, Tim?'

'Flap ahead, then. Flap ahead. Who's hindering?' the senior captain laughed, as we went in.

We held a good lift to clear the coastwise and Continental shipping; and we had need of it. Though our route is in no sense a populated one, there is a steady trickle of traffic this way along. We met Hudson Bay furriers out of the Great Preserve, hurrying to make their departure from Bonavista with sable and black fox for the insatiable markets. We overcossed Keewatin liners, small and cramped; but their captains, who see no land between Trepassy and Blanco, know what gold they bring back from West Africa. Trans-Asiatic Directs we met, soberly ringing the world round the Fiftieth Meridian at an honest seventy knots; and white-painted Ackroyd & Hunt fruiters out of the south fled beneath us, their ventilated hulls whistling like Chinese kites. Their market is in the North among the northern sanatoria where you can smell their grapefruit and bananas across the cold snows. Argentine beef boats we sighted too, of enormous capacity and unlovely outline. They, too, feed the northern health stations in icebound ports where submersibles dare not rise.

Yellow-bellied ore-flats and Ungava petrol-tanks punted down leisurely out of the North, like strings of unfrightened wild duck. It does not pay to fly minerals and oil a mile farther than is necessary; but the risks of transshipping to submersibles in the ice-pack off Nain or Hebron are so great that these heavy freighters fly down to Halifax direct, and scent the air as they go. They are the biggest tramps aloft except the Athabasca grain-tubs. But these last, now that the wheat is moved, are busy, over the world's shoulder, timber-lifting in Siberia.

We held to the St Lawrence (it is astonishing how the old waterways still pull us children of the air), and followed his broad line of black between its drifting ice-blocks, all down the Park that the wisdom of our fathers – but everyone knows the Quebec run.

We dropped to the Heights Receiving Towers twenty minutes ahead of time, and there hung at ease till the Yokohama Intermediate Packet could pull out and give us our proper slip. It was curious to watch the action of the holding-down clips all along the frosty river front as the boats cleared or came to rest. A big Hamburger was leaving Pont Levis, and her crew, unshipping the platform railings, began to sing 'Elsinore' – the oldest of our chanteys. You know it of course:

Mother Rügen's teahouse on the Baltic –
Forty couple waltzing on the floor!
And you can watch my Ray,
For I must go away
And dance with Ella Sweyn at Elsinore!

Then, while they sweated home the covering-plates:

Nor-Nor-Nor-Nor West from Sourabaya
to the Baltic –
Ninety knot an hour to the Skaw!
Mother Rügen's teahouse on the Baltic
And a dance with Ella Sweyn at Elsinore!

The clips parted with a gesture of indignant dismissal, as though Quebec, glittering under her snows, were casting out these light and unworthy lovers. Our signal came from the Heights. Tim turned and floated up, but surely then it was with passionate appeal that the great tower arms flung open – or did I think so because on the upper staging a little hooded figure also opened her arms wide toward her father?

In ten seconds the coach with its clerks clashed down to the receiving-caisson; the hostlers displaced the engineers at the idle turbines, and Tim, prouder of this than all, introduced me to the maiden of the photograph on the shelf. 'And by the way,' said he to her, stepping forth in sunshine under the hat of civil life, 'I saw young Williams in the Mark Boat. I've asked him to tea on Friday.'

Aerial Board of Control

Lights

No changes in English Inland lights for week ending Dec. 18th.

CAPE VERDE Week ending Dec. 18. Verde inclined guide-light changes from 1st proximo to triple flash – green white green – in place of occulting red as heretofore. The warning light for Harmattan winds will be continuous vertical glare (white) on all oases of trans-Saharan N. E. by E. Main Routes.

INVERCARGILL (N.Z.) From 1st prox.: extreme southerly light (double red) will exhibit white beam inclined 45 degrees on approach of Southerly Buster. Traffic flies high off this coast between April and October.

TABLE BAY Devil's Peak Glare removed to Simonsberg. Traffic making Table Mountain coastwise keep all lights from Three Anchor Bay at least two thousand feet under, and do not round to till East of E. shoulder Devil's Peak.

SANDSHEADS LIGHT Green triple vertical marks new private landing-stage for Bay and Burma traffic only.

SNAEFELL JOKUL White occulting light withdrawn for winter.

PATAGONIA No summer light south Cape Pilar. This includes Staten Island and Port Stanley.

C. NAVARIN Quadruple fog flash (white), one minute intervals (new).

EAST CAPE Fog flash: single white with single bomb, 30 sec. intervals (new).

MALAYAN ARCHIPELAGO Lights unreliable owing eruptions. Lay from Cape Somerset to Singapore direct, keeping highest levels.

For the Board:
CATTERTHUN
ST JUST } *Lights*
VAN HEDDER

Casualties

Week ending Dec. 18th.

SABLE ISLAND Green single-barbette tower freighter, number indistinguishable, up-ended, and fore-tank pierced after collision, passed 300-ft level 2 P.M. Dec. 15th. Watched to water and pithed by Mark Boat.

N.F. BANKS Postal packet 162 reports *Halma* freighter (Fowey–St John's) abandoned, leaking after weather, 46° 15' N. 50° 15' W. Crew rescued by Planet liner *Asteroid*. Watched to water and pithed by Postal Packet, Dec. 14th.

KERGUELEN Mark Boat reports last call from *Cymena* freighter (Gayer Tong Huk & Co.) taking water and sinking in snow-storm South McDonald Islands. No wreckage recovered. Messages and wills of crew at all ABC offices.

FEZZAN TAD freighter *Ulema* taken ground during Harmattan on Akakus Range. Under plates strained. Crew at Ghat where repairing Dec. 13th.

BISCAY Mark Boat reports *Carducci* (Valandingham Line) slightly spiked in western gorge Pointe de Benasque. Passengers transferred *Andorra* (Fulton Line). Barcelona Mark Boat salving cargo Dec. 12th.

ASCENSION MARK BOAT Wreck of unknown racing-plane, Parden rudder, wire-stiffened xylonite vans, and Harliss engine-seating, sighted and salved 7° 20' S. 18° 41' W. Dec. 15th. Photos at all ABC offices.

Missing

No answer to General Call having been received during the last week from following overdues, they are posted as missing:

Atlantis, W.17630	Canton–Valparaiso
Audhumla, W.889	Stockholm–Odessa
Berenice, W.2206	Riga–Vladivostock
Draw, E.446	Coventry–Puntas Arenas
Tontine, E.3068	C. Wrath–Ungava
Wu-Sung, E.41776	Hankow–Lobito Bay

General Call (all Mark Boats) out for:

Jane Eyre, W.6990	Port Rupert–City of Mexico
Santander, W.5514	Gobi Desert–Manila
V. Edmundsun, E.9690	Kandahar–Fiume

Broke for Obstruction, and Quitting Levels

VALKYRIE Racing plane, A. J. Hartley owner, New York (twice warned).

GEISHA Racing plane, S. van Cott owner, Philadelphia (twice warned).

MARVEL OF PERU Racing plane, J. X. Peixoto owner, Rio de Janeiro (twice warned).

For the Board:

LAZAREFF
MCKEOUGH } *Traffic*
GOLDBLATT

Notes

High-Level Sleet

The northern weather so far shows no sign of improvement. From all quarters come complaints of the unusual prevalence of sleet at the higher levels. Racing planes and digs alike have suffered severely – the former from unequal deposits of half-frozen slush on their vans (and only those who have 'held up' a badly balanced plane in a cross-wind know what that means), and the latter from loaded bows and snow-cased bodies. As a consequence, the northern and north-western upper levels have been practically abandoned, and the high fliers have returned to the ignoble security of the three, five, and six thousand foot levels. But there remain a few undaunted sun-hunters who, in spite of frozen stays and ice-jammed connecting-rods, still haunt the blue empyrean.

Bat-Boat Racing

The scandals of the past few years have at last moved the yachting world to concerted action in regard to 'bat'-boat racing. We have been treated to the spectacle of what are practically keeled racing planes driven a clear five foot or more above the water, and only eased down to touch their so-called 'native element' as they near the line. Judges and starters have been conveniently blind to this absurdity, but the public demonstration off St Catherine's Light at the Autumn

Regattas has borne ample, if tardy, fruit. In the future the 'bat' is to be a boat, and the long-unheeded demand of the true sportsman for 'no daylight under mid-keel in smooth water' is in a fair way to be conceded. The new rule severely restricts plane area and lift alike. The gas compartments are permitted both fore and aft, as in the old type, but the water-ballast central tank is rendered obligatory. These things work, if not for perfection, at least for the evolution of a sane and wholesome *waterborne* cruiser. The type of rudder is unaffected by the new rules, so we may expect to see the Long-Davidson make (the patent on which has just expired) come largely into use henceforward, though the strain on the sternpost in turning at speeds over sixty miles an hour is admittedly very severe. But bat-boat racing has a great future before it.

Crete and the ABC

The story of the recent Cretan crisis, as told in the *ABC Monthly Report*, is not without humour. Till the 25th October Crete, as all our planet knows, was the sole surviving European repository of 'autonomous institutions', 'local self-government', and the rest of the archaic lumber devised in the past for the confusion of human affairs. She has lived practically on the tourist traffic attracted by her annual pageants of parliaments, boards, municipal councils, etc., etc. Last summer the islanders grew wearied, as their premier explained, of 'playing at being savages for pennies', and proceeded to pull down all the landing-towers on the island and shut off general communication till such time as the ABC should annex them. For side-splitting comedy we would refer our readers to the correspondence between the Board of Control and the Cretan premier during the 'war'. However, all's well that ends well. The ABC have taken over the administration of Crete on normal lines; and tourists must go elsewhere to witness the 'debates', 'resolutions', and 'popular movements' of the old days. The only people to suffer will be the Board of Control, which is grievously overworked already. It is easy enough to condemn the Cretans for their laziness; but when one recalls the large, prosperous, and presumably public-spirited communities which during the last few years have deliberately thrown themselves into the hands of the ABC, one cannot be too hard upon St Paul's old friends.

Correspondence

Skylarking on the Equator

TO THE EDITOR: Only last week, while crossing the Equator (W. 26·15), I became aware of a furious and irregular cannonading some fifteen or twenty knots S. 4 E. Descending to the 5000 ft level, I found a party of Transylvanian tourists engaged in exploding scores of the largest pattern atmospheric bombs (ABC standard) and, in the intervals of their pleasing labours, firing bow and stern smoke-ring swivels. This orgy – I can give it no other name – went on for at least two hours, and naturally produced violent electric derangements. My compasses, of course, were thrown out, my bow was struck twice, and I received two brisk shocks from the lower platform-rail. On remonstrating, I was told that these 'professors' were engaged in scientific experiments. The extent of their 'scientific' knowledge may be judged by the fact that they expected to produce (I give their own words) 'a little blue sky' if 'they went on long enough'. This in the heart of the Doldrums at 4500 feet! I have no objection to any amount of blue sky in its proper place (it can be found at the 4000 level for practically twelve months out of the year), but I submit, with all deference to the educational needs of Transylvania, that 'skylarking' in the centre of a main-travelled road where, at the best of times, electricity literally drips off one's stanchions and screw-blades, is unnecessary. When my friends had finished, the road was seamed, and blown, and pitted with unequal pressure layers, spirals, vortices, and readjustments for at least an hour. I pitched badly twice in an upward rush – solely due to these diabolical throw-downs – that came near to wrecking my propeller. Equatorial work at low levels is trying enough in all conscience without the added terrors of scientific hooliganism in the Doldrums.

Rhyl

J. VINCENT MATHEN

[We entirely sympathise with Professor Mathen's views, but till the Board sees fit to further regulate the Southern areas in which scientific experiments may be conducted, we shall always be exposed to the risk which our correspondent describes. Unfortunately, a chimera bombinating in a vacuum is, nowadays, only too capable of producing secondary causes. – Editor.]

Answers to Correspondents

VIGILANS The Laws of Auroral Derangements are still imperfectly understood. Any overheated motor may of course 'seize' without warning; but so many complaints have reached us of accidents similar to yours while shooting the Aurora that we are inclined to believe with Lavalle that the upper strata of the Aurora Borealis are practically one big electric 'leak', and that the paralysis of your engines was due to complete magnetisation of all metallic parts. Low-flying planes often 'glue up' when near the magnetic pole, and there is no reason in science why the same disability should not be experienced at higher levels when the Auroras are 'delivering' strongly.

INDIGNANT On your own showing, you were not under control. That you could not hoist the necessary NUC lights on approaching a traffic-lane because your electrics had short-circuited is a misfortune which might befall anyone. The ABC, being responsible for the planet's traffic, cannot, however, make allowance for this kind of misfortune. A reference to the Code will show that you were fined on the lower scale.

PLANISTON (1) The Five Thousand Kilometre (overland) was won last year by L. V. Rautsch; R. M. Rautsch, his brother, in the same week pulling off the Ten Thousand (oversea). R. M.'s average worked out at a fraction over 700 kilometres per hour, thus constituting a record. (2) Theoretically, there is no limit to the lift of a dirigible. For commercial and practical purposes 15,000 tons is accepted as the most manageable.

PATERFAMILIAS None whatever. He is liable for direct damage both to your chimneys and any collateral damage caused by fall of bricks into garden, etc., etc. Bodily inconvenience and mental anguish may be included, but the average courts are not, as a rule, swayed by sentiment. If you can prove that his grapnel removed *any* portion of your roof, you had better rest your case on decoverture of domicile (see Parkins *v.* Duboulay). We sympathise with your position, but the night of the 14th was stormy and confused, and – you may have to anchor on a stranger's chimney yourself some night. *Verbum sap.!*

ALDEBARAN (1) War, as a paying concern, ceased in 1967. (2) The Convention of London expressly reserves to every nation the right of waging war so long as it does not interfere with the traffic and all that implies. (3) The ABC was constituted in 1949.

L.M.D. (1) Keep her full head-on at half power, taking advantage of the lulls to speed up and creep into it. She will strain much less this way than in quartering across a gale. (2) Nothing is to be gained by reversing into a following gale, and there is always risk of a turn-over. (3) The formulae for stuns'l brakes are uniformly unreliable, and will continue to be so as long as air is compressible.

PEGAMOID (1) Personally we prefer glass or flux compounds to any other material for winter-work nose-caps as being absolutely non-hygroscopic. (2) We cannot recommend any particular make.

PULMONAR (1) For the symptoms you describe, try the Gobi Desert Sanatoria. The low levels of most of the Saharan Sanatoria are against them except at the outset of the disease. (2) We do not recommend boarding-houses or hotels in this column.

BEGINNER On still days the air above a large inhabited city being slightly warmer – i.e., thinner – than the atmosphere of the surrounding country, a plane drops a little on entering the rarefied area, precisely as a ship sinks a little in fresh water. Hence the phenomena of 'jolt' and your 'inexplicable collisions' with factory chimneys. In air, as on earth, it is safest to fly high.

EMERGENCY There is only one rule of the road in air, earth, and water. Do you want the firmament to yourself?

PICCIOLA Both poles have been overdone in art and

literature. Leave them to science for the next twenty years. You did not send a stamp with your verses.

NORTH NIGERIA The Mark Boat was within her right in warning you off the Reserve. The shadow of a low-flying dirigible scares the game. You can buy all the photos you need at Sokoto.

NEW ERA It is not etiquette to overcross an ABC official's boat without asking permission. He is one of the body responsible for the planet's traffic, and for that reason must not be interfered with. You, presumably, are out on your own business or pleasure, and must leave him alone. For humanity's sake don't try to be 'democratic'.

EXCORIATED All inflators chafe sooner or later. You must go on till your skin hardens by practice. Meantime Vaseline.

Review

The Life of Xavier Lavalle

(Reviewed by René Talland.
École Aéronautique, Paris)

Ten years ago Lavalle, 'that imperturbable dreamer of the heavens', as Lazareff hailed him, gathered together the fruits of a lifetime's labour, and gave it, with well-justified contempt, to a world bound hand and foot to Barald's theory of vertices and 'compensating electric nodes'. 'They shall see,' he wrote – in that immortal postscript to *The Heart of the Cyclone* – 'the laws whose existence they derided written in fire *beneath* them.

'But even here,' he continues, 'there is no finality. Better a thousand times my conclusions should be discredited than that my dead name should lie across the threshold of the temple of science – a bar to further enquiry.'

So died Lavalle – a prince of the powers of the air, and even at his funeral Cellier jested at 'him who had gone to discover the secrets of the Aurora Borealis'.

If I choose thus to be banal, it is only to remind you that Collier's theories are today as exploded as the ludicrous deductions of the Spanish school. In the place of their fugitive and warring dreams we have, definitely, Lavalle's law of the cyclone which he surprised in darkness and cold at the foot of the overarching throne of the Aurora Borealis. It is there that I, intent on my own investigations, have passed and re-passed a hundred times the worn leonine face, white as the snow beneath him, furrowed with wrinkles like the seams and gashes upon the North Cape; the nervous hand, integrally a part of the mechanism of his flighter; and above all, the wonderful lambent eyes turned to the zenith.

'Master,' I would cry as I moved respectfully beneath him, 'what is it you seek today?' and always the answer, clear and without doubt, from above: 'The old secret, my son!'

The immense egotism of youth forced me on my own path, but (cry of the human always!) had I known – if I had known – I would many times have bartered my poor laurels for the privilege, such as Tinsley and Herrera possess, of having aided him in his monumental researches.

It is to the filial piety of Victor Lavalle that we owe the two volumes consecrated to the ground-life of his father, so full of the holy intimacies of the domestic hearth. Once returned from the abysms of the utter North to that little house upon the outskirts of Meudon, it was not the philosopher, the daring observer, the man of iron energy that imposed himself on his family, but a fat and even plaintive jester, a farceur incarnate and kindly, the co-equal of his children, and, it must be written, not seldom the comic despair of Madame Lavalle, who, as she writes five years after the marriage, to her venerable mother, found 'in this unequalled intellect whose name I bear the abandon of a large and very untidy boy'. Here is her letter:

> Xavier returned from I do not know where at midnight, absorbed in calculations on the eternal

question of his Aurora – *la belle Aurore*, whom I begin to hate. Instead of anchoring – I had set out the guide-light above our roof, so he had but to descend and fasten the plane – he wandered, profoundly distracted, above the town with his anchor down! Figure to yourself, dear mother, it is the roof of the mayor's house that the grapnel first engages! That I do not regret, for the mayor's wife and I are not sympathetic; but when Xavier uproots my pet araucaria and bears it across the garden into the conservatory I protest at the top of my voice. Little Victor in his night-clothes runs to the window, enormously amused at the parabolic flight without reason, for it is too dark to see the grapnel, of my prized tree. The Mayor of Meudon thunders at our door in the name of the law, demanding, I suppose, my husband's head. Here is the conversation through the megaphone – Xavier is two hundred feet above us:

> 'M. Lavalle, descend and make reparation for outrage of domicile. Descend, M. Lavalle! [No one answers.] Xavier Lavalle, in the name of the Law, descend and submit to process for outrage of domicile.'
>
> [Xavier, roused from his calculations, comprehending only the last words] 'Outrage of domicile? My dear mayor, who is the man that has corrupted thy Julie?'
>
> [The mayor, furious] 'Xavier Lavalle – '
>
> [Xavier, interrupting] 'I have not that felicity. I am only a dealer in cyclones!'

My faith, he raised one then! All Meudon attended in the streets, and my Xavier, after a long time comprehending what he had done, excused himself in a thousand apologies. At last the reconciliation was effected in our house over a supper at two in the morning – Julie in a wonderful costume of compromises, and I have her and the mayor pacified in bed in the blue room.

And on the next day, while the mayor rebuilds his roof, her Xavier departs anew for the Aurora Borealis, there to commence his life's work. M. Victor Lavalle tells us of that historic collision (*en plane*) on the flank of Hecla between Herrera, then a pillar of the Spanish school, and the man destined to confute his theories and lead him intellectually captive. Even through the years, the immense laugh of Lavalle as he sustains the Spaniard's wrecked plane, and cries: 'Courage! I shall not fall till I have found truth, and I hold *you* fast!' rings like the call of trumpets. This is that Lavalle whom the world, immersed in speculations of immediate gain, did not know nor suspect – the Lavalle whom they adjudged to the last a pedant and a theorist.

The human, as apart from the scientific, side (developed in his own volumes) of his epoch-making discoveries is marked with a simplicity, clarity, and good sense beyond praise. I would specially refer such as doubt the sustaining influence of ancestral faith upon character and will to the eleventh and nineteenth chapters, in which are contained the opening and consummation of the Tellurionical Records extending over nine years. Of their tremendous significance be sure that the modest house at Meudon knew as little as that the records would one day be the planet's standard in all official meteorology. It was enough for them that their Xavier – this son, this father, this husband –

ascended periodically to commune with powers, it might be angelic, beyond their comprehension, and that they united daily in prayers for his safety.

'Pray for me,' he says upon the eve of each of his excursions, and returning, with an equal simplicity, he renders thanks 'after supper in the little room where he kept his barometers'.

To the last Lavalle was a Catholic of the old school, accepting – he who had looked into the very heart of the lightnings – the dogmas of papal infallibility, of absolution, of confession – of relics great and small. Marvellous – enviable contradiction!

The completion of the Tellurionical Records closed what Lavalle himself was pleased to call the theoretical side of his labours – labours from which the youngest and least impressionable planeur might well have shrunk. He had traced through cold and heat, across the deeps of the oceans, with instruments of his own invention, over the inhospitable heart of the polar ice and the sterile visage of the deserts, league by league, patiently, unweariedly, remorselessly, from their ever-shifting cradle under the magnetic pole to their exalted death-bed in the utmost ether of the upper atmosphere – each one of the Isoconical Tellurions – Lavalle's Curves, as we call them today. He had disentangled the nodes of their intersections, assigning to each its regulated period of flux and reflux. Thus equipped, he summons Herrera and Tinsley, his pupils, to the final demonstration as calmly as though he were ordering his flighter for some midday journey to Marseilles.

'I have proved my thesis,' he writes. 'It remains now only that you should witness the proof. We go to Manila tomorrow. A cyclone will form off the

Pescadores S. 17 E. in four days, and will reach its maximum intensity twenty-seven hours after inception. It is there I will show you the Truth.'

A letter heretofore unpublished from Herrera to Madame Lavalle tells us how the Master's prophecy was verified.

I will not destroy its simplicity or its significance by any attempt to quote. Note well, though, that Herrera's preoccupation throughout that day and night of superhuman strain is always for the Master's bodily health and comfort.

'At such a time,' he writes, 'I forced the Master to take the broth'; or 'I made him put on the fur coat as you told me.' Nor is Tinsley (see pp. 184–85) less concerned. He prepares the nourishment. He cooks eternally, imperturbably, suspended in the chaos of which the Master interprets the meaning. Tinsley, bowed down with the laurels of both hemispheres, raises himself to yet nobler heights in his capacity of a devoted *chef*. It is almost unbelievable! And yet men write of the Master as cold, aloof, self-contained. Such characters do not elicit the joyous and unswerving devotion which Lavalle commanded throughout life. Truly, we have changed very little in the course of the ages! The secrets of earth and sky and the links that bind them, we felicitate ourselves we are on the road to discover; but our neighbour's heart and mind we misread, we misjudge, we condemn – now as ever. Let all, then, who love a man read these most human, tender, and wise volumes!

WANTS

REQUIRED IMMEDIATELY, for East Africa, a thoroughly competent Plane and Dirigible Driver, acquainted with Radium and Helium motors and generators. Low-level work only, but must understand heavy-weight digs.

MOSSAMEDES TRANSPORT ASSOC.
84 Palestine Buildings, E.C.

MAN WANTED—DIG DRIVER for Southern Alps with Saharan summer trips. High levels, high speed, high wages.

Apply M. SIDNEY,
Hotel San Stefano, Monte Carlo.

FAMILY DIRIGIBLE. A COMpetent, steady man wanted for slow-speed, low-level Tangye dirigible. No night work, no sea trips. Must be member of the Church of England, and make himself useful in the garden.

M. R.,
The Rectory, Gray's Barton, Wilts.

COMMERCIAL DIG, CENTRAL and Southern Europe. A smart, active man for a L.M.T. Dig. Night work only. Headquarters London and Cairo. Linguist preferred.

BAGMAN,
Charing Cross Hotel, W.C.

FOR SALE — A BARGAIN — Single Plane, narrow-gauge vans, Pinke motor. Restayed this autumn. Hansen air-kit, 38 in. chest, 15½ collar. Can be seen by appointment.

N. 2650. This office.

The Bee-Line Bookshop

BELT'S WAY-BOOKS, giving town lights for all towns over 4000 pop. as laid down by A.B.C.

THE WORLD. Complete 2 vols. Thin Oxford, limp back. 12s. 6d.

BELT'S COASTAL ITINERARY. Shore Lights of the World. 7s. 6d.

THE TRANSATLANTIC AND MEDITERRANEAN TRAFFIC LINES. (By authority of the A.B.C.) Paper, 1s. 6d.; cloth, 2s. 6d. Ready Jan. 15.

ARCTIC AEROPLANING. Siemens and Galt. Cloth, bds. 3s. 6d.

LAVALLE'S HEART OF THE CYCLONE, with supplementary charts. 4s 6d.

RIMINGTON'S PITFALLS IN THE AIR, and Table of Comparative Densities. 3s. 6d.

ANGELO'S DESERT IN A DIRIGIBLE. New edition, revised. 5s. 9d.

VAUGHAN'S PLANE RACING IN CALM AND STORM. 2s. 6d.

VAUGHAN'S HINTS TO THE AIRMATEUR. 1s.

HOFMAN'S LAWS OF LIFT AND VELOCITY. With diagrams, 3s. 6d.

DE VITRE'S THEORY OF SHIFTING BALLAST IN DIRIGIBLES. 2s. 6d.

SANGER'S WEATHERS OF THE WORLD. 4s.

SANGER'S TEMPERATURES AT HIGH ALTITUDES. 4s.

HAWKIN'S FOG AND HOW TO AVOID IT. 3s.

VAN ZUYLAN'S SECONDARY EFFECTS OF THUNDERSTORMS. 4s. 6d.

DAHLGREN'S AIR CURRENTS AND EPIDEMIC DISEASES. 5s. 6d.

REDMAYNE'S DISEASE AND THE BAROMETER 7s. 6d.

WALTON'S HEALTH RESORTS OF THE GOBI AND SHAMO. 3s. 6d.

WALTON'S THE POLE AND PULMONARY COMPLAINTS. 7s. 6d.

MUTLOW'S HIGH LEVEL BACTERIOLOGY. 7s. 6d.

HALLIWELL'S ILLUMINATED STAR MAP, with clockwork attachment, giving apparent motion of heavens, boxed, complete with clamps for binnacle, 36 inch size only, £2 : 2s. (Invaluable for night work.) With A.B.C. certificate, £3 : 10s.

ZALINSKI'S Standard Works:

PASSES OF THE HIMALAYAS. 5s.
PASSES OF THE SIERRAS. 5s.
PASSES OF THE ROCKIES. 5s.
PASSES OF THE URALS. 5s.

The four boxed, limp cloth, with charts, 15s.

GRAY'S AIR CURRENTS IN MOUNTAIN GORGES. 7s. 6d.

A. C. BELT & SON, READING

Flickers! Flickers! Flickers!

High Level Flickers

"He that is down need fear no fall."
Fear not! You will fall lightly as down!

¶ Hansen's air-kits are down in all respects. Tremendous reductions in prices previous to winter stocking. Pure para kit with cellulose seat and shoulder-pads, weighted to balance. Unequalled for all drop-work.

Our trebly resilient heavy kit is the *ne plus ultra* of comfort and safety.

Gas-buoyed, waterproof, hail-proof, non-conducting Flickers with pipe and nozzle fitting all types of generator. Graduated tap on left hip.

Hansen's Flickers Lead the Aerial Flight
197 Oxford Street

The new weighted Flicker with tweed or cheviot surface cannot be distinguished from the ordinary suit till inflated.

Flickers! Flickers! Flickers!

What

"SKID"

was to our forefathers on the ground,

"PITCH"

is to their sons in the air.

The popularity of the large, unwieldy, slow, expensive Dirigible over the light, swift Plane is mainly due to the former's immunity from pitch.

Collison's forward-socketed Air Van renders it impossible for any plane to pitch. The C.F.S. is automatic, simple as a shutter, certain as a power hammer, safe as oxygen. Fitted to any make of plane.

COLLISON
186 Brompton Road
Workshops, *Chiswick*
LUNDIE & MATHERS
Sole Agts for East'n Hemisphere

Starters and Guides

Hotel, club, and private house plane-starters, slips, and guides affixed by skilled workmen in accordance with local building laws.

Rackstraw's forty-foot collapsible steel starters with automatic release at end of travel—prices per foot run, cramps and crampons included. The safest on the market.

Weaver & Denison
Middleboro

C.M.C.

Our Synthetical Mineral

BEARINGS

are chemically and crystallogically identical with the minerals whose names they bear. Any size, any surface. Diamond, Rock-Crystal, Agate and Ruby Bearings—cups, caps, and collars for the higher speeds.

For tractor bearings and spindles—Imperative.

For rear propellers—Indispensable.

For all working parts—Advisable.

Commercial Minerals Co.

107 Minories

Resurgam!

IF YOU HAVE NOT CLOTHED YOURSELF IN A

Normandie Resurgam

YOU WILL PROBABLY NOT BE INTERESTED IN OUR NEXT WEEK'S LIST OF AIR-KIT.

Resurgam Air-Kit Emporium

HYMANS & GRAHAM

1198

Lower Broadway, New York

Remember!

¶ It is now nearly a generation since the Plane was to supersede the Dirigible for all purposes.

¶ TO-DAY *none* of the Planet's freight is carried *en plane.*

¶ Less than two per cent. of the Planet's passengers are carried *en plane.*

We design, equip, and guarantee Dirigibles for all purposes.

Standard Dig Construction Company

MILLWALL and BUENOS AYRES

Flint & Mantel

Southampton

FOR SALE

at the end of Season the following Bat-Boats:

GRISELDA, 65 knt., 42 ft., 430 (nom.) Maginnis Motor, under-rake rudder.

MABELLE, 50 knt., 40 ft., 310 Hargreaves Motor, Douglas' lock-steering gear.

IVEMONA, 50 knt., 35 ft., 300 Hargreaves (Radium accelerator), Miller keel and rudder.

The above are well known on the South Coast as sound, wholesome knockabout boats, with ample cruising accommodation. *Griselda* carries spare set of Hofman racing vans, and can be lifted three foot clear in smooth water with ballast-tank swung aft. The others do not lift clear, and are recommended for beginners.

Also, by private treaty, racing B.B. *Tarpon* (76 winning flags) 120 knt., 60 ft.; Long-Davidson double under-rake rudder, new this season and unstrained. 850 nom. Maginnis motor, Radium relays and Pond generator. Bronze breakwater forward, and treble reinforced forefoot and entry. Talfourd rockered keel. Triple set of Hofman vans, giving maximum lifting surface of 5327 sq. ft.

Tarpon has been lifted *and held* seven feet for four miles between touch and touch.

Our Autumn List of racing and family Bats ready on the 9th January.

CHRISTIAN WR

ESTABLIS

Accessories

Hooded Binnacles with dip-dials automatically recording change of level (illuminated face).

All heights from 50 to 18,000 feet £2 10 0

With Aerial Board of Control certificate £3 11 0

Foot and Hand Fog-horns; Sirens toned to any club note; with air-chest, belt-driven from motor £6 8 0

Wireless installations syntonised to A.B.C. requirements, in neat mahogany case, hundred mile range £3 3 0

Grapnels, mushroom anchors, pithing-irons, winches, hawsers, snaps, shackles, and mooring ropes, for lawn, city, and public installations.

Detachable under-cars, aluminium or stamped steel.

Keeled under-cars for planes: single-action detaching-gear, turning car into boat with one motion of the wrist. Invaluable for sea trips.

Head, side, and riding lights (by size) Nos. 00 to 20 A.B.C. Standard. Rockets and fog-bombs in colours and tones of the principal clubs (boxed).

A selection of twenty £2 17 6

International night-signals (boxed) £1 11 6

Catalogue free

Spare generators guaranteed to lifting power marked on cover (prices according to power).

Wind-noses for dirigibles—Pegamoid, cane-stiffened, lacquered cane or aluminium and flux for winter work.

Smoke-ring cannon for hail-storms, swivel-mounted, bow or stern.

Propeller-blades: metal, tungsten backed; papier-mâché, wire stiffened; ribbed xylonite (Nickson's patent); all razor-edged (price by pitch and diameter).

Compressed steel bow-screws for winter work.

Fused Ruby or Commercial Mineral Co. bearings and collars. Agate-mounted thrust-blocks up to 4 inch.

Magniac's bow-rudders—(Lavalle's patent grooving).

Wove steel beltings for outboard motors (non-magnetic).

Radium batteries, all powers to 150 h.p. (in pairs).

Helium batteries, all powers to 300 h.p. (tandem).

Stuns'l brakes worked from upper or lower platform.

Direct plunge-brakes worked from lower platform only, loaded silk or fibre, wind-tight.

throughout the planet

The Four Angels

As Adam lay a-dreaming beneath the Apple Tree,
The Angel of the Earth came down, and offered
Earth in fee.
But Adam did not need it,
Nor the plough he would not speed it,
Singing: 'Earth and Water, Air and Fire,
What more can mortal man desire?'
(The Apple Tree's in bud.)

As Adam lay a-dreaming beneath the Apple Tree,
The Angel of the Waters offered all the Seas in fee.
But Adam would not take 'em,
Nor the ships he wouldn't make 'em,
Singing: 'Water, Earth and Air and Fire,
What more can mortal man desire?'
(The Apple Tree's in leaf.)

As Adam lay a-dreaming beneath the Apple Tree,
The Angel of the Air he offered all the Air in fee.
But Adam did not crave it,
Nor the voyage he wouldn't brave it,
Singing: 'Air and Water, Earth and Fire,
What more can mortal man desire?'
(The Apple Tree's in bloom.)

As Adam lay a-dreaming beneath the Apple Tree,
The Angel of the Fire rose up and not a word said he.
But he wished a Fire and made it,
And in Adam's heart he laid it,
Singing: 'Fire, Fire, burning Fire,
Stand up and reach your heart's desire!'
(The Apple Blossom's set.)

As Adam was a-working outside of Eden-Wall,
He used the Earth, he used the Seas, he used the
Air and all;
And out of black disaster
He arose to be the master
Of Earth and Water, Air and Fire,
But never reached his heart's desire!
(The Apple Tree's cut down!)

As Easy as ABC

> The ABC, that semi-elected, semi-nominated body of a few score persons, controls the Planet. Transportation is Civilisation, our motto runs. Theoretically we do what we please, so long as we do not interfere with the traffic *and all it implies.* Practically, the ABC confirms or annuls all international arrangements, and, to judge from its last report, finds our tolerant, humorous, lazy little Planet only too ready to shift the whole burden of public administration on its shoulders.
>
> *'With the Night Mail'*

Isn't it almost time that our Planet took some interest in the proceedings of the Aerial Board of Control? One knows that easy communications nowadays, and lack of privacy in the past, have killed all curiosity among mankind, but as the Board's official reporter I am bound to tell my tale.

At 9.30 A.M., August 26, A.D. 2065, the Board, sitting in London, was informed by De Forest that the District of Northern Illinois had riotously cut itself out of all systems and would remain disconnected till the Board should take over and administer it direct.

Every Northern Illinois freight and passenger tower was, he reported, out of action; all District main, local, and guiding lights had been extinguished; all General Communications were dumb, and through traffic had been diverted. No reason had been given, but he gathered unofficially from the Mayor of Chicago that the District complained of 'crowd-making and invasion of privacy'.

As a matter of fact, it is of no importance whether Northern Illinois stay in or out of planetary circuit; as a matter of policy, any complaint of invasion of privacy needs immediate investigation, lest worse follow.

By 9.45 A.M. De Forest, Dragomiroff (Russia), Takahira (Japan), and Pirolo (Italy) were empowered to visit Illinois and 'to take such steps as might be necessary for the resumption of traffic and *all that that implies*'. By 10 A.M. the Hall was empty, and the four Members and I were aboard what Pirolo insisted on calling 'my leetle godchild' – that is to say, the new *Victor Pirolo*. Our Planet prefers to know Victor Pirolo as a gentle, grey-haired enthusiast who spends his time near Foggia, inventing or creating new breeds of Spanish-Italian olive trees; but there is another side to his nature – the manufacture of quaint inventions, of which the *Victor Pirolo* is, perhaps, not the least surprising. She and a few score sister-craft of the same type embody his latest ideas. But she is not comfortable. An ABC boat does not take the air with the level-keeled lift of a liner, but shoots up rocket-fashion like the 'aeroplane' of our ancestors, and makes her height at top-speed from the first. That is why I found myself sitting suddenly on the large lap of Eustace Arnott, who commands the ABC Fleet. One knows vaguely that there is such a thing as a Fleet somewhere on the Planet, and that, theoretically, it exists for the purposes of what used to be known as 'war'. Only a week before, while visiting a glacier sanatorium behind Gothaven, I had seen some squadrons making false auroras far to the north while they manoeuvred round the Pole; but, naturally, it had never occurred to me that the things could be used in earnest.

Said Arnott to De Forest as I staggered to a seat on the chart-room divan: 'We're tremendously grateful to 'em in Illinois. We've never had a chance of exercising all the Fleet together. I've turned in a General Call, and I expect we'll have at least two hundred keels aloft this evening.'

'Well aloft?' De Forest asked.

'Of course, sir. Out of sight till they're called for.'

Arnott laughed as he lolled over the transparent chart-table where the map of the summer-blue Atlantic slid along, degree by degree, in exact answer to our progress. Our dial already showed 320 m.p.h. and we were two thousand feet above the uppermost traffic lines.

'Now, where is this Illinois District of yours?' said Dragomiroff. 'One travels so much, one sees so little. Oh, I remember! It is in North America.'

De Forest, whose business it is to know the out districts, told us that it lay at the foot of Lake Michigan, on a road to nowhere in particular, was about half an hour's run from end to end, and, except in one corner, as flat as the sea. Like most flat countries nowadays, it was heavily guarded against invasion of privacy by forced timber – fifty-foot spruce and tamarack, grown in five years. The population was close on two millions, largely migratory between Florida and California, with a backbone of small farms (they call a thousand acres a farm in Illinois) whose owners come into Chicago for amusements and society during the winter. They were, he said, noticeably kind, quiet folk, but a little exacting, as all flat countries must be, in their notions of privacy.

There had, for instance, been no printed news-sheet in Illinois for twenty-seven years. Chicago argued that engines for printed news sooner or later developed into engines for invasion of privacy, which in turn might bring the old terror of crowds and blackmail back to the Planet. So news-sheets were not.

'And that's Illinois,' De Forest concluded. 'You see, in the Old Days, she was in the forefront of what they used to call "progress", and Chicago – '

'Chicago?' said Takahira. 'That's the little place where there is Salati's Statue of the Nigger in Flames? A fine bit of old work.'

'When did you see it?' asked De Forest quickly. 'They only unveil it once a year.'

'I know. At Thanksgiving. It was then,' said Takahira, with a shudder. 'And they sang MacDonough's Song, too.'

'Whew!' De Forest whistled. 'I did not know that! I wish you'd told me before. MacDonough's Song may have had its uses when it was composed, but it was an infernal legacy for any man to leave behind.'

'It's protective instinct, my dear fellows,' said Pirolo, rolling a cigarette. 'The Planet, she has had her dose of popular government. She suffers from inherited agoraphobia. She has no – ah – use for crowds.'

Dragomiroff leaned forward to give him a light. 'Certainly,' said the white-bearded Russian, 'the Planet has taken all precautions against crowds for the past hundred years. What is our total population today? Six hundred million, we hope; five hundred, we think; but – but if next year's census shows more than four hundred and fifty, I myself will eat all the extra little babies. We have cut the birthrate out – right out!

For a long time we have said to Almighty God, "Thank You, Sir, but we do not much like Your game of life, so we will not play." '

'Anyhow,' said Arnott defiantly, 'men live a century apiece on the average now.'

'Oh, that is quite well! I am rich – you are rich – we are all rich and happy because we are so few and we live so long. Only *I* think Almighty God He will remember what the Planet was like in the time of crowds and the plague. Perhaps He will send us nerves. Eh, Pirolo?'

The Italian blinked into space. 'Perhaps,' he said, 'He has sent them already. Anyhow, you cannot argue with the Planet. She does not forget the Old Days, and – what can you do?'

'For sure we can't remake the world.' De Forest glanced at the map flowing smoothly across the table from west to east. 'We ought to be over our ground by nine tonight. There won't be much sleep afterwards.'

On which hint we dispersed, and I slept till Takahira waked me for dinner. Our ancestors thought nine hours' sleep ample for their little lives. We, living thirty years longer, feel ourselves defrauded with less than eleven out of the twenty-four.

By ten o'clock we were over Lake Michigan. The west shore was lightless, except for a dull ground-glare at Chicago, and a single traffic-directing light – its leading beam pointing north – at Waukegan on our starboard bow. None of the Lake villages gave any sign of life; and inland, westward, so far as we could see, blackness lay unbroken on the level earth. We swooped down and skimmed low across the dark, throwing calls county by county. Now and again we picked up the faint glimmer of a house-light, or heard the rasp and rend of a cultivator being played across the fields, but Northern Illinois as a whole was one inky, apparently uninhabited, waste of high, forced woods. Only our illuminated map, with its little pointer switching from county to county as we wheeled and twisted, gave us any idea of our position. Our calls, urgent, pleading, coaxing or commanding, through the General Communicator brought no answer. Illinois strictly maintained her own privacy in the timber which she grew for that purpose.

'Oh, this is absurd!' said De Forest. 'We're like an owl trying to work a wheat-field. Is this Bureau Creek? Let's land, Arnott, and get hold of someone.'

We brushed over a belt of forced woodland – fifteen-year-old maple sixty feet high – grounded on a private meadow-dock, none too big, where we moored to our own grapnels, and hurried out through the warm dark night towards a light in a verandah. As we neared the garden gate I could have sworn we had stepped knee-deep in quicksand, for we could scarcely drag our feet against the prickling currents that clogged them. After five paces we stopped, wiping our foreheads, as hopelessly stuck on dry smooth turf as so many cows in a bog.

'Pest!' cried Pirolo angrily. 'We are ground-circuited. And it is my own system of ground-circuits too! I know the pull.'

'Good-evening,' said a girl's voice from the verandah. 'Oh, I'm sorry! We've locked up. Wait a minute.'

We heard the click of a switch, and almost fell forward as the currents round our knees were withdrawn.

The girl laughed, and laid aside her knitting. An old-fashioned Controller stood at her elbow, which she reversed from time to time, and we could hear the snort and clank of the obedient cultivator half a mile away, behind the guardian woods.

'Come in and sit down,' she said. 'I'm only playing a plough. Dad's gone to Chicago to – Ah! Then it was *your* call I heard just now!'

She had caught sight of Arnott's Board uniform, leaped to the switch, and turned it full on.

We were checked, gasping, waist-deep in current this time, three yards from the verandah.

'We only want to know what's the matter with Illinois,' said De Forest placidly.

'Then hadn't you better go to Chicago and find out?' she answered. 'There's nothing wrong here. We own ourselves.'

'How can we go anywhere if you won't loose us?' De Forest went on, while Arnott scowled. Admirals of Fleets are still quite human when their dignity is touched.

'Stop a minute – you don't know how funny you look!' She put her hands on her hips and laughed mercilessly.

'Don't worry about that,' said Arnott, and whistled. A voice answered from the *Victor Pirolo* in the meadow.

'Only a single-fuse ground-circuit!' Arnott called. 'Sort it out gently, please.'

We heard the ping of a breaking lamp; a fuse blew out somewhere in the verandah roof, frightening a nestful of birds. The ground-circuit was open. We stooped and rubbed our tingling ankles.

'How rude – how very rude of you!' the maiden cried.

'Sorry, but we haven't time to look funny,' said

Arnott. 'We've got to go to Chicago; and if I were you, young lady, I'd go into the cellars for the next two hours, and take mother with me.'

Off he strode, with us at his heels, muttering indignantly, till the humour of the thing struck and doubled him up with laughter at the foot of the gangway ladder.

'The Board hasn't shown what you might call a fat spark on this occasion,' said De Forest, wiping his eyes. 'I hope I didn't look as big a fool as you did, Arnott! Hullo! What on earth is that? Dad coming home from Chicago?'

There was a rattle and a rush, and a five-plough cultivator, blades in air like so many teeth, trundled itself at us round the edge of the timber, fuming and sparking furiously.

'Jump!' said Arnott, as we bundled ourselves through the none-too-wide door. 'Never mind about shutting it. Up!'

The *Victor Pirolo* lifted like a bubble, and the vicious machine shot just underneath us, clawing high as it passed.

'There's a nice little spit-kitten for you!' said Arnott, dusting his knees. 'We ask her a civil question. First she circuits us and then she plays a cultivator at us!'

'And then we fly,' said Dragomiroff. 'If I were forty years more young, I would go back and kiss her. Ho! Ho!'

'I,' said Pirolo, 'would smack her! My pet ship has been chased by a dirty plough; a – how do you say? – agricultural implement.'

'Oh, that is Illinois all over,' said De Forest. 'They don't content themselves with talking about privacy. They arrange to have it. And now, where's your alleged fleet, Arnott? We must assert ourselves against this wench.'

Arnott pointed to the black heavens.

'Waiting on – up there,' said he. 'Shall I give them the whole installation, sir?'

'Oh, I don't think the young lady is quite worth that,' said De Forest. 'Get over Chicago, and perhaps we'll see something.'

In a few minutes we were hanging at two thousand feet over an oblong block of incandescence in the centre of the little town.

'That looks like the old City Hall. Yes, there's Salati's Statue in front of it,' said Takahira. 'But what on earth are they doing to the place? I thought they used it for a market nowadays! Drop a little, please.'

We could hear the sputter and crackle of road-surfacing machines – the cheap Western type which fuse stone and rubbish into lava-like ribbed glass for their rough country roads. Three or four surfacers worked on each side of a square of ruins. The brick and stone wreckage crumbled, slid forward, and presently spread out into white-hot pools of sticky slag, which the levelling-rods smoothed more or less flat. Already a third of the big block had been so treated, and was cooling to dull red before our astonished eyes.

'It is the Old Market,' said De Forest. 'Well, there's nothing to prevent Illinois from making a road through a market. It doesn't interfere with traffic, that I can see.'

'Hsh!' said Arnott, gripping me by the shoulder. 'Listen! They're singing. Why on the earth are they singing?'

We dropped again till we could see the black fringe of people at the edge of that glowing square.

At first they only roared against the roar of the surfacers and levellers. Then the words came up clearly – the words of the Forbidden Song that all men knew, and none let pass their lips – poor Pat MacDonough's Song, made in the days of the crowds and the plague – every silly word of it loaded to sparking-point with the Planet's inherited memories of horror, panic, fear and cruelty. And Chicago – innocent, contented little Chicago – was singing it aloud to the infernal tune that carried riot, pestilence and lunacy round our Planet a few generations ago!

'Once there was The People – Terror gave it birth;
Once there was The People, and it made a hell of earth!'

(Then the stamp and pause):

'Earth arose and crushed it. Listen, oh, ye slain!
Once there was The People – it shall never be again!'

The levellers thrust in savagely against the ruins as the song renewed itself again, again and again, louder than the crash of the melting walls.

De Forest frowned.

'I don't like that,' he said. 'They've broken back to the Old Days! They'll be killing somebody soon. I think we'd better divert 'em, Arnott.'

'Ay, ay, sir.' Arnott's hand went to his cap, and we heard the hull of the *Victor Pirolo* ring to the command: 'Lamps! Both watches stand by! Lamps! Lamps! Lamps!'

'Keep still!' Takahira whispered to me. 'Blinkers, please, quartermaster.'

'It's all right – all right!' said Pirolo from behind, and

to my horror slipped over my head some sort of rubber helmet that locked with a snap. I could feel thick colloid bosses before my eyes, but I stood in absolute darkness.

'To save the sight,' he explained, and pushed me on to the chart-room divan. 'You will see in a minute.'

As he spoke I became aware of a thin thread of almost intolerable light, let down from heaven at an immense distance – one vertical hairsbreadth of frozen lightning.

'Those are our flanking ships,' said Arnott at my elbow. 'That one is over Galena. Look south – that other one's over Keithburg. Vincennes is behind us, and north yonder is Winthrop Woods. The Fleet's in position, sir' – this to De Forest. 'As soon as you give the word.'

'Ah no! No!' cried Dragomiroff at my side. I could feel the old man tremble. 'I do not know all that you can do, but be kind! I ask you to be a little kind to them below! This is horrible – horrible!'

> 'When a Woman kills a Chicken,
> Dynasties and Empires sicken,'

Takahira quoted. 'It is too late to be gentle now.'

'Then take off my helmet! Take off my helmet!' Dragomiroff began hysterically.

Pirolo must have put his arm round him.

'Hush,' he said, 'I am here. It is all right, Ivan, my dear fellow.'

'I'll just send our little girl in Bureau County a warning,' said Arnott. 'She don't deserve it, but we'll allow her a minute or two to take mamma to the cellar.'

In the utter hush that followed the growling spark after Arnott had linked up his Service Communicator with the invisible Fleet, we heard MacDonough's Song from the city beneath us grow fainter as we rose to position. Then I clapped my hand before my mask lenses, for it was as though the floor of Heaven had been riddled and all the inconceivable blaze of suns in the making was poured through the manholes.

'You needn't count,' said Arnott. I had had no thought of such a thing. 'There are two hundred and fifty keels up there, five miles apart. Full power, please, for another twelve seconds.'

The firmament, as far as eye could reach, stood on pillars of white fire. One fell on the glowing square at Chicago, and turned it black.

'Oh! Oh! Oh! Can men be allowed to do such things?' Dragomiroff cried, and fell across our knees.

'Glass of water, please,' said Takahira to a helmeted shape that leaped forward. 'He is a little faint.'

The lights switched off, and the darkness stunned like an avalanche. We could hear Dragomiroff's teeth on the glass edge.

Pirolo was comforting him.

'All right, all ra-ight,' he repeated. 'Come and lie down. Come below and take off your mask. I give you my word, old friend, it is all right. They are my siege-lights. Little Victor Pirolo's leetle lights. You know *me*! I do not hurt people.'

'Pardon!' Dragomiroff moaned. 'I have never seen Death. I have never seen the Board take action. Shall we go down and burn them alive, or is that already done?'

'Oh, hush,' said Pirolo, and I think he rocked him in his arms.

'Do we repeat, sir?' Arnott asked De Forest.

'Give 'em a minute's break,' De Forest replied. 'They may need it.'

We waited a minute, and then MacDonough's Song, broken but defiant, rose from undefeated Chicago.

'They seem fond of that tune,' said De Forest. 'I should let 'em have it, Arnott.'

'Very good, sir,' said Arnott, and felt his way to the Communicator keys.

No lights broke forth, but the hollow of the skies made herself the mouth for one note that touched the raw fibre of the brain. Men hear such sounds in delirium, advancing like tides from horizons beyond the ruled foreshores of space.

'That's our pitch-pipe,' said Arnott. 'We may be a bit ragged. I've never conducted two hundred and fifty performers before.' He pulled out the couplers, and struck a full chord on the Service Communicators.

The beams of light leaped down again, and danced, solemnly and awfully, a stilt-dance, sweeping thirty or forty miles left and right at each stiff-legged kick, while the darkness delivered itself – there is no scale to measure against that utterance – of the tune to which they kept time. Certain notes – one learnt to expect them with terror – cut through one's marrow, but, after three minutes, thought and emotion passed in indescribable agony.

We saw, we heard, but I think we were in some sort swooning. The two hundred and fifty beams shifted, re-formed, straddled and split, narrowed, widened, rippled in ribbons, broke into a thousand white-hot parallel lines, melted and revolved in interwoven rings like old-fashioned engine-turning, flung up to the zenith, made as if to descend and renew the torment, halted at the last instant, twizzled insanely round the horizon, and vanished, to bring back for the hundredth time darkness more shattering than their instantly renewed light over all Illinois. Then the tune and lights ceased together, and we heard one single devastating wail that shook all the horizon as a rubbed wet finger shakes the rim of a bowl.

'Ah, that is my new siren,' said Pirolo. 'You can break an iceberg in half, if you find the proper pitch. They will whistle by squadrons now. It is the wind through pierced shutters in the bows.'

I had collapsed beside Dragomiroff, broken and snivelling feebly, because I had been delivered before my time to all the terrors of Judgment Day, and the Archangels of the Resurrection were hailing me naked across the Universe to the sound of the music of the spheres.

Then I saw De Forest smacking Arnott's helmet with his open hand. The wailing died down in a long shriek as a black shadow swooped past us, and returned to her place above the lower clouds.

'I hate to interrupt a specialist when he's enjoying himself,' said De Forest. 'But, as a matter of fact, all Illinois has been asking us to stop for these last fifteen seconds.'

'What a pity.' Arnott slipped off his mask. 'I wanted you to hear us really hum. Our lower C can lift street-paving.'

'It is Hell – Hell!' cried Dragomiroff, and sobbed aloud.

Arnott looked away as he answered: 'It's a few thousand volts ahead of the old shoot-'em-and-sink-'em game, but I should scarcely call it *that*. What shall I tell the Fleet, sir?'

'Tell 'em we're very pleased and impressed. I don't think they need wait on any longer. There isn't a spark left down there.' De Forest pointed. 'They'll be deaf and blind.'

'Oh, I think not, sir. The demonstration lasted less than ten minutes.'

'Marvellous!' Takahira sighed. 'I should have said it was half a night. Now, shall we go down and pick up the pieces?'

'But first a small drink,' said Pirolo. 'The Board must not arrive weeping at its own works.'

'I am an old fool – an old fool!' Dragomiroff began piteously. 'I did not know what would happen. It is all new to me. We reason with them in Little Russia.'

Chicago North landing-tower was unlighted, and Arnott worked his ship into the clips by her own lights. As soon as these broke out we heard groanings of horror and appeal from many people below.

'All right,' shouted Arnott into the darkness. 'We aren't beginning again!' We descended by the stairs, to find ourselves knee-deep in a grovelling crowd, some crying that they were blind, others beseeching us not to make any more noises, but the greater part writhing face downward, their hands or their caps before their eyes.

It was Pirolo who came to our rescue. He climbed the side of a surfacing-machine, and there, gesticulating as though they could see, made oration to those afflicted people of Illinois.

'You stchewpids!' he began. 'There is nothing to fuss for. Of course, your eyes will smart and be red tomorrow. You will look as if you and your wives had drunk too much, but in a little while you will see again as well as before. I tell you this, and I – *I* am Pirolo. Victor Pirolo!'

The crowd with one accord shuddered, for many legends attach to Victor Pirolo of Foggia, deep in the secrets of God.

'Pirolo?' An unsteady voice lifted itself. 'Then tell us

was there anything except light in those lights of yours just now?'

The question was repeated from every corner of the darkness.

Pirolo laughed.

'No!' he thundered. (Why have small men such large voices?) 'I give you my word and the Board's word that there was nothing except light – just light! You stchewpids! Your birthrate is too low already as it is. Someday I must invent something to send it up, but send it down – never!'

'Is that true? – We thought – somebody said – '

One could feel the tension relax all round.

'You *too* big fools,' Pirolo cried. 'You could have sent us a call and we would have told you.'

'Send you a call!' a deep voice shouted. 'I wish you had been at our end of the wire.'

'I'm glad I wasn't,' said De Forest. 'It was bad enough from behind the lamps. Never mind! It's over now. Is there anyone here I can talk business with? I'm De Forest – for the Board.'

'You might begin with me, for one – I'm Mayor,' the bass voice replied.

A big man rose unsteadily from the street, and staggered towards us where we sat on the broad turf-edging, in front of the garden fences.

'I ought to be the first on my feet. Am I?' said he.

'Yes,' said De Forest, and steadied him as he dropped down beside us.

'Hello, Andy. Is that you?' a voice called.

'Excuse me,' said the Mayor; 'that sounds like my Chief of Police, Bluthner!'

'Bluthner it is; and here's Mulligan and Keefe – on their feet.'

'Bring 'em up please, Blut. We're supposed to be the Four in charge of this hamlet. What we says, goes. And, De Forest, what do you say?'

'Nothing – yet,' De Forest answered, as we made room for the panting, reeling men. '*You've* cut out of system. Well?'

'Tell the steward to send down drinks, please,' Arnott whispered to an orderly at his side.

'Good!' said the Mayor, smacking his dry lips. 'Now I suppose we can take it, De Forest, that henceforward the Board will administer us direct?'

'Not if the Board can avoid it,' De Forest laughed. 'The ABC is responsible for the planetary traffic only.'

'*And all that that implies.*' The big Four who ran Chicago chanted their Magna Charta like children at school.

'Well, get on,' said De Forest wearily. 'What is your silly trouble anyway?'

'Too much dam' Democracy,' said the Mayor, laying his hand on De Forest's knee.

'So? I thought Illinois had had her dose of that.'

'She has. That's why. Blut, what did you do with our prisoners last night?'

'Locked 'em in the water-tower to prevent the women killing 'em,' the Chief of Police replied. 'I'm too blind to move just yet, but –'

'Arnott, send some of your people, please, and fetch 'em along,' said De Forest.

'They're triple-circuited,' the Mayor called. 'You'll have to blow out three fuses.' He turned to De Forest, his large outline just visible in the paling darkness. 'I hate to throw any more work on the Board. I'm an administrator myself, but we've had a little fuss with our Serviles. What? In a big city there's bound to be a few men and women who can't live without listening to themselves, and who prefer drinking out of pipes they don't own both ends of. They inhabit flats and hotels all the year round. They say it saves 'em trouble. Anyway, it gives 'em more time to make trouble for their neighbours. We call 'em Serviles locally. And they are apt to be tuberculous.'

'Just so!' said the man called Mulligan. Transport–ation is Civilisation. Democracy is Disease. I've proved it by the blood-test, every time.'

'Mulligan's our Health Officer, and a one-idea man,' said the Mayor, laughing. 'But it's true that most Serviles haven't much control. They *will* talk; and when people take to talking as a business, anything may arrive – mayn't it, De Forest?'

'Anything – except the facts of the case,' said De Forest, laughing.

'I'll give you those in a minute,' said the Mayor. 'Our Serviles got to talking – first in their houses and then on the streets, telling men and women how to manage their own affairs. (You can't teach a Servile not to finger his neighbour's soul.) That's invasion of privacy, of course, but in Chicago we'll suffer anything sooner than make crowds. Nobody took much notice, and so I let 'em alone. My fault! I was warned there would be trouble, but there hasn't been a crowd or murder in Illinois for nineteen years.'

'Twenty-two,' said his Chief of Police.

'Likely. Anyway, we'd forgot such things. So, from talking in the houses and on the streets, our Serviles go to calling a meeting at the Old Market yonder.' He nodded across the square where the wrecked buildings heaved up grey in the dawn-glimmer behind the square-cased statue of the Negro in Flames. 'There's nothing to prevent anyone calling meetings except that it's against human nature to stand in a crowd, besides being bad for the health. I ought to have known by the way our men and women attended that first meeting that trouble was brewing. There were as many as a thousand in the marketplace, touching each other. Touching! Then the Serviles turned in all tongue-switches and talked, and we – '

'What did they talk about?' said Takahira.

'First, how badly things were managed in the city. That pleased us Four – we were on the platform – because we hoped to catch one or two good men for City work. You know how rare executive capacity is. Even if we didn't it's – it's refreshing to find anyone interested enough in our job to damn our eyes. You don't know what it means to work, year in, year out, without a spark of difference with a living soul.'

'Oh, don't we!' said De Forest. 'There are times on the Board when we'd give our positions if anyone would kick us out and take hold of things themselves.'

'But they won't,' said the Mayor ruefully. 'I assure you, sir, we Four have done things in Chicago, in the hope of rousing people, that would have discredited Nero. But what do they say? "Very good, Andy. Have it your own way. Anything's better than a crowd. I'll go back to my land." You *can't* do anything with folk who can go where they please, and don't want anything on God's earth except their own way. There isn't a kick or a kicker left on the Planet.'

'Then I suppose that little shed yonder fell down by itself?' said De Forest. We could see the bare and still smoking ruins, and hear the slag-pools crackle as they hardened and set.

'Oh, that's only amusement. 'Tell you later. As I

was saying, our Serviles held the meeting, and pretty soon we had to ground-circuit the platform to save 'em from being killed. And that didn't make our people any more pacific.'

'How d'you mean?' I ventured to ask.

'If you've ever been ground-circuited,' said the Mayor, 'you'll know it don't improve any man's temper to be held up straining against nothing. No, sir! Eight or nine hundred folk kept pawing and buzzing like flies in treacle for two hours, while a pack of perfectly safe Serviles invades their mental and spiritual privacy, may be amusing to watch, but they are not pleasant to handle afterwards.'

Pirolo chuckled.

'Our folk own themselves. They were of opinion things were going too far and too fiery. I warned the Serviles; but they're born house-dwellers. Unless a fact hits 'em on the head they cannot see it. Would you believe me, they went on to talk of what they called "popular government"? They did! They wanted us to go back to the old Voodoo-business of voting with papers and wooden boxes, and word-drunk people and printed formulas, and news-sheets! They said they practised it among themselves about what they'd have to eat in their flats and hotels. Yes, sir! They stood up behind Bluthner's doubled ground-circuits, and they said that, in this present year of grace, *to* self-owning men and women, *on* that very spot! Then they finished' – he lowered his voice cautiously – 'by talking about "The People". And then Bluthner he had to sit up all night in charge of the circuits because he couldn't trust his men to keep 'em shut.'

'It was trying 'em too high,' the Chief of Police

broke in. 'But we couldn't hold the crowd ground-circuited for ever. I gathered in all the Serviles on charge of crowd-making, and put 'em in the water-tower, and then I let things cut loose. I had to! The District lit like a sparked gas-tank!'

'The news was out over seven degrees of country,' the Mayor continued; 'and when once it's a question of invasion of privacy, goodbye to right and reason in Illinois! They began turning out traffic-lights and locking up landing-towers on Thursday night. Friday, they stopped all traffic and asked for the Board to take over. Then they wanted to clean Chicago off the side of the Lake and rebuild elsewhere – just for a souvenir of "The People" that the Serviles talked about. I suggested that they should slag the Old Market where the meeting was held, while I turned in a call to you all on the Board. That kept 'em quiet till you came along. And – and now *you* can take hold of the situation.'

'Any chance of their quieting down?' De Forest asked.

'You can try,' said the Mayor.

De Forest raised his voice in the face of the reviving crowd that had edged in towards us. Day was come.

'Don't you think this business can be arranged?' he began. But there was a roar of angry voices:

'We've finished with crowds! We aren't going back to the Old Days! Take us over! Take the Serviles away! Administer direct or we'll kill 'em! Down with The People!'

An attempt was made to begin MacDonough's Song. It got no further than the first line, for the *Victor Pirolo* sent down a warning drone on one stopped horn. A wrecked side-wall of the Old Market tottered and fell inwards on the slag-pools. None spoke or moved till the last of the dust had settled down again, turning the steel case of Salati's Statue ashy grey.

'You see you'll just *have* to take us over,' the Mayor whispered.

De Forest shrugged his shoulders.

'You talk as if executive capacity could be snatched out of the air like so much horsepower. Can't you manage yourselves on any terms?' he said.

'We can, if you say so. It will only cost those few lives to begin with.'

The Mayor pointed across the square, where Arnott's men guided a stumbling group of ten or twelve men and women to the lake front and halted them under the Statue.

'Now I think,' said Takahira under his breath, 'there will be trouble.'

The mass in front of us growled like beasts.

At that moment the sun rose clear, and revealed the blinking assembly to itself. As soon as it realised that it was a crowd we saw the shiver of horror and mutual repulsion shoot across it precisely as the steely flaws shot across the lake outside. Nothing was said, and, being half blind, of course it moved slowly. Yet in less than fifteen minutes most of that vast multitude – three thousand at the lowest count – melted away like frost on south eaves. The remnant stretched themselves on the grass, where a crowd feels and looks less like a crowd.

'These mean business,' the Mayor whispered to Takahira. 'There are a goodish few women there who've borne children. I don't like it.'

The morning draught off the lake stirred the trees round us with promise of a hot day; the sun reflected itself dazzlingly on the canister-shaped covering of

Salati's Statue; cocks crew in the gardens, and we could hear gate-latches clicking in the distance as people stumblingly resought their homes.

'I'm afraid there won't be any morning deliveries,' said De Forest. 'We rather upset things in the country last night.'

'That makes no odds,' the Mayor returned. 'We're all provisioned for six months. *We* take no chances.'

Nor, when you come to think of it, does anyone else. It must be three-quarters of a generation since any house or city faced a food shortage. Yet is there house or city on the Planet today that has not half a year's provisions laid in? We are like the shipwrecked seamen in the old books, who, having once nearly starved to death, ever afterwards hide away bits of food and biscuit. Truly we trust no crowds, nor system based on crowds!

De Forest waited till the last footstep had died away. Meantime the prisoners at the base of the Statue shuffled, posed, and fidgeted, with the shamelessness of quite little children. None of them were more than six feet high, and many of them were as grey-haired as the ravaged, harassed heads of old pictures. They huddled together in actual touch, while the crowd, spaced at large intervals, looked at them with congested eyes.

Suddenly a man among them began to talk. The Mayor had not in the least exaggerated. It appeared that our Planet lay sunk in slavery beneath the heel of the Aerial Board of Control. The orator urged us to arise in our might, burst our prison doors and break our fetters (all his metaphors, by the way, were of the most medieval). Next he demanded that every matter of daily life, including most of the physical functions, should be submitted for decision at any time of the week, month, or year to, I gathered, anybody who happened to be passing by or residing within a certain radius, and that everybody should forthwith abandon his concerns to settle the matter, first by crowd-making, next by talking to the crowds made, and lastly by describing crosses on pieces of paper, which rubbish should later be counted with certain mystic ceremonies and oaths. Out of this amazing play, he assured us, would automatically arise a higher, nobler, and kinder world, based – he demonstrated this with the awful lucidity of the insane – based on the sanctity of the crowd and the villainy of the single person. In conclusion, he called loudly upon God to testify to his personal merits and integrity. When the flow ceased, I turned bewildered to Takahira, who was nodding solemnly.

'Quite correct,' said he. 'It is all in the old books. He has left nothing out, not even the war-talk.'

'But I don't see how this stuff can upset a child, much less a district,' I replied.

'Ah, you are too young,' said Dragomiroff. 'For another thing, you are not a mamma. Please look at the mammas.'

Ten or fifteen women who remained had separated themselves from the silent men, and were drawing in towards the prisoners. It reminded one of the stealthy encircling, before the rush in at the quarry, of wolves round musk-oxen in the North. The prisoners saw, and drew together more closely. The Mayor covered his face with his hands for an instant. De Forest, bareheaded, stepped forward between the prisoners, and the slowly, stiffly moving line.

'That's all very interesting,' he said to the dry-lipped

orator. 'But the point seems that you've been making crowds and invading privacy.'

A woman stepped forward, and would have spoken, but there was a quick assenting murmur from the men, who realised that De Forest was trying to pull the situation down to ground-line.

'Yes! Yes!' they cried. 'We cut out because they made crowds and invaded privacy! Stick to that! Keep on that switch! Lift the Serviles out of this! The Board's in charge! Hsh!'

'Yes, the Board's in charge,' said De Forest. 'I'll take formal evidence of crowd-making if you like, but the Members of the Board can testify to it. Will that do?'

The women had closed in another pace, with hands that clenched and unclenched at their sides.

'Good! Good enough!' the men cried. 'We're content. Only take them away quickly.'

'Come along up!' said De Forest to the captives, 'Breakfast is quite ready.'

It appeared, however, that they did not wish to go. They intended to remain in Chicago and make crowds. They pointed out that De Forest's proposal was gross invasion of privacy.

'My dear fellow,' said Pirolo to the most voluble of the leaders, 'you hurry, or your crowd that can't be wrong will kill you!'

'But that would be murder,' answered the believer in crowds; and there was a roar of laughter from all sides that seemed to show the crisis had broken.

A woman stepped forward from the line of women, laughing, I protest, as merrily as any of the company. One hand, of course, shaded her eyes, the other was at her throat.

'Oh, they needn't be afraid of being killed!' she called.

'Not in the least,' said De Forest. 'But don't you think that, now the Board's in charge, you might go home while we get these people away?'

'I shall be home long before that. It – it has been rather a trying day.'

She stood up to her full height, dwarfing even De Forest's six-foot-eight, and smiled, with eyes closed against the fierce light.

'Yes, rather,' said De Forest. 'I'm afraid you feel the glare a little. We'll have the ship down.'

He motioned to the *Pirolo* to drop between us and the sun, and at the same time to loop-circuit the prisoners, who were a trifle unsteady. We saw them stiffen to the current where they stood. The woman's voice went on, sweet and deep and unshaken: 'I don't suppose you men realise how much this – this sort of thing means to a woman. I've borne three. We women don't want our children given to crowds. It must be an inherited instinct. Crowds make trouble. They bring back the Old Days. Hate, fear, blackmail, publicity, "The People" – *That! That! That!*' She pointed to the Statue, and the crowd growled once more.

'Yes, if they are allowed to go on,' said De Forest. 'But this little affair – '

'It means so much to us women that this – this little affair should never happen again. Of course, never's a big word, but one feels so strongly that it is important to stop crowds at the very beginning. Those creatures' – she pointed with her left hand at the prisoners swaying like seaweed in a tideway as the circuit pulled them – 'those people have friends and wives and children in the city and elsewhere. One doesn't want anything done to *them*, you know. It's terrible to force a human being out of fifty or sixty years of good life. I'm only forty myself. *I* know. But, at the same time, one feels that an example should be made, because no price is too heavy to pay if – if these people *and all that they imply* can be put an end to. Do you quite understand, or would you be kind enough to tell your men to take the casing off the Statue? It's worth looking at.'

'I understand perfectly. But I don't think anybody here wants to see the Statue on an empty stomach. Excuse me one moment.' De Forest called up to the ship, 'A flying loop ready on the port side, if you please.' Then to the woman he said with some crispness, 'You might leave us a little discretion in the matter.'

'Oh, of course. Thank you for being so patient. I know my arguments are silly, but – ' She half turned away and went on in a changed voice, 'Perhaps this will help you to decide.'

She threw out her right arm with a knife in it. Before the blade could be returned to her throat or her bosom it was twitched from her grip, sparked as it flew out of the shadow of the ship above, and fell flashing in the sunshine at the foot of the Statue fifty yards away. The outflung arm was arrested, rigid as a bar for an instant, till the releasing circuit permitted her to bring it slowly to her side. The other women shrank back silent among the men.

Pirolo rubbed his hands, and Takahira nodded.

'That was clever of you, De Forest,' said he.

'What a glorious pose!' Dragomiroff murmured, for the frightened woman was on the edge of tears.

'Why did you stop me? I would have done it!' she cried.

'I have no doubt you would,' said De Forest. 'But we can't waste a life like yours on these people. I hope the arrest didn't sprain your wrist; it's so hard to regulate a flying loop. But I think you are quite right about those persons' women and children. We'll take them all away with us if you promise not to do anything stupid to yourself.'

'I promise – I promise.' She controlled herself with an effort. 'But it is so important to us women. We know what it means; and I thought if you saw I was in earnest – '

'I saw you were, and you've gained your point. I shall take all your Serviles away with me at once. The Mayor will make lists of their friends and families in the city and the district, and he'll ship them after us this afternoon.'

'Sure,' said the Mayor, rising to his feet. 'Keefe, if you can see, hadn't you better finish levelling off the Old Market? It don't look sightly the way it is now, and we shan't use it for crowds any more.'

'I think you had better wipe out that Statue as well, Mr Mayor,' said De Forest. 'I don't question its merits as a work of art, but I believe it's a shade morbid.'

'Certainly, sir. Oh, Keefe! Slag the Nigger before you go on to fuse the Market. I'll get to the Communicators and tell the District that the Board is in charge. Are you making any special appointments, sir?'

'None. We haven't men to waste on these backwoods. Carry on as before, but under the Board. Arnott, run your Serviles aboard, please. Ground ship and pass them through the bilge-doors. We'll wait till we've finished with this work of art.'

The prisoners trailed past him, talking fluently, but unable to gesticulate in the drag of the current. Then the surfacers rolled up, two on each side of the Statue. With one accord the spectators looked elsewhere, but there was no need. Keefe turned on full power, and the thing simply melted within its case. All I saw was a surge of white-hot metal pouring over the plinth, a glimpse of Salati's inscription, 'To the Eternal Memory of the Justice of the People', ere the stone base itself cracked and powdered into finest lime. The crowd cheered.

'Thank you,' said De Forest; 'but we want our breakfasts, and I expect you do too. Goodbye, Mr Mayor! Delighted to see you at any time, but I hope I shan't have to, officially, for the next thirty years. Goodbye, madam. Yes. We're all given to nerves nowadays. I suffer from them myself. Goodbye, gentlemen all! You're under the tyrannous heel of the Board from this moment, but if ever you feel like breaking your fetters you've only to let us know. This is no treat to us. Good luck!'

We embarked amid shouts, and did not check our lift till they had dwindled into whispers. Then De Forest flung himself on the chart-room divan and mopped his forehead.

'I don't mind men,' he panted, 'but women are the devil!'

'Still the devil,' said Pirolo cheerfully. 'That one would have suicided.'

'I know it. That was why I signalled for the flying loop to be clapped on her. I owe you an apology for that, Arnott. I hadn't time to catch your eye, and you were busy with our caitiffs. By the way, who actually answered my signal? It was a smart piece of work.'

'Ilroy,' said Arnott; 'but he overloaded the wave. It may be pretty gallery-work to knock a knife out of a lady's hand, but didn't you notice how she rubbed 'em? He scorched her fingers. Slovenly, I call it.'

'Far be it from me to interfere with Fleet discipline, but don't be too hard on the boy. If that woman had killed herself they would have killed every Servile and everything related to a Servile throughout the district by nightfall.'

'That was what she was playing for,' Takahira said. 'And with our Fleet gone we could have done nothing to hold them.'

'I may be ass enough to walk into a ground-circuit,' said Arnott, 'but I don't dismiss my Fleet till I'm reasonably sure that trouble is over. They're in position still, and I intend to keep 'em there till the Serviles are shipped out of the district. That last little crowd meant murder, my friends.'

'Nerves! All nerves!' said Pirolo. 'You cannot argue with agoraphobia.'

'And it is not as if they had seen much dead – or *is* it?' said Takahira.

'In all my ninety years I have never seen Death.' Dragomiroff spoke as one who would excuse himself. 'Perhaps that was why – last night – '

Then it came out as we sat over breakfast, that, with the exception of Arnott and Pirolo, none of us had ever seen a corpse, or knew in what manner the spirit passes.

'We're a nice lot to flap about governing the Planet,' De Forest laughed. 'I confess, now it's all over, that my main fear was I mightn't be able to pull it off without losing a life.'

'I thought of that too,' said Arnott; 'but there's no death reported, and I've enquired everywhere. What are we supposed to do with our passengers? I've fed 'em.'

'We're between two switches,' De Forest drawled.

'If we drop them in any place that isn't under the Board the natives will make their presence an excuse for cutting out, same as Illinois did, and forcing the Board to take over. If we drop them in any place under the Board's control they'll be killed as soon as our backs are turned.'

'If you say so,' said Pirolo thoughtfully, 'I can guarantee that they will become extinct in process of time, quite happily. What is their birthrate now?'

'Go down and ask 'em,' said De Forest.

'I think they might become nervous and tear me to bits,' the philosopher of Foggia replied.

'Not really? Well?'

'Open the bilge-doors,' said Takahira with a downward jerk of the thumb.

'Scarcely – after all the trouble we've taken to save 'em,' said De Forest.

'Try London,' Arnott suggested. 'You could turn Satan himself loose there, and they'd only ask him to dinner.'

'Good man! You've given me an idea. Vincent! Oh, Vincent!' He threw the General Communicator open so that we could all hear, and in a few minutes the chart-room filled with the rich, fruity voice of Leopold Vincent, who has purveyed all London her choicest amusements for the last thirty years. We answered with expectant grins, as though we were actually in the stalls of, say, the Combination on a first night.

'We've picked up something in your line,' De Forest began.

'That's good, dear man. If it's old enough. There's nothing to beat the old things for business purposes. Have you seen *London, Chatham, and Dover* at Earl's Court? No? I thought I missed you there. Im–mense!

I've had the real steam locomotive engines built from the old designs and the iron rails cast specially by hand. Cloth cushions in the carriages, too! Im–mense! And paper railway tickets. And Polly Milton.'

'Polly Milton back again!' said Arnott rapturously. 'Book me two stalls for tomorrow night. What's she singing now, bless her?'

'The old songs. Nothing comes up to the old touch. Listen to this, dear men.' Vincent carolled with flourishes:

> 'Oh, cruel lamps of London,
> If tears your light could drown,
> Your victims' eyes would weep them,
> Oh, lights of London Town!'

'Then they weep.'

'You see?' Pirolo waved his hands at us. 'The old world always weeped when it saw crowds together. It did not know why, but it weeped. We know why, but we do not weep, except when we pay to be made to by fat, wicked old Vincent.'

'Old, yourself!' Vincent laughed. 'I'm a public benefactor, I keep the world soft and united.'

'And I'm De Forest of the Board,' said De Forest acidly, 'trying to get a little business done. As I was saying, I've picked up a few people in Chicago.'

'I cut out. Chicago is –'

'Do listen! They're perfectly unique.'

'Do they build houses of baked mudblocks while you wait – eh? That's an old contact.'

'They're an untouched primitive community, with all the old ideas.'

'Sewing-machines and maypole-dances? Cooking on coal-gas stoves, lighting pipes with matches, and driving horses? Gerolstein tried that last year. An absolute blowout!'

De Forest plugged him wrathfully, and poured out the story of our doings for the last twenty-four hours on the top-note.

'And they do it *all* in public,' he concluded. 'You can't stop 'em. The more public, the better they are pleased. They'll talk for hours – like you! Now you can come in again!'

'Do you really mean they know how to vote?' said Vincent. 'Can they act it?'

'Act? It's their life to 'em! And you never saw such faces! Scarred like volcanoes. Envy, hatred, and malice in plain sight. Wonderfully flexible voices. They weep, too.'

'Aloud? In public?'

'I guarantee. Not a spark of shame or reticence in the entire installation. It's the chance of your career.'

'D'you say you've brought their voting props along – those papers and ballot-box things?'

'No, confound you! I'm not a luggage-lifter. Apply direct to the Mayor of Chicago. He'll forward you everything. Well?'

'Wait a minute. Did Chicago want to kill 'em? That 'ud look well on the Communicators.'

'Yes! They were only rescued with difficulty from a howling mob – if you know what that is.'

'But I don't,' answered the Great Vincent simply.

'Well then, they'll tell you themselves. They can make speeches hours long.'

'How many are there?'

'By the time we ship 'em all over they'll be perhaps a hundred, counting children. An old world in miniature. Can't you see it?'

'M–yes; but I've got to pay for it if it's a blowout, dear man.'

'They can sing the old war songs in the streets. They can get word-drunk, and make crowds, and invade privacy in the genuine old-fashioned way; and they'll do the voting trick as often as you ask 'em a question.'

'Too good!' said Vincent.

'You unbelieving Jew! I've got a dozen head aboard here. I'll put you through direct. Sample 'em yourself.'

He lifted the switch and we listened. Our passengers on the lower deck at once, but not less than five at a time, explained themselves to Vincent. They had been taken from the bosom of their families, stripped of their possessions, given food without finger-bowls, and cast into captivity in a noisome dungeon.

'But look here,' said Arnott aghast; 'they're saying what isn't true. My lower deck isn't noisome, and I saw to the finger-bowls myself.'

'My people talk like that sometimes in Little Russia,' said Dragomiroff. 'We reason with them. We never kill. No!'

'But it's not true,' Arnott insisted. 'What can you do with people who don't tell facts? They're mad!'

'Hsh!' said Pirolo, his hand to his ear. 'It is such a little time since all the Planet told lies.'

We heard Vincent silkily sympathetic. Would they, he asked, repeat their assertions in public – before a vast public? Only let Vincent give them a chance, and the Planet, they vowed, should ring with their wrongs. Their aim in life – two women and a man explained it together – was to reform the world. Oddly enough, this also had been Vincent's life-dream. He offered them an arena in which to explain, and by their living example to raise the Planet to loftier levels. He was eloquent on the moral uplift of a simple, old-world life presented in its entirety to a deboshed civilisation.

Could they – would they – for three months certain, devote themselves under his auspices, as missionaries, to the elevation of mankind at a place called Earl's Court, which he said, with some truth, was one of the intellectual centres of the Planet? They thanked him, and demanded (we could hear his chuckle of delight) time to discuss and to vote on the matter. The vote, solemnly managed by counting heads – one head, one vote – was favourable. His offer, therefore, was accepted, and they moved a vote of thanks to him in two speeches – one by what they called the 'proposer' and the other by the 'seconder'.

Vincent threw over to us, his voice shaking with gratitude: 'I've got 'em! Did you hear those speeches? That's Nature, dear men. Art can't teach *that*. And they voted as easily as lying. I've never had a troupe of natural liars before. Bless you, dear men! Remember, you're on my free lists for ever, anywhere – all of you. Oh, Gerolstein will be sick – sick!'

'Then you think they'll do?' said De Forest.

'Do? The Little Village'll go crazy! I'll knock up a series of old-world plays for 'em. Their voices will make you laugh and cry. My God, dear men, where *do* you suppose they picked up all their misery from, on this sweet earth? I'll have a pageant of the world's beginnings, and Mosenthal shall do the music. I'll – '

'Go and knock up a village for 'em by tonight. We'll meet you at No. 15 West Landing Tower,' said De Forest. 'Remember the rest will be coming along tomorrow.'

'Let 'em all come!' said Vincent. 'You don't know

how hard it is nowadays even for me, to find something that really gets under the public's damned iridium-plated hide. But I've got it at last. Goodbye!'

'Well,' said De Forest when we had finished laughing, 'if anyone understood corruption in London I might have played off Vincent against Gerolstein, and sold my captives at enormous prices. As it is, I shall have to be their legal adviser tonight when the contracts are signed. And they won't exactly press any commission on me, either.'

'Meantime,' said Takahira, 'we cannot, of course, confine members of Leopold Vincent's last-engaged company. Chairs for the ladies, please, Arnott.'

'Then I go to bed,' said De Forest. 'I can't face any more women!' And he vanished.

When our passengers were released and given another meal (finger-bowls came first this time) they told us what they thought of us and the Board; and, like Vincent, we all marvelled how they had contrived to extract and secrete so much bitter poison and unrest out of the good life God gives us. They raged, they stormed, they palpitated, flushed and exhausted their poor, torn nerves, panted themselves into silence, and renewed the senseless, shameless attacks.

'But can't you understand,' said Pirolo pathetically to a shrieking woman, 'that if we'd left you in Chicago you'd have been killed?'

'No, we shouldn't. You were bound to save us from being murdered.'

'Then we should have had to kill a lot of other people.'

'That doesn't matter. We were preaching the Truth. You can't stop us. We shall go on preaching in London; and *then* you'll see!'

'You can see now,' said Pirolo, and opened a lower shutter.

We were closing on the Little Village, with her three million people spread out at ease inside her ring of girdling Main-Traffic lights – those eight fixed beams at Chatham, Tonbridge, Redhill, Dorking, Woking, St Albans, Chipping Ongar, and Southend.

Leopold Vincent's new company looked, with small pale faces, at the silence, the size, and the separated houses.

Then some began to weep aloud, shamelessly – always without shame.

MacDonough's Song

Whether the State can loose and bind
  In Heaven as well as on Earth:
If it be wiser to kill mankind
  Before or after the birth –
These are matters of high concern
  Where State-kept schoolmen are;
But Holy State (we have lived to learn)
  Endeth in Holy War.

Whether The People be led by the Lord,
  Or lured by the loudest throat:
If it be quicker to die by the sword
  Or cheaper to die by vote –
These are the things we have dealt with once,
  (And they will not rise from their grave)
For Holy People, however it runs,
  Endeth in wholly Slave.

Whatsoever, for any cause,
  Seeketh to take or give,
Power above or beyond the Laws,
  Suffer it not to live!
Holy State or Holy King –
  Or Holy People's Will –
Have no truck with the senseless thing.
  Order the guns and kill!
    Saying – after – me:

Once there was The People – Terror gave it birth;
Once there was The People and it made a Hell of Earth.
Earth arose and crushed it. Listen, O ye slain!
Once there was The People – it shall never be again!

The Strange Ride of Morrowbie Jukes

Alive or dead – there is no other way.

Native Proverb

There is no invention about this tale. Jukes by accident stumbled upon a village that is well known to exist, though he is the only Englishman who has been there. A somewhat similar institution used to flourish on the outskirts of Calcutta, and there is a story that if you go into the heart of Bikanir, which is in the heart of the Great Indian Desert, you shall come across, not a village, but a town where the Dead who did not die, but may not live, have established their headquarters. And, since it is perfectly true that in the same desert is a wonderful city where all the rich moneylenders retreat after they have made their fortunes (fortunes so vast that the owners cannot trust even the strong hand of the Government to protect them, but take refuge in the waterless sands), and drive sumptuous C-spring barouches, and buy beautiful girls, and decorate their palaces with gold and ivory and Minton tiles and mother-of-pearl, I do not see why Jukes's tale should not be true. He is a civil engineer, with a head for plans and distances and things of that kind, and he certainly would not take the trouble to invent imaginary traps. He could earn more by doing his legitimate work. He never varies the tale in the telling, and grows very hot and indignant when he thinks of the disrespectful treatment he received. He wrote this quite straightforwardly at first, but he has touched it up in places and introduced Moral Reflections: thus:

In the beginning it all arose from a slight attack of fever. My work necessitated my being in camp for some months between Pakpattan and Mubarakpur – a desolate sandy stretch of country as everyone who has had the misfortune to go there may know. My coolies were neither more nor less exasperating than other gangs, and my work demanded sufficient attention to keep me from moping, had I been inclined to so unmanly a weakness.

On the 23rd December 1884 I felt a little feverish. There was a full moon at the time, and, in consequence, every dog near my tent was baying it. The brutes assembled in twos and threes and drove me frantic. A few days previously I had shot one loud-mouthed singer and suspended his carcass *in terrorem* about fifty yards from my tent-door, but his friends fell upon, fought for, and ultimately devoured the body; and, as it seemed to me, sang their hymns of thanksgiving afterwards with renewed energy.

The light-headedness which accompanies fever acts differently on different men. My irritation gave way, after a short time, to a fixed determination to slaughter one huge black-and-white beast who had been foremost in song and first in flight throughout the evening. Thanks to a shaking hand and a giddy head I had already missed him twice with both barrels of my shotgun, when it struck me that my best plan would be to ride him down in the open and finish him off with a hog-spear. This, of course, was merely the semi-delirious notion of a fever-patient; but I remember that it struck me at the time as being eminently practical and feasible.

I therefore ordered my groom to saddle Pornic and bring him round quietly to the rear of my tent. When the pony was ready, I stood at his head prepared to mount and dash out as soon as the dog should again lift up his voice. Pornic, by the way, had not been out of his pickets for a couple of days; the night air was crisp and chilly; and I was armed with a specially long and sharp pair of persuaders with which I had been rousing a sluggish cob that afternoon. You will easily believe, then, that when he was let go he went quickly. In one moment, for the brute bolted as straight as a die, the tent was left far behind, and we were flying over the smooth sandy soil at racing speed. In another we had passed the wretched dog, and I had almost forgotten why it was that I had taken horse and hog-spear.

The delirium of fever and the excitement of rapid motion through the air must have taken away the remnant of my senses. I have a faint recollection of standing upright in my stirrups, and of brandishing my hog-spear at the great white moon that looked down so calmly on my mad gallop; and of shouting challenges to the camel-thorn bushes as they whizzed past. Once or twice, I believe, I swayed forward on Pornic's neck, and literally hung on by my spurs – as the marks next morning showed.

The wretched beast went forward like a thing possessed, over what seemed to be a limitless expanse of moonlit sand. Next, I remember, the ground rose suddenly in front of us, and as we topped the ascent I saw the waters of the Sutlej shining like a silver bar below. Then Pornic blundered heavily on his nose, and we rolled together down some unseen slope.

I must have lost consciousness, for when I recovered I was lying on my stomach in a heap of soft white sand, and the dawn was beginning to break dimly over the edge of the slope down which I had fallen. As the light grew stronger I saw I was at the bottom of a horseshoe-shaped crater of sand, opening on one side directly on to the shoals of the Sutlej. My fever had altogether left me, and, with the exception of a slight dizziness in the head, I felt no bad effects from the fall overnight.

Pornic, who was standing a few yards away, was naturally a good deal exhausted, but had not hurt himself in the least. His saddle, a favourite polo one, was much knocked about, and had been twisted under his belly. It took me some time to put him to rights, and in the meantime I had ample opportunities of observing the spot into which I had so foolishly dropped.

At the risk of being considered tedious, I must describe it at length; inasmuch as an accurate mental picture of its peculiarities will be of material assistance in enabling the reader to understand what follows.

Imagine then, as I have said before, a horseshoe-shaped crater of sand with steeply-graded sand walls about thirty-five feet high. (The slope, I fancy, must have been about 65°.) This crater enclosed a level piece of ground about fifty yards long by thirty at its broadest part, with a rude well in the centre. Round the bottom of the crater, about three feet from the level of the ground proper, ran a series of eighty-three semicircular, ovoid, square, and multilateral holes, all about three feet at the mouth. Each hole on inspection showed that it was carefully shored internally with driftwood and bamboos, and over the mouth a wooden drip-board projected, like the peak of a jockey's cap, for two feet. No sign of life was visible in these tunnels, but a most sickening stench pervaded the entire amphitheatre – a stench fouler than any which my wanderings in Indian villages have introduced me to.

Having remounted Pornic, who was as anxious as I to get back to camp, I rode round the base of the horseshoe to find some place whence an exit would be practicable. The inhabitants, whoever they might be, had not thought fit to put in an appearance, so I was left to my own devices. My first attempt to 'rush' Pornic up the steep sandbanks showed me that I had fallen into a trap exactly on the same model as that which the ant-lion sets for its prey. At each step the shifting sand poured down from above in tons, and rattled on the drip-boards of the holes like small shot. A couple of ineffectual charges sent us both rolling down to the bottom, half choked with the torrents of sand; and I was constrained to turn my attention to the river-bank.

Here everything seemed easy enough. The sand-hills ran down to the river edge, it is true, but there were plenty of shoals and shallows across which I could gallop Pornic, and find my way back to *terra firma* by turning sharply to the right or the left. As I led Pornic over the sands I was startled by the faint pop of a rifle across the river; and at the same moment a bullet dropped with a sharp '*whit*' close to Pornic's head.

There was no mistaking the nature of the missile – a regulation Martini-Henry 'picket'. About five hundred yards away a country-boat was anchored in midstream; and a jet of smoke drifting away from its bows in the still morning air showed me whence the delicate attention had come. Was ever a respectable gentleman in such an *impasse*? The treacherous sand-slope allowed no escape from a spot which I had visited most involuntarily, and a promenade on the river frontage was the signal for a bombardment from some insane native in a boat. I'm afraid that I lost my temper very much indeed.

Another bullet reminded me that I had better save my breath to cool my porridge; and I retreated hastily up the sands and back to the horseshoe, where I saw that the noise of the rifle had drawn sixty-five human beings from the badger-holes which I had up till that point supposed to be untenanted. I found myself in the midst of a crowd of spectators – about forty men, twenty women, and one child who could not have been more than five years old. They were all scantily clothed in that salmon-coloured cloth which one associates with Hindu mendicants, and, at first sight, gave me the impression of a band of loathsome *fakirs*. The filth and repulsiveness of the assembly were beyond all description, and I shuddered to think what their life in the badger-holes must be.

Even in these days, when local self-government has destroyed the greater part of a native's respect for a Sahib, I have been accustomed to a certain amount of civility from my inferiors, and on approaching the crowd naturally expected that there would be some recognition of my presence. As a matter of fact there was, but it was by no means what I had looked for.

The ragged crew actually laughed at me – such laughter I hope I may never hear again. They cackled, yelled, whistled, and howled as I walked into their midst; some of them literally throwing themselves down on the ground in convulsions of unholy mirth. In a moment I had let go Pornic's head, and, irritated beyond expression at the morning's adventure, commenced cuffing those nearest to me with all the force I could. The wretches dropped under my blows like ninepins, and the laughter gave place to wails for mercy; while those yet untouched clasped me round the knees, imploring me in all sorts of uncouth tongues to spare them.

In the tumult, and just when I was feeling very much ashamed of myself for having thus easily given way to my temper, a thin high voice murmured in English from behind my shoulder: 'Sahib! Sahib! Do you not know me? Sahib, it is Gunga Dass, the telegraph-master.'

I spun round quickly and faced the speaker.

Gunga Dass (I have, of course, no hesitation in mentioning the man's real name) I had known four years before as a Deccanee Brahmin lent by the Punjab Government to one of the Khalsia States. He was in charge of a branch telegraph-office there, and when I had last met him was a jovial, full-stomached, portly Government servant with a marvellous capacity for making bad puns in English – a peculiarity which made me remember him long after I had forgotten his services to me in his official capacity. It is seldom that a Hindu makes English puns.

Now, however, the man was changed beyond all recognition. Caste-mark, stomach, slate-coloured continuations, and unctuous speech were all gone. I looked at a withered skeleton, turbanless and almost naked, with long matted hair and deep-set codfish-eyes. But for a crescent-shaped scar on the left cheek – the result of an accident for which I was responsible – I should never have known him. But it was indubitably Gunga Dass, and – for this I was thankful – an English-speaking native who might at least tell me the meaning of all that I had gone through that day.

The crowd retreated to some distance as I turned towards the miserable figure, and ordered him to show me some method of escaping from the crater. He held a freshly-plucked crow in his hand, and in reply to my question climbed slowly to a platform of sand which ran in front of the holes, and commenced lighting a fire there in silence. Dried bents, sand-poppies, and drift-wood burn quickly; and I derived much consolation from the fact that he lit them with an ordinary sulphur match. When they were in a bright glow and the crow was neatly spitted in front thereof, Gunga Dass began without a word of preamble –

'There are only two kinds of men, sar – the alive and the dead. When you are dead you are dead, but when you are alive you live.' (Here the crow demanded his attention for an instant as it twirled before the fire in danger of being burnt to a cinder.) 'If you die at home and do not die when you come to the ghat to be burnt you come here.'

The nature of the reeking village was made plain now, and all that I had known or read of the grotesque and the horrible paled before the fact just communicated by the ex-Brahmin. Sixteen years ago, when I first landed in Bombay, I had been told by a wandering Armenian of the existence, somewhere in India, of a place to which such Hindus as had the misfortune to recover from trance or catalepsy were conveyed and kept, and I recollect laughing heartily at what I was then pleased to consider a traveller's tale. Sitting at the bottom of the sand-trap, the memory of Watson's Hotel, with its swinging punkahs, white-robed servants, and the sallow-faced Armenian, rose up in my mind as vividly as a photograph, and I burst into a loud fit of laughter. The contrast was too absurd!

Gunga Dass, as he bent over the unclean bird, watched me curiously. Hindus seldom laugh, and his surroundings were not such as to move him that way. He removed the crow solemnly from the wooden spit and as solemnly devoured it. Then he continued his story, which I give in his own words.

'In epidemics of the cholera you are carried to be burnt almost before you are dead. When you come to the riverside the cold air, perhaps, makes you alive, and then, if you are only a little alive, mud is put on your nose and mouth and you die conclusively. If you are rather more alive, more mud is put; but if you are too lively they let you go and take you away. I was too lively, and made protestation with anger against the indignities that they endeavoured to press upon me. In those days I was Brahmin and proud man. Now I am dead man and eat' – here he eyed the well-gnawed breastbone with the first sign of emotion that I had seen in him since we met – 'crows, and – other things. They took me from my sheets when they saw that I was too lively and gave me medicines for one week, and I survived successfully. Then they sent me by rail from my place to Okara Station, with a man to take care of me; and at Okara Station we met two other men, and they conducted us three on camels, in the night, from Okara Station to this place, and they propelled me from the top to the bottom, and the other two succeeded, and I have been here ever since two and a half years. Once I was Brahmin and proud man, and now I eat crows.'

'There is no way of getting out?'

'None of what kind at all. When I first came I made experiments frequently, and all the others also, but we have always succumbed to the sand which is precipitated upon our heads.'

'But surely,' I broke in at this point, 'the river-front

is open, and it is worth while dodging the bullets; while at night – '

I had already matured a rough plan of escape which a natural instinct of selfishness forbade me sharing with Gunga Dass. He, however, divined my unspoken thought almost as soon as it was formed; and, to my intense astonishment, gave vent to a long low chuckle of derision – the laughter, be it understood, of a superior or at least of an equal.

'You will not' – he had dropped the 'sir' after his first sentence – 'make any escape that way. But you can try. I have tried. Once only.'

The sensation of nameless terror which I had in vain attempted to strive against overmastered me completely. My long fast – it was now close upon ten o'clock, and I had eaten nothing since tiffin on the previous day – combined with the violent agitation of the ride had exhausted me, and I verily believe that, for a few minutes, I acted as one mad. I hurled myself against the sand-slope. I ran round the base of the crater, blaspheming and praying by turns. I crawled out among the sedges of the river-front, only to be driven back each time in an agony of nervous dread by the rifle-bullets which cut up the sand round me – for I dared not face the death of a mad dog among that hideous crowd – and so fell, spent and raving, at the curb of the well. No one had taken the slightest notice of an exhibition which makes me blush hotly even when I think of it now.

Two or three men trod on my panting body as they drew water, but they were evidently used to this sort of thing, and had no time to waste upon me. Gunga Dass, indeed, when he had banked the embers of his fire with sand, was at some pains to throw half a cupful of fetid water over my head, an attention for which I could have fallen on my knees and thanked him, but he was laughing all the while in the same mirthless, wheezy key that greeted me on my first attempt to force the shoals. And so, in a half-fainting state, I lay till noon. Then, being only a man after all, I felt hungry, and said as much to Gunga Dass, whom I had begun to regard as my natural protector. Following the impulse of the outer world when dealing with natives, I put my hand into my pocket and drew out four annas. The absurdity of the gift struck me at once, and I was about to replace the money.

Gunga Dass, however, cried: 'Give me the money, all you have, or I will get help, and we will kill you!'

A Briton's first impulse, I believe, is to guard the contents of his pockets; but a moment's thought showed me the folly of differing with the one man who had it in his power to make me comfortable; and with whose help it was possible that I might eventually escape from the crater. I gave him all the money in my possession, Rs 9.8.5 – nine rupees, eight annas, and five pice – for I always keep small change as *bakshish* when I am in camp. Gunga Dass clutched the coins, and hid them at once in his ragged loincloth, looking round to assure himself that no one had observed us.

'*Now* I will give you something to eat,' said he.

What pleasure my money could have given him I am unable to say; but inasmuch as it did please him I was not sorry that I had parted with it so readily, for I had no doubt that he would have had me killed if I had refused. One does not protest against the doings of a den of wild beasts; and my companions were lower than any beasts. While I ate what Gunga Dass had provided, a coarse *chapatti* and a cupful of the foul well-water, the people showed not the faintest sign of curiosity – that curiosity which is so rampant, as a rule, in an Indian village.

I could even fancy that they despised me. At all events they treated me with the most chilling indifference, and Gunga Dass was nearly as bad. I plied him with questions about the terrible village, and received extremely unsatisfactory answers. So far as I could gather, it had been in existence from time immemorial – whence I concluded that it was at least a century old – and during that time no one had ever been known to escape from it. (I had to control myself here with both hands, lest the blind terror should lay hold of me a second time and drive me raving round the crater.) Gunga Dass took a malicious pleasure in emphasising this point and in watching me wince. Nothing that I could do would induce him to tell me who the mysterious 'they' were.

'It is so ordered,' he would reply, 'and I do not yet know anyone who has disobeyed the orders.'

'Only wait till my servants find that I am missing,' I retorted, 'and I promise you that this place shall be cleared off the face of the earth, and I'll give you a lesson in civility, too, my friend.'

'Your servants would be torn in pieces before they came near this place; and, besides, you are dead, my dear friend. It is not your fault, of course, but none the less you are dead *and* buried.'

At irregular intervals supplies of food, I was told, were dropped down from the land side into the amphitheatre, and the inhabitants fought for them like wild beasts. When a man felt his death coming on he retreated to his lair and died there. The body was sometimes dragged out of the hole and thrown on to the sand, or allowed to rot where it lay.

The phrase 'thrown on to the sand' caught my attention, and I asked Gunga Dass whether this sort of thing was not likely to breed a pestilence.

'That,' said he, with another of his wheezy chuckles, 'you may see for yourself subsequently. You will have much time to make observations.'

Whereat, to his great delight, I winced once more and hastily continued the conversation: 'And how do you live here from day to day? What do you do?' The question elicited exactly the same answer as before – coupled with the information that 'this place is like your European heaven; there is neither marrying nor giving in marriage'.

Gunga Dass had been educated at a Mission School, and, as he himself admitted, had he only changed his religion 'like a wise man', might have avoided the living grave which was now his portion. But as long as I was with him I fancy he was happy.

Here was a Sahib, a representative of the dominant race, helpless as a child and completely at the mercy of his native neighbours. In a deliberate lazy way he set himself to torture me as a schoolboy would devote a rapturous half-hour to watching the agonies of an impaled beetle, or as a ferret in a blind burrow might glue himself comfortably to the neck of a rabbit. The burden of his conversation was that there was no escape 'of no kind whatever', and that I should stay here till I died and was 'thrown on to the sand'. If it were possible to forejudge the conversation of the Damned on the advent of a new soul in their abode, I should say that they would speak as Gunga Dass did to me throughout that long afternoon. I was powerless to protest or answer; all my energies being devoted to a struggle against the inexplicable terror that threatened to overwhelm me again and again. I can compare the feeling to nothing except the struggles of a man against the overpowering nausea of the Channel passage – only my agony was of the spirit and infinitely more terrible.

As the day wore on, the inhabitants began to appear in full strength to catch the rays of the afternoon sun, which were now sloping in at the mouth of the crater. They assembled by little knots, and talked among themselves without even throwing a glance in my direction. About four o'clock, so far as I could judge, Gunga Dass rose and dived into his lair for a moment, emerging with a live crow in his hands. The wretched bird was in a most draggled and deplorable condition, but seemed to be in no way afraid of its master. Advancing cautiously to the river-front, Gunga Dass stepped from tussock to tussock until he had reached a smooth patch of sand directly in the line of the boat's fire. The occupants of the boat took no notice. Here he stopped, and, with a couple of dexterous turns of the wrist, pegged the bird on its back with outstretched wings. As was only natural, the crow began to shriek at once and beat the air with its claws. In a few seconds the clamour had attracted the attention of a bevy of wild crows on a shoal a few hundred yards away, where they were discussing something that looked like a corpse. Half a dozen crows flew over at once to see what was going on, and also, as it proved, to attack the pinioned bird. Gunga Dass, who had lain down on a tussock, motioned to me to be quiet, though I fancy this was a needless precaution. In a moment, and before I could see how it happened, a wild crow, which had grappled with the shrieking and helpless bird, was entangled in the latter's claws, swiftly disengaged by Gunga Dass, and pegged down beside its companion in adversity. Curiosity, it seemed, overpowered the rest of the flock, and almost before Gunga Dass and I had time to withdraw to the tussock, two more captives were struggling in the upturned claws of the decoys. So the chase – if I can give it so dignified a name – continued until Gunga Dass had captured seven crows. Five of them he throttled at once, reserving two for further operations another day. I was a good deal impressed by this, to me, novel method of securing food, and complimented Gunga Dass on his skill.

'It is nothing to do,' said he. 'Tomorrow you must do it for me. You are stronger than I am.'

This calm assumption of superiority upset me not a little, and I answered peremptorily: 'Indeed, you old ruffian? What do you think I have given you money for?'

'Very well,' was the unmoved reply. 'Perhaps not tomorrow, nor the day after, nor subsequently; but in the end, and for many years, you will catch crows and eat crows, and you will thank your European God that you have crows to catch and eat.'

I could have cheerfully strangled him for this, but judged it best under the circumstances to smother my resentment. An hour later I was eating one of the crows; and, as Gunga Dass had said, thanking my God that I had a crow to eat. Never as long as I live shall I forget that evening meal. The whole population were squatting on the hard sand platform opposite their dens, huddled over tiny fires of refuse and dried rushes. Death having once laid his hand upon these men and forborne to strike, seemed to stand aloof from them now; for most of our company were old men, bent and worn and twisted with years, and women aged to all appearance as the Fates themselves. They sat together in knots and talked – God only knows what they found to discuss – in low equable tones, curiously in contrast to the strident babble with which natives are accustomed to make day hideous. Now and then an access of that sudden fury which had possessed me in the morning would lay hold on a man or woman; and with yells and imprecations the sufferer would attack the steep slope until, baffled and bleeding, he fell back on the platform incapable of moving a limb. The others would never even raise their eyes when this happened, as men too well aware of the futility of their fellows' attempts and wearied with their useless repetition. I saw four such outbursts in the course of that evening.

Gunga Dass took an eminently businesslike view of my situation, and while we were dining – I can afford to laugh at the recollection now, but it was painful enough at the time – propounded the terms on which he would consent to 'do' for me. My nine rupees eight annas, he argued, at the rate of three annas a day, would provide me with food for fifty-one days, or about seven weeks; that is to say, he would be willing to cater for me for that length of time. At the end of it I was to look after myself. For a further consideration – *videlicet* my boots – he would be willing to allow me to occupy the den next to his own, and would supply me with as much dried grass for bedding as he could spare.

'Very well, Gunga Dass,' I replied; 'to the first terms I cheerfully agree, but, as there is nothing on earth to prevent my killing you as you sit here and taking everything that you have' (I thought of the two invaluable crows at the time), 'I flatly refuse to give you my boots and shall take whichever den I please.'

The stroke was a bold one, and I was glad when I saw that it had succeeded. Gunga Dass changed his tone immediately, and disavowed all intention of asking for my boots. At the time it did not strike me as at all strange that I, a civil engineer, a man of thirteen years' standing in the service, and, I trust, an average Englishman, should thus calmly threaten murder and violence against the man who had, for a consideration it is true, taken me under his wing. I had left the world, it seemed, for centuries. I was as certain then as I am now of my own existence, that in the accursed settlement there was no law save that of the strongest; that the living dead men had thrown behind them every canon of the world which had cast them out; and that I had to depend for my own life on my strength and vigilance alone. The crew of the ill-fated *Mignonette* are the only men who would understand my frame of mind. 'At present,' I argued to myself, 'I am strong and a match for six of these wretches. It is imperatively necessary that I should, for my own sake, keep both health and strength until the hour of my release comes – if it ever does.'

Fortified with these resolutions, I ate and drank as much as I could, and made Gunga Dass understand that I intended to be his master, and that the least sign of insubordination on his part would be visited with the only punishment I had it in my power to inflict – sudden and violent death. Shortly after this I went to bed. That is to say, Gunga Dass gave me a double armful of dried bents which I thrust down the mouth of the lair to the right of his, and followed myself, feet foremost; the hole running about nine feet into the sand with a slight downward inclination, and being neatly shored with timbers. From my den, which faced the river-front, I was able to watch the waters of the

Sutlej flowing past under the light of a young moon and compose myself to sleep as best I might.

The horrors of that night I shall never forget. My den was nearly as narrow as a coffin, and the sides had been worn smooth and greasy by the contact of innumerable naked bodies, added to which it smelt abominably. Sleep was altogether out of the question to one in my excited frame of mind. As the night wore on, it seemed that the entire amphitheatre was filled with legions of unclean devils that, trooping up from the shoals below, mocked the unfortunates in their lairs.

Personally I am not of an imaginative temperament – very few engineers are – but on that occasion I was as completely prostrated with nervous terror as any woman. After half an hour or so, however, I was able once more to calmly review my chances of escape. Any exit by the steep sand walls was, of course, impracticable. I had been thoroughly convinced of this some time before. It was possible, just possible, that I might, in the uncertain moonlight, safely run the gauntlet of the rifle shots. The place was so full of terror for me that I was prepared to undergo any risk in leaving it. Imagine my delight, then, when after creeping stealthily to the river-front I found that the infernal boat was not there. My freedom lay before me in the next few steps!

By walking out to the first shallow pool that lay at the foot of the projecting left horn of the horseshoe, I could wade across, turn the flank of the crater, and make my way inland. Without a moment's hesitation I marched briskly past the tussocks where Gunga Dass had snared the crows, and out in the direction of the smooth white sand beyond. My first step from the tufts of dried grass showed me how utterly futile was any hope of escape; for, as I put my foot down, I felt an indescribable drawing, sucking motion of the sand below. Another moment and my leg was swallowed up nearly to the knee. In the moonlight the whole surface of the sand seemed to be shaken with devilish delight at my disappointment. I struggled clear, sweating with terror and exertion, back to the tussocks behind me and fell on my face.

My only means of escape from the semicircle was protected by a quicksand!

How long I lay I have not the faintest idea; but I was roused at last by the malevolent chuckle of Gunga Dass at my ear. 'I would advise you, Protector of the Poor' (the ruffian was speaking English), 'to return to your house. It is unhealthy to lie down here. Moreover, when the boat returns you will most certainly be rifled at.' He stood over me in the dim light of the dawn, chuckling and laughing to himself. Suppressing my first impulse to catch the man by the neck and throw him on to the quicksand, I rose sullenly and followed him to the platform below the burrows.

Suddenly, and futilely as I thought while I spoke, I asked: 'Gunga Dass, what is the good of the boat if I can't get out *anyhow*?' I recollect that even in my deepest trouble I had been speculating vaguely on the waste of ammunition in guarding an already well-protected foreshore.

Gunga Dass laughed again and made answer: 'They have the boat only in daytime. It is for the reason that *there is a way*. I hope we shall have the pleasure of your company for much longer time. It is a pleasant spot when you have been here some years and eaten roast crow long enough.'

I staggered, numbed and helpless, towards the

fetid burrow allotted to me, and fell asleep. An hour or so later I was awakened by a piercing scream – the shrill, high-pitched scream of a horse in pain. Those who have once heard that will never forget the sound. I found some little difficulty in scrambling out of the burrow. When I was in the open, I saw Pornic, my poor old Pornic, lying dead on the sandy soil. How they had killed him I cannot guess. Gunga Dass explained that horse was better than crow, and 'greatest good of greatest number is political maxim. We are now Republic, Mr Jukes, and you are entitled to a fair share of the beast. If you like, we will pass a vote of thanks. Shall I propose?'

Yes, we were a Republic indeed! A Republic of wild beasts penned at the bottom of a pit, to eat and fight and sleep till we died. I attempted no protest of any kind, but sat down and stared at the hideous sight in front of me. In less time almost than it takes me to write this, Pornic's body was divided, in some unclean way or other; the men and women had dragged the fragments on to the platform and were preparing their morning meal. Gunga Dass cooked mine. The almost irresistible impulse to fly at the sand walls until I was wearied laid hold of me afresh, and I had to struggle against it with all my might. Gunga Dass was offensively jocular till I told him that if he addressed another remark of any kind whatever to me I should strangle him where he sat. This silenced him till the silence became insupportable, and I bade him say something.

'You will live here till you die like the other Feringhi,' he said coolly, watching me over the fragment of gristle that he was gnawing.

'What other Sahib, you swine? Speak at once, and don't stop to tell me a lie.'

'He is over there,' answered Gunga Dass, pointing to a burrow-mouth about four doors to the left of my own. 'You can see for yourself. He died in the burrow as you will die, and I will die, and as all these men and women and the one child will also die.'

'For pity's sake tell me all you know about him. Who was he? When did he come, and when did he die?'

This appeal was a weak step on my part. Gunga Dass only leered and replied: 'I will not – unless you give me something first.'

Then I recollected where I was, and struck the man between the eyes, partially stunning him. He stepped down from the platform at once, and, cringing and fawning and weeping and attempting to embrace my feet, led me round to the burrow which he had indicated.

'I know nothing whatever about the gentleman. Your God be my witness that I do not. He was as anxious to escape as you were, and he was shot from the boat, though we all did all things to prevent him from attempting. He was shot here.' Gunga Dass laid his hand on his lean stomach and bowed to the earth.

'Well, and what then? Go on!'

'And then – and then, Your Honour, we carried him into his house and gave him water, and put wet cloths on the wound, and he laid down in his house and gave up the ghost.'

'In how long? In how long?'

'About half an hour after he received his wound. I call Vishnu to witness,' yelled the wretched man, 'that I did everything for him. Everything which was possible, that I did!'

He threw himself down on the ground and clasped my ankles. But I had my doubts about Gunga Dass's benevolence, and kicked him off as he lay protesting.

'I believe you robbed him of everything he had. But I can find out in a minute or two. How long was the Sahib here?'

'Nearly a year and a half. I think he must have gone mad. But hear me swear, Protector of the Poor! Won't Your Honour hear me swear that I never touched an article that belonged to him? What is Your Worship going to do?'

I had taken Gunga Dass by the waist and had hauled him on to the platform opposite the deserted burrow. As I did so I thought of my wretched fellow-prisoner's unspeakable misery among all these horrors for eighteen months, and the final agony of dying like a rat in a hole, with a bullet-wound in the stomach. Gunga Dass fancied I was going to kill him and howled pitifully. The rest of the population, in the plethora that follows a full flesh meal, watched us without stirring.

'Go inside, Gunga Dass,' said I, 'and fetch it out.'

I was feeling sick and faint with horror now. Gunga Dass nearly rolled off the platform and howled aloud.

'But I am Brahmin, Sahib – a high-caste Brahmin. By your soul, by your father's soul, do not make me do this thing!'

'Brahmin or no Brahmin, by my soul and my father's soul, in you go!' I said, and, seizing him by the shoulders, I crammed his head into the mouth of the burrow, kicked the rest of him in, and, sitting down, covered my face with my hands.

At the end of a few minutes I heard a rustle and a creak; then Gunga Dass in a sobbing, choking whisper speaking to himself; then a soft thud – and I uncovered my eyes.

The dry sand had turned the corpse entrusted to its keeping into a yellow-brown mummy. I told Gunga Dass to stand off while I examined it. The body – clad in an olive-green hunting-suit much stained and worn, with leather pads on the shoulders – was that of a man between thirty and forty, above middle height, with light sandy hair, long moustache, and a rough unkempt beard. The left canine of the upper jaw was missing, and a portion of the lobe of the right ear was gone. On the second finger of the left hand was a ring – a shield-shaped bloodstone set in gold, with a monogram that might have been either 'B. K.' or 'B. L.'. On the third finger of the right hand was a silver ring in the shape of a coiled cobra, much worn and tarnished. Gunga Dass deposited a handful of trifles he had picked out of the burrow at my feet, and, covering the face of the body with my handkerchief, I turned to examine these. I give the full list in the hope that it may lead to the identification of the unfortunate man:

1 Bowl of a briarwood pipe, serrated at the edge; much worn and blackened; bound with string at the screw.
2 Two patent-lever keys; wards of both broken.
3 Tortoise-shell-handled penknife, silver or nickel, nameplate marked with monogram 'B. K.'.
4 Envelope, postmark indecipherable, bearing a Victorian stamp, addressed to 'Miss Mon—' (rest illegible) – 'ham' – 'nt'.
5 Imitation crocodile-skin notebook with pencil. First forty-five pages blank; four and a half illegible; fifteen others filled with private memoranda relating chiefly to three persons – a Mrs

L. Singleton, abbreviated several times to 'Lot Single', 'Mrs S. May', and 'Garmison', referred to in places as 'Jerry' or 'Jack'.

6 Handle of small-sized hunting-knife. Blade snapped short. Buck's horn, diamond-cut, with swivel and ring on the butt; fragment of cotton cord attached.

It must not be supposed that I inventoried all these things on the spot as fully as I have here written them down. The notebook first attracted my attention, and I put it in my pocket with a view to studying it later on. The rest of the articles I conveyed to my burrow for safety's sake, and there, being a methodical man, I inventoried them. I then returned to the corpse and ordered Gunga Dass to help me to carry it out to the river-front. While we were engaged in this, the exploded shell of an old brown cartridge dropped out of one of the pockets and rolled at my feet. Gunga Dass had not seen it; and I fell to thinking that a man does not carry exploded cartridge-cases, especially 'browns', which will not bear loading twice, about with him when shooting. In other words, that cartridge-case had been fired inside the crater. Consequently there must be a gun somewhere. I was on the verge of asking Gunga Dass, but checked myself, knowing that he would lie. We laid the body down on the edge of the quicksand by the tussocks. It was my intention to push it out and let it be swallowed up – the only possible mode of burial that I could think of. I ordered Gunga Dass to go away.

Then I gingerly put the corpse out on the quicksand. In doing so – it was lying face downward – I tore the frail and rotten khaki shooting-coat open, disclosing a hideous cavity in the back. I have already told you that the dry sand had, as it were, mummified the body. A moment's glance showed that the gaping hole had been caused by a gunshot wound; the gun must have been fired with the muzzle almost touching the back. The shooting-coat, being intact, had been drawn over the body after death, which must have been instantaneous. The secret of the poor wretch's death was plain to me in a flash. Someone of the crater, presumably Gunga Dass, must have shot him with his own gun – the gun that fitted the brown cartridges. He had never attempted to escape in the face of the rifle-fire from the boat.

I pushed the corpse out hastily, and saw it sink from sight literally in a few seconds. I shuddered as I watched. In a dazed, half-conscious way I turned to peruse the notebook. A stained and discoloured slip of paper had been inserted between the binding and the back, and dropped out as I opened the pages. This is what it contained: '*Four out from crow-clump; three left; nine out; two right; three back; two left; fourteen out; two left; seven out; one left; nine back; two right; six back; four right; seven back.*' The paper had been burnt and charred at the edges. What it meant I could not understand. I sat down on the dried bents turning it over and over between my fingers, until I was aware of Gunga Dass standing immediately behind me with glowing eyes and outstretched hands.

'Have you got it?' he panted. 'Will you not let me look at it also? I swear that I will return it.'

'Got what? Return what?' I asked.

'That which you have in your hands. It will help us both.' He stretched out his long birdlike talons, trembling with eagerness.

'I could never find it,' he continued. 'He had secreted it about his person. Therefore I shot him, but nevertheless I was unable to obtain it.'

Gunga Dass had quite forgotten his little fiction about the rifle-bullet. I heard him calmly. Morality is blunted by consorting with the Dead who are alive.

'What on earth are you raving about? What is it you want me to give you?'

'The piece of paper in the notebook. It will help us both. Oh, you fool! You fool! Can you not see what it will do for us? We shall escape!'

His voice rose almost to a scream, and he danced with excitement before me. I own I was moved at the chance of getting away.

'Do you mean to say that this slip of paper will help us? What does it mean?'

'Read it aloud! Read it aloud! I beg and I pray to you to read it aloud.'

I did so. Gunga Dass listened delightedly, and drew an irregular line in the sand with his fingers.

'See now! It was the length of his gun-barrels without the stock. I have those barrels. Four gun-barrels out from the place where I caught crows. Straight out; do you mind me? Then three left. Ah! Now well I remember how that man worked it out night after night. Then nine out, and so on. Out is always straight before you across the quicksand to the north. He told me so before I killed him.'

'But if you knew all this why didn't you get out before?'

'I did *not* know it. He told me that he was working it out a year and a half ago, and how he was working it out night after night when the boat had gone away, and he could get out near the quicksand safely. Then he said that we would get away together. But I was afraid that he would leave me behind one night when he had worked it all out, and so I shot him. Besides, it is not advisable that the men who once get in here should escape. Only I, and *I* am a Brahmin.'

The hope of escape had brought Gunga Dass's caste back to him. He stood up, walked about, and gesticulated violently. Eventually I managed to make him talk soberly, and he told me how this Englishman had spent six months night after night in exploring, inch by inch, the passage across the quicksand; how he had declared it to be simplicity itself up to within about twenty yards of the river bank after turning the flank of the left horn of the horseshoe. This much he had evidently not completed when Gunga Dass shot him with his own gun.

In my frenzy of delight at the possibilities of escape I recollect shaking hands wildly with Gunga Dass, after we had decided that we were to make an attempt to get away that very night. It was weary work waiting throughout the afternoon.

About ten o'clock, as far as I could judge, when the moon had just risen above the lip of the crater, Gunga Dass made a move for his burrow to bring out the gun-barrels whereby to measure our path. All the other wretched inhabitants had retired to their lairs long ago. The guardian boat drifted downstream some hours before, and we were utterly alone by the crow-clump. Gunga Dass, while carrying the gun-barrels, let slip the piece of paper which was to be our guide. I stooped down hastily to recover it, and, as I did so, I was aware that the creature was aiming a violent blow at the back of my head with the gun-barrels. It was too late to turn round. I must have received the blow somewhere on the nape of my neck, for I fell senseless at the edge of the quicksand.

When I recovered consciousness the moon was going down, and I was sensible of intolerable pain in the back of my head. Gunga Dass had disappeared and my mouth was full of blood. I lay down again and prayed that I might die without more ado. Then the unreasoning fury which I have before mentioned laid hold upon me, and I staggered inland towards the walls of the crater. It seemed that someone was calling to me in a whisper – 'Sahib! Sahib! Sahib!' exactly as my bearer used to call me in the mornings. I fancied that I was delirious until a handful of sand fell at my feet. Then I looked up and saw a head peering down into the amphitheatre – the head of Dunnoo, my dog-boy, who attended to my collies. As soon as he had attracted my attention, he held up his hand and showed a rope. I motioned, staggering to and fro the while, that he should throw it down. It was a couple of leather punkah-ropes knotted together, with a loop at one end. I slipped the loop over my head and under my arms; heard Dunnoo urge something forward; was conscious that I was being dragged, face downward, up the steep sand-slope, and the next instant found myself choked and half-fainting on the sand-hills overlooking the crater. Dunnoo, with his face ashy grey in the moonlight, implored me not to stay, but to get back to my tent at once.

It seems that he had tracked Pornic's footprints fourteen miles across the sands to the crater; had returned and told my servants, who flatly refused to meddle with anyone, white or black, once fallen into the hideous Village of the Dead; whereupon Dunnoo had taken one of my ponies and a couple of punkah ropes, returned to the crater, and hauled me out as I have described.

In the House of Suddhoo

A stone's throw out on either hand
From that well-ordered road we tread,
  And all the world is wild and strange:
Churel and ghoul and *Djinn* and sprite
Shall bear us company tonight,
For we have reached the Oldest Land
  Wherein the Powers of Darkness range.

From the Dusk to the Dawn

The house of Suddhoo, near the Taksali Gate, is two-storeyed, with four carved windows of old brown wood, and a flat roof. You may recognise it by five red handprints arranged like the Five of Diamonds on the whitewash between the upper windows. Bhagwan Dass the grocer and a man who says he gets his living by seal-cutting live in the lower storey with a troop of wives, servants, friends, and retainers. The two upper rooms used to be occupied by Janoo and Azizun and a little black-and-tan terrier that was stolen from an Englishman's house and given to Janoo by a soldier. Today, only Janoo lives in the upper rooms. Suddhoo sleeps on the roof generally, except when he sleeps in the street. He used to go to Peshawar in the cold weather to visit his son who sells curiosities near the Edwardes' Gate, and then he slept under a real mud roof. Suddhoo is a great friend of mine, because his cousin had a son who secured, thanks to my recommendation, the post of head-messenger to a big firm in the station. Suddhoo says that God will make me a

Lieutenant-Governor one of these days. I dare say his prophecy will come true. He is very, very old, with white hair and no teeth worth showing, and he has outlived his wits – outlived nearly everything except his fondness for his son at Peshawar. Janoo and Azizun are Kashmiris, ladies of the city, and theirs was an ancient and more or less honourable profession; but Azizun has since married a medical student from the North-West and has settled down to a most respectable life somewhere near Bareilly. Bhagwan Dass is an extortioner and an adulterator. He is very rich. The man who is supposed to get his living by seal-cutting pretends to be very poor. This lets you know as much as is necessary of the four principal tenants in the house of Suddhoo. Then there is Me of course; but I am only the chorus that comes in at the end to explain things. So I do not count.

Suddhoo was not clever. The man who pretended to cut seals was the cleverest of them all – Bhagwan Dass only knew how to lie – except Janoo. She was also beautiful, but that was her own affair.

Suddhoo's son at Peshawar was attacked by pleurisy, and old Suddhoo was troubled. The seal-cutter man heard of Suddhoo's anxiety and made capital out of it. He was abreast of the times. He got a friend in Peshawar to telegraph daily accounts of the son's health. And here the story begins.

Suddhoo's cousin's son told me, one evening, that Suddhoo wanted to see me; that he was too old and feeble to come personally, and that I should be conferring an everlasting honour on the House of Suddhoo if I went to him. I went; but I think, seeing how well off Suddhoo was then, that he might have sent something better than an *ekka*, which jolted fearfully, to haul out a future Lieutenant-Governor to the City on a muggy April evening. The *ekka* did not run quickly. It was full dark when we pulled up opposite the door of Ranjit Singh's tomb near the main gate of the fort. Here was Suddhoo, and he said that, by reason of my condescension, it was absolutely certain that I should become a Lieutenant-Governor while my hair was yet black. Then we talked about the weather and the state of my health, and the wheat crops, for fifteen minutes, in the Huzuri Bagh, under the stars.

Suddhoo came to the point at last. He said that Janoo had told him that there was an order of the *Sirkar* against magic, because it was feared that magic might one day kill the Empress of India. I didn't know anything about the state of the law; but I fancied that something interesting was going to happen. I said that so far from magic being discouraged by the Government it was highly commended. The greatest officials of the state practised it themselves. (If the financial statement isn't magic, I don't know what is.) Then, to encourage him further, I said that, if there was any *jadoo* afoot, I had not the least objection to giving it my countenance and sanction, and to seeing that it was clean *jadoo* – white magic, as distinguished from the unclean *jadoo* which kills folk. It took a long time before Suddhoo admitted that this was just what he had asked me to come for. Then he told me, in jerks and quavers, that the man who said he cut seals was a sorcerer of the cleanest kind; that every day he gave Suddhoo news of the sick son in Peshawar more quickly than the lightning could fly, and that this news was always corroborated by the letters. Further, that he had told Suddhoo how a great danger was threatening his son, which could be removed by clean *jadoo*; and, of course, heavy payment. I began to see exactly how the land lay, and told Suddhoo that I also understood a little *jadoo* in the Western line, and would go to his house to see that everything was done decently and in order. We set off together; and on the way Suddhoo told me that he had paid the seal-cutter between one hundred and two hundred rupees already; and the *jadoo* of that night would cost two hundred more. Which was cheap, he said, considering the greatness of his son's danger; but I do not think he meant it.

The lights were all cloaked in the front of the house when we arrived. I could hear awful noises from behind the seal-cutter's shop-front, as if someone were groaning his soul out. Suddhoo shook all over, and while we groped our way upstairs told me that the *jadoo* had begun. Janoo and Azizun met us at the stairhead, and told us that the *jadoo*-work was coming off in their rooms, because there was more space there. Janoo is a lady of a freethinking turn of mind. She whispered that the *jadoo* was an invention to get money out of Suddhoo, and that the seal-cutter would go to a hot place when he died. Suddhoo was nearly crying with fear and old age. He kept walking up and down the room in the half-light, repeating his son's name over and over again, and asking Azizun if the seal-cutter ought not to make a reduction in the case of his own landlord. Janoo pulled me over to the shadow in the recess of the carved bow-windows. The boards were up, and the rooms were only lit by one tiny oil-lamp. There was no chance of my being seen if I stayed still.

Presently, the groans below ceased, and we heard steps on the staircase. That was the seal-cutter. He stopped outside the door as the terrier barked and Azizun fumbled at the chain, and he told Suddhoo to blow out the lamp. This left the place in jet darkness, except for the red glow from the two *huqas* that belonged to Janoo and Azizun. The seal-cutter came in, and I heard Suddhoo throw himself down on the floor and groan. Azizun caught her breath, and Janoo backed on to one of the beds with a shudder. There was a clink of something metallic, and then shot up a pale blue-green flame near the ground. The light was just enough to show Azizun, pressed against one corner of the room with the terrier between her knees; Janoo, with her hands clasped, leaning forward as she sat on the bed; Suddhoo, face down, quivering, and the seal-cutter.

I hope I may never see another man like that seal-cutter. He was stripped to the waist, with a wreath of white jasmine as thick as my wrist round his forehead, a salmon-coloured loincloth round his middle, and a steel bangle on each ankle. This was not awe-inspiring. It was the face of the man that turned me cold. It was blue-grey in the first place. In the second, the eyes were rolled back till you could only see the whites of them; and, in the third, the face was the face of a demon – a ghoul – anything you please except of the sleek, oily old ruffian who sat in the daytime over his turning-lathe downstairs. He was lying on his stomach with his arms turned and crossed behind him, as if he had been thrown down pinioned. His head and neck were the only parts of him off the floor. They were nearly at right angles to the body, like the head of a cobra at spring. It was ghastly. In the centre of the room, on the bare earth floor, stood a big, deep, brass basin, with a pale blue-green light floating in the centre like a night-light.

Round that basin the man on the floor wriggled himself three times. How he did it I do not know. I could see the muscles ripple along his spine and fall smooth again; but I could not see any other motion. The head seemed the only thing alive about him, except that slow curl and uncurl of the labouring back-muscles. Janoo from the bed was breathing seventy to the minute; Azizun held her hands before her eyes; and old Suddhoo, fingering at the dirt that had got into his white beard, was crying to himself. The horror of it was that the creeping, crawly thing made no sound – only crawled! And, remember, this lasted for ten minutes, while the terrier whined, and Azizun shuddered, and Janoo gasped, and Suddhoo cried.

I felt the hair lift at the back of my head, and my heart thump like a thermantidote paddle. Luckily, the seal-cutter betrayed himself by his most impressive trick and made me calm again. After he had finished that unspeakable triple crawl, he stretched his head away from the floor as high as he could, and sent out a jet of fire from his nostrils. Now I knew how fire-spouting is done – I can do it myself – so I felt at ease. The business was a fraud. If he had only kept to that crawl without trying to raise the effect, goodness knows what I might not have thought. Both the girls shrieked at the jet of fire and the head dropped, chin-down on the floor, with a thud; the whole body lying then like a corpse with its arms trussed. There was a pause of five full minutes after this, and the blue-green flame died down. Janoo stooped to settle one of her anklets, while Azizun turned her face to the wall and took the terrier in her arms. Suddhoo put out an arm mechanically to Janoo's *huqa*, and she slid it across the floor with her foot. Directly above the body and on the wall, were a couple of flaming portraits, in stamped paper frames, of the Queen and the Prince of Wales. They looked down on the performance, and to my thinking, seemed to heighten the grotesqueness of it all.

Just when the silence was getting unendurable, the body turned over and rolled away from the basin to the side of the room, where it lay stomach-up. There was a faint 'plop' from the basin exactly like the noise a fish makes when it takes a fly – and the green light in the centre revived.

I looked at the basin, and saw, bobbing in the water, the dried, shrivelled, black head of a native baby – open eyes, open mouth, and shaved scalp. It was worse, being so very sudden, than the crawling exhibition. We had no time to say anything before it began to speak.

Read Poe's account of the voice that came from the mesmerised dying man, and you will realise less than one half of the horror of that head's voice.

There was an interval of a second or two between each word, and a sort of 'ring, ring, ring', in the note of the voice, like the timbre of a bell. It pealed slowly, as if talking to itself, for several minutes before I got rid of my cold sweat. Then the blessed solution struck me. I looked at the body lying near the doorway, and saw, just where the hollow of the throat joins on the shoulders, a muscle that had nothing to do with any man's regular breathing twitching away steadily. The whole thing was a careful reproduction of the Egyptian teraphin that one reads about sometimes; and the voice was as clever and as appalling a piece of ventriloquism as one could wish to hear. All this time the head was 'lip-lip-lapping' against the side of the basin, and speaking. It told Suddhoo, on his face again whining, of his son's illness and of the state of the illness up to the evening of that very night. I always shall respect the seal-cutter for keeping so faithfully to the time of the Peshawar telegrams. It went on to say that skilled doctors were night and day watching over the man's life; and that he would eventually recover if the fee to the potent sorcerer, whose servant was the head in the basin, were doubled.

Here the mistake from the artistic point of view came in. To ask for twice your stipulated fee in a voice that Lazarus might have used when he rose from the dead, is absurd. Janoo, who is really a woman of masculine intellect, saw this as quickly as I did. I heard her say '*Asli, nahin! Fareib!*' scornfully under her breath; and just as she said so, the light in the basin died out, the head stopped talking, and we heard the room door creak on its hinges. Then Janoo struck a match, lit the lamp, and we saw that head, basin, and seal-cutter were gone. Suddhoo was wringing his hands and explaining to anyone who cared to listen, that, if his chances of eternal salvation depended on it, he could not raise another two hundred rupees. Azizun was nearly in hysterics in the corner; while Janoo sat down composedly on one of the beds to discuss the probabilities of the whole thing being a *bunao*, or 'make-up'.

I explained as much as I knew of the seal-cutter's way of *jadoo*; but her argument was much more simple – 'The magic that is always demanding gifts is no true magic,' said she. 'My mother told me that the only potent love-spells are those which are told you for love. This seal-cutter man is a liar and a devil. I dare not tell, do anything, or get anything done, because I am in debt to Bhagwan Dass the *bunnia* for two gold rings and a heavy anklet. I must get my food from his shop. The seal-cutter is the friend of Bhagwan Dass, and he would poison my food. A fool's *jadoo* has been going on for ten days, and has cost Suddhoo many rupees each night. The seal-cutter used black hens and lemons and *mantras* before. He never showed us anything like this till tonight. Azizun is a fool, and will be a *purdahnashin* soon. Suddhoo has lost his strength and his wits. See now! I had hoped to get from Suddhoo many rupees while he lived, and many more after his death; and behold, he is spending everything on that offspring of a devil and a she-ass, the seal-cutter!'

Here I said, 'But what induced Suddhoo to drag me into the business? Of course I can speak to the seal-cutter, and he shall refund. The whole thing is child's talk – shame – and senseless.'

'Suddhoo *is* an old child,' said Janoo. 'He has lived on the roofs these seventy years and is as senseless as a milch-goat. He brought you here to assure himself that he was not breaking any law of the *Sirkar*, whose salt he ate many years ago. He worships the dust off the feet of the seal-cutter, and that cow-devourer has forbidden him to go and see his son. What does Suddhoo know of your laws or the lightning-post? I have to watch his money going day by day to that lying beast below.'

Janoo stamped her foot on the floor and nearly cried with vexation; while Suddhoo was whimpering under a blanket in the corner, and Azizun was trying to guide the pipe-stem to his foolish old mouth.

* * *

Now, the case stands thus. Unthinkingly, I have laid myself open to the charge of aiding and abetting the seal-cutter in obtaining money under false pretences, which is forbidden by Section 420 of the Indian Penal Code. I am helpless in the matter for these reasons. I cannot inform the police. What witnesses would support my statements? Janoo refuses flatly, and Azizun is a veiled woman somewhere near Bareilly – lost in this big India of ours. I dare not again take the law into my own hands, and speak to the seal-cutter; for certain am I that, not only would Suddhoo disbelieve me, but this step would end in the poisoning of Janoo, who is bound hand and foot by her debt to the *bunnia*. Suddhoo is an old dotard; and whenever we meet mumbles my idiotic joke that the *Sirkar* rather patronises the Black Art than otherwise. His son is well now; but Suddhoo is completely under the influence of the seal-cutter, by whose advice he regulates the affairs of his life. Janoo watches daily the money that she hoped to wheedle out of Suddhoo taken by the seal-cutter, and becomes daily more furious and sullen.

She will never tell, because she dare not; but, unless something happens to prevent her, I am afraid that the seal-cutter will die of cholera – the white arsenic kind – about the middle of May. And thus I shall be privy to a murder in the House of Suddhoo.

Slaves of the Lamp

The music room on the top floor of number five was filled with the 'Aladdin' company at rehearsal. Dickson Quartus, commonly known as Dick Four, was Aladdin, stage manager, ballet master, half the orchestra, and largely librettist, for the 'book' had been rewritten and filled with local allusions. The pantomime was to be given next week, in the downstairs study occupied by Aladdin, Abanazar, and the Emperor of China. The Slave of the Lamp, with the Princess Badroulbadour and the Widow Twankey, owned number five study across the same landing, so that the company could be easily assembled. The floor shook to the stamp-and-go of the ballet, while Aladdin, in pink cotton tights, a blue and tinsel jacket, and a plumed hat, banged alternately on the piano and his banjo. He was the moving spirit of the game, as befitted a senior who had passed his army preliminary and hoped to enter Sandhurst next spring.

Aladdin came to his own at last, Abanazar lay poisoned on the floor, the Widow Twankey danced her dance, and the company decided it would 'come all right on the night'.

'What about the last song, though?' said the Emperor, a tallish, fair-headed boy with a ghost of a moustache, at which he pulled manfully. 'We need a rousing old tune.'

' "John Peel"? "Drink, Puppy, Drink"?' suggested Abanazar, smoothing his baggy lilac pyjamas. 'Pussy' Abanazar never looked more than one-half awake, but he owned a soft, slow smile which well suited the part of the Wicked Uncle.

'Stale,' said Aladdin. 'Might as well have "Grandfather's Clock". What's that thing you were humming at prep last night, Stalky?'

Stalky, the Slave of the Lamp, in black tights and doublet, a black silk half-mask on his forehead, whistled lazily where he lay on the top of the piano. It was a catchy music-hall tune.

Dick Four cocked his head critically, and squinted down a large red nose.

'Once more, and I can pick it up,' he said, strumming. 'Sing the words.'

'Arrah, Patsy, mind the baby! Arrah, Patsy, mind the child!
Wrap him in an overcoat, he's surely goin' wild!
Arrah, Patsy, mind the baby! just ye mind the child awhile!
He'll kick an' bite an' cry all night! Arrah, Patsy, mind the child!'

'Rippin'! Oh, rippin'!' said Dick Four. 'Only we shan't have any piano on the night. We must work it with the banjos – play an' dance at the same time. You try, Tertius.'

The Emperor pushed aside his pea-green sleeves of state, and followed Dick Four on a heavy nickel-plated banjo.

'Yes, but I'm dead all this time. Bung in the middle of the stage, too,' said Abanazar.

'Oh, that's Beetle's biznai,' said Dick Four. 'Vamp it up, Beetle. Don't keep us waiting all night. You've got to get Pussy out of the light somehow, and bring us all in dancin' at the end.'

'All right. You two play it again,' said Beetle, who, in a grey skirt and a wig of chestnut sausage-curls, set slantwise above a pair of spectacles mended with an old bootlace, represented the Widow Twankey. He waved one leg in time to the hammered refrain, and the banjos grew louder.

'Um! Ah! Er – "Aladdin now has won his wife," ' he sang, and Dick Four repeated it.

' "Your Emperor is appeased." ' Tertius flung out his chest as he delivered his line.

'Now jump up, Pussy! Say, "I think I'd better come to life!" Then we all take hands and come forward: "We hope you've all been pleased." *Twiggez-vous?*'

'*Nous twiggons*. Good enough. What's the chorus for the final ballet? It's four kicks and a turn,' said Dick Four.

'Oh! Er!

John Short will ring the curtain down.
  And ring the prompter's bell;
We hope you know before you go
  That we all wish you well.'

'Rippin'! Rippin'! Now for the Widow's scene with the Princess. Hurry up, Turkey.'

McTurk, in a violet silk skirt and a coquettish blue turban, slouched forward as one thoroughly ashamed of himself. The Slave of the Lamp climbed down from the piano, and dispassionately kicked him. 'Play up, Turkey,' he said; 'this is serious.' But there fell on the door the knock of authority. It happened to be King, in gown and mortar-board, enjoying a Saturday evening prowl before dinner.

'Locked doors! Locked doors!' he snapped with a scowl. 'What's the meaning of this; and what, may

I ask, is the intention of this – this epicene attire?'

'Pantomime, sir. The Head gave us leave,' said Abanazar, as the only member of the Sixth concerned. Dick Four stood firm in the confidence born of well-fitting tights, but Beetle strove to efface himself behind the piano. A grey princess-skirt borrowed from a day-boy's mother and a spotted cotton bodice unsystematically padded with imposition-paper make one ridiculous. And in other regards Beetle had a bad conscience.

'As usual!' sneered King. 'Futile foolery just when your careers, such as they may be, are hanging in the balance. I see! Ah, I see! The old gang of criminals – allied forces of disorder – Corkran' – the Slave of the Lamp smiled politely – 'McTurk' – the Irishman smiled – 'and, of course, the unspeakable Beetle, our friend Gigadibs.' Abanazar, the Emperor, and Aladdin had more or less of characters, and King passed them over. 'Come forth, my inky buffoon, from behind yonder instrument of music! You supply, I presume, the doggerel for this entertainment. Esteem yourself to be, as it were, a poet?'

'He's found one of 'em,' thought Beetle, noting the flush on King's cheekbone.

'I have just had the pleasure of reading an effusion of yours to my address, I believe – an effusion intended to rhyme. So – so you despise me, Master Gigadibs, do you? I am quite aware – you need not explain – that it was ostensibly not intended for my edification. I read it with laughter – yes, with laughter. These paper pellets of inky boys – still a boy we are, Master Gigadibs – do not disturb my equanimity.'

'Wonder which it was,' thought Beetle. He had launched many lampoons on an appreciative public ever since he discovered that it was possible to convey reproof in rhyme.

In sign of his unruffled calm, King proceeded to tear Beetle, whom he called Gigadibs, slowly asunder. From his untied shoestrings to his mended spectacles (the life of a poet at a big school is hard) he held him up to the derision of his associates – with the usual result. His wild flowers of speech – King had an unpleasant tongue – restored him to good humour at the last. He drew a lurid picture of Beetle's latter end as a scurrilous pamphleteer dying in an attic, scattered a few compliments over McTurk and Corkran, and, reminding Beetle that he must come up for judgement when called upon, went to common room, where he triumphed anew over his victims.

'And the worst of it,' he explained in a loud voice over his soup, 'is that I waste such gems of sarcasm on their thick heads. It's miles above them, I'm certain.'

'We–ell,' said the school chaplain slowly, 'I don't know what Corkran's appreciation of your style may be, but young McTurk reads Ruskin for his amusement.'

'Nonsense! He does it to show off. I mistrust the dark Celt.'

'He does nothing of the kind. I went into their study the other night, unofficially, and McTurk was gluing up the back of four odd numbers of *Fors Clavigera*.'

'I don't know anything about their private lives,' said a mathematical master hotly, 'but I've learned by bitter experience that number five study are best left alone. They are utterly soulless young devils.' He blushed as the others laughed.

But in the music room there was wrath and bad language. Only Stalky, Slave of the Lamp, lay on the piano unmoved.

'That little swine Manders minor must have shown him your stuff. He's always suckin' up to King. Go and kill him,' he drawled. 'Which one was it, Beetle?'

'Dunno,' said Beetle, struggling out of the skirt. 'There was one about his hunting for popularity with the small boys, and the other one was one about him in hell, tellin' the Devil he was a Balliol man. I swear both of 'em rhymed all right. By gum! P'raps Manders minor showed him both! *I'll* correct his caesuras for him.'

He disappeared down two flights of stairs, flushed a small pink and white boy in a form-room next door to King's study, which, again, was immediately below his own, and chased him up the corridor into a form-room sacred to the revels of the Lower Third. Thence he came back, greatly disordered, to find McTurk, Stalky, and the others of the company in his study enjoying an unlimited 'brew' – coffee, cocoa, buns, new bread hot and steaming, sardine, sausage, ham-and-tongue paste, pilchards, three jams, and at least as many pounds of Devonshire cream.

'My hat!' said he, throwing himself upon the banquet. 'Who stumped up for this, Stalky?' It was within a month of term end, and blank starvation had reigned in the studies for weeks.

'You,' said Stalky, serenely.

'Confound you! You haven't been popping my Sunday bags, then?'

'Keep your hair on. It's only your watch.'

'Watch! I lost it – weeks ago. Out on the Burrows, when we tried to shoot the old ram – the day our pistol burst.'

'It dropped out of your pocket (you're so beastly careless, Beetle), and McTurk and I kept it for you. I've been wearing it for a week, and you never noticed.

Took it into Bideford after dinner today. Got thirteen and sevenpence. Here's the ticket.'

'Well, that's pretty average cool,' said Abanazar behind a slab of cream and jam, as Beetle, reassured upon the safety of his Sunday trousers, showed not even surprise, much less resentment. Indeed, it was McTurk who grew angry, saying: 'You gave him the ticket, Stalky? You pawned it? You unmitigated beast! Why, last month you and Beetle sold mine! Never got a sniff of any ticket.'

'Ah, that was because you locked your trunk, and we wasted half the afternoon hammering it open. We might have pawned it if you'd behaved like a Christian, Turkey.'

'My aunt!' said Abanazar, 'you chaps are communists. Vote of thanks to Beetle, though.'

'That's beastly unfair,' said Stalky, 'when I took all the trouble to pawn it. Beetle never knew he had a watch. Oh, I say, Rabbits-Eggs gave me a lift into Bideford this afternoon.'

Rabbits-Eggs was the local carrier – an outcrop of the early Devonian formation. It was Stalky who had invented his unlovely name. 'He was pretty average drunk, or he wouldn't have done it. Rabbits-Eggs is a little shy of me, somehow. But I swore it was *pax* between us, and gave him a bob. He stopped at two pubs on the way in, so he'll be howling drunk tonight. Oh, don't begin reading, Beetle; there's a council of war on. What the deuce is the matter with your collar?'

'Chivvied Manders minor into the Lower Third box room. Had all his beastly little friends on top of me,' said Beetle from behind a jar of pilchards and a book.

'You ass! Any fool could have told you where Manders would bunk to,' said McTurk.

'I didn't think,' said Beetle meekly, scooping out pilchards with a spoon.

''Course you didn't. You never do.' McTurk adjusted Beetle's collar with a savage tug. 'Don't drop oil all over my *Fors* or I'll scrag you!'

'Shut up, you – you Irish biddy! 'Tisn't your beastly *Fors*. It's one of mine.'

The book was a fat, brown-backed volume of the later sixties, which King had once thrown at Beetle's head that Beetle might see whence the name Gigadibs came. Beetle had quietly annexed the book, and had seen – several things. The quarter-comprehended verses lived and ate with him, as the be-dropped pages showed. He removed himself from all that world, drifting at large with wondrous men and women, till McTurk hammered the pilchard spoon on his head and he snarled.

'Beetle! You're oppressed and insulted and bullied by King. Don't you feel it?'

'Let me alone! I can write some more poetry about him if I am, I suppose.'

'Mad! Quite mad!' said Stalky to the visitors, as one exhibiting strange beasts. 'Beetle reads an ass called Brownin', and McTurk reads an ass called Ruskin, and – '

'Ruskin isn't an ass,' said McTurk. 'He's almost as good as the Opium Eater. He says "we're children of noble races trained by surrounding art". That means me, and the way I decorated the study when you two badgers would have stuck up brackets and Christmas cards. Child of a noble race, trained by surrounding art, stop reading, or I'll shove a pilchard down your neck!'

'It's two to one,' said Stalky, warningly, and Beetle

closed the book, in obedience to the law under which he and his companions had lived for six checkered years.

The visitors looked on delighted. Number five study had a reputation for more variegated insanity than the rest of the school put together; and so far as its code allowed friendship with outsiders it was polite and open-hearted to its neighbours on the same landing.

'What rot do you want now?' said Beetle.

'King! War!' said McTurk, jerking his head toward the wall, where hung a small wooden West African war drum, a gift to McTurk from a naval uncle.

'Then we shall be turned out of the study again,' said Beetle, who loved his fleshpots. 'Mason turned us out for – just warbling on it.' Mason was the mathematical master who had testified in common room.

'Warbling? – Oh, Lord!' said Abanazar. 'We couldn't hear ourselves speak in our study when you played the infernal thing. What's the good of getting turned out of your study, anyhow?'

'We lived in the form-rooms for a week, too,' said Beetle, tragically. 'And it was beastly cold.'

'Ye–es, but Mason's rooms were filled with rats every day we were out. It took him a week to draw the inference,' said McTurk. 'He loathes rats. Minute he let us go back the rats stopped. Mason's a little shy of us now, but there was no evidence.'

'Jolly well there wasn't,' said Stalky, 'when I got out on the roof and dropped the beastly things down his chimney. But, look here – question is, are our characters good enough just now to stand a study row?'

'Never mind mine,' said Beetle. 'King swears I haven't any.'

'I'm not thinking of you,' Stalky returned scornfully.

'You aren't going up for the army, you old bat. I don't want to be expelled – and the head's getting rather shy of us, too.'

'Rot!' said McTurk. 'The Head never expels except for beastliness or stealing. But I forgot; you and Stalky *are* thieves – regular burglars.'

The visitors gasped, but Stalky interpreted the parable with large grins.

'Well, you know, that little beast Manders minor saw Beetle and me hammerin' McTurk's trunk open in the dormitory when we took his watch last month. Of course Manders sneaked to Mason, and Mason solemnly took it up as a case of theft, to get even with us about the rats.'

'That just put Mason into our giddy hands,' said McTurk, blandly. 'We were nice to him, because he was a new master and wanted to win the confidence of the boys. Pity he draws inferences, though. Stalky went to his study and pretended to blub, and told Mason he'd lead a new life if Mason would let him off this time, but Mason wouldn't. Said it was his duty to report him to the Head.'

'Vindictive swine!' said Beetle. 'It was all those rats! Then *I* blubbed, too, and Stalky confessed that he'd been a thief in regular practice for six years, ever since he came to the school; and that I'd taught him – *à la* Fagin. Mason turned white with joy. He thought he had us on toast.'

'Gorgeous! Gorgeous!' said Dick Four. 'We never heard of this.'

' 'Course not. Mason kept it jolly quiet. He wrote down all our statements on impot-paper. There wasn't anything he wouldn't believe,' said Stalky.

'And handed it all up to the Head, *with* an extempore

prayer. It took about forty pages,' said Beetle. 'I helped him a lot.'

'And then, you crazy idiots?' said Abanazar.

'Oh, we were sent for; and Stalky asked to have the "depositions" read out, and the Head knocked him spinning into a wastepaper basket. Then he gave us eight cuts apiece – welters – for – for – takin' unheard-of liberties with a new master. I saw his shoulders shaking when we went out. Do you know,' said Beetle, pensively, 'that Mason can't look at us now in second lesson without blushing? We three stare at him sometimes till he regularly trickles. He's an awfully sensitive beast.'

'He read *Eric, or Little by Little*,' said McTurk; 'so we gave him *St Winifred's, or The World of School*. They spent all their spare time stealing at St Winifred's, when they weren't praying or getting drunk at pubs. Well, that was only a week ago, and the Head's a little bit shy of us. He called it constructive devilry. Stalky invented it all.'

'Not the least good having a row with a master unless you can make an ass of him,' said Stalky, extended at ease on the hearthrug. 'If Mason didn't know number five – well, he's learnt, that's all. Now, my dearly beloved 'earers' – Stalky curled his legs under him and addressed the company – 'we've got that strong, perseverin' man King on our hands. He went miles out of his way to provoke a conflict.' (Here Stalky snapped down the black silk domino and assumed the air of a judge.) 'He has oppressed Beetle, McTurk, and me, *privatim et seriatim*, one by one, as he could catch us. But now, he has insulted number five up in the music room, and in the presence of these – these ossifers of the Ninety-third, wot look like hairdressers.

Binjimin, we must make him cry, "*Capivi!*"'

Stalky's reading did not include Browning or Ruskin.

'And, besides,' said McTurk, 'he's a Philistine, a basket-hanger. He wears a tartan tie. Ruskin says that any man who wears a tartan tie will, without doubt, be damned everlastingly.'

'Bravo, McTurk,' said Tertius; 'I thought he was only a beast.'

'He's that, too, of course, but he's worse. He has a china basket with blue ribbons and a pink kitten on it, hung up in his window to grow musk in. You know when I got all that old oak carvin' out of Bideford Church, when they were restoring it (Ruskin says that any man who'll restore a church is an unmitigated sweep), and stuck it up here with glue? Well, King came in and wanted to know whether we'd done it with a fretsaw! Yah! He is the king of basket-hangers!'

Down went McTurk's inky thumb over an imaginary arena full of bleeding Kings. '*Placente*, child of a generous race!' he cried to Beetle.

'Well,' began Beetle, doubtfully, 'he comes from Balliol, but I'm going to give the beast a chance. You see I can always make him hop with some more poetry. He can't report me to the Head, because it makes him ridiculous. (Stalky's quite right.) But he shall have his chance.'

Beetle opened the book on the table, ran his finger down a page, and began at random:

> 'Or who in Moscow toward the Czar
> With the demurest of footfalls,
> Over the Kremlin's pavement white
> With serpentine and syenite,
> Steps with five other generals – '

'That's no good. Try another,' said Stalky.

'Hold on a shake; I know what's coming.' McTurk was reading over Beetle's shoulder.

'That simultaneously take snuff,
For each to have pretext enough,
And kerchiefwise unfold his sash,
Which – softness' self – is yet the stuff

(Gummy! What a sentence!)

To hold fast where a steel chain snaps
And leave the grand white neck no gash.

(Full stop.)'

'Don't understand a word of it,' said Stalky.

'More fool you! Construe,' said McTurk. 'Those six bargees scragged the Czar, and left no evidence. *Actum est* with King.'

'He gave me that book, too,' said Beetle, licking his lips:

'There's a great text in Galatians,
  Once you trip on it entails
Twenty-nine distinct damnations,
  One sure if another fails.'

Then irrelevantly:

'Setebos! Setebos! and Setebos!
Thinketh he liveth in the cold of the moon.'

'He's just come in from dinner,' said Dick Four, looking through the window. 'Manders minor is with him.'

'Safest place for Manders minor just now,' said Beetle.

'Then you chaps had better clear out,' said Stalky

politely to the visitors. ' 'Tisn't fair to mix you up in a study row. Besides, we can't afford to have evidence.'

'Are you going to begin at once?' said Aladdin.

'Immediately, if not sooner,' said Stalky, and turned out the gas. 'Strong, perseverin' man – King. Make him cry, "*Capivi!*" G'way, Binjimin.'

The company retreated to their own neat and spacious study with expectant souls.

'When Stalky blows out his nostrils like a horse,' said Aladdin to the Emperor of China, 'he's on the warpath. Wonder what King will get.'

'Beans,' said the Emperor. 'Number five generally pays in full.'

'Wonder if I ought to take any notice of it officially,' said Abanazar, who had just remembered he was a prefect.

'It's none of your business, Pussy. Besides, if you did, we'd have them hostile to us; and we shouldn't be able to do any work,' said Aladdin. 'They've begun already.'

Now, that West African war drum had been made to signal across estuaries and deltas. Number five was forbidden to wake the engine within earshot of the school. But a deep, devastating drone filled the passages as McTurk and Beetle scientifically rubbed its top. Anon it changed to the blare of trumpets – of savage pursuing trumpets. Then, as McTurk slapped one side, smooth with the blood of ancient sacrifice, the roar broke into short coughing howls such as the wounded gorilla throws in his native forest. These were followed by the wrath of King – three steps at a time, up the staircase, with a dry whirr of the gown. Aladdin and company, listening, squeaked with excitement as the door crashed open. King stumbled into the darkness, and cursed those performers by the gods of Balliol and quiet repose.

'Turned out for a week,' said Aladdin, holding the study door on the crack. 'Key to be brought down to his study in five minutes. "Brutes! Barbarians! Savages! Children!" He's rather agitated. "Arrah, Patsy, mind the baby," ' he sang in a whisper as he clung to the doorknob, dancing a noiseless war-dance.

King went downstairs again, and Beetle and McTurk lit the gas to confer with Stalky. But Stalky had vanished.

'Looks like no end of a mess,' said Beetle, collecting his books and mathematical instrument case. 'A week in the form-room isn't any advantage to us.'

'Yes, but don't you see that Stalky isn't here, you owl!' said McTurk. 'Take down the key, and look sorrowful. King'll only jaw you for half an hour. I'm going to read in the lower form-room.'

'But it's always me,' mourned Beetle.

'Wait till we see,' said McTurk hopefully. 'I don't know any more than you do what Stalky means, but it's something. Go down and draw King's fire. You're used to it.'

No sooner had the key turned in the door than the lid of the coal-box, which was also the window seat, lifted cautiously. It had been a tight fit, even for the lithe Stalky, his head between his knees, and his stomach under his right ear. From a drawer in the table he took a well-worn catapult, a handful of buckshot, and a duplicate key of the study; noiselessly he raised the window and kneeled by it, his face turned to the road, the wind-sloped trees, the dark levels of the Burrows, and the white line of breakers falling nine-deep along the Pebbleridge. Far down the steep-banked Devonshire lane he heard the husky hoot of the carrier's horn. There was a ghost of melody in it, as it might have been the wind in a gin bottle essaying to sing, 'It's a way we have in the army.'

Stalky smiled a tight-lipped smile, and at extreme range opened fire: the old horse half wheeled in the shafts.

'Where be gwaine tu?' hiccoughed Rabbits-Eggs. Another buckshot tore through the rotten canvas tilt with a vicious zipp.

'*Habet!*' murmured Stalky, as Rabbits-Eggs swore into the patient night, protesting that he saw the 'dommed colleger' who was assaulting him.

'And so,' King was saying in a high head voice to Beetle, whom he had kept to play with before Manders minor, well knowing that it hurts a Fifth-form boy to be held up to a fag's derision, 'and so, Master Beetle, in spite of all our verses, which we are so proud of, when we presume to come into direct conflict with even so humble a representative of authority as myself, for instance, we are turned out of our studies, are we not?'

'Yes, sir,' said Beetle, with a sheepish grin on his lips and murder in his heart. Hope had nearly left him, but he clung to a well-established faith that never was Stalky so dangerous as when he was invisible.

'You are not required to criticise, thank you. Turned out of our studies, we are, just as if we were no better than little Manders minor. Only inky schoolboys we are, and must be treated as such.'

Beetle pricked up his ears, for Rabbits-Eggs was swearing savagely on the road, and some of the language entered at the upper sash. King believed in ventilation. He strode to the window, gowned and majestic, very visible in the gaslight.

'I zee 'un! I zee 'un!' roared Rabbits-Eggs, now that he had found a visible foe – another shot from the darkness above. 'Yiss, yeou, yeou long-nosed, fower-eyed, gingy-whiskered beggar! Yeu'm tu old for such goin's on. Aie! Poultice yeour nose, I tall 'ee! Poultice yeour long nose!'

Beetle's heart leaped up within him. Somewhere, somehow, he knew, Stalky moved behind these manifestations. There was hope and the prospect of revenge. He would embody the suggestion about the nose in deathless verse. King threw up the window, and sternly rebuked Rabbits-Eggs. But the carrier was beyond fear or fawning. He had descended from the cart, and was stooping by the roadside.

It all fell swiftly as a dream. Manders minor raised his hand to his head with a cry, as a jagged flint cannoned on to some rich tree-calf bindings in the bookshelf. Another quoited along the writing table. Beetle made zealous feint to stop it, and in that endeavour overturned a student's lamp, which dripped, *via* King's papers and some choice books, greasily on to a Persian rug. There was much broken glass on the window seat; the china basket – McTurk's aversion – cracked to flinders, had dropped her musk plant and its earth over the red rep cushions; Manders minor was bleeding profusely from a cut on the cheekbone; and King, using strange words, every one of which Beetle treasured, ran forth to find the school-sergeant, that Rabbits-Eggs might be instantly cast into jail.

'Poor chap!' said Beetle, with a false, feigned

sympathy. 'Let it bleed a little. That'll prevent apoplexy,' and he held the blind head skilfully over the table, and the papers on the table, as he guided the howling Manders to the door.

Then did Beetle, alone with the wreckage, return good for evil. How, in that office, a complete set of 'Gibbon' was scarred all along the back as by a flint; how so much black and copying ink came to be mingled with Manders's gore on the tablecloth; why the big gum bottle, unstoppered, had rolled semicircularly across the floor; and in what manner the white china doorknob grew to be painted with yet more of Manders's young blood, were matters which Beetle did not explain when the rabid King returned to find him standing politely over the reeking hearthrug.

'You never told me to go, sir,' he said, with the air of Casabianca, and King consigned him to the outer darkness.

But it was to a boot cupboard under the staircase on the ground floor that he hastened, to loose the mirth that was destroying him. He had not drawn breath for a first whoop of triumph when two hands choked him dumb.

'Go to the dormitory and get me my things. Bring 'em to number five lavatory. I'm still in tights,' hissed Stalky, sitting on his head. 'Don't run. Walk.'

But Beetle staggered into the form-room next door, and delegated his duty to the yet unenlightened McTurk, with an hysterical precis of the campaign thus far. So it was McTurk, of the wooden visage, who brought the clothes from the dormitory while Beetle panted on a form. Then the three buried themselves in number five lavatory, turned on all the taps, filled the place with steam, and dropped weeping into the baths, where they pieced out the war.

'*Moi! Je! Ich! Ego!*' gasped Stalky. 'I waited till I couldn't hear myself think, while you played the drum! Hid in the coal-locker – and tweaked Rabbits-Eggs – and Rabbits-Eggs rocked King. Wasn't it beautiful? Did you hear the glass?'

'Why, he – he – he,' shrieked McTurk, one trembling finger pointed at Beetle.

'Why, I – I – I was through it all,' Beetle howled; 'in his study, being jawed.'

'Oh, my soul!' said Stalky with a yell, disappearing under water.

'The – the glass was nothing. Manders minor's head's cut open. La–la–lamp upset all over the rug. Blood on the books and papers. The gum! The gum! The gum! The ink! The ink! The ink! Oh, Lord!'

Then Stalky leaped out, all pink as he was, and shook Beetle into some sort of coherence; but his tale prostrated them afresh.

'I bunked for the boot cupboard the second I heard King go downstairs. Beetle tumbled in on top of me. The spare key's hid behind the loose board. There isn't a shadow of evidence,' said Stalky. They were all chanting together.

'And he turned us out himself – himself – him*self*!' This from McTurk. 'He can't begin to suspect us. Oh, Stalky, it's the loveliest thing we've ever done.'

'Gum! Gum! Dollops of gum!' shouted Beetle, his spectacles gleaming through a sea of lather. 'Ink and blood all mixed. I held the little beast's head all over the Latin proses for Monday. Golly, how the oil stunk! And Rabbits-Eggs told King to poultice his nose! Did you hit Rabbits-Eggs, Stalky?'

'Did I jolly well not? Tweaked him all over. Did you hear him curse? Oh, I shall be sick in a minute if I don't stop.'

But dressing was a slow process, because McTurk was obliged to dance when he heard that the musk basket was broken, and, moreover, Beetle retailed all King's language with emendations and purple insets.

'Shockin'!' said Stalky, collapsing in a helpless welter of half-hitched trousers. 'So dam' bad, too, for innocent boys like us! Wonder what they'd say at *St Winifred's, or The World of School.* By gum! That reminds me, we owe the Lower Third one for assaultin' Beetle when he chivvied Manders minor. Come on! It's an alibi, Samivel; and, besides, if we let 'em off they'll be worse next time.'

The Lower Third had set a guard upon their form-room for the space of a full hour, which to a boy is a lifetime. Now they were busy with their Saturday evening businesses – cooking sparrows over the gas with rusty nibs; brewing unholy drinks in gallipots; skinning moles with pocket-knives; attending to paper trays full of silkworms, or discussing the iniquities of their elders with a freedom, fluency, and point that would have amazed their parents. The blow fell without warning. Stalky upset a form crowded with small boys among their own cooking utensils, McTurk raided the untidy lockers as a terrier digs at a rabbit-hole, while Beetle poured ink upon such heads as he could not appeal to with a Smith's *Classical Dictionary*. Three brisk minutes accounted for many silkworms, pet larvae, French exercises, school caps, half-prepared bones and skulls, and a dozen pots of home-made sloe jam. It was a great wreckage, and the form-room looked as though three conflicting tempests had smitten it.

'Phew!' said Stalky, drawing breath outside the door (amid groans of 'Oh, you beastly ca–ads! You think yourselves awful funny,' and so forth). '*That's* all right. Never let the sun go down upon your wrath. Rummy little devils, fags. Got no notion o' combinin'.'

'Six of 'em sat on my head when I went in after Manders minor,' said Beetle. 'I warned 'em what they'd get, though.'

'Everybody paid in full – beautiful feelin',' said McTurk absently, as they strolled along the corridor. 'Don't think we'd better say much about King, though, do you, Stalky?'

'Not much. Our line is injured innocence, of course – same as when old Faxibus reported us on suspicion of smoking in the bunkers. If I hadn't thought of buyin' the pepper and spillin' it all over our clothes, he'd have smelt us. King was gha–astly facetious about that. Called us bird-stuffers in form for a week.'

'Ah, King hates the Natural History Society because little Hartopp is president. Mustn't do anything in the coll. without glorifyin' King,' said McTurk. 'But he must be a putrid ass, you know, to suppose at our time o' life we'd go and stuff birds like fags.'

'Poor old King!' said Beetle. 'He's awf'ly unpopular in common room, and they'll chaff his head off about Rabbits-Eggs. Golly! How lovely! How beautiful! How holy! But you should have seen his face when the first rock came in! *And* the earth from the basket!'

So they were all stricken helpless for five minutes.

They repaired at last to Abanazar's study, and were received reverently.

'What's the matter?' said Stalky, quick to realise new atmospheres.

'You know jolly well,' said Abanazar. 'You'll be expelled if you get caught. King is a gibbering maniac.'

'Who? Which? What? Expelled for how? We only played the war drum. We've got turned out for that already.'

'Do you chaps mean to say you didn't make Rabbits-Eggs drunk and bribe him to rock King's rooms?'

'Bribe him? No, that I'll swear we didn't,' said Stalky, with a relieved heart, for he loved not to tell lies. 'What a low mind you've got, Pussy! We've been down having a bath. Did Rabbits-Eggs rock King? Strong, perseverin' man King? Shockin'!'

'Awf'ly. King's frothing at the mouth. There's bell for prayers. Come on.'

'Wait a sec,' said Stalky, continuing the conversation in a loud and cheerful voice, as they descended the stairs. 'What did Rabbits-Eggs rock King for?'

'I know,' said Beetle, as they passed King's open door. 'I was in his study.'

'Hush, you ass!' hissed the Emperor of China.

'Oh, he's gone down to prayers,' said Beetle, watching the shadow of the housemaster on the wall. 'Rabbits-Eggs was only a bit drunk, swearin' at his horse, and King jawed him through the window, and then, of course, he rocked King.'

'Do you mean to say,' said Stalky, 'that King began it?'

King was behind them, and every well-weighed word went up the staircase like an arrow. 'I can only swear,' said Beetle, 'that King cursed like a bargee. Simply disgustin'. I'm goin' to write to my father about it.'

'Better report it to Mason,' suggested Stalky. 'He knows our tender consciences. Hold on a shake. I've got to tie my bootlace.'

The other study hurried forward. They did not wish to be dragged into stage asides of this nature. So it was left to McTurk to sum up the situation beneath the guns of the enemy.

'You see,' said the Irishman, hanging on the banister, 'he begins by bullying little chaps; then he bullies the big chaps; then he bullies someone who isn't connected with the college, and then he catches it. Serves him jolly well right . . . I beg your pardon, sir. I didn't see you were coming down the staircase.'

The black gown tore past like a thunderstorm, and in its wake, three abreast, arms linked, the Aladdin company rolled up the big corridor to prayers, singing with most innocent intention:

> 'Arrah, Patsy, mind the baby! Arrah, Patsy, mind the child!
> Wrap him up in an overcoat, he's surely goin' wild!
> Arrah, Patsy, mind the baby; just ye mind the child awhile!
> He'll kick an' bite an' cry all night! Arrah, Patsy, mind the child!'

Kaspar's Song in 'Varda'

(*from the Swedish of Stagnelius*)

Eyes aloft, over dangerous places,
  The children follow where Psyche flies,
And, in the sweat of their upturned faces,
  Slash with a net at the empty skies.

So it goes they fall amid brambles,
  And sting their toes on the nettle-tops,
Till after a thousand scratches and scrambles
  They wipe their brows, and the hunting stops.

Then to quiet them comes their father
  And stills the riot of pain and grief,
Saying, 'Little ones, go and gather
  Out of my garden a cabbage leaf.

'You will find on it whorls and clots of
  Dull grey eggs that, properly fed,
Turn, by way of the worm, to lots of
  Radiant Psyches raised from the dead.'

* * *

'Heaven is beautiful, Earth is ugly,'
  The three-dimensioned preacher saith,
So we must not look where the snail and
                the slug lie
  For Psyche's birth . . . And that is our death!

'Wireless'

'It's a funny thing, this Marconi business, isn't it?' said Mr Shaynor, coughing heavily. 'Nothing seems to make any difference, by what they tell me – storms, hills, or anything; but if that's true we shall know before morning.'

'Of course it's true,' I answered, stepping behind the counter. 'Where's old Mr Cashell?'

'He's had to go to bed on account of his influenza. He said you'd very likely drop in.'

'Where's his nephew?'

'Inside, getting the things ready. He told me that the last time they experimented they put the pole on the roof of one of the big hotels here, and the batteries electrified all the water-supply, and' – he giggled – 'the ladies got shocks when they took their baths.'

'I never heard of that.'

'The hotel wouldn't exactly advertise it, would it? Just now, by what Mr Cashell tells me, they're trying to signal from here to Poole, and they're using stronger batteries than ever. But, you see, he being the guvnor's nephew and all that (and it will be in the papers too), it doesn't matter how they electrify things in this house. Are you going to watch?'

'Very much. I've never seen this game. Aren't you going to bed?'

'We don't close till ten on Saturdays. There's a good deal of influenza in town, too, and there'll be a dozen prescriptions coming in before morning. I generally sleep in the chair here. It's warmer than jumping out of bed every time. Bitter cold, isn't it?'

'Freezing hard. I'm sorry your cough's worse.'

'Thank you. I don't mind cold so much. It's this wind that fair cuts me to pieces.' He coughed again hard and hackingly, as an old lady came in for ammoniated quinine. 'We've just run out of it in bottles, madam,' said Mr Shaynor, returning to the professional tone, 'but if you will wait two minutes, I'll make it up for you, madam.'

I had used the shop for some time, and my acquaintance with the proprietor had ripened into friendship. It was Mr Cashell who revealed to me the purpose and power of Apothecaries' Hall what time a fellow-chemist had made an error in a prescription of mine, had lied to cover his sloth, and when error and lie were brought home to him had written vain letters.

'A disgrace to our profession,' said the thin, mild-eyed man, hotly, after studying the evidence. 'You couldn't do a better service to the profession than report him to Apothecaries' Hall.'

I did so, not knowing what djinns I should evoke; and the result was such an apology as one might make who had spent a night on the rack. I conceived great respect for Apothecaries' Hall, and esteem for Mr Cashell, a zealous craftsman who magnified his calling. Until Mr Shaynor came down from the North his assistants had by no means agreed with Mr Cashell. 'They forget,' said he, 'that, first and foremost, the compounder is a medicine-man. On him depends the physician's reputation. He holds it literally in the hollow of his hand, sir.'

Mr Shaynor's manners had not, perhaps, the polish of the grocery and Italian warehouse next door, but he knew and loved his dispensary work in every detail. For relaxation he seemed to go no farther afield than the romance of drugs – their discovery, preparation, packing, and export – but it led him to the ends of the earth, and on this subject, and the Pharmaceutical Formulary, and Nicholas Culpeper, most confident of physicians, we met.

Little by little I grew to know something of his beginnings and his hopes – of his mother, who had been a schoolteacher in one of the northern counties, and of his red-headed father, a small job-master at Kirby Moors, who died when he was a child; of the examinations he had passed and of their exceeding and increasing difficulty; of his dreams of a shop in London; of his hate for the price-cutting Co-operative stores; and, most interesting, of his mental attitude towards customers.

'There's a way you get into,' he told me, 'of serving them carefully, and I hope, politely, without stopping your own thinking. I've been reading Christie's *New Commercial Plants* all this autumn, and that needs keeping your mind on it, I can tell you. So long as it isn't a prescription, of course, I can carry as much as half a page of Christie in my head, and at the same time I could sell out all that window twice over, and not a penny wrong at the end. As to prescriptions, I think I could make up the general run of 'em in my sleep, almost.'

For reasons of my own, I was deeply interested in Marconi experiments at their outset in England; and it was of a piece with Mr Cashell's unvarying thoughtfulness that, when his nephew the electrician appropriated the house for a long-range installation, he should, as I have said, invite me to see the result.

The old lady went away with her medicine, and Mr Shaynor and I stamped on the tiled floor behind the counter to keep ourselves warm. The shop, by the light of the many electrics, looked like a Paris-diamond mine, for Mr Cashell believed in all the ritual of his craft. Three superb glass jars – red, green, and blue – of the sort that led Rosamund to parting with her shoes – blazed in the broad plate-glass windows, and there was a confused smell of orris, Kodak films, vulcanite, tooth-powder, sachets, and almond-cream in the air. Mr Shaynor fed the dispensary stove, and we sucked cayenne-pepper jujubes and menthol lozenges. The brutal east wind had cleared the streets, and the few passers-by were muffled to their puckered eyes. In the Italian warehouse next door some gay feathered birds and game, hung upon hooks, sagged to the wind across the left edge of our window-frame.

'They ought to take these poultry in – all knocked about like that,' said Mr Shaynor. 'Doesn't it make you feel fair perishing? See that old hare! The wind's nearly blowing the fur off him.'

I saw the belly-fur of the dead beast blown apart in ridges and streaks as the wind caught it, showing bluish skin underneath. 'Bitter cold,' said Mr Shaynor, shuddering. 'Fancy going out on a night like this! Oh, here's young Mr Cashell.'

The door of the inner office behind the dispensary opened, and an energetic, spade-bearded man stepped forth, rubbing his hands.

'I want a bit of tinfoil, Shaynor,' he said. 'Good-evening. My uncle told me you might be coming.' This to me, as I began the first of a hundred questions.

'I've everything in order,' he replied. 'We're only waiting until Poole calls us up. Excuse me a minute.

You can come in whenever you like – but I'd better be with the instruments. Give me that tinfoil. Thanks.'

While we were talking, a girl – evidently no customer – had come into the shop, and the face and bearing of Mr Shaynor changed. She leaned confidently across the counter.

'But I can't,' I heard him whisper uneasily – the flush on his cheek was dull red, and his eyes shone like a drugged moth's. 'I can't. I tell you I'm alone in the place.'

'No, you aren't. Who's *that*? Let him look after it for half an hour. A brisk walk will do you good. Ah, come now, John.'

'But he isn't –'

'I don't care. I want you to; we'll only go round by St Agnes. If you don't –'

He crossed to where I stood in the shadow of the dispensary counter, and began some sort of broken apology about a lady-friend.

'Yes,' she interrupted. 'You take the shop for half an hour – to oblige *me*, won't you?'

She had a singularly rich and promising voice that well matched her outline.

'All right,' I said. 'I'll do it – but you'd better wrap yourself up, Mr Shaynor.'

'Oh, a brisk walk ought to help me. We're only going round by the church.' I heard him cough grievously as they went out together.

I refilled the stove, and, after reckless expenditure of Mr Cashell's coal, drove some warmth into the shop. I explored many of the glass-knobbed drawers that lined the walls, tasted some disconcerting drugs, and, by the aid of a few cardamoms, ground ginger, chloric-ether, and dilute alcohol, manufactured a new and wildish drink, of which I bore a glassful to young Mr Cashell, busy in the back office. He laughed shortly when I told him that Mr Shaynor had stepped out – but a frail coil of wire held all his attention, and he had no word for me bewildered among the batteries and rods. The noise of the sea on the beach began to make itself heard as the traffic in the street ceased. Then briefly, but very lucidly, he gave me the names and uses of the mechanism that crowded the tables and the floor.

'When do you expect to get the message from Poole?' I demanded, sipping my liquor out of a graduated glass.

'About midnight, if everything is in order. We've got our installation-pole fixed to the roof of the house. I shouldn't advise you to turn on a tap or anything tonight. We've connected up with the plumbing, and all the water will be electrified.' He repeated to me the history of the agitated ladies at the hotel at the time of the first installation.

'But what *is* it?' I asked. 'Electricity is out of my beat altogether.'

'Ah, if you knew *that* you'd know something nobody knows. It's just It – what we call Electricity, but the magic – the manifestations – the Hertzian waves – are all revealed by *this*. The coherer, we call it.'

He picked up a glass tube not much thicker than a thermometer, in which, almost touching, were two tiny silver plugs, and between them an infinitesimal pinch of metallic dust. 'That's all,' he said, proudly, as though himself responsible for the wonder. 'That is the thing that will reveal to us the Powers – whatever the Powers may be – at work – through space – a long distance away.'

Just then Mr Shaynor returned alone and stood coughing his heart out on the mat.

'Serves you right for being such a fool,' said young Mr Cashell, as annoyed as myself at the interruption. 'Never mind – we've all the night before us to see wonders.'

Shaynor clutched the counter, his handkerchief to his lips. When he brought it away I saw two bright red stains.

'I – I've got a bit of a rasped throat from smoking cigarettes,' he panted. 'I think I'll try a cubeb.'

'Better take some of this. I've been compounding while you've been away.' I handed him the brew.

' 'Twon't make me drunk, will it? I'm almost a teetotaller. My word! That's grateful and comforting.'

He set down the empty glass to cough afresh.

'Brr! But it was cold out there! I shouldn't care to be lying in my grave a night like this. Don't *you* ever have a sore throat from smoking?' He pocketed the handkerchief after a furtive peep.

'Oh, yes, sometimes,' I replied, wondering, while I spoke, into what agonies of terror I should fall if ever I saw those bright-red danger-signals under my nose. Young Mr Cashell among the batteries coughed slightly to show that he was quite ready to continue his scientific explanations, but I was thinking still of the girl with the rich voice and the significantly cut mouth, at whose command I had taken charge of the shop. It flashed across me that she distantly resembled the seductive shape on a gold-framed toilet-water advertisement whose charms were unholily heightened by the glare from the red bottle in the window. Turning to make sure, I saw Mr Shaynor's eyes bent in the same direction, and by instinct recognised that the flamboyant thing was to him a shrine. 'What do you take for your – cough?' I asked.

'Well, I'm the wrong side of the counter to believe much in patent medicines. But there are asthma cigarettes and there are pastilles. To tell you the truth, if you don't object to the smell, which is very like incense, I believe, though I'm not a Roman Catholic, Blaudett's Cathedral Pastilles relieve me as much as anything.'

'Let's try.' I had never raided a chemist's shop before, so I was thorough. We unearthed the pastilles – brown, gummy cones of benzoin – and set them alight under the toilet-water advertisement, where they fumed in thin blue spirals.

'Of course,' said Mr Shaynor, to my question, 'what one uses in the shop for one's self comes out of one's pocket. Why, stocktaking in our business is nearly the same as with jewellers – and I can't say more than that. But one gets them' – he pointed to the pastille-box – 'at trade-prices.' Evidently the censing of the gay, seven-tinted wench with the teeth was an established ritual which cost something.

'And when do we shut up shop?'

'We stay like this all night. The guv – old Mr Cashell – doesn't believe in locks and shutters as compared with electric light. Besides, it brings trade. I'll just sit here in the chair by the stove and write a letter, if you don't mind. Electricity isn't my prescription.'

The energetic young Mr Cashell snorted within, and Shaynor settled himself up in his chair over which he had thrown a staring red, black, and yellow Austrian jute blanket, rather like a table-cover. I cast about, amid patent-medicine pamphlets, for something to read, but finding little, returned to the manufacture of the new drink. The Italian warehouse took down its game and went to bed. Across the street blank shutters flung back the gaslight in cold smears; the dried pavement seemed to rough up in goose-flesh under the scouring of the savage wind, and we could hear, long ere he passed, the policeman flapping his arms to keep himself warm. Within, the flavours of cardamoms and chloric-ether disputed those of the pastilles and a score of drugs and perfume and soap scents. Our electric lights, set low down in the windows before the tun-bellied Rosamund jars, flung inward three monstrous daubs of red, blue, and green, that broke into kaleidoscopic lights on the faceted knobs of the drug-drawers, the cut-glass scent flagons, and the bulbs of the sparklet bottles. They flushed the white-tiled floor in gorgeous patches; splashed along the nickel-silver counter-rails, and turned the polished mahogany counter-panels to the likeness of intricate grained marbles – slabs of porphyry and malachite. Mr Shaynor unlocked a drawer, and ere he began to write, took out a meagre bundle of letters. From my place by the stove, I could see the scalloped edges of the paper with a flaring monogram in the corner and could even smell the reek of chypre. At each page he turned toward the toilet-water lady of the advertisement and devoured her with over-luminous eyes. He had drawn the Austrian blanket over his shoulders, and among those warring lights he looked more than ever the incarnation of a drugged moth – a tiger-moth as I thought.

He put his letter into an envelope, stamped it with stiff mechanical movements, and dropped it in the drawer. Then I became aware of the silence of a great city asleep – the silence that underlaid the even voice of the breakers along the seafront – a thick, tingling quiet of warm life stilled down for its appointed time, and unconsciously I moved about the glittering shop as one moves in a sickroom. Young Mr Cashell was adjusting some wire that crackled from time to time with the tense, knuckle-stretching sound of the electric spark. Upstairs, where a door shut and opened swiftly, I could hear his uncle coughing abed.

'Here,' I said, when the drink was properly warmed, 'take some of this, Mr Shaynor.'

He jerked in his chair with a start and a wrench, and held out his hand for the glass. The mixture, of a rich port-wine colour, frothed at the top.

'It looks,' he said, suddenly, 'it looks – those bubbles – like a string of pearls winking at you – rather like the pearls round that young lady's neck.' He turned again to the advertisement where the female in the dove-coloured corset had seen fit to put on all her pearls before she cleaned her teeth.

'Not bad, is it?' I said.

'Eh?'

He rolled his eyes heavily full on me, and, as I stared, I beheld all meaning and consciousness die out of the swiftly dilating pupils. His figure lost its stark rigidity, softened into the chair, and, chin on chest, hands dropped before him, he rested open-eyed, absolutely still.

'I'm afraid I've rather cooked Shaynor's goose,' I said, bearing the fresh drink to young Mr Cashell. 'Perhaps it was the chloric-ether.'

'Oh, he's all right.' The spade-bearded man glanced at him pityingly. 'Consumptives go off in those sort of dozes very often. It's exhaustion . . . I don't wonder. I dare say the liquor will do him good. It's grand stuff,' he finished his share appreciatively. 'Well, as I was saying – before he interrupted – about this little coherer. The pinch of dust, you see, is nickel-filings. The Hertzian waves, you see, come out of space from the station that despatches 'em, and all these little particles are attracted together – cohere, we call it – for just so long as the current passes through them. Now, it's important to remember that the current is an induced current. There are a good many kinds of induction – '

'Yes, but what *is* induction?'

'That's rather hard to explain untechnically. But the long and the short of it is that when a current of electricity passes through a wire there's a lot of magnetism present round that wire; and if you put another wire parallel to, and within what we call its magnetic field – why then, the second wire will also become charged with electricity.'

'On its own account?'

'On its own account.'

'Then let's see if I've got it correctly. Miles off, at Poole, or wherever it is – '

'It will be anywhere in ten years.'

'You've got a charged wire – '

'Charged with Hertzian waves which vibrate, say, two hundred and thirty million times a second.' Mr Cashell snaked his forefinger rapidly through the air.

'All right – a charged wire at Poole, giving out these waves into space. Then this wire of yours sticking out into space – on the roof of the house – in some mysterious way gets charged with those waves from Poole – '

'Or anywhere – it only happens to be Poole tonight.'

'And those waves set the coherer at work, just like an ordinary telegraph-office ticker?'

'No! That's where so many people make the mistake. The Hertzian waves wouldn't be strong enough to work a great heavy Morse instrument like ours. They can only just make that dust cohere, and while it coheres (a little while for a dot and a longer while for a dash) the current from this battery – the home battery' – he laid his hand on the thing – 'can get through to the Morse printing-machine to record the dot or dash. Let me make it clearer. Do you know anything about steam?'

'Very little. But go on.'

'Well, the coherer is like a steam-valve. Any child can open a valve and start a steamer's engines, because a turn of the hand lets in the main steam, doesn't it? Now, this home battery here ready to print is the main steam. The coherer is the valve, always ready to be turned on. The Hertzian wave is the child's hand that turns it.'

'I see. That's marvellous.'

'Marvellous, isn't it? And, remember, we're only at the beginning. There's nothing we shan't be able to do in ten years. I want to live – my God, how I want to live, and see it develop!' He looked through the door at Shaynor breathing lightly in his chair. 'Poor beast! And he wants to keep company with Fanny Brand.'

'Fanny *who*?' I said, for the name struck an obscurely familiar chord in my brain – something connected with a stained handkerchief, and the word 'arterial'.

'Fanny Brand – the girl you kept shop for.' He laughed. 'That's all I know about her, and for the life of me I can't see what Shaynor sees in her, or she in him.'

'*Can't* you see what he sees in her?' I insisted.

'Oh, yes, if *that's* what you mean. She's a great, big, fat lump of a girl, and so on. I suppose that's why he's so crazy after her. She isn't his sort. Well, it doesn't matter. My uncle says he's bound to die before the year's out. Your drink's given him a good sleep, at any rate.' Young Mr Cashell could not catch Mr Shaynor's face, which was half turned to the advertisement.

I stoked the stove anew, for the room was growing cold, and lighted another pastille. Mr Shaynor in his chair, never moving, looked through and over me with eyes as wide and lustreless as those of a dead hare.

'Poole's late,' said young Mr Cashell, when I stepped back. 'I'll just send them a call.'

He pressed a key in the semidarkness, and with a rending crackle there leaped between two brass knobs a spark, streams of sparks, and sparks again.

'Grand, isn't it? *That's* the Power – our unknown Power – kicking and fighting to be let loose,' said young Mr Cashell. 'There she goes – kick – kick – kick into space. I never get over the strangeness of it when I work a sending-machine – waves going into space, you know. T. R. is our call. Poole ought to answer with L. L. L.'

We waited two, three, five minutes. In that silence, of which the boom of the tide was an orderly part, I caught the clear '*kiss – kiss – kiss*' of the halliards on the roof, as they were blown against the installation-pole.

'Poole is not ready. I'll stay here and call you when he is.'

I returned to the shop, and set down my glass on a marble slab with a careless clink. As I did so, Shaynor rose to his feet, his eyes fixed once more on the advertisement, where the young woman bathed in the light from the red jar simpered pinkly over her pearls. His lips moved without cessation. I stepped nearer to listen. 'And threw – and threw – and threw,' he repeated, his face all sharp with some inexplicable agony.

I moved forward astonished. But it was then he

found words – delivered roundly and clearly. These: 'And threw warm gules on Madeleine's young breast.'

The trouble passed off his countenance, and he returned lightly to his place, rubbing his hands.

It had never occurred to me, though we had many times discussed reading and prize-competitions as a diversion, that Mr Shaynor ever read Keats, or could quote him at all appositely. There was, after all, a certain stained-glass effect of light on the high bosom of the highly-polished picture which might, by stretch of fancy, suggest, as a vile chromo recalls some incomparable canvas, the line he had spoken. Night, my drink, and solitude were evidently turning Mr Shaynor into a poet. He sat down again and wrote swiftly on his villainous notepaper, his lips quivering.

I shut the door into the inner office and moved up behind him. He made no sign that he saw or heard. I looked over his shoulder, and read, amid half-formed words, sentences, and wild scratches:

> Very cold it was. Very cold
> The hare – the hare – the hare –
> The birds –

He raised his head sharply, and frowned toward the blank shutters of the poulterer's shop where they jutted out against our window. Then one clear line came: 'The hare, in spite of fur, was very cold.'

The head, moving machine-like, turned right to the advertisement where the Blaudett's Cathedral Pastille reeked abominably. He grunted, and went on:

> Incense in a censer –
> Before her darling picture framed in gold –
> Maiden's picture – angel's portrait –

'Hsh!' said Mr Cashell guardedly from the inner office, as though in the presence of spirits. 'There's something coming through from somewhere; but it isn't Poole.' I heard the crackle of sparks as he depressed the keys of the transmitter. In my own brain, too, something crackled, or it might have been the hair on my head. Then I heard my own voice, in a harsh whisper: 'Mr Cashell, there is something coming through here, too. Leave me alone till I tell you.'

'But I thought you'd come to see this wonderful thing – sir,' indignantly at the end.

'Leave me alone till I tell you. Be quiet.'

I watched – I waited. Under the blue-veined hand – the dry hand of the consumptive – came away clear, without erasure:

> And my weak spirit fails
> To think how the dead must freeze –

he shivered as he wrote –

> Beneath the churchyard mould.

Then he stopped, laid the pen down, and leaned back.

For an instant, that was half an eternity, the shop spun before me in a rainbow-tinted whirl, in and through which my own soul most dispassionately considered my own soul as that fought with an overmastering fear. Then I smelt the strong smell of cigarettes from Mr Shaynor's clothing, and heard, as though it had been the rending of trumpets, the rattle of his breathing. I was still in my place of observation, much as one would watch a rifle-shot at the butts, half-bent, hands on my knees, and head within a few inches of the black, red, and yellow blanket of his shoulder. I was whispering encouragement, evidently to my other self, sounding sentences, such as men pronounce in dreams.

'If he has read Keats, it proves nothing. If he hasn't – like causes *must* beget like effects. There is no escape from this law. *You* ought to be grateful that you know "St Agnes' Eve" without the book; because, given the circumstances, such as Fanny Brand, who is the key of the enigma, and approximately represents the latitude and longitude of Fanny Brawne; allowing also for the bright red colour of the arterial blood upon the handkerchief, which was just what you were puzzling over in the shop just now; and counting the effect of the professional environment, here almost perfectly duplicated – the result is logical and inevitable. As inevitable as induction.'

Still, the other half of my soul refused to be comforted. It was cowering in some minute and inadequate corner – at an immense distance.

Hereafter, I found myself one person again, my hands still gripping my knees, and my eyes glued on the page before Mr Shaynor. As dreamers accept and explain the upheaval of landscapes and the resurrection of the dead, with excerpts from the evening hymn or the multiplication-table, so I had accepted the facts, whatever they might be, that I should witness, and had devised a theory, sane and plausible to my mind, that explained them all. Nay, I was even in advance of my facts, walking hurriedly before them, assured that they would fit my theory. And all that I now recall of that epoch-making theory are the lofty words: 'If he has read Keats it's the chloric-ether. If he hasn't, it's the identical bacillus, or Hertzian wave of tuberculosis, *plus* Fanny Brand and the professional status which, in conjunction with the mainstream of subconscious thought common to all mankind, has throwm up temporarily an induced Keats.'

Mr Shaynor returned to his work, erasing and rewriting as before with swiftness. Two or three blank pages he tossed aside. Then he wrote, muttering: 'The little smoke of a candle that goes out.'

'No,' he muttered. 'Little smoke – little smoke – little smoke. What else?' He thrust his chin forward toward the advertisement, whereunder the last of the Blaudett's Cathedral Pastilles fumed in its holder. 'Ah!' Then with relief: 'The little smoke that dies in moonlight cold.'

Evidently he was snared by the rhymes of his first verse, for he wrote and rewrote 'gold – cold – mould' many times. Again he sought inspiration from the advertisement, and set down, without erasure, the line I had overheard: 'And threw warm gules on Madeleine's young breast.' As I remembered the original it is 'fair' – a trite word – instead of 'young', and I found myself nodding approval, though I admitted that the attempt to reproduce 'its little smoke in pallid moonlight died' was a failure.

Followed without a break ten or fifteen lines of bald prose – the naked soul's confession of its physical yearning for its beloved – unclean as we count uncleanliness; unwholesome, but human exceedingly; the raw material, so it seemed to me in that hour and in that place, whence Keats wove the twenty-sixth, -seventh and -eighth stanzas of his poem. Shame I had none in overseeing this revelation; and my fear had gone with the smoke of the pastille.

'That's it,' I murmured. 'That's how it's blocked out. Go on! Ink it in, man. Ink it in!'

Mr Shaynor returned to broken verse wherein

'loveliness' was made to rhyme with a desire to look upon 'her empty dress'. He picked up a fold of the gay, soft blanket, spread it over one hand, caressed it with infinite tenderness, thought, muttered, traced some snatches which I could not decipher, shut his eyes drowsily, shook his head, and dropped the stuff. Here I found myself at fault, for I could not then see (as I do now) in what manner a red, black, and yellow Austrian blanket coloured his dreams.

In a few minutes he laid aside his pen, and, chin on hand, considered the shop with thoughtful and intelligent eyes. He threw down the blanket, rose, passed along a line of drug-drawers, and read the names on the labels aloud. Returning, he took from his desk Christie's *New Commercial Plants* and the old Culpeper that I had given him, opened and laid them side by side with a clerky air, all trace of passion gone from his face, read first in one and then in the other, and paused with pen behind his ear.

'What wonder of Heaven's coming now?' I thought.

'Manna – manna – manna,' he said at last, under wrinkled brows. 'That's what I wanted. Good! Now then! Now then! Good! Good! Oh, by God, that's good!' His voice rose and he spoke rightly and fully without a falter:

> Candied apple, quince and plum and gourd,
> And jellies smoother than the creamy curd,
> And lucent syrups tinct with cinnamon,
> Manna and dates in Argosy transferred
> From Fez; and spiced dainties, every one
> From silken Samarkand to cedared Lebanon.

He repeated it once more, using 'blander' for 'smoother' in the second line; then wrote it down without erasure, but this time (my set eyes missed no stroke of any word) he substituted 'soother' for his atrocious second thought, so that it came away under his hand as it is written in the book – as it is written in the book.

A wind went shouting down the street, and on the heels of the wind followed a spurt and rattle of rain.

After a smiling pause – and good right had he to smile – he began anew, always tossing the last sheet over his shoulder:

> The sharp rain falling on the windowpane,
> Rattling sleet – the windblown sleet.

Then prose: 'It is very cold of mornings when the wind brings rain and sleet with it. I heard the sleet on the windowpane outside, and thought of you, my darling. I am always thinking of you. I wish we could both run away like two lovers into the storm and get that little cottage by the sea which we are always thinking about, my own dear darling. We could sit and watch the sea beneath our windows. It would be a fairyland all of our own – a fairy sea – a fairy sea . . . '

He stopped, raised his head, and listened. The steady drone of the Channel along the seafront that had borne us company so long leaped up a note to the sudden fuller surge that signals the change from ebb to flood. It beat in like the change of step throughout an army – this renewed pulse of the sea – and filled our ears till they, accepting it, marked it no longer.

> A fairyland for you and me
> Across the foam – beyond . . .
> A magic foam, a perilous sea.

He grunted again with effort and bit his underlip. My throat dried, but I dared not gulp to moisten it lest I should break the spell that was drawing him nearer and nearer to the high-water mark but two of the sons of Adam have reached. Remember that in all the millions permitted there are no more than five – five little lines – of which one can say: 'These are the pure Magic. These are the clear Vision. The rest is only poetry.' And Mr Shaynor was playing hot and cold with two of them!

I vowed no unconscious thought of mine should influence the blindfold soul, and pinned myself desperately to the other three, repeating and re-repeating:

A savage spot as holy and enchanted
As e'er beneath a waning moon was haunted
By woman wailing for her demon lover.

But though I believed my brain thus occupied, my every sense hung upon the writing under the dry, bony hand, all brown-fingered with chemicals and cigarette-smoke.

Our windows fronting on the dangerous foam,

(he wrote, after long, irresolute snatches), and then –

Our open casements facing desolate seas
Forlorn – forlorn –

Here again his face grew peaked and anxious with that sense of loss I had first seen when the Power snatched him. But this time the agony was tenfold keener. As I watched it mounted like mercury in the tube. It lighted his face from within till I thought the visibly scourged soul must leap forth naked between his jaws, unable to endure. A drop of sweat trickled from my forehead down my nose and splashed on the back of my hand.

> Our windows facing on the desolate seas
> And pearly foam of magic fairyland –

'Not yet – not yet,' he muttered, 'wait a minute. *Please* wait a minute. I shall get it then:

> Our magic windows fronting on the sea,
> The dangerous foam of desolate seas . . .
> For aye.

Ouh, my God!'

From head to heel he shook – shook from the marrow of his bones outwards – then leaped to his feet with raised arms, and slid the chair screeching across the tiled floor where it struck the drawers behind and fell with a jar. Mechanically, I stooped to recover it.

As I rose, Mr Shaynor was stretching and yawning at leisure.

'I've had a bit of a doze,' he said. 'How did I come to knock the chair over? You look rather –'

'The chair startled me,' I answered. 'It was so sudden in this quiet.'

Young Mr Cashell behind his shut door was offendedly silent.

'I suppose I must have been dreaming,' said Mr Shaynor.

'I suppose you must,' I said. 'Talking of dreams – I – I noticed you writing – before –'

He flushed consciously.

'I meant to ask you if you've ever read anything written by a man called Keats.'

'Oh! I haven't much time to read poetry, and I can't

say that I remember the name exactly. Is he a popular writer?'

'Middling. I thought you might know him because he's the only poet who was ever a druggist. And he's rather what's called the lover's poet.'

'Indeed. I must dip into him. What did he write about?'

'A lot of things. Here's a sample that may interest you.'

Then and there, carefully, I repeated the verse he had twice spoken and once written not ten minutes ago.

'Ah! Anybody could see he was a druggist from that line about the tinctures and syrups. It's a fine tribute to our profession.'

'I don't know,' said young Mr Cashell, with icy politeness, opening the door one half-inch, 'if you still happen to be interested in our trifling experiments. But, should such be the case – '

I drew him aside, whispering, 'Shaynor seemed going off into some sort of fit when I spoke to you just now. I thought, even at the risk of being rude, it wouldn't do to take you off your instruments just as the call was coming through. Don't you see?'

'Granted – granted as soon as asked,' he said, unbending. 'I *did* think it a shade odd at the time. So that was why he knocked the chair down?'

'I hope I haven't missed anything,' I said.

'I'm afraid I can't say that, but you're just in time for the end of a rather curious performance. You can come in too, Mr Shaynor. Listen, while I read it off.'

The Morse instrument was ticking furiously. Mr Cashell interpreted: ' "K.K.V. Can make nothing of your signals." ' A pause. ' "M.M.V. M.M.V. Signals unintelligible. Purpose anchor Sandown Bay. Examine instruments tomorrow." Do you know what that means? It's a couple of men-o'-war working Marconi signals off the Isle of Wight. They are trying to talk to each other. Neither can read the other's messages, but all their messages are being taken in by our receiver here. They've been going on for ever so long. I wish you could have heard it.'

'How wonderful!' I said. 'Do you mean we're overhearing Portsmouth ships trying to talk to each other – that we're eavesdropping across half South England?'

'Just that. Their transmitters are all right, but their receivers are out of order, so they only get a dot here and a dash there. Nothing clear.'

'Why is that?'

'God knows – and Science will know tomorrow. Perhaps the induction is faulty; perhaps the receivers aren't tuned to receive just the number of vibrations per second that the transmitter sends. Only a word here and there. Just enough to tantalise.'

Again the Morse sprang to life.

'That's one of 'em complaining now. Listen: "Disheartening – most disheartening." It's quite pathetic. Have you ever seen a spiritualistic seance? It reminds me of that sometimes – odds and ends of messages coming out of nowhere – a word here and there – no good at all.'

'But mediums are all impostors,' said Mr Shaynor, in the doorway, lighting an asthma-cigarette. 'They only do it for the money they can make. I've seen 'em.'

'Here's Poole, at last – clear as a bell. L.L.L. *Now* we shan't be long.' Mr Cashell rattled the keys merrily. 'Anything you'd like to tell 'em?'

'No, I don't think so,' I said. 'I'll go home and get to bed. I'm feeling a little tired.'

The Bee Boy's Song

Bees! Bees! Hark to your bees!
'Hide from your neighbours as much as you please,
But all that has happened, to us you must tell.
Or else we will give you no honey to sell!'

A maiden in her glory,
Upon her wedding-day,
Must tell her Bees the story,
Or else they'll fly away.
Fly away – die away –
Dwindle down and leave you!
But if you don't deceive your Bees,
Your Bees will not deceive you.

Marriage, birth or buryin',
News across the seas,
All you're sad or merry in,
You must tell the Bees.
Tell 'em coming in an' out,
Where the Fanners fan,
'Cause the Bees are justabout
As curious as a man!

Don't you wait where trees are,
When the lightnings play;
Nor don't you hate where Bees are,
Or else they'll pine away.
Pine away – dwine away –
Anything to leave you!
But if you never grieve your Bees,
Your Bees'll never grieve you!

'Dymchurch Flit'

Just at dusk, a soft September rain began to fall on the hop-pickers. The mothers wheeled the bouncing perambulators out of the gardens; bins were put away, and tally-books made up. The young couples strolled home, two to each umbrella, and the single men walked behind them laughing. Dan and Una, who had been picking after their lessons, marched off to roast potatoes at the oast house, where old Hobden, with Blue-eyed Bess, his lurcher dog, lived all the month through, drying the hops.

They settled themselves, as usual, on the sack-strewn cot in front of the fires, and, when Hobden drew up the shutter, stared, as usual, at the flameless bed of coals spouting its heat up the dark well of the old-fashioned roundel. Slowly he cracked off a few fresh pieces of coal, packed them, with fingers that never flinched, exactly where they would do most good; slowly he reached behind him till Dan tilted the potatoes into his iron scoop of a hand; carefully he arranged them round the fire, and then stood for a moment, black against the glare. As he closed the shutter, the oast house seemed dark before the day's end, and he lit the candle in the lanthorn. The children liked all these things because they knew them so well.

The Bee Boy, Hobden's son, who is not quite right in his head, though he can do anything with bees, slipped in like a shadow. They only guessed it when Bess's stump-tail wagged against them.

A big voice began singing outside in the drizzle:

'Old Mother Laidinwool had nigh twelve
months been dead,
She heard the hops were doin' well, and
then popped up her head.'

'There can't be two people made to holler like that!' cried old Hobden, wheeling round.

'For, says she, "The boys I've picked
with when I was young and fair,
They're bound to be at hoppin', and I'm – " '

A man showed at the doorway.

'Well, well! They do say hoppin'll draw the very deadest, and now I belieft 'em. You, Tom? Tom Shoesmith?' Hobden lowered his lanthorn.

'You're a hem of a time makin' your mind to it, Ralph!' The stranger strode in – three full inches taller than Hobden, a grey-whiskered, brown-faced giant with clear blue eyes. They shook hands, and the children could hear the hard palms rasp together.

'You ain't lost none o' your grip,' said Hobden. 'Was it thirty or forty year back you broke my head at Peasmarsh Fair?'

'Only thirty, an' no odds 'tween us regardin' heads, neither. You had it back at me with a hop-pole. How did we get home that night? Swimmin'?'

'Same way the pheasant come into Gubbs's pocket – by a little luck an' a deal o' conjurin'.' Old Hobden laughed in his deep chest.

'I see you've not forgot your way about the woods. D'ye do any o' *this* still?' The stranger pretended to look along a gun.

Hobden answered with a quick movement of the

hand as though he were pegging down a rabbit-wire.

'No. *That's* all that's left me now. Age she must as Age she can. An' what's your news since all these years?'

'Oh, I've bin to Plymouth, I've bin to Dover –
I've bin ramblin', boys, the wide world over,'

the man answered cheerily. 'I reckon I know as much of Old England as most.' He turned towards the children and winked boldly.

'I lay they told you a sight o' lies, then. I've been into England fur as Wiltsheer once. I was cheated proper over a pair of hedgin'-gloves,' said Hobden.

'There's fancy-talkin' everywhere. You've cleaved to your own parts pretty middlin' close, Ralph.'

'Can't shift an old tree 'thout it dyin',' Hobden chuckled. 'An' I be no more anxious to die than you look to be to help me with my hops tonight.'

The great man leaned against the brickwork of the roundel, and swung his arms abroad. 'Hire me!' was all he said, and they stumped upstairs laughing.

The children heard their shovels rasp on the cloth where the yellow hops lie drying above the fires, and all the oast house filled with the sweet, sleepy smell as they were turned.

'Who is it?' Una whispered to the Bee Boy.

'Dunno, no more'n you – if *you* dunno,' said he, and smiled.

The voices on the drying-floor talked and chuckled together, and the heavy footsteps moved back and forth. Presently a hop-pocket dropped through the press-hole overhead, and stiffened and fattened as they shovelled it full. 'Clank!' went the press, and rammed the loose stuff into tight cake.

'Gently!' they heard Hobden cry. 'You'll bust her crop if you lay on so. You be as careless as Gleason's bull, Tom. Come an' sit by the fires. She'll do now.'

They came down, and as Hobden opened the shutter to see if the potatoes were done Tom Shoesmith said to the children, 'Put a plenty salt on 'em. That'll show you the sort o' man *I* be.' Again he winked, and again the Bee Boy laughed and Una stared at Dan.

'*I* know what sort o' man you be,' old Hobden grunted, groping for the potatoes round the fire.

'Do ye?' Tom went on behind his back. 'Some of us can't abide Horseshoes, or Church Bells, or Running Water; an', talkin' o' runnin' water' – he turned to Hobden, who was backing out of the roundel – 'd'you mind the great floods at Robertsbridge, when the miller's man was drowned in the street?'

'Middlin' well.' Old Hobden let himself down on the coals by the fire-door. 'I was courtin' my woman on the Marsh that year. Carter to Mus' Plum I was, gettin' ten shillin's week. Mine was a Marsh woman.'

'Won'erful odd-gates place – Romney Marsh,' said Tom Shoesmith. 'I've heard say the world's divided like into Europe, Ashy, Afriky, Ameriky, Australy, an' Romney Marsh.'

'The Marsh folk think so,' said Hobden. 'I had a hem o' trouble to get my woman to leave it.'

'Where did she come out of? I've forgot, Ralph.'

'Dymchurch under the Wall,' Hobden answered, a potato in his hand.

'Then she'd be a Pett – or a Whitgift, would she?'

'Whitgift.' Hobden broke open the potato and ate it with the curious neatness of men who make most of their meals in the blowy open. 'She growed to be quite reasonable-like after livin' in the Weald awhile, but our first twenty year or two she was odd-fashioned, no bounds. And she was a won'erful hand with bees.' He cut away a little piece of potato and threw it out to the door.

'Ah! I've heard say the Whitgifts could see further through a millstone than most,' said Shoesmith. 'Did she, now?'

'She was honest-innocent of any nigromancin',' said Hobden. 'Only she'd read signs and sinnifications out o' birds flyin', stars fallin', bees hivin', and such. An, she'd lie awake – listenin' for calls, she said.'

'That don't prove naught,' said Tom. 'All Marsh folk has been smugglers since time everlastin'. 'Twould be in her blood to listen out o' nights.'

'Nature-ally,' old Hobden replied, smiling. 'I mind when there was smugglin' a sight nearer us than what the Marsh be. But that wasn't my woman's trouble. 'Twas a passel o' no-sense talk' – he dropped his voice – 'about Pharisees.'

'Yes. I've heard Marsh men belieft in 'em.' Tom looked straight at the wide-eyed children beside Bess.

'Pharisees,' cried Una. 'Fairies? Oh, *I* see!'

'People o' the Hills,' said the Bee Boy, throwing half of his potato towards the door.

'There you be!' said Hobden, pointing at him. 'My boy – he has her eyes and her out-gate senses. That's what *she* called 'em!'

'And what did you think of it all?'

'Um – um,' Hobden rumbled. 'A man that uses fields an' shaws after dark as much as I've done, he don't go out of his road excep' for keepers.'

'But settin' that aside?' said Tom, coaxingly. 'I saw ye throw the Good Piece out-at-doors just now. Do ye believe or – *do* ye?'

'There was a great black eye to that tater,' said Hobden indignantly.

'My liddle eye didn't see un, then. It looked as if you meant it for – for anyone that might need it. But settin' that aside, d'ye believe or – *do* ye?'

'I ain't sayin' nothin', because I've heard naught, an' I've see naught. But if you was to say there was more things after dark in the shaws than men, or fur, or feather, or fin, I dunno as I'd go far about to call you a liar. Now turn again, Tom. What's your say?'

'I'm like you. I say nothin'. But I'll tell you a tale, an' you can fit it *as* how you please.'

'Passel o' no-sense stuff,' growled Hobden, but he filled his pipe.

'The Marsh men they call it Dymchurch Flit,' Tom went on slowly. 'Hap you have heard it?'

'My woman she've told it me scores o' times. Dunno as I didn't end by belieftin' it – sometimes.'

Hobden crossed over as he spoke, and sucked with his pipe at the yellow lanthorn flame. Tom rested one great elbow on one great knee, where he sat among the coal.

'Have you ever bin in the Marsh?' he said to Dan.

'Only as far as Rye, once,' Dan answered.

'Ah, that's but the edge. Back behind of her there's steeples settin' beside churches, an' wise women settin' beside their doors, an' the sea settin' above the land, an' ducks herdin' wild in the diks' (he meant ditches). 'The Marsh is justabout riddled with diks an' sluices, an' tide-gates an' water-lets. You can hear 'em bubblin' an' grummelin' when the tide works in 'em, an' then you hear the sea rangin' left and right-handed all up along the Wall. You've seen how flat she is – the Marsh? You'd think nothin' easier than to walk eend-on acrost her? Ah, but the diks an' the water-lets, they twists the roads about as ravelly as witch-yarn on the spindles. So ye get all turned round in broad daylight.'

'That's because they've dreened the waters into the diks,' said Hobden. 'When I courted my woman the rushes was green – Eh me! the rushes was green – an' the Bailiff o' the Marshes he rode up and down as free as the fog.'

'Who was he?' said Dan.

'Why, the Marsh fever an' ague. He've clapped me on the shoulder once or twice till I shook proper. But now the dreenin' off of the waters have done away with the fevers; so they make a joke, like, that the Bailiff o' the Marshes broke his neck in a dik. A won'erful place for bees an' ducks 'tis too.'

'An' old,' Tom went on. 'Flesh an' Blood have been there since Time Everlastin' Beyond. Well, now, speakin' among themselves, the Marsh men say that from Time Everlastin' Beyond, the Pharisees favoured the Marsh above the rest of Old England. I lay the Marsh men ought to know. They've been out after dark, father an' son, smugglin' some one thing or t'other, since ever wool grew to sheep's backs. They say there was always a middlin' few Pharisees to be seen on the Marsh. Impident as rabbits, they was. They'd dance on the nakid roads in the nakid daytime; they'd flash their liddle green lights along the diks, comin' an' goin', like honest smugglers. Yes, an' times they'd lock the church doors against parson an' clerk of Sundays.'

'That 'ud be smugglers layin' in the lace or the brandy till they could run it out o' the Marsh. I've told my woman so,' said Hobden.

'I'll lay she didn't belieft it, then – not if she was a Whitgift. A won'erful choice place for Pharisees, the Marsh, by all accounts, till Queen Bess's father he come in with his Reformatories.'

'Would that be a Act o' Parliament like?' Hobden asked.

'Sure–ly. Can't do nothing in Old England without Act, Warrant, an' Summons. He got his Act allowed him, an', they say, Queen Bess's father he used the parish churches something shameful. Justabout tore the gizzards out of I dunnamany. Some folk in England they held with 'en; but some they saw it different, an' it eended in 'em takin' sides an' burnin' each other no bounds, accordin' which side was top, time bein'. That tarrified the Pharisees: for Goodwill among Flesh an' Blood is meat an' drink to 'em, an' ill-will is poison.'

'Same as bees,' said the Bee Boy. 'Bees won't stay by a house where there's hating.'

'True,' said Tom. 'This Reformatories tarrified the Pharisees same as the reaper goin' round a last stand o' wheat tarrifies rabbits. They packed into the Marsh from all parts, and they says, "Fair or foul, we must flit out o' this, for Merry England's done with, an' we're reckoned among the Images." '

'Did they *all* see it that way?' said Hobden.

'All but one that was called Robin – if you've heard of him. What are you laughin' at?' Tom turned to Dan. 'The Pharisees's trouble didn't tech Robin, because he'd cleaved middlin' close to people, like. No more he never meant to go out of Old England – not he; so he was sent messagin' for help among Flesh an' Blood. But Flesh an' Blood must always think of their own concerns, an' Robin couldn't get *through* at 'em, ye see. They thought it was tide-echoes off the Marsh.'

'What did you – what did the fai – Pharisees want?' Una asked.

'A boat, to be sure. Their liddle wings could no more cross Channel than so many tired butterflies. A boat an' a crew they desired to sail 'em over to France, where yet awhile folks hadn't tore down the Images. They couldn't abide cruel Canterbury Bells ringin' to Bulverhithe for more pore men an' women to be burnded, nor the King's proud messenger ridin' through the land givin' orders to tear down the Images. They couldn't abide it no shape. Nor yet they couldn't get their boat an' crew to flit by without Leave an' Goodwill from Flesh an' Blood; an' Flesh an' Blood came an' went about its own business the while the Marsh was swarvin' up, an' swarvin' up with Pharisees from all England over, strivin' all means to get *through* at Flesh an' Blood to tell 'em their sore need . . . I don't know as you've ever heard say Pharisees are like chickens?'

'My woman used to say that too,' said Hobden, folding his brown arms.

'They be. You run too many chickens together, an' the ground sickens, like, an' you get a squat, an' your chickens die. Same way, you crowd Pharisees all in one place – *they* don't die, but Flesh an' Blood walkin' among 'em is apt to sick up an' pine off. *They* don't mean it, an' Flesh an' Blood don't know it, but that's the truth – as I've heard. The Pharisees through bein' all stenched up an' frighted, an' trying' to come *through* with their supplications, they nature-ally changed the thin airs an' humours in Flesh an' Blood. It lay on the Marsh like thunder. Men saw their churches ablaze with the wildfire in the windows after dark; they saw their cattle scatterin' an' no man scarin'; their sheep flockin' an' no man drivin'; their horses latherin' an' no man leadin'; they saw the liddle low green lights more than ever in the dik-sides; they heard the liddle feet patterin' more than ever round the houses; an' night an' day, day an' night, 'twas all as though they were bein' creeped up on, an' hinted at by Someone or other that couldn't rightly shape their trouble. Oh, I lay they sweated! Man an' maid, woman an' child, their nature done 'em no service all the weeks while the Marsh was swarvin' up with Pharisees. But they was Flesh an' Blood, an' Marsh men before all. They reckoned the signs sinnified trouble for the Marsh. Or that the sea 'ud rear up against Dymchurch Wall an' they'd be drownded like Old Winchelsea; or that the Plague was comin'. So they looked for the meanin' in the sea or in the clouds – far an' high up. They never thought to look near an' knee-high, where they could see naught.

'Now there was a poor widow at Dymchurch under the Wall, which, lacking man or property, she had the more time for feeling; and she come to feel there was a Trouble outside her doorstep bigger an' heavier than aught she'd ever carried over it. She had two sons – one born blind, an' t'other struck dumb through fallin' off the Wall when he was liddle. They was men grown, but not wage-earnin', an' she worked for 'em, keepin' bees and answerin' Questions.'

'What sort of questions?' said Dan.

'Like where lost things might be found, an' what to put about a crooked baby's neck, an' how to join parted sweethearts. She felt the Trouble on the Marsh same as eels feel thunder. She was a wise woman.'

'My woman was won'erful weather-tender, too,' said Hobden. 'I've seen her brish sparks like off an anvil out of her hair in thunderstorms. But she never laid out to answer Questions.'

'This woman was a Seeker, like, an' Seekers they sometimes find. One night, while she lay abed, hot an' achin', there come a Dream an' tapped at her window, an' "Widow Whitgift," it said, "Widow Whitgift!"

'First, by the wings an' the whistlin', she thought it was peewits, but last she arose an' dressed herself, an' opened her door to the Marsh, an' she felt the Trouble an' the Groanin' all about her, strong as fever an' ague, an' she calls: "What is it? Oh, what is it?"

'Then 'twas all like the frogs in the diks peepin'; then 'twas all like the reeds in the diks clip-clappin'; an' then the great Tide-wave rummelled along the Wall, an' she couldn't hear proper.

'Three times she called, an' three times the Tide-wave did her down. But she catched the quiet between, an' she cries out, "What is the Trouble on the Marsh that's been lying down with my heart an' arising with my body this month gone?" She felt a liddle hand lay hold on her gown-hem, an' she stooped to the pull o' that liddle hand.'

Tom Shoesmith spread his huge fist before the fire and smiled at it as he went on.

' "Will the sea drown the Marsh?" she says. She was a Marsh woman first an' foremost.

' "No," says the liddle voice. "Sleep sound for all o' that."

' "Is the Plague comin' to the Marsh?" she says. Them was all the ills she knowed.

' "No. Sleep sound for all o' that," says Robin.

'She turned about, half mindful to go in, but the liddle voices grieved that shrill an' sorrowful she turns back, an' she cries: "If it is not a Trouble of Flesh an' Blood, what can I do?"

'The Pharisees cried out upon her from all round to fetch them a boat to sail to France, an' come back no more.

' "There's a boat on the Wall," she says, "but I can't push it down to the sea, nor sail it when 'tis there."

' "Lend us your sons," says all the Pharisees. "Give 'em Leave an' Goodwill to sail it for us, Mother – O Mother!"

' "One's dumb, an' t'other's blind," she says. "But all the dearer me for that; and you'll lose them in the big sea." The voices justabout pierced through her; an' there was children's voices too. She stood out all she could, but she couldn't rightly stand against *that*. So she says: "If you can draw my sons for your job, I'll not hinder 'em. You can't ask no more of a Mother."

'She saw them liddle green lights dance an' cross till she was dizzy; she heard them liddle feet patterin' by the thousand; she heard cruel Canterbury Bells ringing to Bulverhithe, an' she heard the great Tide-wave ranging along the Wall. That was while the Pharisees was workin' a Dream to wake her two sons asleep: an' while she bit on her fingers she saw them two she'd bore come out an' pass her with never a word. She followed 'em, cryin' pitiful, to the old boat on the Wall, an' that they took an' runned down to the Sea.

'When they'd stepped mast an' sail the blind son speaks: "Mother, we're waitin' your Leave an' Goodwill to take Them over." '

Tom Shoesmith threw back his head and half shut his eyes.

'Eh, me!' he said. 'She was a fine, valiant woman, the Widow Whitgift. She stood twistin' the ends of her long hair over her fingers, an' she shook like a poplar, makin' up her mind. The Pharisees all about they hushed their children from cryin' an' they waited dumb-still. She was all their dependence. 'Thout her Leave an' Goodwill they could not pass; for she was the Mother. So she shook like a aps tree makin' up her mind. 'Last she drives the word past her teeth, an' "Go!" she says. "Go with my Leave an' Goodwill."

'Then I saw – then, they say, she had to brace back same as if she was wadin' in tide water; for the Pharisees just about flowed past her – down the beach to the boat, *I* dunnamany of 'em – with their wives an' childern an' valooables, all escapin' out of cruel Old England. Silver you could hear clinkin', an' liddle bundles hove down dunt on the bottom-boards, an' passels o' liddle swords an' shields raklin', an' liddle fingers an' toes scratchin' on the boatside to board her when the two sons pushed her off. That boat she sunk lower an' lower, but all the Widow could see in it was her boys movin' hampered-like to get at the tackle. Up sail they did, an' away they went, deep as a Rye barge, away into the offshore mists, an' the Widow Whitgift she sat down an' eased her grief till mornin' light.'

'I never heard she was *all* alone,' said Hobden.

'I remember now. The one called Robin, he stayed with her, they tell. She was all too grievous to listen to his promises.'

'Ah! She should ha' made her bargain beforehand. I allus told my woman so!' Hobden cried.

'No. She loaned her sons for a pure love-loan, bein' as she sensed the Trouble on the Marshes, an' was simple good-willin' to ease it.' Tom laughed softly. 'She done that. Yes, she done that! From Hithe to Bulverhithe, fretty man an' petty maid, ailin' woman an' wailin' child, they took the advantage of the change in the thin airs just about *as* soon as the Pharisees flitted. Folks come out fresh an' shinin' all over the Marsh like snails after wet. An' that while the Widow Whitgift sat grievin' on the Wall. She might have belieft us – she might have trusted her sons would be sent back! She fussed, no bounds, when their boat come in after three days.'

'And, of course, the sons were both quite cured?' said Una.

'No–o. That would have been out o' nature. She got 'em back *as* she sent 'em. The blind man he hadn't seen naught of anythin', an' the dumb man nature-ally he couldn't say aught of what he'd seen. I reckon that was why the Pharisees pitched on 'em for the ferryin' job.'

'But what did you – what did Robin promise the Widow?' said Dan.

'What *did* he promise, now?' Tom pretended to think. 'Wasn't your woman a Whitgift, Ralph? Didn't she ever say?'

'She told me a passel o' no-sense stuff when he was born.' Hobden pointed at his son. 'There was always to be one of 'em that could see further into a millstone than most.'

'Me! That's me!' said the Bee Boy so suddenly that they all laughed.

'I've got it now!' cried Tom, slapping his knee. 'So long as Whitgift blood lasted, Robin promised there would allers be one o' her stock that – that no Trouble 'ud lie on, no Maid 'ud sigh on, no Night could frighten, no Fright could harm, no Harm could make sin, an' no Woman could make a fool of.'

'Well, ain't that just me?' said the Bee Boy, where he

sat in the silver square of the great September moon that was staring into the oast house door.

'They was the exact words she told me when we first found he wasn't like others. But it beats me how you known 'em,' said Hobden.

'Aha! There's more under my hat besides hair!' Tom laughed and stretched himself. 'When I've seen these two young folk home, we'll make a night of old days, Ralph, with passin' old tales – eh? An' where might you live?' he said, gravely, to Dan. 'An' do you think your Pa 'ud give me a drink for takin' you there, Missy?'

They giggled so at this that they had to run out. Tom picked them both up, set one on each broad shoulder, and tramped across the ferny pasture where the cows puffed milky puffs at them in the moonlight.

'Oh, Puck! Puck! I guessed you right from when you talked about the salt. How could you ever do it?' Una cried, swinging along delighted.

'Do what?' he said, and climbed the stile by the pollard oak.

'Pretend to be Tom Shoesmith,' said Dan, and they ducked to avoid the two little ashes that grow by the bridge over the brook. Tom was almost running.

'Yes. That's my name, Mus' Dan,' he said, hurrying over the silent shining lawn, where a rabbit sat by the big white-thorn near the croquet ground. 'Here you be.' He strode into the old kitchen yard, and slid them down as Ellen came to ask questions.

'I'm helping in Mus' Spray's oast house,' he said to her. 'No, I'm no foreigner. I knowed this country 'fore your mother was born; an' – yes, it's dry work oastin', Miss. Thank you.'

Ellen went to get a jug, and the children went in – magicked once more by Oak, Ash, and Thorn!

A Three-Part Song

I'm just in love with all these three,
The Weald an' the Marsh an' the Down countrie;
Nor I don't know which I love the most,
The Weald or the Marsh or the white chalk coast!

I've buried my heart in a ferny hill,
Twix' a liddle low shaw an' a great high gill.
Oh, hop-bine yaller an' wood-smoke blue,
I reckon you'll keep her middling true!

I've loosed my mind for to out an' run
On a Marsh that was old when Kings begun:
Oh, Romney level an' Brenzett reeds,
I reckon you know what my mind needs!

I've given my soul to the Southdown grass,
An' sheep-bells tinkled where you pass.
Oh, Firle an' Ditchling an' sails at sea,
I reckon you keep my soul for me!

The House Surgeon

On an evening after Easter Day, I sat at a table in a homeward bound steamer's smoking-room, where half a dozen of us told ghost stories. As our party broke up, a man, playing patience in the next alcove, said to me: 'I didn't quite catch the end of that last story about the curse on the family's first-born.'

'It turned out to be drains,' I explained. 'As soon as new ones were put into the house the curse was lifted, I believe. I never knew the people myself.'

'Ah! I've had *my* drains up twice; I'm on gravel too.'

'You don't mean to say you've a ghost in your house? Why didn't you join our party?'

'Any more orders, gentlemen, before the bar closes?' the steward interrupted.

'Sit down again, and have one with me,' said the patience player. 'No, it isn't a ghost. Our trouble is more depression than anything else.'

'How interesting! Then it's nothing anyone can see?'

'It's – it's nothing worse than a little depression. And the odd part is that there hasn't been a death in the house since it was built – in 1863. The lawyer said so. That decided me – my good lady, rather – and he made me pay an extra thousand for it.'

'How curious! Unusual, too!' I said.

'Yes, ain't it? It was built for three sisters – Moultrie was the name – three old maids. They all lived together; the eldest owned it. I bought it from her lawyer a few years ago, and if I've spent a pound on the place first and last, I must have spent five thousand. Electric light, new servants' wing, garden – all that sort of thing. A man and his family ought to be happy after so much expense, ain't it?' He looked at me through the bottom of his glass.

'Does it affect your family much?'

'My good lady – she's a Greek, by the way – and myself are middle-aged. We can bear up against depression; but it's hard on my little girl. I say little; but she's twenty. We send her visiting to escape it. She almost lived at hotels and hydros, last year, but that isn't pleasant for her. She used to be a canary – a perfect canary – always singing. You ought to hear her. She doesn't sing now. That sort of thing's unwholesome for the young, ain't it?'

'Can't you get rid of the place?' I suggested.

'Not except at a sacrifice, and we are fond of it. Just suits us three. We'd love it if we were allowed.'

'What do you mean by not being allowed?'

'I mean because of the depression. It spoils everything.'

'What's it like exactly?'

'I couldn't very well explain. It must be seen to be appreciated, as the auctioneers say. Now, I was much impressed by the story you were telling just now.'

'It wasn't true,' I said.

'My tale is true. If you would do me the pleasure to come down and spend a night at my little place, you'd learn more than you would if I talked till morning. Very likely 'twouldn't touch your good self at all. You might be – immune, ain't it? On the other hand, if this influenza-influence *does* happen to affect you, why, I think it will be an experience.'

While he talked he gave me his card, and I read his name was L. Maxwell McLeod, Esq., of Holmescroft. A City address was tucked away in a corner.

'My business,' he added, 'used to be furs. If you are interested in furs – I've given thirty years of my life to 'em.'

'You're very kind,' I murmured.

'Far from it, I assure you. I can meet you next Saturday afternoon anywhere in London you choose to name, and I'll be only too happy to motor you down. It ought to be a delightful run at this time of year – the rhododendrons will be out. I mean it. You don't know how truly I mean it. Very probably – it won't affect you at all. And – I think I may say I have the finest collection of narwhal tusks in the world. All the best skins and horns have to go through London, and L. Maxwell McLeod, he knows where they come from, and where they go to. That's his business.'

For the rest of the voyage up-channel Mr McLeod talked to me of the assembling, preparation, and sale of the rarer furs; and told me things about the manufacture of fur-lined coats which quite shocked me. Somehow or other, when we landed on Wednesday, I found myself pledged to spend that weekend with him at Holmescroft.

On Saturday he met me with a well-groomed motor, and ran me out in an hour and a half to an exclusive residential district of dustless roads and elegantly designed country villas, each standing in from three to five acres of perfectly appointed land. He told me land was selling at eight hundred pounds the acre, and the new golf links, whose Queen Anne pavilion we passed, had cost nearly twenty-four thousand pounds to create.

Holmescroft was a large, two-storeyed, low, creeper-covered residence. A verandah at the south side gave on to a garden and two tennis courts, separated by a tasteful iron fence from a most park-like meadow of five or six acres, where two Jersey cows grazed. Tea was ready in the shade of a promising copper beech, and I could see groups on the lawn of young men and maidens appropriately clothed, playing lawn tennis in the sunshine.

'A pretty scene, ain't it?' said Mr McLeod. 'My good lady's sitting under the tree, and that's my little girl in pink on the far court. But I'll take you to your room, and you can see 'em all later.'

He led me through a wide parquet-floored hall furnished in pale lemon, with huge cloisonné vases, an ebonised and gold grand piano, and banks of pot flowers in Benares brass bowls, up a pale oak staircase to a spacious landing, where there was a green velvet settee trimmed with silver. The blinds were down, and the light lay in parallel lines on the floors.

He showed me my room, saying cheerfully: 'You may be a little tired. One often is without knowing it after a run through traffic. Don't come down till you feel quite restored. We shall all be in the garden.'

My room was rather warm, and smelt of perfumed soap. I threw up the window at once, but it opened so close to the floor and worked so clumsily that I came within an ace of pitching out, where I should certainly have ruined a rather lopsided laburnum below. As I set about washing off the journey's dust, I began to feel a little tired. But, I reflected, I had not come down here in this weather and among these new surroundings to be depressed; so I began to whistle.

And it was just then that I was aware of a little grey

shadow, as it might have been a snowflake seen against the light, floating at an immense distance in the background of my brain. It annoyed me, and I shook my head to get rid of it. Then my brain telegraphed that it was the forerunner of a swift-striding gloom which there was yet time to escape if I would force my thoughts away from it, as a man leaping for life forces his body forward and away from the fall of a wall. But the gloom overtook me before I could take in the meaning of the message. I moved toward the bed, every nerve already aching with the foreknowledge of the pain that was to be dealt it, and sat down, while my amazed and angry soul dropped, gulf by gulf, into that horror of great darkness which is spoken of in the Bible, and which, as auctioneers say, must be experienced to be appreciated.

Despair upon despair, misery upon misery, fear after fear, each causing their distinct and separate woe, packed in upon me for an unrecorded length of time, until at last they blurred together, and I heard a click in my brain like the click in the ear when one descends in a diving bell, and I knew that the pressures were equalised within and without, and that, for the moment, the worst was at an end. But I knew also that at any moment the darkness might come down anew; and while I dwelt on this speculation precisely as a man torments a raging tooth with his tongue, it ebbed away into the little grey shadow on the brain of its first coming, and once more I heard my brain, which knew what would recur, telegraph to every quarter for help, release or diversion.

The door opened, and McLeod reappeared. I thanked him politely, saying I was charmed with my room, anxious to meet Mrs McLeod, much refreshed with my wash, and so on and so forth. Beyond a little stickiness at the corners of my mouth, it seemed to me that I was managing my words admirably; the while that I myself cowered at the bottom of unclimbable pits. McLeod laid his hand on my shoulder, and said: 'You've got it now already, ain't it?'

'Yes,' I answered. 'It's making me sick!'

'It will pass off when you come outside. I give you my word it will then pass off. Come!'

I shambled out behind him, and wiped my forehead in the hall.

'You musn't mind,' he said. 'I expect the run tired you. My good lady is sitting there under the copper beech.'

She was a fat woman in an apricot-coloured gown, with a heavily powdered face, against which her black long-lashed eyes showed like currants in dough. I was introduced to many fine ladies and gentlemen of those parts. Magnificently appointed landaus and covered motors swept in and out of the drive, and the air was gay with the merry outcries of the tennis players.

As twilight drew on they all went away, and I was left alone with Mr and Mrs McLeod, while tall men-servants and maidservants took away the tennis and tea things. Miss McLeod had walked a little down the drive with a light-haired young man, who apparently knew everything about every South American railway stock. He had told me at tea that these were the days of financial specialisation.

'I think it went off beautifully, my dear,' said Mr McLeod to his wife; and to me: 'You feel all right now, ain't it? Of course you do.'

Mrs McLeod surged across the gravel. Her husband skipped nimbly before her into the south verandah, turned a switch, and all Holmescroft was flooded with light.

'You can do that from your room also,' he said as they went in. 'There is something in money, ain't it?'

Miss McLeod came up behind me in the dusk. 'We have not yet been introduced,' she said, 'but I suppose you are staying the night?'

'Your father was kind enough to ask me,' I replied.

She nodded. 'Yes, *I* know; and you know too, don't you? I saw your face when you came to shake hands with mamma. You felt the depression very soon. It is simply frightful in that bedroom sometimes. What do you think it is – bewitchment? In Greece, where I was a little girl, it might have been; but not in England, do you think? Or *do* you?'

'I don't know what to think,' I replied. 'I never felt anything like it. Does it happen often?'

'Yes, sometimes. It come and goes.'

'Pleasant!' I said, as we walked up and down the gravel at the lawn edge. 'What has been your experience of it?'

'That is difficult to say, but – sometimes that – that depression is like as it were' – she gesticulated in most un-English fashion – 'a light. Yes, like a light turned into a room – only a light of blackness, do you understand? – into a happy room. For sometimes we are so happy, all we three – so *very* happy. Then this blackness, it is turned on us just like – ah, I know what I mean now – like the headlamp of a motor, and we are eclip–sed. And there is another thing – '

The dressing-gong roared, and we entered the over-lighted hall. My dressing was a brisk athletic performance, varied with outbursts of song – careful attention paid to articulation and expression. But nothing happened. As I hurried downstairs, I thanked heaven that nothing had happened.

Dinner was served breakfast-fashion; the dishes were placed on the sideboard over heaters and we helped ourselves.

'We always do this when we are alone, so we talk better,' said Mr McLeod.

'And we are always alone,' said the daughter.

'Cheer up, Thea. It will all come right,' he insisted.

'No, papa.' She shook her dark head. 'Nothing is right while *it* comes.'

'It is nothing that we ourselves have ever done in our lives – that I will swear to you,' said Mrs McLeod suddenly. 'And we have changed our servants several times. So we know it is not *them*.'

'Never mind. Let us enjoy ourselves while we can,' said Mr McLeod, opening the champagne.

But we did not enjoy ourselves. The talk failed. There were long silences.

'I beg your pardon,' I said, for I thought someone at my elbow was about to speak.

'Ah! That is the other thing!' said Miss McLeod. Her mother groaned.

We were silent again, and, in a few seconds it must have been, a live grief beyond words – not ghostly dread or horror, but aching, helpless grief – overwhelmed us, each, I felt, according to his or her nature, and held steady like the beam of a burning-glass. Behind that pain I was conscious there was a desire on somebody's part to explain something on which some tremendously important issue hung.

Meantime I rolled bread pills and remembered my sins; McLeod considered his own reflection in a spoon; his wife seemed to be praying, and the girl fidgeted desperately with hands and feet, till the darkness passed on – as though the malignant rays of a burning-glass had been shifted from us.

'There,' said Miss McLeod, half rising. 'Now you see what makes a happy home. Oh, sell it – sell it, father mine, and let us go away!'

'But I've spent thousands on it. You shall go to Harrogate next week, Thea dear.'

'I'm only just back from hotels. I am *so* tired of packing.'

'Cheer up, Thea. It is over. You know it does not often come here twice in the same night. I think we shall dare now to be comfortable.'

He lifted a dish-cover, and helped his wife and daughter. His face was lined and fallen like an old man's after a debauch, but his hand did not shake, and his voice was clear. As he worked to restore us by speech and action, he reminded me of a grey-muzzled collie herding demoralised sheep.

After dinner we sat round the dining-room fire – the drawing-room might have been under the Shadow for aught we knew – talking with the intimacy of gypsies by the wayside, or of wounded comparing notes after a skirmish. By eleven o'clock the three between them had given me every name and detail they could recall that in any way bore on the house, and what they knew of its history.

We went to bed in a fortifying blaze of electric light. My one fear was that the blasting gust of depression would return – the surest way, of course, to bring it. I lay awake till dawn, breathing quickly and sweating lightly, beneath what De Quincey inadequately describes as 'the oppression of inexpiable guilt'. Now as soon as the lovely day was broken, I fell into the most terrible of all dreams – that joyous one in which all past evil has not only been wiped out of our lives, but has never been committed; and in the very bliss of our assured innocence, before our loves shriek and change countenance, we wake to the day we have earned.

It was a coolish morning, but we preferred to breakfast in the south verandah. The forenoon we spent in the garden, pretending to play games that come out of boxes, such as croquet and clock golf. But most of the time we drew together and talked. The young man who knew all about South American railways took Miss McLeod for a walk in the afternoon, and at five McLeod thoughtfully whirled us all up to dine in town.

'Now, don't say you will tell the Psychological Society, and that you will come again,' said Miss McLeod, as we parted. 'Because I know you will not.'

'You should not say that,' said her mother. 'You should say, "Goodbye, Mr Perseus. Come again." '

'Not him!' the girl cried. 'He has seen the Medusa's head!'

Looking at myself in the restaurant's mirrors, it seemed to me that I had not much benefited by my weekend. Next morning I wrote out all my Holmescroft notes at fullest length, in the hope that by so doing I could put it all behind me. But the experience worked on my mind, as they say certain imperfectly understood rays work on the body.

I am less calculated to make a Sherlock Holmes than any man I know, for I lack both method and patience, yet the idea of following up the trouble to its source fascinated me. I had no theory to go on, except a vague idea that I had come between two poles of a discharge, and had taken a shock meant for someone else. This was followed by a feeling of intense irritation. I waited cautiously on myself, expecting to be overtaken by horror of the supernatural, but my self persisted in being humanly indignant, exactly as though it had been the victim of a practical joke. It was in great pains and upheavals – that I felt in every fibre – but its dominant idea, to put it coarsely, was to get back a bit of its own. By this I knew that I might go forward if I could find the way.

After a few days it occurred to me to go to the office of Mr J. M. M. Baxter – the solicitor who had sold Holmescroft to McLeod. I explained I had some notion of buying the place. Would he act for me in the matter?

Mr Baxter, a large, greyish, throaty-voiced man, showed no enthusiasm. 'I sold it to Mr McLeod,' he said. 'It 'ud scarcely do for me to start on the running-down tack now. But I can recommend – '

'I know he's asking an awful price,' I interrupted, 'and atop of it he wants an extra thousand for what he calls your clean bill of health.'

Mr Baxter sat up in his chair. I had all his attention.

'Your guarantee with the house. Don't you remember it?'

'Yes, yes. That no death had taken place in the house since it was built. I remember perfectly.'

He did not gulp as untrained men do when they lie, but his jaws moved stickily, and his eyes, turning towards the deed boxes on the wall, dulled. I counted seconds, one, two, three – one, two, three – up to ten. A man, I knew, can live through ages of mental depression in that time.

'I remember perfectly.' His mouth opened a little as though it had tasted old bitterness.

'Of course *that* sort of thing doesn't appeal to me,' I went on. '*I* don't expect to buy a house free from death.'

'Certainly not. No one does. But it was Mr McLeod's fancy – his wife's rather, I believe; and since we could meet it – it was my duty to my clients – at whatever cost to my own feelings – to make him pay.'

'That's really why I came to you. I understood from him you knew the place well.'

'Oh, yes. Always did. It originally belonged to some connections of mine.'

'The Misses Moultrie, I suppose. How interesting! They must have loved the place before the country round about was built up.'

'They were very fond of it indeed.'

'I don't wonder. So restful and sunny. I don't see how they could have brought themselves to part with it.'

Now it is one of the most constant peculiarities of the English that in polite conversation – and I had striven to be polite – no one ever does or sells anything for mere money's sake.

'Miss Agnes – the youngest – fell ill' (he spaced his words a little), 'and, as they were very much attached to each other, that broke up the home.'

'Naturally. I fancied it must have been something of that kind. One doesn't associate the Staffordshire Moultries' (my Demon of Irresponsibility at that instant created 'em) 'with – with being hard up.'

'I don't know whether we're related to them,' he answered importantly. 'We may be, for our branch of the family comes from the Midlands.'

I give this talk at length, because I am so proud of my first attempt at detective work. When I left him, twenty minutes later, with instructions to move against the owner of Holmescroft, with a view to purchase, I was more bewildered than any Dr Watson at the opening of a story.

Why should a middle-aged solicitor turn plover's-egg colour and drop his jaw when reminded of so innocent and festal a matter as that no death had ever occurred in a house that he had sold? If I knew my English vocabulary at all, the tone in which he said the youngest sister 'fell ill' meant that she had gone out of her mind. That might explain his change of countenance, and it was just possible that her demented influence still hung about Holmescroft; but the rest was beyond me.

I was relieved when I reached McLeod's City office, and could tell him what I had done – not what I thought.

McLeod was quite willing to enter into the game of the pretended purchase, but did not see how it would help if I knew Baxter.

'He's the only living soul I can get at who was connected with Holmescroft,' I said.

'Ah! Living soul is good,' said McLeod. 'At any rate our little girl will be pleased that you are still interested in us. Won't you come down some day this week?'

'How is it there now?' I asked.

He screwed up his face. 'Simply frightful!' he said. 'Thea is at Droitwich.'

'I should like it immensely, but I must cultivate Baxter for the present. You'll be sure and keep him busy your end, won't you?'

He looked at me with quiet contempt. 'Do not be afraid. I shall be a good Jew. I shall be my own solicitor.'

Before a fortnight was over, Baxter admitted ruefully that McLeod was better than most firms in the business. We buyers were coy, argumentative, shocked at the price of Holmescroft, inquisitive, and cold by turns, but Mr McLeod the seller easily met and surpassed us; and Mr Baxter entered every letter, telegram, and consultation at the proper rates in a cinematograph-film of a bill. At the end of a month he said it looked as though McLeod, thanks to him, were really going to listen to reason. I was many pounds out of pocket, but I had learned something of Mr Baxter on the human side. I deserved it. Never in my life have I worked to conciliate, amuse, and flatter a human being as I worked over my solicitor.

It appeared that he golfed. Therefore, I was an enthusiastic beginner, anxious to learn. Twice I invaded his office with a bag (McLeod lent it) full of the spelicans needed in this detestable game, and a vocabulary to match. The third time the ice broke, and Mr Baxter took me to his links, quite ten miles off, where in a maze of tramway lines, railroads, and nursery maids, we skelped our divoted way round nine holes like barges plunging through head seas. He played vilely and had never expected to meet anyone worse; but as he realised my form, I think he began to like me, for he took me in hand by the two hours together. After a fortnight he could give me no more than a stroke a hole, and when, with this allowance, I once managed to beat him by one, he was honestly glad, and assured me that I should be a golfer if I stuck to it. I was sticking to it for my own ends, but now and again my conscience pricked me; for the man was a nice man. Between games he supplied me with odd pieces of evidence, such as that he had known the Moultries all his life, being their cousin, and that Miss Mary, the eldest, was an unforgiving woman who would never let bygones be. I naturally wondered what she might have against him; and somehow connected him unfavourably with mad Agnes.

'People ought to forgive and forget,' he volunteered one day between rounds. 'Specially where, in the nature of things, they can't be sure of their deductions. Don't you think so?'

'It all depends on the nature of the evidence on which one forms one's judgment,' I answered.

'Nonsense!' he cried. 'I'm lawyer enough to know that there's nothing in the world so misleading as circumstantial evidence. Never was.'

'Why? Have you ever seen men hanged on it?'

'Hanged? People have been supposed to be eternally lost on it.' His face turned grey again. 'I don't know how it is with you, but my consolation is that God must know. He must! Things that seem on the face of 'em like murder, or say suicide, may appear different to God. Heh?'

'That's what the murderer and the suicide can always hope – I suppose.'

'I have expressed myself clumsily as usual. The facts as God knows 'em – may *be* different – even after the most clinching evidence. I've always said that – both as a lawyer and a man, but some people won't – I don't want to judge 'em – we'll say they can't – believe it; whereas *I* say there's always a working chance – a certainty – that the worst hasn't happened.' He stopped and cleared his throat. 'Now, let's come on! This time next week I shall be taking my holiday.'

'What links?' I asked carelessly, while twins in a perambulator got out of our line of fire.

'A potty little nine-hole affair at a hydro in the Midlands. My cousins stay there. Always will. Not but what the fourth and the seventh holes take some doing.

You could manage it, though,' he said encouragingly. 'You're doing much better. It's only your approach shots that are weak.'

'You're right. I can't approach for nuts! I shall go to pieces while you're away – with no one to coach me,' I said mournfully.

'I haven't taught you anything,' he said, delighted with the compliment.

'I owe all I've learned to you, anyhow. When will you come back?'

'Look here,' he began. 'I don't know your engagements, but I've no one to play with at Burry Mills. Never have. Why couldn't you take a few days off and join me there? I warn you it will be rather dull. It's a throat and gout place – baths, massage, electricity, and so forth. But the fourth and the seventh holes really take some doing.'

'I'm for the game,' I answered valiantly; Heaven well knowing that I hated every stroke and word of it.

'That's the proper spirit. As their lawyer I must ask you not to say anything to my cousins about Holmescroft. It upsets 'em. Always did. But speaking as man to man, it would be very pleasant for me if you could see your way to – '

I saw it as soon as decency permitted, and thanked him sincerely. According to my now well-developed theory he had certainly misappropriated his aged cousins' monies under power of attorney, and had probably driven poor Agnes Moultrie out of her wits, but I wished that he was not so gentle, and good-tempered, and innocent-eyed.

Before I joined him at Burry Mills Hydro, I spent a night at Holmescroft. Miss McLeod had returned from her hydro, and first we made very merry on the open lawn in the sunshine over the manners and customs of the English resorting to such places. She knew dozens of hydros, and warned me how to behave in them, while Mr and Mrs McLeod stood aside and adored her.

'Ah! That's the way she always comes back to us,' he said. 'Pity it wears off so soon, ain't it? You ought to hear her sing "With mirth, thou pretty bird".'

We had the house to face through the evening, and there we neither laughed nor sang. The gloom fell on us as we entered, and did not shift till ten o'clock, when we crawled out, as it were, from beneath it.

'It has been bad this summer,' said Mrs McLeod in a whisper after we realised that we were freed. 'Sometimes I think the house will get up and cry out – it is so bad.'

'How?'

'Have you forgotten what comes after the depression?'

So then we waited about the small fire, and the dead air in the room presently filled and pressed down upon us with the sensation (but words are useless here) as though some dumb and bound power were striving against gag and bond to deliver its soul of an articulate word. It passed in a few minutes, and I fell to thinking about Mr Baxter's conscience and Agnes Moultrie, gone mad in the well-lit bedroom that awaited me. These reflections secured me a night during which I rediscovered how, from purely mental causes, a man can be physically sick; but the sickness was bliss compared to my dreams when the birds waked. On my departure, McLeod gave me a beautiful narwhal's horn, much as a nurse gives a child sweets for being brave at a dentist's.

'There's no duplicate of it in the world,' he said,

'else it would have come to old Max McLeod,' and he tucked it into the motor. Miss McLeod on the far side of the car whispered, 'Have you found out anything, Mr Perseus?'

I shook my head.

'Then I shall be chained to my rock all my life,' she went on. 'Only don't tell papa.'

I supposed she was thinking of the young gentleman who specialised in South American rails, for I noticed a ring on the third finger of her left hand.

I went straight from that house to Burry Mills Hydro, keen for the first time in my life on playing golf, which is guaranteed to occupy the mind. Baxter had taken me a room communicating with his own, and after lunch introduced me to a tall, horse-headed elderly lady of decided manners, whom a white-haired maid pushed along in a bath-chair through the park-like grounds of the hydro. She was Miss Mary Moultrie, and she coughed and cleared her throat just like Baxter. She suffered – she told me it was a Moultrie caste mark – from some obscure form of chronic bronchitis, complicated with spasm of the glottis; and, in a dead, flat voice, with a sunken eye that looked and saw not, told me what washes, gargles, pastilles, and inhalations she had proved most beneficial. From her I was passed on to her younger sister, Miss Elizabeth, a small and withered thing with twitching lips, victim, she told me, to very much the same sort of throat, but secretly devoted to another set of medicines. When she went away with Baxter and the bath-chair, I fell across a major of the Indian army with gout in his glassy eyes, and a stomach which he had taken all round the Continent. He laid everything before me; and him I escaped only to be confided in by a matron with a tendency to follicular tonsillitis and eczema. Baxter waited hand and foot on his cousins till five o'clock, trying, as I saw, to atone for his treatment of the dead sister. Miss Mary ordered him about like a dog.

'I warned you it would be dull,' he said when we met in the smoking-room.

'It's tremendously interesting,' I said. 'But how about a look round the links?'

'Unluckily damp always affects my eldest cousin. I've got to buy her a new bronchitis-kettle. Arthurs broke her old one yesterday.'

We slipped out to the chemist's shop in the town, and he bought a large glittering tin thing whose workings he explained.

'I'm used to this sort of work. I come up here pretty often,' he said. 'I've the family throat too.'

'You're a good man,' I said. 'A very good man.'

He turned towards me in the evening light among the beeches, and his face was changed to what it might have been a generation before.

'You see,' he said huskily, 'there was the youngest – Agnes. Before she fell ill, you know. But she didn't like leaving her sisters. Never would.' He hurried on with his odd-shaped load and left me among the ruins of my black theories. The man with that face had done Agnes Moultrie no wrong.

We never played our game. I was waked between two and three in the morning from my hygienic bed by Baxter in an ulster over orange and white pyjamas, which I should never have suspected from his character.

'My cousin has had some sort of a seizure,' he said.

'Will you come? I don't want to wake the doctor. Don't want to make a scandal. Quick!'

So I came quickly, and led by the white-haired Arthurs in a jacket and petticoat, entered a double-bedded room reeking with steam and Friar's Balsam. The electrics were all on. Miss Mary – I knew her by her height – was at the open window, wrestling with Miss Elizabeth, who gripped her round the knees. Miss Mary's hand was at her own throat, which was streaked with blood.

'She's done it. She's done it too!' Miss Elizabeth panted. 'Hold her! Help me!'

'Oh, I say! Women don't cut their throats,' Baxter whispered.

'My God! Has she cut her throat?' the maid cried out, and with no warning rolled over in a faint. Baxter pushed her under the washbasins, and leaped to hold the gaunt woman who crowed and whistled as she struggled towards the window. He took her by the shoulder, and she struck out wildly.

'All right! She's only cut her hand,' he said. 'Wet towel – quick!'

While I got that he pushed her backward. Her strength seemed almost as great as his. I swabbed at her throat when I could, and found no mark; then helped him to control her a little. Miss Elizabeth leaped back to bed, wailing like a child.

'Tie up her hand somehow,' said Baxter. 'Don't let it drip about the place. She – ' he stepped on broken glass in his slippers, 'she must have smashed a pane.'

Miss Mary lurched towards the open window again, dropped on her knees, her head on the sill, and lay quiet, surrendering the cut hand to me.

'What did she do?' Baxter turned towards Miss Elizabeth in the far bed.

'She was going to throw herself out of the window,' was the answer. 'I stopped her, and sent Arthurs for you. Oh, we can never hold up our heads again!'

Miss Mary writhed and fought for breath. Baxter found a shawl which he threw over her shoulders.

'Nonsense!' said he. 'That isn't like Mary'; but his face worked when he said it.

'You wouldn't believe about Aggie, John. Perhaps you will now!' said Miss Elizabeth. 'I *saw* her do it, and she's cut her throat too!'

'She hasn't,' I said. 'It's only her hand.'

Miss Mary suddenly broke from us with an indescribable grunt, flew, rather than ran, to her sister's bed, and there shook her as one furious schoolgirl would shake another.

'No such thing,' she croaked. 'How dare you think so, you wicked little fool?'

'Get into bed, Mary,' said Baxter. 'You'll catch a chill.'

She obeyed, but sat up with the grey shawl round her lean shoulders, glaring at her sister. 'I'm better now,' she panted. 'Arthurs let me sit out too long. Where's Arthurs? The kettle.'

'Never mind Arthurs,' said Baxter. '*You* get the kettle.' I hastened to bring it from the side table. 'Now, Mary, as God sees you, tell me what you've done.'

His lips were dry, and he could not moisten them with his tongue.

Miss Mary applied herself to the mouth of the kettle, and between in-draws of steam said: 'The spasm came on just now, while I was asleep. I was nearly choking to death. So I went to the window. I've done it often before, without waking anyone. Bessie's such an old maid about draughts! I tell you I was choking to death. I couldn't manage the catch, and I nearly fell out. That window opens too low. I cut my hand trying to save myself. Who has tied it up in this filthy handkerchief? I wish you had had my throat, Bessie. I never was nearer dying!' She scowled on us all impartially, while her sister sobbed.

From the bottom of the bed we heard a quivering voice: 'Is she dead? Have they took her away? Oh, I never could bear the sight o' blood!'

'Arthurs,' said Miss Mary, 'you are an hireling. Go away!'

It is my belief that Arthurs crawled out on all fours, but I was busy picking up broken glass from the carpet.

Then Baxter, seated by the side of the bed, began to cross-examine in a voice I scarcely recognised. No one could for an instant have doubted the genuine rage of Miss Mary against her sister, her cousin, or her maid; and that a doctor should have been called in – for she did me the honour of calling me doctor – was the last drop. She was choking with her throat; had rushed to the window for air; had near pitched out, and in catching at the window bars had cut her hand. Over and over she made this clear to the intent Baxter. Then she turned on her sister and tongue-lashed her savagely.

'You mustn't blame me,' Miss Bessie faltered at last. 'You know what we think of night and day.'

'I'm coming to that,' said Baxter. 'Listen to me. What *you* did, Mary, misled four people into thinking you – you meant to do away with yourself.'

'Isn't one suicide in the family enough? Oh God, help and pity us! You *couldn't* have believed that!' she cried.

'The evidence was complete. Now, don't you think,' Baxter's finger wagged under her nose – '*can't* you think that poor Aggie did the same thing at Holmescroft when she fell out of the window?'

'She had the same throat,' said Miss Elizabeth. 'Exactly the same symptoms. Don't you remember, Mary?'

'Which was her bedroom?' I asked of Baxter in an undertone.

'Over the south verandah, looking on to the tennis lawn.'

'I nearly fell out of that very window when I was at Holmescroft – opening it to get some air. The sill doesn't come much above your knees,' I said.

'You hear that, Mary? Mary, do you hear what this gentleman says? Won't you believe that what nearly happened to you must have happened to poor Aggie that night? For God's sake – for her sake – Mary, *won't* you believe?'

There was a long silence while the steam kettle puffed.

'If I could have proof – if I could have proof,' said she, and broke into most horrible tears.

Baxter motioned to me, and I crept away to my room, and lay awake till morning, thinking more specially of the dumb Thing at Holmescroft which wished to explain itself. I hated Miss Mary as perfectly as though I had known her for twenty years, but I felt that, alive or dead, I should not like her to condemn me.

Yet at midday, when I saw Miss Mary in her bath-chair, Arthurs behind and Baxter and Miss Elizabeth on either side, in the park-like grounds of the hydro, I found it difficult to arrange my words.

'Now that you know all about it,' said Baxter aside,

after the first strangeness of our meeting was over, 'it's only fair to tell you that my poor cousin did not die *in* Holmescroft at all. She was dead when they found her under the window in the morning. Just dead.'

'Under that laburnum outside the window?' I asked, for I suddenly remembered the crooked evil thing.

'Exactly. She broke the tree in falling. But no death has ever taken place *in* the house, so far as we were concerned. You can make yourself quite easy on that point. Mr McLeod's extra thousand for what you called the "clean bill of health" was something towards my cousins' estate when we sold. It was my duty as their lawyer to get it for them – at any cost to my own feelings.'

I know better than to argue when the English talk about their duty. So I agreed with my solicitor.

'Their sister's death must have been a great blow to your cousins,' I went on. The bath-chair was behind me.

'Unspeakable,' Baxter whispered. 'They brooded on it day and night. No wonder. If their theory of poor Aggie making away with herself was correct, she was eternally lost!'

'Do you believe that she made away with herself?'

'No, thank God! Never have! And after what happened to Mary last night, I see perfectly what happened to poor Aggie. She had the family throat too. By the way, Mary thinks you are a doctor. Otherwise she wouldn't like your having been in her room.'

'Very good. Is she convinced now about her sister's death?'

'She'd give anything to be able to believe it, but she's a hard woman, and brooding along certain lines makes one groovy. I have sometimes been afraid for her reason – on the religious side, don't you know.

Elizabeth doesn't matter. Brain of a hen. Always had.'

Here Arthurs summoned me to the bath-chair, and the ravaged face, beneath its knitted Shetland wool hood, of Miss Mary Moultrie.

'I need not remind you, I hope, of the seal of secrecy – absolute secrecy – in your profession,' she began. 'Thanks to my cousin's and my sister's stupidity, you have found out – ' She blew her nose.

'Please don't excite her, sir,' said Arthurs at the back.

'But, my dear Miss Moultrie, I only know what I've seen, of course, but it seems to me that what you thought was a tragedy in your sister's case, turns out, on your own evidence, so to speak, to have been an accident – a dreadfully sad one – but absolutely an accident.'

'Do you believe that too?' she cried. 'Or are you only saying it to comfort me?'

'I believe it from the bottom of my heart. Come down to Holmescroft for an hour – for half an hour – and satisfy yourself.'

'Of what? You don't understand. I see the house every day – every night. I am always there in spirit – waking or sleeping. I couldn't face it in reality.'

'But you must,' I said. 'If you go there in the spirit the greater need for you to go there in the flesh. Go to your sister's room once more, and see the window – I nearly fell out of it myself. It's – it's awfully low and dangerous. That would convince you,' I pleaded.

'Yet Aggie had slept in that room for years,' she interrupted.

'You've slept in your room here for a long time, haven't you? But you nearly fell out of the window when you were choking.'

'That is true. That is one thing true,' she nodded. 'And I might have been killed as – perhaps – Aggie was killed.'

'In that case your own sister and cousin and maid would have said you had committed suicide, Miss Moultrie. Come down to Holmescroft, and go over the place just once.'

'You are lying,' she said quite quietly. 'You don't want me to come down to see a window. It is something else. I warn you we are Evangelicals. We don't believe in prayers for the dead. "As the tree falls – " '

'Yes. I dare say. But you persist in thinking that your sister committed suicide – '

'No! No! I have always prayed that I might have misjudged her.'

Arthurs at the bath-chair spoke up: 'Oh, Miss Mary! you would 'ave it from the first that poor Miss Aggie 'ad made away with herself; an', of course, Miss Bessie took the notion from you. Only Master – Mister John stood out, and – and I'd 'ave taken my Bible oath *you* was making away with yourself last night.'

Miss Mary leaned towards me, one finger on my sleeve.

'If going to Holmescroft kills me,' she said, 'you will have the murder of a fellow-creature on your conscience for all eternity.'

'I'll risk it,' I answered. Remembering what torment the mere reflection of her torments had cast on Holmescroft, and remembering, above all, the dumb Thing that filled the house with its desire to speak, I felt that there might be worse things.

Baxter was amazed at the proposed visit, but at a nod from that terrible woman went off to make arrangements. Then I sent a telegram to McLeod bidding him and his vacate Holmescroft for that afternoon. Miss Mary should be alone with her dead, as I had been alone.

I expected untold trouble in transporting her, but to do her justice, her promise given for the journey, she underwent it without murmur, spasm, or unnecessary word. Miss Bessie, pressed in a corner by the window, wept behind her veil, and from time to time tried to take hold of her sister's hand. Baxter wrapped himself in his newly found happiness as selfishly as a bridegroom, for he sat still and smiled.

'So long as I know that Aggie didn't make away with herself,' he explained, 'I tell you frankly I don't care what happened. She's as hard as a rock – Mary. Always was. *She* won't die.'

We led her out on to the platform like a blind woman, and so got her into the fly. The half-hour crawl to Holmescroft was the most racking experience of the day. McLeod had obeyed my instructions. There was no one visible in the house or the gardens; and the front door stood open.

Miss Mary rose from beside her sister, stepped forth first, and entered the hall.

'Come, Bessie,' she cried.

'I daren't. Oh, I daren't.'

'Come!' Her voice had altered. I felt Baxter start. 'There's nothing to be afraid of.'

'Good heavens!' said Baxter. 'She's running up the stairs. We'd better follow.'

'Let's wait below. She's going to the room.'

We heard the door of the bedroom I knew open and shut, and we waited in the lemon-coloured hall, heavy with the scent of flowers.

'I've never been into it since it was sold,' Baxter

sighed. 'What a lovely, restful place it is! Poor Aggie used to arrange the flowers.'

'Restful?' I began, but stopped of a sudden, for I felt all over my bruised soul that Baxter was speaking truth. It was a light, spacious, airy house, full of the sense of well-being and peace – above all things, of peace. I ventured into the dining-room where the thoughtful McLeods had left a small fire. There was no terror there, present or lurking; and in the drawing-room, which for good reasons we had never cared to enter, the sun and the peace and the scent of the flowers worked together as is fit in an inhabited house. When I returned to the hall, Baxter was sweetly asleep on a couch, looking most unlike a middle-aged solicitor who had spent a broken night with an exacting cousin.

There was ample time for me to review it all – to felicitate myself upon my magnificent acumen (barring some errors about Baxter as a thief and possibly a murderer), before the door above opened, and Baxter, evidently a light sleeper, sprang awake.

'I've had a heavenly little nap,' he said, rubbing his eyes with the backs of his hands like a child. 'Good Lord! That's not *their* step!'

But it was. I had never before been privileged to see the Shadow turned backward on the dial – the years ripped bodily off poor human shoulders – old sunken eyes filled and alight – harsh lips moistened and human.

'John,' Miss Mary called, 'I know now. Aggie didn't do it!' and, 'She didn't do it!' echoed Miss Bessie, and giggled.

'I did not think it wrong to say a prayer,' Miss Mary continued. 'Not for her soul, but for our peace. Then I was convinced.'

'Then we got conviction,' the younger sister piped.

'We've misjudged poor Aggie, John. But I feel she knows now. Wherever she is, she knows that we know she is guiltless.'

'Yes, she knows. I felt it too,' said Miss Elizabeth.

'I never doubted,' said John Baxter, whose face was beautiful at that hour. 'Not from the first. Never have!'

'You never offered me proof, John. Now, thank God, it will not be the same any more. I can think henceforward of Aggie without sorrow.' She tripped, absolutely tripped, across the hall. 'What ideas these Jews have of arranging furniture!' She spied me behind a big cloisonné vase.

'I've seen the window,' she said remotely. 'You took a great risk in advising me to undertake such a journey. However, as it turns out . . . I forgive you, and I pray you may never know what mental anguish means! Bessie! Look at this peculiar piano! Do you suppose, doctor, these people would offer one tea? I miss mine.'

'I will go and see,' I said, and explored McLeod's new-built servants' wing. It was in the servants' hall that I unearthed the McLeod family, bursting with anxiety.

'Tea for three, quick,' I said. 'If you ask me any questions now, I shall have a fit!' So Mrs McLeod got it, and I was butler, amid murmured apologies from Baxter, still smiling and self-absorbed, and the cold disapproval of Miss Mary, who thought the pattern of the china vulgar. However, she ate well, and even asked me whether I would not like a cup of tea for myself.

They went away in the twilight – the twilight that I had once feared. They were going to a hotel in London to rest after the fatigues of the day, and as their fly turned down the drive, I capered on the doorstep, with the all-darkened house behind me.

Then I heard the uncertain feet of the McLeods and bade them not to turn on the lights, but to feel – to feel what I had done; for the Shadow was gone, with the dumb desire in the air. They drew short, but afterwards deeper, breaths, like bathers entering chill water, separated one from the other, moved about the hall, tiptoed upstairs, raced down, and then Miss McLeod, and I believe her mother, though she denies this, embraced me. I know McLeod did.

It was a disgraceful evening. To say we rioted through the house is to put it mildly. We played a sort of Blind Man's Buff along the darkest passages, in the unlighted drawing-room, and little dining-room, calling cheerily to each other after each exploration that here, and here, and here, the trouble had removed itself. We came up to *the* bedroom – mine for the night again – and sat, the women on the bed, and we men on chairs, drinking in blessed draughts of peace and comfort and cleanliness of soul, while I told them my tale in full, and received fresh praise, thanks, and blessings.

When the servants, returned from their day's outing, gave us a supper of cold fried fish, McLeod had sense enough to open no wine. We had been practically drunk since nightfall, and grew incoherent on water and milk.

'I like that Baxter,' said McLeod. 'He's a sharp man. The death wasn't *in* the house, but he ran it pretty close, ain't it?'

'And the joke of it is that he supposes I want to buy the place from you,' I said. 'Are you selling?'

'Not for twice what I paid for it – now,' said McLeod. 'I'll keep you in furs all your life; but not our Holmescroft.'

'No – never our Holmescroft,' said Miss McLeod. 'We'll ask *him* here on Tuesday, mamma.' They squeezed each other's hands.

'Now tell me,' said Mrs McLeod – 'that tall one I saw out of the scullery window – did *she* tell you she was always here in the spirit? I hate her. She made all this trouble. It was *not* her house after she had sold it. What do you think?'

'I suppose,' I answered, 'she brooded over what she believed was her sister's suicide night and day – she confessed she did – and her thoughts being concentrated on this place, they felt like a – like a burning-glass.'

'Burning-glass is good,' said McLeod.

'I said it was like a light of blackness turned on us,' cried the girl, twiddling her ring. 'That must have been when the tall one thought worst about her sister and the house.'

'Ah, the poor Aggie!' said Mrs McLeod. 'The poor Aggie, trying to tell everyone it was not so! No wonder we felt Something wished to say Something. Thea, Max, do you remember that night – ?'

'We need not remember any more,' McLeod interrupted. 'It is not our trouble. They have told each other now.'

'Do you think, then,' said Miss McLeod, 'that those two, the living ones, were actually told something – upstairs – in your – in the room?'

'I can't say. At any rate they were made happy, and they ate a big tea afterwards. As your father says, it is not our trouble any longer – thank God!'

'Amen!' said McLeod. 'Now, Thea, let us have

some music after all these months. "With mirth, thou pretty bird", ain't it? You ought to hear that.'

And in the half-lighted hall, Thea sang an old English song that I had never heard before.

> With mirth, thou pretty bird, rejoice
>   Thy Maker's praise enhancèd;
> Lift up thy shrill and pleasant voice,
>   Thy God is high advancèd!
> Thy food before He did provide,
> And gives it in a fitting side,
>   Wherewith be thou sufficèd!
> Why shouldst thou now unpleasant be,
>   Thy wrath against God venting,
> That He a little bird made thee,
>   Thy silly head tormenting,
> Because He made thee not a man?
> Oh, Peace! He hath well thought thereon,
>   Therewith be thou sufficèd!

The Man who would be King

Brother to a Prince and fellow to a
beggar if he be found worthy

The Law, as quoted, lays down a fair conduct of life, and one not easy to follow. I have been fellow to a beggar again and again under circumstances which prevented either of us finding out whether the other was worthy. I have still to be brother to a Prince, though I once came near to kinship with what might have been a veritable King, and was promised the reversion of a Kingdom – army, law-courts, revenue, and policy all complete. But, today, I greatly fear that my King is dead, and if I want a crown I must go hunt it for myself.

The beginning of everything was in a railway train upon the road to Mhow from Ajmir. There had been a deficit in the budget, which necessitated travelling, not second-class, which is only half as dear as first-class, but by intermediate, which is very awful indeed. There are no cushions in the intermediate class, and the population are either intermediate, which is Eurasian, or native, which for a long night journey is nasty, or loafer, which is amusing though intoxicated. Intermediates do not buy from refreshment-rooms. They carry their food in bundles and pots, and buy sweets from the native sweetmeat-sellers, and drink the roadside water. That is why in the hot weather intermediates are taken out of the carriages dead, and in all weathers are most properly looked down upon.

My particular intermediate happened to be empty till I reached Nasirabad, when a big black-browed gentleman in shirtsleeves entered, and, following the custom of intermediates, passed the time of day. He was a wanderer and a vagabond like myself, but with an educated taste for whisky. He told tales of things he had seen and done, of out-of-the-way corners of the Empire into which he had penetrated, and of adventures in which he risked his life for a few days' food.

'If India was filled with men like you and me, not knowing more than the crows where they'd get their next day's rations, it isn't seventy millions of revenue the land would be paying – it's seven hundred millions,' said he; and as I looked at his mouth and chin I was disposed to agree with him.

We talked politics – the politics of loaferdom, that sees things from the underside where the lath and plaster is not smoothed off – and we talked postal arrangements because my friend wanted to send a telegram back from the next station to Ajmir, the turning-off place from the Bombay to the Mhow line as you travel westward. My friend had no money beyond eight annas, which he wanted for dinner, and I had no money at all, owing to the hitch in the budget before mentioned. Further, I was going into a wilderness where, though I should resume touch with the treasury, there were no telegraph offices. I was, therefore, unable to help him in any way.

'We might threaten a station-master, and make him send a wire on tick,' said my friend, 'but that'd mean enquiries for you and for me, and *I*'ve got my hands full these days. Did you say you are travelling back along this line within any days?'

'Within ten,' I said.

'Can't you make it eight?' said he. 'Mine is rather urgent business.'

'I can send your telegram within ten days if that will serve you,' I said.

'I couldn't trust the wire to fetch him, now I think of it. It's this way. He leaves Delhi on the 23rd for Bombay. That means he'll be running through Ajmir about the night of the 23rd.'

'But I'm going into the Indian Desert,' I explained.

'Well *and* good,' said he. 'You'll be changing at Marwar Junction to get into Jodhpore territory – you must do that – and he'll be coming through Marwar Junction in the early morning of the 24th by the Bombay Mail. Can you be at Marwar Junction on that time? 'Twon't be inconveniencing you because I know that there's precious few pickings to be got out of these Central India States – even though you pretend to be correspondent of the *Backwoodsman*.'

'Have you ever tried that trick?' I asked.

'Again and again, but the Residents find you out, and then you get escorted to the border before you've time to get your knife into them. But about my friend here. I *must* give him a word o' mouth to tell him what's come to me or else he won't know where to go. I would take it more than kind of you if you was to come out of Central India in time to catch him at Marwar Junction, and say to him: "He has gone south for the week." He'll know what that means. He's a big man with a red beard, and a great swell he is. You'll find him sleeping like a gentleman with all his luggage round him in a second-class compartment. But don't you be afraid. Slip down the window, and say: "He has gone south for the week," and he'll tumble. It's only cutting your time of stay in those parts by two days. I ask you as a stranger – going to the west,' he said with emphasis.

'Where have *you* come from?' said I.

'From the east,' said he, 'and I am hoping that you will give him the message on the square – for the sake of my mother as well as your own.'

Englishmen are not usually softened by appeals to the memory of their mothers, but for certain reasons, which will be fully apparent, I saw fit to agree.

'It's more than a little matter,' said he, 'and that's why I asked you to do it – and now I know that I can depend on you doing it. A second-class carriage at Marwar Junction, and a red-haired man asleep in it. You'll be sure to remember. I get out at the next station, and I must hold on there till he comes or sends me what I want.'

'I'll give the message if I catch him,' I said, 'and for the sake of your mother as well as mine I'll give you a word of advice. Don't try to run the Central India States just now as the correspondent of the *Backwoodsman*. There's a real one knocking about here, and it might lead to trouble.'

'Thank you,' said he simply, 'and when will the swine be gone? I can't starve because he's ruining my work. I wanted to get hold of the Degumber Rajah down here about his father's widow, and give him a jump.'

'What did he do to his father's widow, then?'

'Filled her up with red pepper and slippered her to death as she hung from a beam. I found that out myself, and I'm the only man that would dare going into the state to get hush-money for it. They'll try to poison me, same as they did in Chortumna when I went on the loot there. But you'll give the man at Marwar Junction my message?'

He got out at a little roadside station, and I reflected. I had heard, more than once, of men personating correspondents of newspapers and bleeding small native states with threats of exposure, but I had never met any of the caste before. They lead a hard life, and generally die with great suddenness. The native states have a wholesome horror of English newspapers which may throw light on their peculiar methods of government, and do their best to choke correspondents with champagne, or drive them out of their mind with four-in-hand barouches. They do not understand that nobody cares a straw for the internal administration of native states so long as oppression and crime are kept within decent limits, and the ruler is not drugged, drunk, or diseased from one end of the year to the other. They are the dark places of the earth, full of unimaginable cruelty, touching the railway and the telegraph on one side, and, on the other, the days of Harun-al-Raschid. When I left the train I did business with divers Kings, and in eight days passed through many changes of life. Sometimes I wore dress-clothes and consorted with princes and politicals, drinking from crystal and eating from silver. Sometimes I lay out upon the ground and devoured what I could get, from a plate made of leaves, and drank the running water, and slept under the same rug as my servant. It was all in the day's work.

Then I headed for the Great Indian Desert upon the proper date, as I had promised, and the night mail set me down at Marwar Junction, where a funny, little, happy-go-lucky, native-managed railway runs to Jodhpore. The Bombay Mail from Delhi makes a short halt at Marwar. She arrived as I got in, and I had just time to hurry to her platform and go down the carriages. There was only one second-class on the train. I slipped the window and looked down upon a flaming red beard, half covered by a railway rug. That was my man, fast asleep, and I dug him gently in the ribs. He woke with a grunt, and I saw his face in the light of the lamps. It was a great and shining face.

'Tickets again?' said he.

'No,' said I. 'I am to tell you that he is gone south for the week. He has gone south for the week!'

The train had begun to move out. The red man rubbed his eyes. 'He has gone south for the week,' he repeated. 'Now that's just like his impidence. Did he say that I was to give you anything? 'Cause I won't.'

'He didn't,' I said, and dropped away, and watched the red lights die out in the dark. It was horribly cold because the wind was blowing off the sands. I climbed into my own train – not an intermediate carriage this time – and went to sleep.

If the man with the beard had given me a rupee I should have kept it as a memento of a rather curious affair. But the consciousness of having done my duty was my only reward.

Later on I reflected that two gentlemen like my friends could not do any good if they forgathered and personated correspondents of newspapers, and might, if they blackmailed one of the little rat trap states of Central India or Southern Rajputana, get themselves into serious difficulties. I therefore took some trouble to describe them as accurately as I could remember to people who would be interested in deporting them; and succeeded, so I was later informed, in having them headed back from the Degumber borders.

Then I became respectable, and returned to an

office where there were no kings and no incidents outside the daily manufacture of a newspaper. A newspaper office seems to attract every conceivable sort of person, to the prejudice of discipline. Zenana-mission ladies arrive, and beg that the editor will instantly abandon all his duties to describe a Christian prize-giving in a back-slum of a perfectly inaccessible village; colonels who have been over-passed for command sit down and sketch the outline of a series of ten, twelve, or twenty-four leading articles on seniority *versus* selection; missionaries wish to know why they have not been permitted to escape from their regular vehicles of abuse and swear at a brother-missionary under special patronage of the editorial We; stranded theatrical companies troop up to explain that they cannot pay for their advertisements, but on their return from New Zealand or Tahiti will do so with interest; inventors of patent punkah-pulling machines, carriage couplings, and unbreakable swords and axle-trees, call with specifications in their pockets and hours at their disposal; tea-companies enter and elaborate their prospectuses with the office pens; secretaries of ball-committees clamour to have the glories of their last dance more fully described; strange ladies rustle in and say, 'I want a hundred lady's cards printed *at once*, please,' which is manifestly part of an editor's duty; and every dissolute ruffian that ever tramped the Grand Trunk Road makes it his business to ask for employment as a proofreader. And, all the time, the telephone-bell is ringing madly, and kings are being killed on the Continent, and empires are saying, 'You're another,' and Mr Gladstone is calling down brimstone upon the British Dominions, and the little black copy-boys are whining, '*kaa-pi chay-ha-yeh*' [copy wanted], like tired bees, and most of the paper is as blank as Modred's shield.

But that is the amusing part of the year. There are six other months when none ever comes to call, and the thermometer walks inch by inch up to the top of the glass, and the office is darkened to just above reading-light, and the press-machines are red-hot of touch, and nobody writes anything but accounts of amusements in the hill-stations or obituary notices. Then the telephone becomes a tinkling terror, because it tells you of the sudden deaths of men and women that you knew intimately, and the prickly-heat covers you with a garment, and you sit down and write: 'A slight increase of sickness is reported from the Khuda Janta Khan District. The outbreak is purely sporadic in its nature, and, thanks to the energetic efforts of the District authorities, is now almost at an end. It is, however, with deep regret we record the death, etc.'

Then the sickness really breaks out, and the less recording and reporting the better for the peace of the subscribers. But the empires and the kings continue to divert themselves as selfishly as before, and the foreman thinks that a daily paper really ought to come out once in twenty-four hours, and all the people at the hill-stations in the middle of their amusements say: 'Good gracious! Why can't the paper be sparkling? I'm sure there's plenty going on up here.'

That is the dark half of the moon, and, as the advertisements say, 'must be experienced to be appreciated'.

It was in that season, and a remarkably evil season, that the paper began running the last issue of the week on Saturday night, which is to say Sunday morning, after the custom of a London paper. This was a great convenience, for immediately after the paper was put to bed, the dawn would lower the thermometer from 96° to almost 84° for half an hour, and in that chill – you have no idea how cold is 84° on the grass until you begin to pray for it – a very tired man could get off to sleep ere the heat roused him.

One Saturday night it was my pleasant duty to put the paper to bed alone. A king or courtier or a courtesan or a community was going to die or get a new constitution, or do something that was important on the other side of the world, and the paper was to be held open till the latest possible minute in order to catch the telegram.

It was a pitchy black night, as stifling as a June night can be, and the *loo*, the red-hot wind from the westward, was booming among the tinder-dry trees and pretending that the rain was on its heels. Now and again a spot of almost boiling water would fall on the dust with the flop of a frog, but all our weary world knew that was only pretence. It was a shade cooler in the press-room than the office, so I sat there, while the type ticked and clicked, and the nightjars hooted at the windows, and the all but naked compositors wiped the sweat from their foreheads, and called for water. The thing that was keeping us back, whatever it was, would not come off, though the *loo* dropped and the last type was set, and the whole round earth stood still in the choking heat, with its finger on its lip, to wait the event. I drowsed, and wondered whether the telegraph was a blessing, and whether this dying man, or struggling people, might be aware of the inconvenience the delay was causing. There was no special reason beyond the heat and worry to make tension, but, as the clock-hands crept up to three o'clock, and the machines spun their flywheels two or three times to see that all was in order before I said the word that would set them off, I could have shrieked aloud.

Then the roar and rattle of the wheels shivered the quiet into little bits. I rose to go away, but two men in white clothes stood in front of me. The first one said: 'It's him!' The second said: 'So it is!' And they both laughed almost as loudly as the machinery roared, and mopped their foreheads. 'We seed there was a light burning across the road, and we were sleeping in that ditch there for coolness, and I said to my friend here, "The office is open. Let's come along and speak to him as turned us back from the Degumber State," ' said the smaller of the two. He was the man I had met in the Mhow train, and his fellow was the red-bearded man of Marwar Junction. There was no mistaking the eyebrows of the one or the beard of the other.

I was not pleased, because I wished to go to sleep, not to squabble with loafers. 'What do you want?' I asked.

'Half an hour's talk with you, cool and comfortable, in the office,' said the red-bearded man. 'We'd *like* some drink – the contrack doesn't begin yet, Peachey, so you needn't look – but what we really want is advice. We don't want money. We ask you as a favour, because we found out you did us a bad turn about Degumber State.'

I led from the press-room to the stifling office with the maps on the walls, and the red-haired man rubbed his hands. 'That's something like,' said he. 'This was the proper shop to come to. Now, sir, let me introduce to you Brother Peachey Carnehan, that's him, and Brother Daniel Dravot, that is *me*, and the less said about our professions the better, for we have been most things in our time. Soldier, sailor, compositor, photographer, proofreader, street-preacher, *and* correspondent of the *Backwoodsman* when we thought the paper wanted one. Carnehan is sober, and so am I. Look at us first, and see that's sure. It will save you cutting into my talk. We'll take one of your cigars apiece, and you shall see us light up.'

I watched the test. The men were absolutely sober, so I gave them each a tepid whisky and soda.

'Well *and* good,' said Carnehan of the eyebrows, wiping the froth from his moustache. 'Let *me* talk now, Dan. We have been all over India, mostly on foot. We have been boiler-fitters, engine-drivers, petty contractors, and all that, and we have decided that India isn't big enough for such as us.'

They certainly were too big for the office. Dravot's beard seemed to fill half the room and Carnehan's shoulders the other half, as they sat on the big table. Carnehan continued: 'The country isn't half worked out because they that governs it won't let you touch it. They spend all their blessed time in governing it, and you can't lift a spade, nor chip a rock, nor look for oil, nor anything like that, without all the Government saying, "Leave it alone, and let us govern." Therefore, such *as* it is, we will let it alone, and go away to some other place where a man isn't crowded and can come to his own. We are not little men, and there is nothing that we are afraid of except drink, and we have signed a contrack on that. *Therefore*, we are going away to be kings.'

'Kings in our own right,' muttered Dravot.

'Yes, of course,' I said. 'You've been tramping in the sun, and it's a very warm night, and hadn't you better sleep over the notion? Come tomorrow.'

'Neither drunk nor sun-struck,' said Dravot. 'We have slept over the notion half a year, and require to see books and atlases, and we have decided that there is only one place now in the world that two strong men can Sar-a-*whack*. They call it Kafiristan. By my reckoning it's the top right-hand corner of Afghanistan, not more than three hundred miles from Peshawar. They have two-and-thirty heathen idols there, and we'll be the thirty-third and -fourth. It's a mountainous country, and the women of those parts are very beautiful.'

'But that is provided against in the contrack,' said Carnehan. 'Neither woman nor liqu–or, Daniel.'

'And that's all we know, except that no one has gone there, and they fight, and in any place where they fight, a man who knows how to drill men can always be a king. We shall go to those parts and say to any king we find – "D'you want to vanquish your foes?" and we will show him how to drill men; for that we know better than anything else. Then we will subvert that king and seize his throne and establish a dy–nasty.'

'You'll be cut to pieces before you're fifty miles across the border,' I said. 'You have to travel through Afghanistan to get to that country. It's one mass of mountains and peaks and glaciers, and no Englishman has been through it. The people are utter brutes, and even if you reached them you couldn't do anything.'

'That's more like,' said Carnehan. 'If you could think us a little more mad we would be more pleased. We have come to you to know about this country, to read a book about it, and to be shown maps. We want you to tell us that we are fools and to show us your books.' He turned to the bookcases.

'Are you at all in earnest?' I said.

'A little,' said Dravot sweetly. 'As big a map as you have got, even if it's all blank where Kafiristan is, and any books you've got. We can read, though we aren't very educated.'

I uncased the big thirty-two-miles-to-the-inch map of India, and two smaller frontier maps, hauled down volume INF–KAN of the *Encyclopaedia Britannica*, and the men consulted them.

'See here!' said Dravot, his thumb on the map. 'Up to Jagdallak, Peachey and me know the road. We was there with Roberts' Army. We'll have to turn off to the right at Jagdallak through Laghman territory. Then we get among the hills – fourteen thousand feet – fifteen thousand – it will be cold work there, but it don't look very far on the map.'

I handed him Wood on the *Sources of the Oxus*. Carnehan was deep in the *Encyclopaedia*.

'They're a mixed lot,' said Dravot reflectively; 'and it won't help us to know the names of their tribes. The more tribes the more they'll fight, and the better for us. From Jagdallak to Ashang. H'mm!'

'But all the information about the country is as sketchy and inaccurate as can be,' I protested. 'No one knows anything about it really. Here's the file of the United Services' Institute. Read what Bellew says.'

'Blow Bellew!' said Carnehan. 'Dan, they're a stinkin' lot of heathens, but this book here says they think they're related to us English.'

I smoked while the men pored over Raverty, Wood, the maps, and the *Encyclopaedia*.

'There is no use your waiting,' said Dravot politely. 'It's about four o'clock now. We'll go before six o'clock if you want to sleep, and we won't steal any of the papers. Don't you sit up. We're two harmless lunatics, and if you come tomorrow evening down to the serai we'll say goodbye to you.'

'You *are* two fools,' I answered. 'You'll be turned back at the frontier or cut up the minute you set foot in Afghanistan. Do you want any money or a recommendation down-country? I can help you to the chance of work next week.'

'Next week we shall be hard at work ourselves, thank you,' said Dravot. 'It isn't so easy being a king as it looks. When we've got our kingdom in going order we'll let you know, and you can come up and help us to govern it.'

'Would two lunatics make a contrack like that?' said Carnehan, with subdued pride, showing me a greasy half-sheet of notepaper on which was written the following. I copied it, then and there, as a curiosity:

This Contract between me and you persuing witnesseth in the name of God – Amen and so forth.

(One) That me and you will settle this matter together; i.e. to be Kings of Kafiristan.

(Two) That you and me will not, while this matter is being settled, look at any Liquor, nor any Woman black, white, or brown, so as to get mixed up with one or the other harmful.

(Three) That we conduct ourselves with Dignity and Discretion, and if one of us gets into trouble the other will stay by him.

Signed by you and me this day.

PEACHEY TALIAFERRO CARNEHAN

DANIEL DRAVOT

Both Gentlemen at Large

'There was no need for the last article,' said Carnehan, blushing modestly; 'but it looks regular. Now you know the sort of men that loafers are – we *are* loafers, Dan, until we get out of India – and *do* you think that we would sign a contrack like that unless we was in earnest? We have kept away from the two things that make life worth having.'

'You won't enjoy your lives much longer if you are going to try this idiotic adventure. Don't set the office on fire,' I said, 'and go away before nine o'clock.'

I left them still poring over the maps and making notes on the back of the 'contrack'. 'Be sure to come down to the serai tomorrow,' were their parting words.

The Kumharsen serai is the great foursquare sink of humanity where the strings of camels and horses from the north load and unload. All the nationalities of Central Asia may be found there, and most of the folk of India proper. Balkh and Bokhara there meet Bengal and Bombay, and try to draw eyeteeth. You can buy ponies, turquoises, Persian pussy-cats, saddle-bags, fat-tailed sheep and musk in the Kumharsen serai, and get many strange things for nothing. In the afternoon I went down to see whether my friends intended to keep their word or were lying there drunk.

A priest attired in fragments of ribbons and rags stalked up to me, gravely twisting a child's paper whirligig. Behind him was his servant bending under the load of a crate of mud toys. The two were loading up two camels, and the inhabitants of the serai watched them with shrieks of laughter.

'The priest is mad,' said a horse-dealer to me. 'He is going up to Kabul to sell toys to the Amir. He will either be raised to honour or have his head cut off. He came in here this morning and has been behaving madly ever since.'

'The witless are under the protection of God,' stammered a flat-cheeked Usbeg in broken Hindi. 'They foretell future events.'

'Would they could have foretold that my caravan would have been cut up by the Shinwaris almost within shadow of the pass!' grunted the Yusufzai agent of a Rajputana trading-house whose goods had been diverted into the hands of other robbers just across the border, and whose misfortunes were the laughing-stock of the bazar. 'Ohé, priest, whence come you and whither do you go?'

'From Roum have I come,' shouted the priest, waving his whirligig; 'from Roum, blown by the breath of a hundred devils across the sea! O thieves, robbers, liars, the blessing of Pir Khan on pigs, dogs, and perjurers! Who will take the Protected of God to the north to sell charms that are never still to the Amir? The camels shall not gall, the sons shall not fall sick, and the wives shall remain faithful while they are away, of the men who give me place in their caravan. Who will assist me to slipper the King of the Roos with a golden slipper with a silver heel? The protection of Pir Khan be upon his labours!' He spread out the skirts of his gaberdine and pirouetted between the lines of tethered horses.

'There starts a caravan from Peshawar to Kabul in twenty days, *Huzrut*,' said the Yusufzai trader. 'My camels go therewith. Do thou also go and bring us good luck.'

'I will go even now!' shouted the priest. 'I will depart upon my winged camels, and be at Peshawar in a day! Ho! Hazar Mir Khan,' he yelled to his servant, 'drive out the camels, but let me first mount my own.'

He leaped on the back of his beast as it knelt, and, turning round to me, cried: 'Come thou also, Sahib, a little along the road, and I will sell thee a charm – an amulet that shall make thee King of Kafiristan.'

Then the light broke upon me, and I followed the two camels out of the serai till we reached open road and the priest halted.

'What d'you think o' that?' said he in English. 'Carnehan can't talk their patter, so I've made him my servant. He makes a handsome servant. 'Tisn't for nothing that I've been knocking about the country for fourteen years. Didn't I do that talk neat? We'll hitch on to a caravan at Peshawar till we get to Jagdallak, and then we'll see if we can get donkeys for our camels, and strike into Kafiristan. Whirligigs for the Amir, O Lor! Put your hand under the camel-bags and tell me what you feel.'

I felt the butt of a Martini, and another and another.

'Twenty of 'em,' said Dravot placidly. 'Twenty of 'em and ammunition to correspond, under the whirligigs and the mud dolls.'

'Heaven help you if you are caught with those things!' I said. 'A Martini is worth her weight in silver among the Pathans.'

'Fifteen hundred rupees of capital – every rupee we could beg, borrow, or steal – are invested on these two camels,' said Dravot. 'We won't get caught. We're going through the Khyber with a regular caravan. Who'd touch a poor mad priest?'

'Have you got everything you want?' I asked, overcome with astonishment.

'Not yet, but we shall soon. Give us a memento of your kindness, *Brother*. You did me a service, yesterday, and that time in Marwar. Half my kingdom shall you have, as the saying is.' I slipped a small charm compass from my watch-chain and handed it up to the priest.

'Goodbye,' said Dravot, giving me hand cautiously. 'It's the last time we'll shake hands with an Englishman these many days. Shake hands with him, Carnehan,' he cried, as the second camel passed me.

Carnehan leaned down and shook hands. Then the camels passed away along the dusty road, and I was left alone to wonder. My eye could detect no failure in the disguises. The scene in the serai proved that they were complete to the native mind. There was just the chance, therefore, that Carnehan and Dravot would be able to wander through Afghanistan without detection. But, beyond, they would find death – certain and awful death.

Ten days later a native correspondent, giving me the news of the day from Peshawar, wound up his letter with: 'There has been much laughter here on account of a certain mad priest who is going in his estimation to sell petty gauds and insignificant trinkets which he ascribes as great charms to H.H. the Amir of Bokhara. He passed through Peshawar and associated himself to the second summer caravan that goes to Kabul. The merchants are pleased because through super–stition they imagine that such mad fellows bring good fortune.'

The two, then, were beyond the border. I would have prayed for them, but, that night, a real king died in Europe, and demanded an obituary notice.

The wheel of the world swings through the same phases again and again. Summer passed and winter thereafter, and came and passed again. The daily paper continued and I with it, and upon the third summer there fell a hot night, a night-issue, and a strained waiting for something to be telegraphed from the other side of the world, exactly as had happened before. A few great men had died in the past two years, the machines worked with more clatter, and some of the trees in the office garden were a few feet taller. But that was all the difference.

I passed over to the press-room, and went through just such a scene as I have already described. The nervous tension was stronger than it had been two years before, and I felt the heat more acutely. At three o'clock I cried, 'Print off,' and turned to go, when there crept to my chair what was left of a man. He was bent into a circle, his head was sunk between his shoulders, and he moved his feet one over the other like a bear. I could hardly see whether he walked or crawled – this rag-wrapped, whining cripple who addressed me by name, crying that he was come back. 'Can you give me a drink?' he whimpered. 'For the Lord's sake give me a drink!'

I went back to the office, the man following with groans of pain, and I turned up the lamp.

'Don't you know me?' he gasped, dropping into a chair, and he turned his drawn face, surmounted by a shock of grey hair, to the light.

I looked at him intently. Once before had I seen eyebrows that met over the nose in an inch-broad black band, but for the life of me I could not tell where.

'I don't know you,' I said, handing him the whisky. 'What can I do for you?'

He took a gulp of the spirit raw, and shivered in spite of the suffocating heat.

'I've come back,' he repeated; 'and I was the King of

Kafiristan – me and Dravot – crowned kings we was! In this office we settled it – you setting there and giving us the books. I am Peachey – Peachey Taliaferro Carnehan, and you've been setting here ever since – O Lord!'

I was more than a little astonished, and expressed my feelings accordingly.

'It's true,' said Carnehan, with a dry cackle, nursing his feet, which were wrapped in rags. 'True as gospel. Kings we were, with crowns upon our heads – me and Dravot – poor Dan – oh, poor, poor Dan, that would never take advice, not though I begged of him!'

'Take the whisky,' I said, 'and take your own time. Tell me all you can recollect of everything from beginning to end. You got across the border on your camels, Dravot dressed as a mad priest and you his servant. Do you remember that?'

'I ain't mad – yet, but I shall be that way soon. Of course I remember. Keep looking at me, or maybe my words will go all to pieces. Keep looking at me in my eyes and don't say anything.'

I leaned forward and looked into his face as steadily as I could. He dropped one hand upon the table and I grasped it by the wrist. It was twisted like a bird's claw, and upon the back was a ragged red diamond-shaped scar.

'No, don't look there. Look at *me*,' said Carnehan. 'That comes afterwards, but for the Lord's sake don't distrack me. We left with that caravan, me and Dravot playing all sorts of antics to amuse the people we were with. Dravot used to make us laugh in the evenings when all the people was cooking their dinners – cooking their dinners, and . . . what did they do then? They lit little fires with sparks that went into Dravot's beard, and we all laughed – fit to die. Little red fires they was, going into Dravot's big red beard – so funny.' His eyes left mine and he smiled foolishly.

'You went as far as Jagdallak with that caravan,' I said at a venture, 'after you had lit those fires. To Jagdallak, where you turned off to try to get into Kafiristan.'

'No, we didn't neither. What are you talking about? We turned off before Jagdallak, because we heard the roads was good. But they wasn't good enough for our two camels – mine and Dravot's. When we left the caravan, Dravot took off all his clothes and mine too, and said we would be heathen, because the Kafirs didn't allow Mohammedans to talk to them. So we dressed betwixt and between, and such a sight as Daniel Dravot I never saw yet nor expect to see again. He burned half his beard, and slung a sheepskin over his shoulder, and shaved his head into patterns. He shaved mine, too, and made me wear outrageous things to look like a heathen. That was in a most mountaineous country, and our camels couldn't go along any more because of the mountains. They were tall and black, and coming home I saw them fight like wild goats – there are lots of goats in Kafiristan. And these mountains, they never keep still, no more than the goats. Always fighting they are, and don't let you sleep at night.'

'Take some more whisky,' I said very slowly. 'What did you and Daniel Dravot do when the camels could go no farther because of the rough roads that led into Kafiristan?'

'What did which do? There was a party called Peachey Taliaferro Carnehan that was with Dravot. Shall I tell you about him? He died out there in the cold. Slap from the bridge fell old Peachey, turning and twisting in the air like a penny whirligig that you can sell to the Amir. – No; they was two for three-ha'pence, those whirligigs, or I am much mistaken and woeful sore . . . And then these camels were no use, and Peachey said to Dravot – "For the Lord's sake let's get out of this before our heads are chopped off," and with that they killed the camels all among the mountains, not having anything in particular to eat, but first they took off the boxes with the guns and the ammunition, till two men came along driving four mules. Dravot up and dances in front of them, singing – "Sell me four mules." Says the first man – "If you are rich enough to buy, you are rich enough to rob"; but before ever he could put his hand to his knife, Dravot breaks his neck over his knee, and the other party runs away. So Carnehan loaded the mules with the rifles that was taken off the camels, and together we starts forward into those bitter cold mountainous parts, and never a road broader than the back of your hand.'

He paused for a moment, while I asked him if he could remember the nature of the country through which he had journeyed.

'I am telling you as straight as I can, but my head isn't as good as it might be. They drove nails through it to make me hear better how Dravot died. The country was mountaineous and the mules were most contrary, and the inhabitants was dispersed and solitary. They went up and up, and down and down, and that other party, Carnehan, was imploring of Dravot not to sing and whistle so loud, for fear of bringing down the tremenjus avalanches. But Dravot says that if a king couldn't sing it wasn't worth being king, and whacked the mules over the rump, and never took no heed for ten cold days. We came to a big level valley all among the mountains, and the mules were near dead, so we killed them, not having anything in special for them or us to eat. We sat upon the boxes, and played odd and even with the cartridges that was jolted out.

'Then ten men with bows and arrows ran down that valley, chasing twenty men with bows and arrows, and the row was tremenjus. They was fair men – fairer than you or me – with yellow hair and remarkable well built. Says Dravot, unpacking the guns – "This is the beginning of the business. We'll fight for the ten men," and with that he fires two rifles at the twenty men, and drops one of them at two hundred yards from the rock where he was sitting. The other men began to run, but Carnehan and Dravot sits on the boxes picking them off at all ranges, up and down the valley. Then we goes up to the ten men that had run across the snow too, and they fires a footy little arrow at us. Dravot he shoots above their heads and they all falls down flat. Then he walks over them and kicks them, and then he lifts them up and shakes hands all round to make them friendly like. He calls them and gives them the boxes to carry, and waves his hand for all the world as though he was king already. They takes the boxes and him across the valley and up the hill into a pine wood on the top, where there was half a dozen big stone idols. Dravot he goes to the biggest – a fellow they call Imbra – and lays a rifle and a cartridge at his feet, rubbing his nose respectful with his own nose, patting him on the head, and saluting in front of it. He turns round to the men and nods his head, and says – "That's all right. I'm in the know too, and all these old jim-jams are my friends." Then he opens his mouth and points down it, and when the first man brings him food, he says – "No"; and when the second man brings him food he says – "No"; but when one of the old priests and the boss of the village brings him food, he says – "Yes," very haughty, and eats it slow. That was how we came to our first village, without any trouble, just as though we had tumbled from the skies. But we tumbled from one of those damned rope-bridges, you see, and – you couldn't expect a man to laugh much after that?'

'Take some more whisky and go on,' I said. 'That was the first village you came into. How did you get to be king?'

'I wasn't king,' said Carnehan. 'Dravot he was the king, and a handsome man he looked with the gold crown on his head and all. Him and the other party stayed in that village, and every morning Dravot sat by the side of old Imbra, and the people came and worshipped. That was Dravot's order. Then a lot of men came into the valley, and Carnehan and Dravot picks them off with the rifles before they knew where they was, and runs down into the valley and up again the other side and finds another village, same as the first one, and the people all falls down flat on their faces, and Dravot says – "Now what is the trouble between you two villages?" and the people points to a woman, as fair as you or me, that was carried off, and Dravot takes her back to the first village and counts up the dead – eight there was. For each dead man Dravot pours a little milk on the ground and waves his arms like a whirligig, and "That's all right," says he. Then he and Carnehan takes the big boss of each village by the arm and walks them down into the valley, and shows them how to scratch a line with a spear right down the valley, and gives each a sod of turf from both sides of the line. Then all the people comes down and shouts like the devil and all, and Dravot says – "Go and dig the land, and be fruitful and multiply," which they did, though they didn't understand. Then we asks the names of things in their lingo – bread and water and fire and idols and such, and Dravot leads the priest of each village up to the idol, and says he must sit there and judge the people, and if anything goes wrong he is to be shot.

'Next week they was all turning up the land in the valley as quiet as bees and much prettier, and the priests heard all the complaints and told Dravot in dumb show what it was about. "That's just the beginning," says Dravot. "They think we're gods." He and Carnehan picks out twenty good men and shows them how to click off a rifle, and form fours, and advance in line, and they was very pleased to do so, and clever to see the hang of it. Then he takes out his pipe and his baccy-pouch and leaves one at one village, and one at the other, and off we two goes to see what was to be done in the next valley. That was all rock, and there was a little village there, and Carnehan says – "Send 'em to the old valley to plant," and takes 'em there, and gives 'em some land that wasn't took before. They were a poor lot, and we blooded 'em with a kid before letting 'em into the new kingdom. That was to impress the people, and then they settled down quiet, and Carnehan went back to Dravot who had got into another valley, all snow and ice and most mountaineous. There was no people there and the army got afraid, so Dravot shoots one of them, and goes on till he finds some people in a village, and the army explains that unless the people wants to be killed they had better not shoot their little matchlocks; for they had matchlocks. We makes friends with the priest, and I stays there alone with two of the army, teaching the men how to drill, and a thundering big chief comes across the snow with kettle-drums and horns twanging, because he heard there was a new god kicking about. Carnehan sights for the brown of the men half a mile across the snow and wings one of them. Then he sends a message to the chief that, unless he wished to be killed, he must come and shake hands with me and leave his arms behind. The chief comes alone first, and Carnehan shakes hands with him and whirls his arms about, same as Dravot used, and very much surprised that chief was, and strokes my eyebrows. Then Carnehan goes alone to the chief, and asks him in dumb show if he had an enemy he hated. "I have," says the chief. So Carnehan weeds out the pick of his men, and sets the two of the army to show them drill, and at the end of two weeks the men can manoeuvre about as well as volunteers. So he marches with the chief to a great big plain on the top of a mountain, and the chief's men rushes into a village and takes it; we three Martinis firing into the brown of the enemy. So we took that village too, and I gives the chief a rag from my coat and says, "Occupy till I come"; which was scriptural. By way of a reminder, when me and the army was eighteen hundred yards away, I drops a bullet near him standing on the snow, and all the people falls flat on their faces. Then I sends a letter to Dravot wherever he be by land or by sea.'

At the risk of throwing the creature out of train I interrupted – 'How could you write a letter up yonder?'

'The letter? – Oh! – The letter! Keep looking at me

between the eyes, please. It was a string-talk letter, that we'd learned the way of it from a blind beggar in the Punjab.'

I remember that there had once come to the office a blind man with a knotted twig and a piece of string which he wound round the twig according to some cipher of his own. He could, after the lapse of days or hours, repeat the sentence which he had reeled up. He had reduced the alphabet to eleven primitive sounds, and tried to teach me his method, but I could not understand.

'I sent that letter to Dravot,' said Carnehan; 'and told him to come back because this kingdom was growing too big for me to handle, and then I struck for the first valley, to see how the priests were working. They called the village we took along with the chief, Bashkai, and the first village we took, Er-Heb. The priests at Er-Heb was doing all right, but they had a lot of pending cases about land to show me, and some men from another village had been firing arrows at night. I went out and looked for that village, and fired four rounds at it from a thousand yards. That used all the cartridges I cared to spend, and I waited for Dravot, who had been away two or three months, and I kept my people quiet.

'One morning I heard the devil's own noise of drums and horns, and Dan Dravot marches down the hill with his army and a tail of hundreds of men, and, which was the most amazing, a great gold crown on his head. "My Gord, Carnehan," says Daniel, "this is a tremenjus business, and we've got the whole country as far as it's worth having. I am the son of Alexander by Queen Semiramis, and you're my younger brother and a god too! It's the biggest thing we've ever seen.

I've been marching and fighting for six weeks with the army, and every footy little village for fifty miles has come in rejoiceful; and more than that, I've got the key of the whole show, as you'll see, and I've got a crown for you! I told 'em to make two of 'em at a place called Shu, where the gold lies in the rock like suet in mutton. Gold I've seen, and turquoise I've kicked out of the cliffs, and there's garnets in the sands of the river, and here's a chunk of amber that a man brought me. Call up all the priests and, here, take your crown."

'One of the men opens a black hair bag, and I slips the crown on. It was too small and too heavy, but I wore it for the glory. Hammered gold it was – five pound weight, like a hoop of a barrel.

' "Peachey," says Dravot, "we don't want to fight no more. The Craft's the trick, so help me!" and he brings forward that same chief that I left at Bashkai – Billy Fish we called him afterwards, because he was so like Billy Fish that drove the big tank-engine at Mach on the Bolan in the old days. "Shake hands with him," says Dravot, and I shook hands and nearly dropped, for Billy Fish gave me the Grip. I said nothing, but tried him with the Fellow Craft Grip. He answers all right, and I tried the Master's Grip, but that was a slip. "A Fellow Craft he is!" I says to Dan. "Does he know the word?" – "He does," says Dan, "and all the priests know. It's a miracle! The chiefs and the priests can work a Fellow Craft Lodge in a way that's very like ours, and they've cut the marks on the rocks, but they don't know the Third Degree, and they've come to find out. It's Gord's Truth! I've known these long years that the Afghans knew up to the Fellow Craft Degree, but this is a miracle. A god and a Grand-Master of the Craft am I, and a Lodge in the Third

Degree I will open, and we'll raise the head priests and the chiefs of the villages."

' "It's against all the law," I says, "holding a Lodge without warrant from anyone; and you know we never held office in any Lodge."

' "It's a masterstroke o' policy," says Dravot. "It means running the country as easy as a four-wheeled bogie on a down grade. We can't stop to enquire now, or they'll turn against us. I've forty chiefs at my heel, and passed and raised according to their merit they shall be. Billet these men on the villages, and see that we run up a Lodge of some kind. The temple of Imbra will do for the Lodge-room. The women must make aprons as you show them. I'll hold a levee of chiefs tonight and Lodge tomorrow."

'I was fair run off my legs, but I wasn't such a fool as not to see what a pull this Craft business gave us. I showed the priests' families how to make aprons of the degrees, but for Dravot's apron the blue border and marks was made of turquoise lumps on white hide, not cloth. We took a great square stone in the temple for the Master's chair, and little stones for the officers' chairs, and painted the black pavement with white squares, and did what we could to make things regular.

'At the levee which was held that night on the hillside with big bonfires, Dravot gives out that him and me were gods and sons of Alexander, and Past Grand-Masters in the Craft, and was come to make Kafiristan a country where every man should eat in peace and drink in quiet, and 'specially obey us. Then the chiefs come round to shake hands, and they were so hairy and white and fair it was just shaking hands with old friends. We gave them names according as they was like men we had known in India – Billy Fish, Holly Dilworth, Pikky Kergan, that was bazar-master when I was at Mhow, and so on, and so on.

'*The* most amazing miracles was at Lodge next night. One of the old priests was watching us continuous, and I felt uneasy, for I knew we'd have to fudge the Ritual, and I didn't know what the men knew. The old priest was a stranger come in from beyond the village of Bashkai. The minute Dravot puts on the Master's apron that the girls had made for him, the priest fetches a whoop and a howl, and tries to overturn the stone that Dravot was sitting on. "It's all up now," I says. "That comes of meddling with the Craft without warrant!" Dravot never winked an eye, not when ten priests took and tilted over the Grand-Master's chair – which was to say the stone of Imbra. The priests begins rubbing the bottom end of it to clear away the black dirt, and presently he shows all the other priests the Master's Mark, same as was on Dravot's apron, cut into the stone. Not even the priests of the temple of Imbra knew it was there. The old chap falls flat on his face at Dravot's feet and kisses 'em. "Luck again," says Dravot, across the Lodge to me; "they say it's the missing Mark that no one could understand the why of. We're more than safe now." Then he bangs the butt of his gun for a gavel and says: "By virtue of the authority vested in me by my own right hand and the help of Peachey, I declare myself Grand-Master of all Freemasonry in Kafiristan in this the Mother Lodge o' the country, and King of Kafiristan equally with Peachey!" At that he puts on his crown and I puts on mine – I was doing Senior Warden – and we opens the Lodge in most ample form. It was a amazing miracle! The priests moved in Lodge through the first two degrees almost without telling, as if the memory was coming back to them. After that, Peachey and Dravot raised such as was worthy – high priests and chiefs of far-off villages. Billy Fish was the first, and I can tell you we scared the soul out of him. It was not in any way according to Ritual, but it served our turn. We didn't raise more than ten of the biggest men, because we didn't want to make the Degree common. And they was clamouring to be raised.

' "In another six months," says Dravot, "we'll hold another Communication, and see how you are working." Then he asks them about their villages, and learns that they was fighting one against the other, and were sick and tired of it. And when they wasn't doing that they was fighting with the Mohammedans. "You can fight those when they come into our country," says Dravot. "Tell off every tenth man of your tribes for a frontier guard, and send two hundred at a time to this valley to be drilled. Nobody is going to be shot or speared any more so long as he does well, and I know that you won't cheat me, because you're white people – sons of Alexander – and not like common, black Mohammedans. You are *my* people, and by God," says he, running off into English at the end – "I'll make a damned fine nation of you, or I'll die in the making!"

'I can't tell all we did for the next six months, because Dravot did a lot I couldn't see the hang of, and he learned their lingo in a way I never could. My work was to help the people plough, and now and again go out with some of the army and see what the other villages were doing, and make 'em throw rope-bridges across the ravines which cut up the country horrid. Dravot was very kind to me, but when he walked up and down in the pine wood pulling that bloody red beard of his with both fists I knew he was thinking plans I could not advise about, and I just waited for orders.

'But Dravot never showed me disrespect before the people. They were afraid of me and the army, but they loved Dan. He was the best of friends with the priests and the chiefs; but anyone could come across the hills with a complaint, and Dravot would hear him out fair, and call four priests together and say what was to be done. He used to call in Billy Fish from Bashkai, and Pikky Kergan from Shu, and an old chief we called Kafuzelum – it was like enough to his real name – and hold councils with 'em when there was any fighting to be done in small villages. That was his council of war, and the four priests of Bashkai, Shu, Khawak, and Madora was his privy council. Between the lot of 'em they sent me, with forty men and twenty rifles and sixty men carrying turquoises, into the Ghorband country to buy those handmade Martini rifles, that come out of the Amir's workshops at Kabul, from one of the Amir's Herati regiments that would have sold the very teeth out of their mouths for turquoises.

'I stayed in Ghorband a month, and gave the Governor there the pick of my baskets for hush-money, and bribed the colonel of the regiment some more, and, between the two and the tribespeople, we got more than a hundred handmade Martinis, a hundred good Kohat *jezails* that'll throw to six hundred yards, and forty man-loads of very bad ammunition for the rifles. I came back with what I had, and distributed 'em among the men that the chiefs sent in to me to drill. Dravot was too busy to attend to those things, but the old army that we first made helped me, and we turned out five hundred men that could drill, and two hundred that knew how to hold arms pretty straight. Even those cork-screwed, handmade guns was a miracle to them. Dravot talked big about powder-shops and factories, walking up and down in the pine wood when the winter was coming on.

' "I won't make a nation," says he. "I'll make an empire! These men aren't niggers; they're English! Look at their eyes – look at their mouths. Look at the way they stand up. They sit on chairs in their own houses. They're the Lost Tribes, or something like it, and they've grown to be English. I'll take a census in the spring if the priests don't get frightened. There must be a fair two million of 'em in these hills. The villages are full o' little children. Two million people – two hundred and fifty thousand fighting men – and all English! They only want the rifles and a little drilling. Two hundred and fifty thousand men, ready to cut in on Russia's right flank when she tries for India! Peachey, man," he says, chewing his beard in great hunks, "we shall be emperors – emperors of the earth! Rajah Brooke will be a suckling to us. I'll treat with the Viceroy on equal terms. I'll ask him to send me twelve picked English – twelve that I know of – to help us govern a bit. There's Mackray, sergeant-pensioner at Segowli – many's the good dinner he's given me, and his wife a pair of trousers. There's Donkin, the warder of Tounghoo jail; there's hundreds that I could lay my hand on if I was in India. The Viceroy shall do it for me. I'll send a man through in the spring for those men, and I'll write for a dispensation from the Grand Lodge for what I've done as Grand-Master. That – and all the Sniders that'll be thrown out when the native troops in India take up the Martini. They'll be worn smooth, but they'll do for fighting in these hills. Twelve English, a hundred thousand Sniders run through the Amir's country in driblets – I'd be content with twenty thousand in one year – and we'd be an empire. When everything was shipshape, I'd hand over the crown – this crown I'm wearing now – to Queen Victoria on my knees, and she'd say: 'Rise up, Sir Daniel Dravot.' Oh, it's big! It's big, I tell you! But there's so much to be done in every place – Bashkai, Khawak, Shu, and everywhere else."

' "What is it?" I says. "There are no more men coming in to be drilled this autumn. Look at those fat, black clouds. They're bringing the snow."

' "It isn't that," says Daniel, putting his hand very hard on my shoulder; "and I don't wish to say anything that's against you, for no other living man would have followed me and made me what I am as you have done. You're a first-class commander-in-chief, and the people know you; but – it's a big country, and somehow you can't help me, Peachey, in the way I want to be helped."

' "Go to your blasted priests, then!" I said, and I was sorry when I made that remark, but it did hurt me sore to find Daniel talking so superior when I'd drilled all the men, and done all he told me. "Don't let's quarrel, Peachey," says Daniel without cursing. "You're a king too, and the half of this kingdom is yours; but can't you see, Peachey, we want cleverer men than us now – three or four of 'em, that we can scatter about for our deputies. It's a hugeous great state, and I can't always tell the right thing to do, and I haven't time for all I want to do, and here's the winter coming on and all." He put half his beard into his mouth, all red like the gold of his crown.

' "I'm sorry, Daniel," says I. "I've done all I could. I've drilled the men and shown the people how to stack their oats better; and I've brought in those tinware rifles from Ghorband – but I know what you're driving at. I take it kings always feel oppressed that way."

' "There's another thing too," says Dravot, walking up and down. "The winter's coming and these people won't be giving much trouble, and if they do we can't move about. I want a wife."

' "For Gord's sake leave the women alone!" I says. "We've both got all the work we can, though I *am* a fool. Remember the contrack, and keep clear o' women."

' "The contrack only lasted till such time as we was kings; and kings we have been these months past," says Dravot, weighing his crown in his hand. "You go get a wife too, Peachey – a nice, strappin', plump girl that'll keep you warm in the winter. They're prettier than English girls, and we can take the pick of 'em. Boil 'em once or twice in hot water and they'll come out like chicken and ham."

' "Don't tempt me!" I says. "I will not have any dealings with a woman not till we are a dam' side more settled than we are now. I've been doing the work o' two men, and you've been doing the work o' three. Let's lie off a bit, and see if we can get some better tobacco from Afghan country and run in some good liquor; but no women."

' "Who's talking o' *women*?" says Dravot. "I said *wife* – a queen to breed a king's son for the king. A queen out of the strongest tribe, that'll make them your blood-brothers, and that'll lie by your side and tell you all the people thinks about you and their own affairs. That's what I want."

' "Do you remember that Bengali woman I kept at Mogul serai when I was a platelayer?" says I. "A fat lot o' good she was to me. She taught me the lingo and one or two other things; but what happened? She ran away with the station-master's servant and half my month's pay. Then she turned up at Dadur Junction in tow of a half-caste, and had the impidence to say I was her husband – all among the drivers in the running-shed too!"

' "We've done with that," says Dravot; "these women are whiter than you or me, and a queen I will have for the winter months."

' "For the last time o' asking, Dan, do *not*," I says. "It'll only bring us harm. The Bible says that kings ain't to waste their strength on women, 'specially when they've got a new raw kingdom to work over."

' "For the last time of answering, I will," said Dravot, and he went away through the pine trees looking like a big red devil, the sun being on his crown and beard and all.

'But getting a wife was not as easy as Dan thought. He put it before the council, and there was no answer till Billy Fish said that he'd better ask the girls. Dravot damned them all round. "What's wrong with me?" he shouts, standing by the idol Imbra. "Am I a dog or am I not enough of a man for your wenches? Haven't I put the shadow of my hand over this country? Who stopped the last Afghan raid?" It was me really, but Dravot was too angry to remember. "Who bought your guns? Who repaired the bridges? Who's the Grand-Master of the sign cut in the stone?" says he, and he thumped his hand on the block that he used to sit on in Lodge, and at council, which opened like Lodge always. Billy Fish said nothing and no more did the others. "Keep your hair on, Dan," said I; "and ask the girls. That's how it's done at home, and these people are quite English."

' "The marriage of the king is a matter of state," says Dan, in a white-hot rage, for he could feel, I hope, that he was going against his better mind. He walked out of the council-room, and the others sat still, looking at the ground.

' "Billy Fish," says I to the Chief of Bashkai, "what's the difficulty here? A straight answer to a true friend."

' "You know," says Billy Fish. "How should a man tell you who knows everything? How can daughters of men marry gods or devils? It's not proper."

'I remembered something like that in the Bible; but if, after seeing us as long as they had, they still believed we were gods, it wasn't for me to undeceive them.

' "A god can do anything," says I. "If the king is fond of a girl he'll not let her die." – "She'll have to," said Billy Fish. "There are all sorts of gods and devils in these mountains, and now and again a girl marries one of them and isn't seen any more. Besides, you two know the mark cut in the stone. Only the gods know that. We thought you were men till you showed the sign of the Master."

'I wished then that we had explained about the loss of the genuine secrets of a Master-Mason at the first go-off; but I said nothing. All that night there was a blowing of horns in a little dark temple halfway down the hill, and I heard a girl crying fit to die. One of the priests told us that she was being prepared to marry the king.

' "I'll have no nonsense of that kind," says Dan. "I don't want to interfere with your customs, but I'll take my own wife." – "The girl's a little bit afraid," says the priest. "She thinks she's going to die, and they are a-heartening of her up down in the temple."

' "Hearten her very tender, then," says Dravot, "or I'll hearten you with the butt of a gun so you'll never want to be heartened again." He licked his lips, did Dan, and stayed up walking about more than half the night, thinking of the wife that he was going to get in the morning. I wasn't any means comfortable, for I knew that dealings with a woman in foreign parts, though you was a crowned king twenty times over, could not but be risky. I got up very early in the morning while Dravot was asleep, and I saw the priests talking together in whispers, and the chiefs talking together too, and they looked at me out of the corners of their eyes.

' "What is up, Fish?" I says to the Bashkai man, who was wrapped up in his furs and looking splendid to behold.

' "I can't rightly say," says he; "but if you can make the king drop all this nonsense about marriage, you'll be doing him and me and yourself a great service."

' "That I do believe," says I. "But sure, you know, Billy, as well as me, having fought against and for us, that the king and me are nothing more than two of the finest men that God Almighty ever made. Nothing more, I do assure you."

' "That may be," says Billy Fish, "and yet I should be sorry if it was." He sinks his head upon his great fur cloak for a minute and thinks. "King," says he, "be you man or god or devil, I'll stick by you today. I have twenty of my men with me, and they will follow me. We'll go to Bashkai until the storm blows over."

'A little snow had fallen in the night, and everything was white except the greasy fat clouds that blew down and down from the north. Dravot came out with his crown on his head, swinging his arms and stamping his feet, and looking more pleased than Punch.

' "For the last time, drop it, Dan," says I in a whisper, "Billy Fish here says that there will be a row."

' "A row among my people!" says Dravot. "Not much. Peachey, you're a fool not to get a wife too. Where's the girl?" says he with a voice as loud as the braying of a jackass. "Call up all the chiefs and priests, and let the emperor see if his wife suits him."

'There was no need to call anyone. They were all there leaning on their guns and spears round the clearing in the centre of the pine wood. A lot of priests went down to the little temple to bring up the girl, and the horns blew fit to wake the dead. Billy Fish saunters round and gets as close to Daniel as he could, and behind him stood his twenty men with matchlocks. Not a man of them under six feet. I was next to Dravot, and behind me was twenty men of the regular army. Up comes the girl, and a strapping wench she was, covered with silver and turquoises, but white as death, and looking back every minute at the priests.

' "She'll do," said Dan, looking her over. "What's to be afraid of, lass? Come and kiss me." He puts his arm round her. She shuts her eyes, gives a bit of a squeak, and down goes her face in the side of Dan's flaming red beard.

' "The slut's bitten me!" says he, clapping his hand to his neck, and, sure enough, his hand was red with blood. Billy Fish and two of his matchlock-men catches hold of Dan by the shoulders and drags him into the Bashkai lot, while the priests howl in their lingo – "Neither God nor Devil but a man!" I was all taken aback, for a priest cut at me in front, and the army behind began firing into the Bashkai men.

' "God A'mighty!" says Dan. "What is the meaning o' this?"

' "Come back! Come away!" says Billy Fish. "Ruin and mutiny is the matter. We'll break for Bashkai if we can."

'I tried to give some sort of orders to my men – the men o' the regular army – but it was no use, so I fired into the brown of 'em with an English Martini and drilled three beggars in a line. The valley was full of shouting, howling creatures, and every soul was shrieking, "Not a god nor a devil but only a man!" The Bashkai troops stuck to Billy Fish all they were worth, but their matchlocks wasn't half as good as the Kabul breech-loaders, and four of them dropped. Dan was bellowing like a bull, for he was very wrathy; and Billy Fish had a hard job to prevent him running out at the crowd.

' "We can't stand," says Billy Fish. "Make a run for it down the valley! The whole place is against us." The matchlock-men ran, and we went down the valley in spite of Dravot. He was swearing horrible and crying out he was a king. The priests rolled great stones on us, and the regular army fired hard, and there wasn't more than six men, not counting Dan, Billy Fish, and me, that came down to the bottom of the valley alive.

'Then they stopped firing and the horns in the temple blew again. "Come away – for God's sake come away!" says Billy Fish. "They'll send runners out to all the villages before ever we get to Bashkai. I can protect you there, but I can't do anything now."

'My own notion is that Dan began to go mad in his head from that hour. He stared up and down like a stuck pig. Then he was all for walking back alone and killing the priests with his bare hands; which he could have done. "An emperor am I," says Daniel, "and next year I shall be a knight of the queen."

' "All right, Dan," says I; "but come along now while there's time."

' "It's your fault," says he, "for not looking after your army better. There was mutiny in the midst, and you didn't know – you damned engine-driving, plate-laying, missionary's-pass-hunting hound!" He sat upon a rock and called me every foul name he could lay tongue to. I was too heart-sick to care, though it was all his foolishness that brought the smash.

' "I'm sorry, Dan," says I, "but there's no accounting for natives. This business is our 'Fifty-Seven. Maybe we'll make something out of it yet, when we've got to Bashkai."

' "Let's get to Bashkai, then," says Dan, "and, by God, when I come back here again I'll sweep the valley so there isn't a bug in a blanket left!"

'We walked all that day, and all that night Dan was stumping up and down on the snow, chewing his beard and muttering to himself.

' "There's no hope o' getting clear," said Billy Fish. "The priests will have sent runners to the villages to say that you are only men. Why didn't you stick on as gods till things was more settled? I'm a dead man," says Billy Fish, and he throws himself down on the snow and begins to pray to his gods.

'Next morning we was in a cruel bad country – all up and down, no level ground at all, and no food either. The six Bashkai men looked at Billy Fish hungry-ways as if they wanted to ask something, but they said never a word. At noon we came to the top of a flat mountain all covered with snow, and when we climbed up into it, behold, there was an army in position waiting in the middle!

' "The runners have been very quick," says Billy Fish, with a little bit of a laugh. "They are waiting for us."

'Three or four men began to fire from the enemy's side, and a chance shot took Daniel in the calf of the leg. That brought him to his senses. He looks across the snow at the army, and sees the rifles that we had brought into the country.

' "We're done for," says he. "They are Englishmen, these people, – and it's my blasted nonsense that has brought you to this. Get back, Billy Fish, and take your men away; you've done what you could, and now cut for it. Carnehan," says he, "shake hands with me and go along with Billy. Maybe they won't kill you. I'll go and meet 'em alone. It's me that did it. Me, the king!"

' "Go!" says I. "Go to hell, Dan! I'm with you here. Billy Fish, you clear out, and we two will meet those folk."

' "I'm a chief," says Billy Fish, quite quiet. "I stay with you. My men can go."

'The Bashkai fellows didn't wait for a second word, but ran off, and Dan and me and Billy Fish walked across to where the drums were drumming and the horns were horning. It was cold – awful cold. I've got that cold in the back of my head now. There's a lump of it there.'

The punkah-coolies had gone to sleep. Two kerosene lamps were blazing in the office, and the perspiration poured down my face and splashed on the blotter as I leaned forward. Carnehan was shivering, and I feared that his mind might go. I wiped my face, took a fresh grip of the piteously mangled hands, and said: 'What happened after that?'

The momentary shift of my eyes had broken the clear current.

'What was you pleased to say?' whined Carnehan. 'They took them without any sound. Not a little whisper all along the snow, not though the king knocked down the first man that set hand on him – not though old Peachey fired his last cartridge into the brown of 'em. Not a single solitary sound did those swines make. They just closed up tight, and I tell you their furs stunk. There was a man called Billy Fish, a good friend of us all, and they cut his throat, sir, then and there, like a pig; and the king kicks up the bloody snow and says: "We've had a dashed fine run for our money. What's coming next?" But Peachey, Peachey Taliaferro, I tell you, sir, in confidence as betwixt two friends, he lost his head, sir. No, he didn't neither. The king lost his head, so he did, all along o' one of those cunning rope-bridges. Kindly let me have the paper-cutter, sir. It tilted this way. They marched him a mile across that snow to a rope-bridge over a ravine with a river at the bottom. You may have seen such. They prodded him behind like an ox. "Damn your eyes!" says the king. "D'you suppose I can't die like a gentleman?" He turns to Peachey – Peachey that was crying like a child. "I've brought you to this, Peachey," says he. "Brought you out of your happy life to be killed in Kafiristan, where you was late commander-in-chief of the emperor's forces. Say you forgive me, Peachey." – "I do," says Peachey. "Fully and freely do I forgive you, Dan." – "Shake hands, Peachey," says he. "I'm going now." Out he goes, looking neither right nor left, and when he was plumb in the middle of those dizzy dancing ropes – "Cut, you beggars," he shouts; and they cut, and old Dan fell, turning round and round and round, twenty thousand miles, for he took half an hour to fall till he struck the water, and I could see his body caught on a rock with the gold crown close beside.

'But do you know what they did to Peachey between two pine trees? They crucified him, sir, as Peachey's hands will show. They used wooden pegs for his hands and his feet; and he didn't die. He hung there and screamed, and they took him down next day, and said it was a miracle that he wasn't dead. They took him down – poor old Peachey that hadn't done them any harm – that hadn't done them any – '

He rocked to and fro and wept bitterly, wiping his eyes with the back of his scarred hands and moaning like a child for some ten minutes.

'They was cruel enough to feed him up in the temple, because they said he was more of a god than old Daniel that was a man. Then they turned him out on the snow, and told him to go home, and Peachey came home in about a year, begging along the roads quite safe; for Daniel Dravot he walked before and said: "Come along, Peachey. It's a big thing we're doing." The mountains they danced at night, and the mountains they tried to fall on Peachey's head, but Dan he held up his hand, and Peachey came along bent double. He never let go of Dan's hand, and he never let go of Dan's head. They gave it to him as a present in the temple, to remind him not to come again, and though the crown was pure gold, and Peachey was starving, never would Peachey sell the same. You knew Dravot, sir! You knew Right Worshipful Brother Dravot! Look at him now!'

He fumbled in the mass of rags round his bent waist;

brought out a black horsehair bag embroidered with silver thread, and shook therefrom on to my table – the dried, withered head of Daniel Dravot! The morning sun that had long been paling the lamps struck the red beard and blind sunken eyes; struck, too, a heavy circlet of gold studded with raw turquoises, that Carnehan placed tenderly on the battered temples.

'You be'old now,' said Carnehan, 'the emperor in his 'abit as he lived – the King of Kafiristan with his crown upon his head. Poor old Daniel that was a monarch once!'

I shuddered, for, in spite of defacements manifold, I recognised the head of the man of Marwar Junction. Carnehan rose to go. I attempted to stop him. He was not fit to walk abroad. 'Let me take away the whisky, and give me a little money,' he gasped. 'I was a king once. I'll go to the Deputy Commissioner and ask to set in the poorhouse till I get my health. No, thank you, I can't wait till you get a carriage for me. I've urgent private affairs – in the south – at Marwar.'

He shambled out of the office and departed in the direction of the Deputy Commissioner's house. That day at noon I had occasion to go down the blinding hot mall, and I saw a crooked man crawling along the white dust of the roadside, his hat in his hand, quavering dolorously after the fashion of street-singers at home. There was not a soul in sight, and he was out of all possible earshot of the houses. And he sang through his nose, turning his head from right to left –

'The Son of Man goes forth to war,
  A kingly crown to gain;
His blood-red banner streams afar!
  Who follows in his train?'

I waited to hear no more, but put the poor wretch into my carriage and drove him off to the nearest missionary for eventual transfer to the asylum. He repeated the hymn twice while he was with me, whom he did not in the least recognise, and I left him singing it to the missionary.

Two days later I enquired after his welfare of the superintendent of the asylum.

'He was admitted suffering from sunstroke. He died early yesterday morning,' said the superintendent. 'Is it true that he was half an hour bareheaded in the sun at midday?'

'Yes,' said I, 'but do you happen to know if he had anything upon him by any chance when he died?'

'Not to my knowledge,' said the superintendent.

And there the matter rests.

Afterword

Perhaps no other major English-language writer has suffered such a widely varying critical reputation as Rudyard Kipling. He was lionised during his early years as the natural heir to Dickens's mantle – oddly, because his novels are generally his least successful works. He was regarded as largely a spent force during his later years, especially – and ironically – after his receipt of the Nobel Prize for Literature in 1907. He was vilified throughout much of the latter half of the twentieth century as a racist aggrandiser of the dead days of the British Empire. It is only relatively recently that the eye of criticism has begun to re-evaluate Kipling as what he was: one of the most astonishing, important, versatile and gifted figures in literary history. Further, those remarks and observations in his fictions which were for so long taken literally – as denigrations of the non-white races, in particular the peoples of the Indian subcontinent – can now be seen as quietly subversive of the prevalent, racist, milieu of his day. Kipling was someone who had no trouble in acknowledging that Gunga Din could be a better man than he himself, and in thereby sliding a shiv – oh, so smoothly – into the spine of his age's bigotry.

When one reads any collection of Kipling's short stories today, the first thing that strikes one is their seeming modernity. The narrative techniques which Kipling deployed without any seeming consciousness that he was doing something 'special' are often much the same as those being rediscovered by the short-story writers of today. He exploited as a matter of course the technique known as the frame story (whereby the main tale is contained within and interacts with a subsidiary narrative). He had no compunction about using himself as a character in his own stories, usually under the thin veil of an invented name. And, unlike most of his predecessors, he was content in his descriptions to leave many of the gaps to be filled in by the reader's imagination (which is not to say that Kipling could not fill in those gaps when he felt it essential to do so).

In none of these (or other) respects could Kipling be said to be a pioneer – there are plenty of precedents for all of them – but what he managed to do was amalgamate them all with an apparent ease that brought about a new form of naturalism in tale-telling. When we read today something by such contemporaries – and friends – of his as Rider Haggard and Henry James, we are all too aware that we are reading something consciously *written*, complete with passages whose elegance the author intended his readers to admire. In the case of Kipling, while there are examples galore of passages that can indeed be admired for their beauty, the accent instead was on the painting of a picture and the telling of a tale. It is symptomatic of his approach that many of his tales benefit from being read out loud: they belong, in a sense, more to the oral tradition than that of written literature. This is all the more surprising in that Kipling was, after all, a highly accomplished – and prolific – poet, and as such might have been expected to empurple his tales more, rather than less.

The stories in this selection show Kipling operating in a wide diversity of the styles which he made his own. There are fantasies and adventure tales, a couple of ghost stories, a school story, a fairytale and even a couple of pieces of science fiction.

The Phantom 'Rickshaw

The driving force behind this powerful ghost story is – as in all the best ghost stories – not so much the ghost but the guilt of the living, in this case of the unfortunate Pansay, who acted appallingly to his mistress Mrs Keith-Wessington and is unable to escape from her piteous entreaties even after her death. That Pansay quite insouciantly engaged in an adulterous relationship with her was a sin scandalous enough, but that he then rejected her so miserably was a sin unforgivable. Because Pansay's belated sense of guilt is the mainspring of the tale, it is left deliciously uncertain as to whether the haunting is an objective or a subjective one – that is, if it is genuinely a supernatural manifestation or more a matter of mental affliction. Heatherlegh, the no-nonsense doctor and Good Samaritan who treated Pansay, believes unequivocally that the latter is the case. We, as readers, must instead surely agree with the narrator of Kipling's frame story that 'there was a crack in Pansay's head and a little bit of the Dark World came through and pressed him to death'. Interestingly in view of Kipling's use of the phrase 'pressed him to death', it is less the spectral presence that scares us than the suffocating pressure of Pansay's own guilt.

'The Phantom 'Rickshaw' was first published in 1885 in *Quartette*, the Christmas Annual of the *Civil & Military Gazette*, and was revised for its publication in the story collection *The Phantom 'Rickshaw and Other Tales* (1888).

'The Finest Story in the World'

In a sense this story is an extended joke, a tall tale told with a considerable richness of humour and humanity, deriving its quasi-plausibility from its accurate dissection of the foibles of those who are in love with the notion of being a writer but lack, however industrious they might appear, the mental application – and perhaps the talent – to create anything of any worth. Young Charlie Mears is perfectly prepared to spend all his energies and spare time ripping out reams of prose and poetry, but never has the patience, whatever his protests to the contrary, to attempt to *learn* his chosen art. He is destined to a lifetime of mediocrity, except . . . The 'except' is the basis of this superb tale.

No writer can fail to fall into wry laughter at Kipling's portrait of the author *manqué*, which is spared from cruelty only by its fundamental compassion:

> He desired to make himself an undying name chiefly through verse, though he was not above sending stories of love and death to the penny-in-the-slot journals. It was my fate to sit still while Charlie read me poems of many hundred lines, and bulky fragments of plays that would surely shake the world. My reward was his unreserved confidence, and the self-revelations and troubles of a young man are almost as holy as those of a maiden. Charlie had never fallen in love, but was anxious to do so on the first opportunity; he believed in all things good and all things honourable, but at the same time, was curiously careful to let me see that he knew his way about the world as befitted a bank-clerk on twenty-five shillings a week. He rhymed

'dove' with 'love' and 'moon' with 'June', and devoutly believed that they had never so been rhymed before. The long lame gaps in his plays he filled up with hasty words of apology and description, and swept on, seeing all that he intended to do so clearly that he esteemed it already done, and turned to me for applause.

What can be missed as we grin at the inadequacies of Charlie and the ever-increasing desperation of the mendacious narrator, a professional writer eager to make a quick buck out of the strange ability of his young protégé to recall past lives, is that this is also a remarkably sophisticated fantasy story. If not itself the finest story in the world, it is certainly one of them.

' "The Finest Story in the World" ' was first published in 1891 in the *Contemporary Review*, and collected in *Many Inventions* (1893).

With the Night Mail and As Easy as ABC

These two related science-fiction stories concern themselves with the doings of the Aerial Board of Control (the ABC of the latter story's title). The first is subtitled 'A Story of 2000 AD'; the second is seemingly set far further in the future, when plague and slaughter have rendered the world significantly less populated than it is today.

'With the Night Mail' is not so much a story as a narrative designed to evoke the reader's sense of wonder at the marvels technology will soon be ushering in; it can be regarded as Kipling's response to the highly popular quasi-predictive fictions of H. G. Wells. The narrator rides with the night mail, which is carried across the Atlantic at seemingly astonishing speed by airship; he and his companions have various adventures. But there is a subtext to the tale that would be more fully explored in 'As Easy as ABC': that whoever controls the air will also control the land:

> . . . that semi-elected, semi-nominated body [the Aerial Board of Control] of a few score of persons of both sexes, controls this planet. 'Transportation is Civilisation', our motto runs. Theoretically, we do what we please so long as we do not interfere with the traffic *and all it implies*. Practically , the ABC confirms or annuls all international arrangements and, to judge from its last report, finds our tolerant, humorous, lazy little planet only too ready to shift the whole burden of public administration on its shoulders.

Without that subtext, Kipling's vision of the world in the year 2000 might seem with hindsight somewhat timid – after all, by the real year 2000 dirigibles had largely become curios and antiquities, the night mail was likely to be transported by supersonic jet, and the cutting edge of transport was the Space Shuttle. However, it's clear that he was envisaging, as backdrop to the story, an astonishing measure of social change: his implication was that, to all intents and purposes, sovereign nations had become a thing of the past.

He expanded upon this theme in 'As Easy as ABC', the more ambitious of the two stories, which depicts what the narrator regards as a near-utopia while presenting a disturbingly dystopian vision of the future. The technological armoury of the ABC has become such as to dwarf any other human endeavours; by now the ABC has become a substitute for God, but a

God able and reasonably willing to play an active part in the doings of mortals. War is a thing of the past; democracy is reviled as merely another guise for mob rule. All the ingredients are there for a sort of quasi-benevolent fascist tyranny in which everyone is so militant in the defence of their own 'freedom' and 'individuality' that they have squeezed out any possibility of either: dissenters are at risk of savage repression at the hands of the mob whose members detest the very concept of mob rule.

'With the Night Mail: A Story of 2000 AD' was first published in *McClure's Magazine* in 1905 and collected in *Actions and Reactions* (1909). 'As Easy as ABC' was first published in 1912 in the *London Magazine* and collected in *A Diversity of Creatures* (1917). On original publication both were accompanied by supposedly contemporary (to the tale) advertisements, written by Kipling; these have today lost much of their pith.

The Strange Ride of Morrowbie Jukes

Stories about the afterlife are almost by definition fantasies, although many revisionist writers have attempted to depict 'the next world' as a thoroughly domesticated, humdrum place, thereby making the fantasy mundane – usually for no good reason other than to demonstrate their own cleverness. Here Kipling adopted an entirely different approach to the afterlife story. The afterlife – one of several purported – in 'The Strange Ride of Morrowbie Jukes' is as real and rationalised as one could ask of it: there is no logical reason at all why such places should not physically exist in the real world. The conceit of the tale is that Hindu victims of coma and other forms of pseudo-death who unobligingly reveal themselves to be still very much alive at the start of the funeral ceremonies are regarded as dead in all but the actual condition, and consequently banished for the rest of their existences to isolated hell-holes where they must subsist as best they can, all hopes of escape cut off. What the writer achieved was an astonishing paradox: through rationalising every element of his story he rendered it inordinately fantasticated.

It cannot be denied that 'The Strange Ride of Morrowbie Jukes' is the work of the immature Kipling: the racist attitude of Jukes to Gunga Dass and the other Indian denizens of the afterlife is deeply objectionable to the modern reader, and must have been so to many in Kipling's own time; and the ending of the story is rushed and arbitrary, as if the writer had run out of either time or space – or both. In mitigation, it should be pointed out that, at the time he wrote the story, Kipling was only just out of his teens, if indeed he was out of them at all. What is more important than the story's defects is the vividness of its central image, which lasts long in the mind.

'The Strange Ride of Morrowbie Jukes' was first published in 1885 in *Quartette*, the Christmas Annual of the *Civil & Military Gazette*, the same issue as 'The Phantom 'Rickshaw'. Also like that story, it was collected in *The Phantom 'Rickshaw and Other Tales* (1888).

In the House of Suddhoo

The quirkiest of the tales in this volume, 'In the House of Suddhoo' is one of Kipling's many stories about the wiliness of the Indians among whom he spent much of his early life. It is the tale of a con trick – and a rather cruel con trick at that – which relies for its working on the credulity and superstition of the simple, good and honest man who is the only person to emerge from the account with very much credit; even the narrator in effect betrays, through pusillanimity, his 'great friend' Suddhoo. Ironically, since Kipling was in later life accused of being misogynist, the most strikingly and affectionately portrayed character in the story is the lovely and intelligent whore Janoo.

'In the House of Suddhoo' was first published in 1886 in the *Civil & Military Gazette* under the title 'Section 420, I.P.C.' (I.P.C. = Indian Penal Code), and was collected in *Plain Tales from the Hills* (1888).

Slaves of the Lamp

Kipling spent five largely happy years during his teens at boarding school, at the United Services College at Westward Ho!, Devon; the tales in the book *Stalky & Co.* (1899) are derived from his experiences there, with himself cast in the role of Beetle. The story 'Slaves of the Lamp' is given as 'Slaves of the Lamp, Part I' in those editions of the book that contain also an 'afterstory', called 'Slaves of the Lamp, Part II', set long after schooldays and demonstrating how the lessons learned from the school adventures bear fruit in the context of adult life: Stalky, leading a small band of Sikh soldiers against two Afghan tribes, is able to defeat the latter by setting his foes against each other, much as he did in 'Slaves of the Lamp'.

'Slaves of the Lamp', the first of the Stalky stories to be published, appeared originally in *Cosmopolis* in 1897.

'Wireless'

Another fantasy story, and a very clever one. While young Mr Cashell is attempting to participate in an early radio ('wireless') experiment, the narrator observes that pharmacist's assistant Mr Shaynor has fallen into a trance owing to a combination of consumption, the cold night air, the exhilaration of young love, and an *ad hoc* alcoholic cocktail the narrator has concocted from the pharmacy shelves. In his trance, Shaynor's brain appears to have induced a signal, much as Cashell is attempting to induce a radio signal in his apparatus. But the signal Shaynor is picking up is a mental one, and it is transcending the barriers of time: all the circumstances are right for his brain to induce the mental set of another pharmacist's assistant who suffered from both consumption and the toils of romantic love: the poet John Keats.

Kipling seems to have been fascinated by time fantasies, and in particular by what are technically called time-slip fantasies – tales in which it is the mind rather than the physical body that travels through time. ' "The Finest Story in the World' " is another example of him writing in this vein, as (arguably) are the tales in *Puck of Pook's Hill* (1906). Time-slip fantasies enjoyed a long vogue from about the 1920s to the end of the twentieth century, and are still immensely popular in the cinema today – a recent (and very good) example is *Frequency* (2000), starring Dennis Quaid and Jim Caviezel. (Oddly enough, its tale too is based on amateur radio.) However, Kipling pioneered the sub-genre with such stories as the two in this book, which preceded almost all the other early examples by as much as a decade.

'"Wireless"' was first published in 1902 in *Scribner's Magazine* and was collected in *Traffics and Discoveries* (1904).

'Dymchurch Flit'

In *Puck of Pook's Hill* (1906) Kipling let two children, Dan and Una, explore real and mythical British history through the agency of Robin Goodfellow – Puck – who was able to transport them at least mentally backwards through time to witness events as they unfolded. (The text leaves it open as to whether they actually travelled through time or just had the subjective experience of doing so.) '"Dymchurch Flit"' is the odd one out among the tales in *Puck of Pook's Hill* in that the children are not transported into the middle of the events; instead Puck – in the guise of Tom Shoesmith – merely tells them the tale of how the fairy folk departed Britain to avoid the otherwise inevitable confrontation with mortals (the 'Flesh and Blood'). There are allusions to the parallels that could be drawn between the Fairy/Flesh and Blood schism and, in genuine history, the wedge driven between the folk of Britain by the Reformation.

'"Dymchurch Flit"' is a fine fairytale, probably based on a Sussex folk tradition. Much of it is told in light dialect. Dialect was probably an over-obsession of Kipling's; he was intent on capturing speech as it was spoken, which he did admirably . . . but on occasion with the effect of making his stories hard to comprehend on the printed page. This is an example of a Kipling tale that works much better when read aloud – the meanings of the various 'difficult' dialect words become completely transparent on their being sounded.

' "Dymchurch Flit" ' was written especially for *Puck of Pook's Hill*.

The House Surgeon

Again a ghost story driven less by the ghost than by surviving guilt – indeed, the house of the punning title boasts no apparitions but is instead haunted by the crushing sense of gloom, guilt and depression that afflicts anyone who tries to stay in it. The guilt is really two-directional: on the one side there is the rather irrational guilt experienced by the soul of the dead Agnes Moultrie; on the other there is the subliminal guilt of the remaining two Misses Moultrie, who must know that they are unreasonable in thinking the worst of their deceased sister but carry on thinking it anyway. Once the guilt of the living sisters is brought out into the open and confronted – exorcised through the demonstration of its folly rather than that their beliefs are groundless (it is shown that Agnes's death *could* have been accidental, which they accept as proof that it *must* have been so) – then so too is the house itself exorcised. In effect, the agent carrying out the haunting isn't so much a ghost or a discarnate soul as the memories the two living sisters possess.

'The House Surgeon' was first published in 1909 in *Harper's Magazine* and collected in *Actions and Reactions* (1909).

The Man who would be King

Widely regarded as Kipling's masterpiece, 'The Man who would be King' is too often seen as purely an adventure story – perhaps because that was the approach John Huston took in his excellent 1975 screen adaptation. In fact, it works very well at the adventure-story level, but far more important is its function as an allegory.

While the con-men Dravot and Carnehan are at the outset complete scapegraces, with no thought for anything except to make a good living at someone else's expense, by the time they've fully established their little kingdom in the back of beyond they've become capable of being first-rate rulers. The justice they dispense is fair and relatively honest, while also relatively compassionate. They have brought peace among the warring tribes, who are enjoying an era of plenty unlike any they have known before. In short, the two men have civilised the natives, who have come to regard them as gods because of the arcane Freemasonry mumbo-jumbo Dravot and Carnehan have deployed as a tool in the subjugation. This is in accordance with the 'Contrack' the pair drew up before they departed on their quest for fortune:

> This Contract between me and you persuing witnesseth in the name of God – Amen and so forth.
>
> (One) That me and you will settle this matter together; i.e. to be Kings of Kafiristan.
>
> (Two) That you and me will not, while this matter is being settled, look at any Liquor, nor any Woman black, white, or brown, so as to get mixed up with one or the other harmful.

(Three) That we conduct ourselves with Dignity and Discretion, and if one of us gets into trouble the other will stay by him.

Signed by you and me this day.
PEACHEY TALIAFERRO BARNEHAN
DANIEL DRAVOT
Both Gentlemen at Large

(As Peachey asks the narrator plaintively, ' . . . and *do* you think that we would sign a Contrack like that unless we was in earnest? We have kept away from the two things that make life worth having.')

It is only when Dravot decides he can with impunity ignore Clause Two of the Contrack and take one of the tribeswomen to be his wife that everything falls apart: she demonstrates for all to see that he is no god but all too mortal.

The allegory intended by Kipling is with the British occupation of India. Whatever their origins and motives, the British, he is saying, have become damn' fine emperors, and the Indian people are the better off for the presence of the colonial power. For the spreading of Christianity by the British among the Indians he substitutes Dravot's and Peachey's use of Freemasonic ritual that is understood by neither natives nor rulers; the point Kipling seems to be making is that it matters not at all *what* religion colonial powers rely on as their aid in the task of civilising savages, just so long as there *is* one – just so long as there's some appropriately impressive mumbo-jumbo to turn everyone's attention toward a supposed higher power. (This was actually a very subversive view for its day.) If the Indians know what's good for them they'll accept British rule for all the bounties it has brought them, rather than rebel against what they perceive as its yoke . . .

At the same time, the British can continue to rule only if they determinedly adhere to the highest possible moral and ethical standards in their dealings with the subject peoples. This is the other half of the tacit contract – or Contrack – between rulers and ruled. Should they slip from those standards, then they will deserve to lose their pre-eminence on the subcontinent.

These arguments in favour of the unending day of the British Empire are not fashionable views today, and the world is a better place that this is so: there is about them something of the skewed logic used by those who plead that cigarette smoking isn't actually bad for you. But the young Kipling (he was still in his early twenties when he wrote this story) argued his case with fervour and quite probably believed it – believed that British rule was the best thing that had happened to India, no matter the injustices, abominations and petty tyrannies that came with it. His naïve faith in the staunch moral integrity of the average British colonial might seem laughable to us now, especially since – as this story itself illustrates – he was perfectly aware how unethically many of them behaved; but nations and the individuals within them do tend to brainwash themselves with their own propaganda ('The land of the free'; 'God is on our side') to the extent that reality is relegated to second fiddle, and the British Empire of the time was no different.

Kipling was right about one thing, though. Just like Dravot and Peachey, only so long as the British kept their administration, if not its individual officers, relatively clear of corruption could they cling on to the subcontinent. While their expulsion would inevitably have come one day, the process was much accelerated by their failure at all times to observe the Contrack.

'The Man who would be King' was first published in *The Phantom 'Rickshaw and Other Tales* (1888) and collected in *Wee Willie Winkie and Other Stories* (1895).

In the Cinema

The works of Rudyard Kipling have proved a rich source for the cinema. Well over fifty screen presentations have been based on his novels, stories and even poems, with more constantly being added to that total; in particular, several movies have been based on *The Jungle Book*, famously including the Disney animated travesty of 1967. Screen productions relevant to the stories in this collection are two.

The Man Who Would Be King (1975) was directed by John Huston; it starred Sean Connery as Dan Dravot and Michael Caine as Peachey Carnehan, with Christopher Plummer playing the role of the written tale's narrator – assumed by the screenplay to be Kipling himself. While concerned more with adventure than subtext, the movie is an excellent late example of the Hollywood epic, distinguished by surprisingly good performances from the two leads.

Also of note is the 1982 six-part BBC television series based on *Stalky & Co.*, directed by Rodney Bennett and starring Robert Addie as Stalky, Robert Burbage as McTurk and David Parfitt as Beetle. The adaptation of the six stories concerned is fairly faithful, and the direction and acting are excellent.

Further Reading

Bauer, Helen Pike, *Rudyard Kipling: A Study in Short Fiction*, Twayne, New York, 1994

Bloom, Harold (ed.), *Rudyard Kipling (Modern Critical Views)*, Chelsea House, Langhorne (PA), 2000

Fido, Martin, *Rudyard Kipling: An Illustrated Biography*, Book Sales, New York, 1988

Harrison, James, *Rudyard Kipling*, Twayne, New York, 1982

Leibfried, Philip, *Rudyard Kipling and Sir Henry Rider Haggard on Screen, Stage, Radio and Television*, McFarland, Jefferson (NC) and London, 1999

Martindell, Ernest Walter, *A Bibliography of the Works of Rudyard Kipling (1881–1921)*, Haskell House, New York, 1972

Orel, Harold (ed.), *Critical Essays on Rudyard Kipling*, G. K. Hall, Boston, 1989

Rao, K. Bhaskara, *Rudyard Kipling's India*, University of Oklahoma Press, Norman (OK), 1967

Ricketts, Harry, *Kipling: A Life,* Carroll & Graf, New York, 2001

Shahane, Vasant Anant, *Rudyard Kipling: Activist and Artist*, Southern Illinois University Press, Carbondale (IL), 1973

Biography

Born in Mumbai (Bombay), India, in 1865, Joseph Rudyard Kipling was the son of an art teacher and museum curator; an aunt married the painter Edward Burne-Jones; another aunt was the mother of Stanley Baldwin. Rudyard was sent to England in 1871 and eventually, in 1878, to the United Services College at Westward Ho!, Devon; he later fictionalised his adventures at this school in *Stalky & Co.* (1899). In 1882 he returned to India, working in Lahore for the *Civil & Military Gazette*, for which journal he wrote numerous poems and stories. In 1889 he came to live in Britain, where his literary star rose rapidly. Having married an American, between 1892 and 1896 he lived in Vermont, before returning once more to Britain. He was awarded the Nobel Prize for Literature in 1907, the first British writer to be so honoured; the presentation banquet was, however, cancelled owing to the death the previous day of the Swedish king, Oscar II. He declined to accept the position of Poet Laureate, and also declined the Order of Merit, but did accept the Gold Medal of the Royal Society of Literature, previously awarded only to Sir Walter Scott, George Meredith and Thomas Hardy. He died in 1936.

His major prose works were *The Jungle Book* (1894), *The Second Jungle Book* (1895), *Captains Courageous* (1897), *Stalky & Co.* (1899), *Kim* (1901), *Just So Stories* (1902), *Traffics and Discoveries* (1904), *Puck of Pook's Hill* (1906) and *Rewards and Fairies* (1910). His autobiographical *Something of Myself* (1937) was published posthumously.